LETHAL
TREASURE

LETHAL
TREASURE

• JANE K. CLELAND •

W⊕RLDWIDE®

TORONTO • NEW YORK • LONDON
AMSTERDAM • PARIS • SYDNEY • HAMBURG
STOCKHOLM • ATHENS • TOKYO • MILAN
MADRID • WARSAW • BUDAPEST • AUCKLAND

This is for librarians, the rock stars of my world. When I was young, librarians welcomed me and encouraged my curiosity, so libraries became, to me, a place of solace and hope. Today, libraries remain a safe haven in times of strife, and librarians continue to be my heroes. And, of course, for Joe.

Recycling programs
for this product may
not exist in your area.

Lethal Treasure

A Worldwide Mystery/December 2015

First published by Minotaur Books, an imprint of St. Martin's Press.

ISBN-13: 978-0-373-26972-3

Copyright © 2013 by Jane K. Cleland

All rights reserved. No part of this book may be reproduced or transmitted in any form or by any means, electronic or mechanical, including photocopying, recording or by any information storage and retrieval system, without permission in writing from the publisher. For information, contact: St. Martin's Press, 175 Fifth Avenue, New York, N.Y. 10010, U.S.A.

This is a work of fiction. Names, characters, places and incidents are either the product of the author's imagination or are used fictitiously, and any resemblance to actual persons, living or dead, business establishments, events or locales is entirely coincidental.

® and TM are trademarks of Harlequin Enterprises Limited. Trademarks indicated with ® are registered in the United States Patent and Trademark Office, the Canadian Intellectual Property Office and in other countries.

Printed in U.S.A.

Author's Note

This is a work of fiction. While there is a Seacoast Region in New Hampshire, there is no town called Rocky Point, and many other geographic liberties have been taken.

ONE

"SUZANNE DYRE—SHE's the new manager of the Blue Dolphin," Leigh Ann Dubois said. "Do you know her, Josie? She hired us to help her redo her condo."

"I don't know the name, but if she's bringing the Blue Dolphin back to life, she's got to be good people!"

"She's new to town and just as sweet as sweet potato pie. If only she'd consider other color options…she's decided to do her living room in mauve and teal. Can you imagine? Those colors went out of style when I was in nursery school. Well, first grade, anyway."

"I think you're looking at it backwards, Leigh Ann. It's good news that she's so clear on what she wants. The more specific she is, the greater the chance she'll be happy with the finished product. Which means she'll tell all her friends what good interior designers you and Henri are."

"You're so practical. I admire that. And I think you're right, now that I reflect on it. Mama always said, 'Once you stop trying to get people to change, life gets easier.' You'd think I'd have learned it by now. Suzanne collects thimbles, by the way. I wonder if she's been to your tag sale."

"We sure carry a lot of them." I smiled, not the least bit shy when it came to touting my business, Prescott's Antiques and Auctions. "Just in case she doesn't know about us, will you suggest she stop by? Maybe give her one of my cards?"

"Absolutely! I should have thought of it myself." She fluffed her short blond hair. "I'm so excited about tonight."

The Dubois were new friends. They'd opened Dubois Interior Designs about six months earlier, right after they'd moved from New York City to tiny Rocky Point, New Hampshire. We'd met when they stopped by my company to introduce themselves, and we'd hit it off right away. Leigh Ann, a bubbly Southern belle, always had a kind word to say and usually had me laughing at her fun, unique take on the world. I liked her husband, Henri, too. A recent immigrant from France, he was a charmer and a hard worker. Over the months, my boyfriend, Ty, and I had hung out with them half a dozen times, and the four of us were well on our way to becoming true friends.

Their shop fronted Rocky Point Green, with a clear view of meandering paths and flowering bushes and the gazebo where bands played familiar tunes on hot summer nights. Today, everything in sight was buried in snow. This February we'd shattered records for both snow accumulation and cold.

Ty and I had asked them to join us in celebrating the reopening of my favorite restaurant, the Blue Dolphin, a change in plans from our original invitation to come to my place for a kitchen clambake. After reading the unqualified praise for the restaurant in this morning's Rocky Point Foodies blog, I asked if they'd mind a rain check on the clambake. The blogger, a retired chef named Mac who seemed to know all the local food-related gossip, usually before everyone else, wrote that the former executive chef, Chef Ray, had returned to his previous job, along with several other employees. It was like hearing you could go home again after all. I'd come in early, just to visit a while with Leigh Ann. We sat on either side of her ultramodern glass and steel desk.

"I'm more than excited about tonight," I said, sipping Earl Grey tea from a glass mug. "I'm completely thrilled!

I sure hope Mac's blog is right, and that the restaurant is the same as before."

"You can give that hope a bye-bye wave as it disappears from sight," she said, her tone unexpectedly bitter. "Nothing stays the same, no matter how hard you pray."

I wondered what in her life had changed for the worse, but I didn't want to ask. We weren't that sort of friends, not yet. I waited for a few seconds, offering her the opportunity to volunteer more information, but she didn't. She was staring out the window, a million miles away, remembering something perhaps, or dreaming or planning. I followed her gaze. All the bushes and trees were capped with snow. The streets had been plowed, but a packed white coating covered the asphalt. The sky was overcast. No one was in sight. *Leigh Ann is right,* I thought. *Change is the constant, not stability.* I turned back to face her and found that she was looking at me, smiling.

"Sorry," she said. "Mama always said I could turn a sunny day to rain when I got thinking too hard. I'm betting the food at the Blue Dolphin will be even tastier than you remember. Since we did the redecoration, I know the atmosphere is more elegant than ever."

"I can't wait to see what you've done," I said, then paused to come up with a less emotionally loaded subject than change and rejuvenation. "So…are you thinking florals for Suzanne's living room?"

"I'm not thinking yet," she said. "I'm still in the cranky phase."

I laughed. "How long does the cranky phase typically last?"

"It depends. Once, when a client wanted fire-engine red zebra stripes on top of neon pink walls, I was cranky for a week. Mauve and teal…my guess is I'll be fine in a day or two. Actually, I'll be fine by tomorrow. I have an old friend coming in for the weekend, and I'm looking forward to seeing him, so I won't let mauve and teal spoil my mood."

The antique sleigh bells Leigh Ann had purchased at one of my company's antiques auctions and hung on their shop door tinkled merrily. I looked up in time to see Henri push his way in, bringing a blast of frigid air with him. He had a small opaque plastic tub tucked under his arm. I cupped the mug to warm my fingers.

"Josie," he said, smiling. His English was fluent, but his accent was strong, and when he spoke my name, it came out as "Zhozee," as if the *J* were pronounced like the *g* in mirage. As he hung his heavy parka on a standing rack by the front door, he glanced toward Leigh Ann. "Ma cherie."

"Hello, darlin'!" Leigh Ann said. "What's in the tub?"

Henri slid it onto a black-granite-topped table positioned against one wall and said, "Hearts...perfect, non? One week before Valentine's Day? I found them at the back of the storage unit."

"Oooh!" she said, hurrying across the showroom. "Show me!"

I heard my phone buzz and dug into my tote bag to find it. Ty texted that he was running a little late. He'd be here in half an hour and couldn't wait to see me. I replied with "xo" and tossed the unit back in my bag.

"That's so pretty!" Leigh Ann said, holding up a bulbous ceramic heart, glazed a deep bloodred. At its widest point, it was about three inches across. A small gold metal eye was embedded at the top, so it could be hung as a Christmas decoration or wall art.

I joined them at the table, wishing I'd found a box of hearts in the storage unit I'd won earlier that day. Not that I had any complaints. After I'd won the bidding—I'd paid $150, a reasonable amount based on what I could see, which was nothing much—I'd rushed to open the unlabeled cardboard boxes and was thrilled to discover a dozen unsigned but distinctive brass bookends, each one featuring a different forest animal; an orange carnival glass punch bowl set in excellent condition; half a dozen serviceable cast-iron pots and pans; and a collection of Agatha Christie hardback novels, no first editions, but several early printings. Taken together, I calculated that everything would fetch more than $750 at my company's weekly tag sale, a great return on investment.

Usually my take was less lucrative. Buying abandoned storage units sold at auction wasn't exactly a blind gamble; it was more of an educated gamble. Based on the visible contents, you took your best guess and went at it. No surprise, it didn't always pan out. Sometimes, despite neat stacks of clean cardboard boxes, a solid indicator of potential value, I found inexplicable valueless oddities, like half-used bars of soap or rolls of old twine. Other times, amid what appeared to be piles of trash, I'd come across a valuable antique. Usually, though, the units I bought were filled with salable utilitarian pieces and collectibles, and over time, the lockers had become a consistent source of inventory for the tag sale, which, since I'd doubled the size of the venue last fall, and sales were brisk, was seriously good news. The truth was that buying antiques and collectibles was a constant battle because it's harder by far to buy than it is to sell.

Two or three times a week, I found myself at an auction somewhere in New Hampshire, Massachusetts, or Maine, often bidding against Henri. Our competition was friendly, more cooperative than antagonistic. In fact, we'd begun to work together more closely than either of us could have predicted. Since their firm specialized in contemporary design, Henri often called on my company to appraise objects that didn't fit their point of view but might have resale value, and generally he and Leigh Ann were as eager to sell or consign them as I was to acquire them.

Henri extracted another ceramic heart from a bubble-wrap sleeve and placed it on his palm for us to view. This one featured white glaze, decorated with lemon yellow polka dots, very jazzy.

"There are twenty of them, all different," Henri said.

"They're lovely," I said, meaning it.

"Are they antiques?" Leigh Ann asked.

I leaned in to read the small print. "Probably not," I said, pointing at the writing. "Do you see here? 'Made in West Germany.' West Germany was formed when? Nineteen forty-nine, wasn't it?"

"Oui," Henri said, nodding. "I see. East and West Germany reunited in 1990, so that means the hearts, they were crafted between those two dates. You are very clever, Josie, to notice this thing."

"Thanks. It's what I do, actually—I notice things."

"When did labeling laws come to pass?" Leigh Ann asked. "Maybe we can narrow the span some."

"Good thought," I said, "but no. Companies have had to publish the country of origin since 1890."

"So these hearts don't qualify as antiques, right?" she asked.

"My company's policy is that we don't call anything an antique unless it's a hundred years old." I shrugged and smiled. "To get a better date estimate, you'd need to conduct a materials analysis that probably isn't worth it."

"Maybe the artist is famous," Henri said.

"Why don't we check for a signature. Do you have a loupe handy?"

Leigh Ann said she'd get one and slid open a panel in her credenza in back of her desk. She selected a loupe from a wicker catchall box near her all-in-one scanner/printer/

fax. In addition to the loupe, I noticed a few screwdrivers, several wrenches from socket to tension and from pipe to lug, a hammer, and four kinds of glue, from wood to ceramic and from Gorilla to spray mount, tools of the trade.

I examined the heart millimeter by millimeter, searching for a maker's mark, then turned it over, repeating the process. There was no name or mark. I repeated the process with another of the hearts.

"Nothing," I said, handing Henri the loupe so he could check for himself. They might not be one-of-a-kind rare trinkets, but it was for sure the right piece at the right time. Priced right, somewhere around twenty dollars, I thought, they would sell in a flash.

He took a cursory look. "I understand…they're jolie… pretty…but not valuable. Would you like to buy them?"

"I'd love to."

"What do you think is a fair price?"

My dad taught me that if you start the negotiation, you lose. Let the other guy be the first to name his price.

"You tell me," I said. "What do you think is fair?"

He named a price I thought was too high, and I countered with a lower offer, explaining my logic—that what with overhead and marketing and appraising costs, Prescott's never paid more than 30 percent of our estimated sales price for anything. We fussed back and forth, and after a while, Leigh Ann drifted back to her desk and started tapping away on her computer. A minute or two later, Henri and I settled on a price I hoped he thought was as reasonable as I did, $120. We unwrapped all the hearts so I could be certain none was chipped or cracked, then repacked them carefully and shook on the deal.

"Did you show Josie the Merian?" Henri asked Leigh Ann as he handed me the tub.

Leigh Ann was staring out the window again, just as she

had earlier, unseeing, absorbed, glum. Leigh Ann wasn't putting on any airs that I could see. From where I stood, it seemed evident that all was not well in Leigh Ann's world.

"No," I said, to spare him having to repeat his question, to spare her having her wandering mind recalled in public. "What edition?"

"Come," Henri said, "I'll show you."

"What a terrific find," I said, sliding the tub near my tote bag under Leigh Ann's desk and following him into the back, feeling another ding of envy. "Merian prints are always popular."

He smiled, and I recognized his expression—he thought he'd hit pay dirt.

TWO

"THIS MERIAN," HENRI SAID, holding open the door to the back room, waiting for me to join him, "this I do not sell, not as a book. This we use for prints. It is a twentieth-century reproduction, with many pages missing, it is true, but with enough remaining that we can make many beautiful prints." He pointed to an oversized volume, a thick art book. "This is a special find, non?"

Old botanical prints weren't particularly valuable, retailing for only about twenty dollars each matted and slipped into a plastic sleeve, fifty dollars or more if framed, but they sold steadily. An old Maria Sibylla Merian book in good condition showcasing her astonishingly lifelike color plant and insect engravings, even a twentieth-century repro, would sell at auction for several thousand dollars. A broken book, with pages missing, had no value as a book, but the individual prints were money in the bank. I had just begun to flip through the pages when I heard the distant tinkle of the sleigh bells. A customer, perhaps, or Ty.

"The drawings are incredible," I said. "What talent she had."

"Yes. The detail is astounding. Look at this one." Henri opened the book to show me one of the most famous of Merian's engravings, *Metamorphosis Insectorum Surinamensium*.

"Beautiful," I said.

"I can cut this part off, non?" he asked, pointing to a reddish brown stain near the outer edge.

"Foxing," I said. "Yes. It's good that it doesn't touch the illustration itself."

Leigh Ann pushed through into the back room. "Suzanne is here—she thought she could get a head start at picking her paint colors." She reached for a heavy swatch book. "Here's to mauve and teal!" She started back into the showroom, then paused, resting the book against the table's edge, to ask me, "What do you think of the Merian?"

"It's a wonderful find."

"Even though so many pages are in such rough shape?" she asked.

She was right—it was in bad shape. The leather binding was rubbed thin and dried out. Many pages were chipped, ripped, or foxed. Even with my cursory examination, though, I could tell that with careful trimming, fifty or more of the color illustrations could be salvaged. Matted and framed, their damage could be hidden, and buyers would treasure them for their beauty, not condemn them for their flaws. Conservatively they were looking at $2,500 or more. My ding of envy chimed louder.

"They can be trimmed," I said. "Once they're matted and framed...you'll get at least a couple of thousand dollars for the prints."

"A good unit, then!" she said, flashing a dazzling smile at Henri, heading toward the front, swatch book in hand. "Well done!"

"Thank you, ma cherie," he said.

"Are you sure you don't want to save yourself the work and sell the book as is?" I asked, grinning. "I'll be glad to take it off your hands."

He smiled, on to me. "I think not, ma chère amie."

"No harm in trying," I said as I followed him back to the showroom.

"These prints...they never go out of style," Henri remarked as we walked. "Why is that, do you think?"

"I've often wondered the same thing," I said. "Why some things we think of as trendy end up enduring, while others don't. Critical mass, maybe. If enough people like something, it's no longer trendy. It becomes a standard, and if it lasts long enough, a classic."

"An interesting thought."

He held open the door for me to precede him.

"Suzanne!" he said, approaching a tall woman, younger than me by five or six years, sitting on the guest side of Leigh Ann's desk. A welter of paint chips covered the desk.

I'd seen her before, but it took me a few seconds to recall where and when. At last month's annual Rocky Point Winter Festival, she'd taken a seat a few tables away from me. I'd been struck by her delicate beauty and wondered who she was. Once the evening was over, I hadn't thought of her again.

"Henri!" she said, standing, extending her hands to greet him.

He squeezed her hands, then embraced her, kissing her on both cheeks, four times, Parisian-style.

For reasons that weren't immediately apparent, Suzanne reminded me of my mother, an odd and disconcerting feeling since she bore no resemblance to her. My mom had been shorter than me, which was saying something, whereas Suzanne was taller by half a foot. My mom had dressed for what she called country comfort—jeans and heavy cable-knit sweaters and tweed skirts—whereas Suzanne was dressed with city polish. Her moss green suit fit her like a dream. My mom's smooth brown hair had hung straight to her shoulders. Suzanne's auburn hair was twisted into a stylish chignon. She wore more makeup than my mother had used in a year, but it was so well applied, it was almost invisible. The overall impression I had of Suzanne was one of quiet sophistication. Then I saw how affable Suzanne looked as she chatted with Leigh Ann and Henri, her eyes full of interest, communicating an ineffable graciousness. She exuded sincerity and warmth—just like my mom.

The sleigh bells tinkled, and Ty walked in. He saw me and smiled, a special one, just for me, and I smiled back, a high-wattage one, just for him. Standing just over six feet, Ty had broad shoulders and craggy features and deep dark piercing eyes. Since he'd been organizing outdoor training exercises for Homeland Security, his skin had weathered and browned.

"Hey, gorgeous," he said.

"Hey, handsome," I replied, moving forward, reaching him, and taking his hand.

He brushed his lips against mine, a tease, then greeted Leigh Ann and Henri and turned expectantly toward Suzanne.

"Have you met Suzanne yet?" Leigh Ann asked us. "Suzanne Dyre. The new manager of the Blue Dolphin. This is Josie Prescott, owner of the best antiques auction house in the region, and this is Ty Alverez, a big-cheese training guru for Homeland Security."

"You're new to the area," I said, smiling. "Are you settling in all right?"

"Actually, I'm settling in beautifully, largely because of friends like Leigh Ann and Henri."

"I can believe that," I said. "They're very special."

Leigh Ann looked pleased. "You two! You're making me blush. Suzanne, tell Josie about your thimbles."

"There's not much to tell." She laughed, setting her eyes twinkling. "I collect thimbles."

"Do you specialize in a certain style or a specific material or anything?" I asked.

"No, I just go with what attracts me. My grandmother was quite a seamstress, and she had the most beautiful sterling silver thimble. There was a peacock on top." She shook her head, some special memory taking hold. "I loved my grandmother very much."

"I think that's about the best reason to start a collection I've ever heard," I said. I handed her a card and told her about the weekly tag sales.

"I'll add my welcome," Ty said when I was done. "Where did you move from?"

"Los Angeles," she said, smiling as she explained that she'd been reassigned by the holding company that had purchased the Blue Restaurant chain, an investment group that specialized in restaurant turnarounds. Since the Blue Dolphin had closed three years ago, it had languished, the building boarded up, waiting for someone to come to its rescue. "There was definitely a bit of culture shock moving from L.A. to New Hampshire. Don't get me wrong—I'm having a great time!"

Ty asked what about Rocky Point was working for her. Suzanne said all the right things, the things you say to natives when you're a newcomer on their turf, but I had the sense that she meant them, which was either true or a tribute to her polished professionalism.

"It's great news that the Blue Dolphin has reopened," I said after hearing how much she liked the rugged New Hampshire coast and how friendly she found the people. "It was my favorite restaurant."

"I hope it lives up to your expectations," she said, sounding confident that it would.

"It's got to be hard trying to re-create something," Ty said. "You have to wear a lot of hats."

She laughed. "You've got that right. To do this job you need to know as much about wielding a screwdriver as you do about managing personnel. Luckily, the building itself was in better shape than I'd expected, and a lot of the staff came back, including the head chef. Between that and the way Leigh Ann and Henri cleverly re-created the inside decor...well, let's just say I got a real leg up."

"We're the lucky ones," Henri said. "It is a wonderful tribute to you, to your company, that you gave us, newcomers, such an important job, working on Rocky Point's top restaurant. We are so grateful for your trust."

"You won the bid fair and square," Suzanne said. "You earned the opportunity."

As she spoke, I scanned the dusky rose and purplish mauve paint chips spread over Leigh Ann's desk.

"Where are you with your color choices?" I asked Suzanne.

"Somewhere between Victorian Rose and Sunset." She glanced at her watch. "Well, break's over. I'm sorry, Leigh Ann, that I can't make up my mind. Oh, well! Tomorrow's another day."

Henri's jacket shimmied, then buzzed.

"My phone," Henri said, reaching into a side pocket. He glanced at the display. "I must take this call. Excusez-moi."

He hurried to the far side of the room, moving with lithe grace, like a fencer, and stood by the glass table with his back to us.

Leigh Ann cocked her head, watching Henri for a moment, then turned to Suzanne.

"You'll see us in about ten minutes," Leigh Ann said. "Josie brags on the Blue Dolphin's food like nobody's business. I can't wait to see what all the fuss is about."

Suzanne smiled at me. "Thanks for giving us a try."

She reached for her to-the-ankle faux-mink coat, hanging next to Henri's.

"Is it still like an ice chest out there?" she asked Ty.

I heard Ty say that it was colder than an ice chest, but nothing else. My attention was on Henri. He shook his head, *no, no, no.* I glanced at Leigh Ann, but her focus was on Suzanne. Both women were laughing as Ty held Suzanne's coat and she struggled to find the armhole.

Henri's call ended abruptly barely a minute after it began, and he half-turned toward us, then stopped midstep, his eyes on his phone, maybe willing it to ring again, perhaps reliving a patently difficult conversation. As if he could feel my scrutiny, he looked up and met my eyes. After a second, maybe two, he smiled, a shallow attempt to cover up his true feelings. I didn't return his smile. I hoped he could read my expression, understand that I perceived his dismay, and know that I would help him if I could. Henri glanced at Leigh Ann and his faux happiness gave way to something closer to dejection. He took in a deep breath and smiled again, and this one stayed frozen in place. He expected Leigh Ann to be as troubled by whatever he'd just learned as he was, and he hoped not to have to tell her about it, at least not now.

"I'm sorry," Henri said to us all. "Business. Always business."

"Good news?" Leigh Ann asked.

"Of course," he said, giving her a shoulder-squeeze.

"See you soon!" Suzanne called, pulling a matching hat over her head. She looked like a million bucks, as chic as if she'd walked off the pages of *Vogue,* and cute as a bug.

Everyone called good-bye; then Henri leaned over Leigh Ann and kissed the top of her head, casting a quick conspiratorial glance in my direction. I turned to see if Ty had witnessed any part of the minidrama, but he was looking at his watch.

"How about if we put the hearts in my car before heading over to the Blue Dolphin?" I asked. "I'm in the garage."

"Sounds like a plan," Ty said.

I picked up my tote bag and the tub of hearts. Ty and Leigh Ann were chatting about whether it was too cold to snow. When I glanced at Henri, he was staring at me again, and he raised his finger to his lips. I nodded.

Two minutes later, bundled up against the bitter late-afternoon air, the four of us headed out. I was silent the whole way to the garage and then to the Blue Dolphin, thinking that Henri and I shared an approach to receiving bad news. I usually wanted to keep my own counsel, as it seemed he did, to think things through at my own pace before discussing them with Ty. I hoped my nod had reassured Henri. If he knew me better, he'd have known that he had nothing to worry about. I was discreet, and nothing if not a loyal friend.

THREE

THE BLUE DOLPHIN was housed in an eighteenth-century brick building originally designed to fit into the curved corner of Bow and Market streets in downtown Rocky Point. The restaurant appeared wonderfully unchanged.

The dome-shaped hammered-copper awning gleamed under the golden recessed lighting. The heavy wooden door, embellished with wrought-iron hinges, was just as I remembered it. Standing at the hostess stand, I could see through into the dining room, and smiled. A wood fire crackled in the five-foot-wide fireplace, the aroma scenting the air. The wide-plank oak flooring, burnished to a rich golden brown through generations of use and polishing, was original to the building. The walls were painted the same antique white with Colonial blue trim that I recalled. Even the curtains were identical, toile, featuring a blue and white pastoral French country theme. The tables were familiar, too—laid with the same crisp white linen and set with the same lustrous silver flatware and sparkling cut crystal as before. The crystal wall sconces, chandeliers, and table lamps also appeared unchanged. Flickering bulbs cast a shimmering glow throughout the room. The design of the Blue Dolphin's main dining room communicated security and substance. Stepping inside felt as warming and comforting as my mother's kitchen on days when she'd baked bread.

"Unbelievable," I said to Leigh Ann and Henri. "It's as

beautiful as I remember. More beautiful than I remember. What an accomplishment."

"Thanks, Josie," Leigh Ann said, squeezing my hand.

I turned to Frieda, the hostess I'd known for years and hadn't seen since the restaurant had closed. "Yay! You're here, and everything looks the same."

"Josie!" she said, leaning in for an air kiss. "Welcome back. We're so pumped! Jimmy's here, too, and Chef Ray is ruling the kitchen like he never left. Have you met Suzanne Dyre, our new general manager? Suzanne, this is Josie Prescott and Ty Alverez, two of our favorite customers."

"We just met," Suzanne said, extending her hands. "Welcome!" She and Leigh Ann exchanged a fluttering butterfly kiss; then she introduced Leigh Ann and Henri to Frieda as the magicians who'd brought the Blue Dolphin back to life. As we handed our coats over to a woman I didn't know working the coat check room, Suzanne turned her radiant attention toward me. "We open for dinner in about fifteen minutes, at five. Were you thinking of having a drink first?"

"Yes, indeed!" I said. "I love the lounge!"

"You are making my day, Josie, what with your enthusiasm and support."

"Mama always said dinner tastes better when you've had a cocktail first," Leigh Ann said as we got situated at my favorite table by the bow-shaped window that overlooked the Piscataqua River. "But that might have been because she was such a bad cook."

I laughed. "I want to meet your mom someday. She sounds like a hoot."

"You'll have to go to Thibodaux then. Mama doesn't trust Yankees, so it's thanks, anyway, but I'll stay here in Louisiana."

"How do you feel being around all us northerners?" I asked.

"Like a fish out of water, if the truth be told. Don't get me wrong—I liked New York City just fine, and I like it here, too. But I think for most people, where you're reared is where you feel most at home. Even when you hated it and couldn't wait to get out." She turned toward Henri and smiled. "Maybe that's why Henri and I get along so well. We're both out of our element, what with Henri coming from Paris and me from down south."

"Good to see ya, Joze," Jimmy said, approaching the table. "You too, Ty. What can I getcha?"

"A French martini, please," I said. To Leigh Ann and Henri, I added, "This is Jimmy, the best bartender in town."

Jimmy greeted them with practiced warmth. He hadn't aged at all. His hair was just as red, his smile just as easy, and his trick of flipping cocktail napkins as if he were skimming rocks across the ocean surface was just as familiar and predictable as the tide. I felt myself relax. To some people, familiarity might breed contempt; to me, it bred contentment.

"I'll have a French martini, too," Leigh Ann said, patting Henri's hand. "Not that I know what it is, but if it's French, it must be wonderful."

Henri raised her hand to his lips and kissed her fingertips. "Ma cherie."

Ty ordered a White Birch ale, and Henri ordered Johnnie Walker Black. Half the tables in the lounge were occupied, a good sign, I thought, since a large segment of the happy hour crowd would just now be getting out of work.

"You don't think of Rocky Point as being a place people move to," I said, "yet we all have come here from somewhere else, Suzanne included."

"That is true," Henri. "All of us for business."

"As well as I know you... I can't believe I've never asked—when you decided to open your own design firm, why did you come to Rocky Point?" I wondered if their story was anything like mine, a tale of escape. "Why didn't you open the company in New York?"

"I moved to New York to be an actress," Leigh Ann said. "I moved to New Hampshire to get away from failure."

"Non, ma cherie," Henri said, squeezing her hand. "We left for a new opportunity. There was no talk of failure. Not for you. Not for me. We moved together to this place, and it is exactly right for us."

Leigh Ann shrugged and smiled, but this one lacked conviction. "Makes no never mind at this point, that's for sure."

"New York's loss is Rocky Point's gain," I said, touching her elbow.

Tales of disappointment ended there. We spent the rest of the evening exchanging opinions about winter sports (oddly, no one skied and everyone skated), winter cookouts (we were all fans), and winter vacations (none for them; the Bahamas in March for us). We ate steak and salad and potatoes and creamed spinach, and then Suzanne bought us a complimentary dessert sampler for the table, chocolate lava cake and crème brûlée and apple pie with Stilton cheese and butterscotch cream puffs—a thank-you, she said, for giving the restaurant a whirl during its reopening week. Everything was delicious, better than before, or maybe I just thought it was better. Recovering something you'd loved and lost was rare. My dad always said to never cry over something that could be replaced with money, so I understood why I felt emotional. There were scores of restaurants up and down the seacoast, but there was only one Blue Dolphin. When I'd first arrived in Rocky Point, a stranger, reeling from loss, facing an uncertain future, the Blue Dolphin had been my sanctuary. And now it was back.

By the end of the evening, I'd reached two conclusions: I liked Leigh Ann and Henri more than ever, and Suzanne Dyre was maybe the best restaurateur I'd ever met.

The next morning, Friday, just after nine, I stood in the front office listening as Cara, our grandmotherly receptionist, updated me on my staff's schedules. Gretchen, my administrative manager, and Eric, my facilities manager and jack-of-all-trades, were walking the tag sale venue floor to discuss setup ways and means. Fred, one of my company's antiques appraisers, was en route to Durham. He had an appointment with a museum curator about an antique lute we were featuring in an upcoming auction called Music for Life.

Cara nodded to where Sasha, my chief appraiser, sat reading an antiques journal. "Sasha is researching something about a cello for Fred," she whispered.

"Which means you don't need to whisper!" I said. "You know Sasha! When she's in research mode, it would take a battalion of buglers to rouse her."

"That's true, isn't it?" Cara said, smiling. "Her ability to focus is a wonderful thing."

"You have it, too. I've seen you proofreading catalogue copy, and if that doesn't take focus, I don't know what does." I picked up my ankle-length down coat. "I'm going to run an errand en route to the—"

I broke off as Suzanne Dyre pushed through the door, setting the wind chimes Gretchen had hung there years earlier jangling.

Seeing that I had my coat in hand, she said, "Oh, no! I knew I should have called for an appointment."

"Not a bit! We welcome visitors anytime."

I glanced at the Mickey Mouse clock that Gretchen kept on her desk. It was 9:10. I had a good half an hour before I had to leave for yet another abandoned-storage-room auction. I'd planned on dropping off some dry cleaning, but I could do that after the auction just as easily as before.

Cara helped Suzanne settle in at the round guest table, taking her red wool coat and matching pillbox hat, and told her it was nice to see her again. As I tossed my coat and tote bag onto one of the guest chairs, they chatted about the record-breaking cold and dreary sky. Cara brought her a cup of tea and a plate of homemade gingersnaps.

"Before you say anything," I told her, "I want to tell you how truly fabulous dinner was last night. Everything was as good as before, and maybe better."

Suzanne smiled and nodded. "That's so great to hear. That—exactly that—is my job."

"You said your company specializes in turnarounds. Are you here just to get the Blue Dolphin started back up again?"

"My commitment is eighteen months, long enough to get the place back on track and take it through an annual cycle, and then we'll see. I'm a city girl, but I must say, Rocky Point is so… I don't know…warm and welcoming, well…we'll see. It might be time to settle down." She paused again, and this time her expression turned wistful. After a few seconds, she shook off her dreamy mood and smiled again. "Bottom line—so far, I love it here. Which is why I'm paying so much attention to my condo. I want it to be a home, not just a place I'm staying for a while." She laughed. "Leigh Ann is delightful, but she doesn't share my taste in home decor. I thought she was going to faint when I told her my color choices for the living room."

I laughed, too. "Let's just say she was surprised."

"That's very good, Josie. Very polite." She paused, a slight smile drawing up the corners of her mouth. "The truth is I'm not interested in trends. Those were the colors I grew up with, and to me, they represent love and comfort and stability."

"You're a traditional gal, and you know that about yourself. There's nothing wrong with that. If you don't mind my asking—why did you select Dubois Interior Designs? They're known for their contemporary work."

"I'm a woman of many talents, but interior design isn't one of them! Once I decided to bring in professional designers, I thought using them made sense. Not only did they do a great job with the restaurant's traditional decor, they came in under budget, which, as I'm sure you know, almost never happens. I figured that if they could do a traditional design for a restaurant, they could do it for a condo." She laughed. "Clearly Henri and Leigh Ann aren't as comfortable with my personal taste as they were with the classic French country look we wanted to re-create for the Blue Dolphin, but—" She held up a hand. "I don't want to imply I'm less than happy. I adore working with Leigh Ann and Henri. I never would have been able to update my kitchen so cleverly without them." She paused again, her eyes shining. "This is a roundabout way of saying that I want wall art I know Leigh Ann is going to hate, and rather than get into a fuss about it, I'd like to present the object to her as a fait accompli. That's where your company comes in." She looked around, noting the two empty workstations, the desks where Gretchen and Fred worked. "Is Fred here?"

"No, he just left for an appointment. Sorry. Can I help?"

She smiled conspiratorially. "Maybe. I want one of those metal birds-in-flight wall art pieces, and Fred told me you had some in stock."

I smiled, too, knowing she was right—Leigh Ann was definitely going to hate it. "Sasha?"

Sasha looked up from her computer, startled.

"I have a question," I continued. "This is Suzanne Dyre. Suzanne, this is Sasha, Prescott's chief antiques appraiser. Suzanne is interested in metal wall art. Specifically, birds in flight."

Sasha tucked her straight brown hair behind her ears and smiled. Normally self-effacing, when talking about art and antiques, Sasha was transformed into a confident powerhouse.

"Hi," she said, then tapped something into her computer. "Oh, yes! We have a wonderful four-piece set and a single panel." She stood up. "I'll be right back."

"That's too much to carry in one trip," I said. "I'll help." To Suzanne, I added, "We'll be back in a flash."

The phone rang as we stepped into the warehouse, and Cara answered with her typical friendly greeting.

Sasha handed me the single panel and carried the four-pack herself. Back in the front, we laid them out on the guest table, placing the single unit at the top and aligning the four panels so the overall picture they created was clear. The single piece was cast from a mold and showed waves rolling in to shore, the sun hanging low in the sky. A pair of seagulls was swooping down, fishing. The four-panel set was artisan-made of copper and designed to replicate four panes of a window. Branches of a tree crisscrossed the panes. A bird's nest perched high atop one limb. The mother bird was about to land, ready to care for her nestlings. In the background, a flock of birds flew across the sky in a chevron pattern.

Suzanne pointed to the ocean scene. "This one looks, I don't know, too simple, or something." She looked at the

four-piece set and nodded. "This one is more complex...
I love it."

I agreed with her assessment. The first piece was
crudely crafted, a basic design. The second piece was
subtle and detailed, creating a peek into a world. Placed
against a painted wall, the effect would be vivid and evoc-
ative.

Sasha told Suzanne the price of the 1985-ish handmade
but unsigned piece, $450, and she wrote a check on the
spot.

"I'm meeting Leigh Ann at two to finalize the paint
colors," she said, her eyes sparkling. "I'll show it to her
then. Wouldn't you love to be a fly on the wall during that
conversation?"

I laughed. "Truthfully...yes!"

I left Sasha to package it up and headed out to the auction, admiring Suzanne's silver Mercedes as I hurried to
my car.

I planned on wiping out the competition today. I was
loaded with cash and ready to buy. *Look out, Henri,* I
thought with a determined smile.

Crawford Self Storage in Rocky Point was located on
Route 1, just south of Portsmouth. As I pulled into the lot
the facility shared with an office building, I saw that Henri
was already there.

"Henri!" I called as I stepped out of my car onto the
crusty remnants of rock salt.

He waved and smiled. "Josie," he said, waiting for me
to catch up. "We had a grand time last night. Now today,
here we are. We fight together for the lockers."

"You could just let me win everything," I joked.

"Moi? Non. Sorry, my friend. I play to win." As we
crunched our way across the lot, walking quickly in the
bitter cold, he added, "About that phone call yesterday...

a contract, a deal I'd almost finalized fell through. I'd
hoped to surprise Leigh Ann with some good news, but…
oh, well!"

"I'm sorry to hear that."

"It would have been a nice extra."

"I understand," I said, thinking that those were words
to live by. When you owned a business, it was always nice
to have extra.

FOUR

VICKI CRAWFORD, THE CRAWFORD Self Storage facility's owner, was a big-boned woman twice my age. She stood by her office door holding a clipboard talking in an undertone to a man I knew to be a top auctioneer. His name was Tom, and he sometimes worked for Prescott's. He was astute and competent and grumpy all the time. Vicki wasn't grumpy, but she sure was by-the-book and no-nonsense. Everything about her, from her pugnacious stance to her take-no-prisoners glare, communicated that she hadn't taken a wooden nickel in a year or two and didn't plan on starting now.

I stamped my feet a couple of times, trying to counteract the icy cold leaching through my heavy work boots and woolen socks. The temperature had risen to nearly twenty, which, while better than yesterday's single digits, was still cold enough to make standing around on asphalt a penance. Crawford Self Storage's units opened directly into the parking lot, handy for renters, but not so nice for us. Some high-end facilities included heated waiting rooms, but not Crawford's, where the entire auction would take place outside.

At one minute to ten, there were five of us gathered together in a ragged line, waiting for the auction to begin. In addition to Henri and me, there were two other local antiques dealers, one a chatty woman named CiCi, the other an old-timer named Caleb. CiCi was wearing an ankle-length faux-leopard coat with a matching beret and black wool mittens. Caleb wore an old anorak and an even older wool watch cap. The fifth bidder was a newbie. He was about my age, midthirties, with small brown eyes set close together and a stubble of beard. Both his Red Sox baseball cap and his dark blue parka were smeared with grease.

"Listen up," Vicki said. "We have three units to auction off today. You know the rules. I'll open the door and you can look in for five minutes, but you can't go in or reach in to open anything. You can't touch anything." She paused to stare at each of us, issuing a personalized warning. "Everything is sold as is and all sales are final. Cash and carry. You've got to pay in cash and you've got to carry it out by the end of the day, trash and all. You've all left a deposit. That gets you the right to bid. If you win a locker and don't have the cash, I keep the deposit. If you don't clear your lockers out on time, I keep the deposit. If you have the cash and leave the room broom clean, I give the cash back. Simple. Once we're done, I take the winning bidders' payments first, then give back outstanding deposits. You can wait or you come back later. Any questions?" No one said anything. "All right, then. The first unit up for sale is number twenty-three, around the other side. Follow me."

We tramped along behind Vicki. The storage facility was shaped like a T, and the first unit was on the far side of the crossbar. CiCi ran to join me, slapping her upper arms with her mittened hands.

"Brrr!" she said. "It's a cold one! They said the temperature was rising, but I don't feel it, do you? My uncle says his bones are acting up—that means a storm is coming, a bad one."

"The weatherman said it would only be a dusting."

"Ha! Who are you going to believe? My infallible Uncle Willy or a meteorologist with wavy hair and a fake smile?"

"Uncle Willy," I said, laughing. "No question. How bad does he say it's going to be?"

"He says the ache is wicked deep and in both legs. One arm, so far, not both. That means two feet, maybe more. Starting tomorrow night, lasting for at least a full day."

"Wow... Uncle Willy is very specific, isn't he?"

"He's been calling storms for close on sixty years."

"All right, then. I better get to the store and stock up. Please thank Uncle Willy for me."

I'd planned on picking up a chicken. If we were going to be snowbound for the weekend, though, I needed more than one chicken. I offered a private prayer that the storm would hold off until six tomorrow evening, after our weekly tag sale, and after Ty got back from overseeing the training exercises he'd scheduled upstate. Intellectually, I understood why Ty often planned training exercises over weekends—their work was easier when venues were empty, plus, of course, it caused less disruption to business. But emotionally, I hated to have him gone, especially on Sundays, the family day. This week, he was only supposed to work on Saturday—good news.

Vicki used metal cutters to shear off the padlock.

"Here we go," she said. "This is a small locker, five by six." She swung the door wide. "You've got five minutes, starting now."

The five of us crowded together in front of the unit aiming our flashlights into dark corners and narrow crevices, trying to intuit value. Rocky Point was an amalgam of wealthy and not, so the neighborhood offered no hint of what the unit might contain, and this locker offered up no obvious clues on its own. Two rows of oversized trash bags were stuffed full of angular somethings, like boxes or storage tubs, and piled to the ceiling. In the very back, I spotted a pair of wooden ladder-back chairs, the kind we could sell at the tag sale for twenty dollars or more each depending on their age and condition.

"What's in those bags?" CiCi whispered, a rhetorical question.

"Nothing," Caleb replied, disgusted, turning away. "A lot of nothing."

I didn't think it was nothing. Those bags hadn't been tossed in haphazardly. Someone had taken the time to pack and stack them carefully, and those angles…it could be excess inventory for some small business, now defunct. Or winter clothes someone put away last spring, then never retrieved, who knew why. Or kitchen goods. Or jigsaw puzzles or toys or games. Or electronics. It could be anything, but I thought it was something, and my competitive dander was up.

Tom started the auction, his patter rhythmic and constant. Henri jumped in with a $50 bid, the minimum. CiCi ran him up to $110, then Caleb entered the fray with a bid of $120. Evidently he didn't think it was nothing after all. I bid $130, and Caleb countered. CiCi dropped out at $160, and Caleb at $170, and I won the unit for $180.

I won room 18, too, a large one, stuffed to the rafters with reproduction British Colonial bamboo furniture and matching decorative elements, like monkey-themed picture frames and plates. I paid $720 and couldn't wait to dig in.

"Reproductions," Henri said, wrinkling his nose.

I laughed. "You're an antiques snob, my friend," I said, thinking he shared that quality with Fred. To Fred, collectibles were like unwanted stepchildren. Sasha was more open-minded.

"And proud. I am a very proud man," Henri said, smiling.

The last room up for auction was huge, the largest Crawford offered, 15' by 10' by 10', and it was packed. In addition to boxes and plastic tubs, I spotted what appeared to be a nineteenth-century ornately carved mahogany occasional table. It looked pristine, and I felt my pulse quicken. Tallying my guesstimates of what the visible goods would sell for, I determined that I could bid as much as $1,300 for the unit and still meet my company's 30 percent max protocol.

The other four bidders leaped into a fierce battle. I stayed on the side until Caleb stepped out, which happened the moment Henri bid $700. He stomped off to his car without a word. I jumped in with a $900 bid, trying to shut down the bidding then and there. It didn't work.

Henri called out his hallmark "Oui," raising me to $950.

The four of us went around and around and the price went up and up until finally I hit my max and shook my head, signaling I was out. CiCi bid one more time, raising her offer to $1,350. Henri bid $1,400, and CiCi waved her arms back in forth in front of her, communicating she was done.

"Darn!" she said, turning to leave. "Next time I'll win one!"

I was chilled to the bone, but despite my discomfort, I decided to stay and see who won the bidding, then take a quick look at my units. Curiosity trumps cold every day of the week.

The newcomer in the Red Sox hat went toe to toe with Henri until the end, finally dropping out at $2,200. When he heard Henri's "Oui!" raising the bid one last time, he stomped off toward his car. *Maybe he's embarrassed at losing his first time out of the gate,* I thought. Bidding on abandoned storage units wasn't for the faint of heart. *He'll be back for his deposit in an hour or two, after he's cooled down, just like CiCi and Caleb.* Seconds later, he revved up his engine and tore out of the lot.

After about a minute and a half rummaging through

the smaller of my two lockers and finding delicate glassware of no particular value, I decided that I wasn't so
curious after all. It was just too cold for outdoor work.
I snapped the padlocks I'd brought with me into place,
knowing I could trust Eric to oversee the move-out process. I jogged around the corner and passed Henri's unit
in time to see him slit open a sealed cardboard box with
a small box cutter. I shouted good-bye as I passed, but he
didn't respond. He was deep in acquisition mode. Probably he didn't even hear me.

The best find from the first load Eric brought back was
a box of vintage jewelry, some obviously costume, some
maybe not. I reached into the box and, under a warped
old cardboard gift box, uncovered a Fulco di Verdura–
style wrapped heart, a brooch, about three inches high.
The stones appeared to be cabochon rubies and diamonds
set in white gold or platinum, with thick strands of what,
from the rich color, I suspected was 18-karat gold, draped
like ribbon over and around the heart. The ribbon was
creased and shone like gilt. It was breathtakingly beautiful. I turned it over and used a loupe to examine the back
for hallmarks and signatures. I spotted the mark indicating
it was made of platinum, Pt999, and then saw faint etch
marks. I moved closer to the light, and only by squinting
was I able to make out a code: C-136. I didn't know what it
meant, but I knew it meant something. I soft-whistled and
used the wall phone intercom to summon Sasha.

"Take a gander at this," I said, handing it to her as she
approached the worktable.

Sasha's eyes lit up as she turned it this way and that.
"It's magnificent, isn't it? Is it marked?"

"Yes. It looks like a Verdura, don't you think?"

"Yes," she said, nodding, "and I know he did a series
of wrapped hearts back in the forties."

"We need to get it over to Nate, pronto."

Nate, the third-generation Blackmore to work at the jewelry store his grandfather founded, was our go-to guy for jewelry appraisals. Blackmore's Jewelers was the best jewelry store on the coast, bar none.

She nodded. "I'll take it myself."

"There's a boxful of jewelry. Jade earrings. Rope necklaces. All sorts of things. Take everything—you never know. If Nate thinks this heart might be real, we should call Verdura's in New York. I remember them from when I worked at Frisco's; they were able to authenticate a brooch from one of Verdura's original drawings. They have something like ten thousand of those drawings, and all the original bills of sale. And almost nothing is computerized, or at least it wasn't back then. Can you imagine?"

"How can they find anything?"

"They're organized! If the piece is unique, and many of Verdura's were, since he designed one-of-a-kind pieces for Coco Chanel and Babe Paley and Greta Garbo and the Duchess of Windsor and so on, the process is pretty straight ahead. On the other hand, there are thousands of gold crisscross bracelets, for instance—it was one of his most popular designs—and those are, obviously, harder to authenticate. But let's not get ahead of ourselves. The first thing to do is get Nate's opinion."

She nodded and glanced at the clock mounted nearby. It was 11:55.

"I'll call him right away," she said.

I left Sasha with the jewelry and went to the far side of the warehouse, where Hank, Prescott's Maine Coon cat, was curled up in his basket. He mewed in his sleep as I approached, and his paws twitched. I smiled, thinking he was dreaming of chasing a mouse, or maybe a bird.

"Hi, Hank," I said softly. I didn't want to wake him.

"There may be a storm this weekend, so we'll get you all set up with extra food and water, okay?"

His paws twitched again.

"Good boy," I said, leaning in for a kiss. I pecked the top of his head. "I love you, Hank."

I was halfway up the spiral stairs that led to my private office when Cara's voice crackled over the PA system. "Josie, come to the front, please."

I paused at the heavy door that led from the warehouse to the front office with my hand on the push bar to peek through the security window I'd had installed at my insurance company's behest. The one-way glass was bulletproof, like the steel-reinforced door. It allowed us to see who was in the unsecured office before leaving the fortresslike warehouse, but no one standing or hiding in the office could see in.

Maybe it was a trick of light, but from where I stood, it looked as if Henri's eyes were boring into mine, as if he were somehow able to see through the mirrored glass, a disconcerting feeling. He was laughing at something Fred said, and I felt myself smile in response, as if I were sharing in the joke even though I couldn't hear a word.

FIVE

I STEPPED INTO the front office in time to hear Henri finishing a comment.

"...such weather. I am lucky, non, that I prefer cold to hot. In Paris, we have winter, certainly, but not like this. So cold for so many days in a row, and so much snow, it is not typical. Paris weather is more like New York, although my time in New York was not long, so I should not generalize."

"It's not really typical here, either," Fred said. "New Hampshire weather is always harsher than New York's, though."

Fred was a transplant from New York City, having joined my team about a year after I'd opened the business, and he looked the part. He wore Italian-made suits and skinny ties and cool-kid square-framed glasses that were always slipping down his nose. I'd been worried that Fred would have a rough time adjusting to small-town living, but he had taken to it as quickly and easily as Hank had taken to living at Prescott's, which is to say in no time at all.

"You, too, prefer the cold?" Henri asked him.

"Personally," Fred said with a crooked grin, "I prefer Bermuda."

Henri laughed, and Fred pushed up his glasses.

"Hey, Henri!" I said. "I didn't expect to see you again today. Are you here to brag on your unit?"

"Non," Henri said, smiling. "I come to you for help.

Look what I found in my locker." Henri opened an old scrapbook he'd placed on the guest table and pointed to two vintage restaurant menus tucked behind plastic sleeves on facing pages. One was from the venerable Four Seasons, the other from the equally famous Delmonico's. "Voilà!"

"Nice," I said.

"You will appraise them for me, oui? At your usual rate?"

"Thank you, Henri. We'd be pleased to. Is there anything else in the album we should look at?"

"You tell me. I saw only ticket stubs and playbills for Broadway shows, newspaper clippings of show openings, that sort of thing. Maybe they have value. I rely on you, mon ami." He smiled again, this one conveying devilish delight. "That is not all I found."

He opened a triangular post office poster mailer he'd leaned against a wall, and turned it upside down. A round poster tube fell out. He thumbed off the plastic lid and shook out a cylinder covered in brown wrapping paper, secured in three places with small bits of masking tape. The ends of all three sections of tape had been folded over, leaving nonsticky handles about an inch long, an easy way of ensuring you could remove the tape gently. Someone had packed whatever was about to be revealed with care. Henri peeled the tape back, then unfurled a thin stack of colorful posters. He moved the album to a chair so he could stretch the posters out across the guest table. Placing the triangular poster pack across the top and two Minnie Mouse paperweights I commandeered from Gretchen's desk on the bottom made the posters lie flat.

"Would you look at that," I said. Greta Garbo gazed at me from under blue-tinted lids, meeting my eyes and holding them. Her expression was knowing and brazen and dangerous. I glanced at Sasha and Fred, both staring at their computer monitors. "Fred? Sasha? Come here a sec and take a look at this. It's a poster for the movie *The Mysterious Lady.* What do you think?"

"I think it's no wonder she was the biggest star of her day," Fred said as he approached.

"It's in wonderful condition," Sasha added. "So good, it makes me wonder if it might be a repro."

"There's more." Henri deftly moved the Garbo poster to the back of the stack, revealing Lillian Gish dressed in bridal white in *Way Down East.* From the pout of her ruby lips to the sensual gaze of her limpid brown eyes, her expression defined ingenuous.

"Now, that's hot," Fred said.

"She's dressed like a bride," Sasha said. "I think she looks virginal, not hot."

Fred laughed. "Virginal *is* hot."

"Oh," she said, casting him a sideways glance.

I was always amazed how well Sasha and Fred got along, when on the face of it, they had so little in common. Sasha was a small-town girl, local to Rocky Point. She didn't like cities and didn't really understand how anyone could. Fred liked Rocky Point just fine but spent many of his days off in New York or Boston. Sasha was reserved. Fred was gregarious. Sasha dressed for comfort. Fred dressed for style. While they were as dissimilar in demeanor as any two people could be, the qualities they shared transcended their differences. They treasured the artifacts we appraised not only for their beauty but for their history, and they were both analytical truth seekers. Their disagreements, which to the uninitiated might smack of bickering, were never personal.

The third poster featured a Ku Klux Klansman riding a rearing horse, both horse and man clad in white, including head coverings. The man held a burning cross high above his head. The background swirled in fiery yellow-green. Oblongs of red-flecked gold dappled the man's thigh and arm and head. Evidently, the fire, though out of the frame, had just been ignited. The image was bone-chillingly fearsome, more so for what couldn't be seen. The text read "D.W. Griffith's *The Clansman*."

"That's terrifying," Sasha said, twirling a strand of hair, a sign of anxiety.

"Completely," I agreed. "The coloration is incredible, though. That green makes no sense, but it works. And that coppery gold from the flames…it's spectacular."

"Very distinctive," Fred said.

"The posters aren't all drawn by the same hand," I noted. "This style is much more dramatic than the others. The one with Lillian Gish is downright delicate."

"The color penetration is different, too," Sasha said, "and the palettes."

"Do either of you recognize any of the artists?" I asked.

Sasha shook her head. Fred said no.

"Here's the last one," Henri said, showing us a poster advertising Charlie Chaplin's *The Gold Rush*.

The image showed Chaplin shivering inside a rustic wood shack. The composition and coloration told the tale: Chaplin's feet were off the ground, his shoulders and hat covered in snow, his nose red. It wasn't the red of a drinking man; it was the red of a man frozen and frostbit. Chaplin's expression was fearful yet determined.

I searched the margins for copyright or printing information but saw none.

"These colors were more muted than the others," Sasha noted.

"Let's turn the posters over," I said.

Printing attribution or ordering information was absent

on the backs, too, encouraging me to think they weren't modern reproductions.

"They are valuable, non?" Henri asked.

"I don't know," I replied, smiling. "You know appraisals take time!"

"I'm an impatient man."

"We'll be as quick as we can." I turned to Gretchen. "Please give Henri a receipt for everything."

Henri and I watched as Sasha helped Gretchen take photos for the receipt; then Fred helped gather the scrapbook and posters together.

"Are these your packing materials, or did you find the posters wrapped this way?" Fred asked.

"The posters came that way. Why?"

Fred nodded and added the tubes and wrapping paper to the pile.

"You never know what might give up clues to ownership or value," Fred said.

Sasha and Fred said good-bye and, laden with Henri's objects, disappeared into the warehouse.

"Do you have a moment?" Henri asked in a near-whisper. "To talk privately?"

"Of course," I said. "Come upstairs."

As I led the way across the cold concrete to the spiral staircase, Fred and Sasha's voices drifted across the echoing span.

"Let's start with an analysis of the movies' production dates and locations," Fred said.

"No. I think we should examine the materials first," Sasha replied.

Their voices faded as we climbed the steps to the mezzanine level.

Back when the building housed a manufacturer of canvas products, the mezzanine had allowed managers to observe the production process. When I'd renovated the space, I'd converted it into a private office. What had been the factory floor was now the warehouse.

Henri sat in one of the two yellow brocade Queen Anne wing chairs positioned at one end of the room. I sat across from him on the matching love seat and waited for him to speak. Henri stared at his clasped hands for several seconds. When he looked up, his eyes conveyed sorrow.

"I have not told Leigh Ann about the call," he said. "I decided not to tell her ever. She has no need to know we lost a contract. I don't want to worry her."

He paused, perhaps hoping I'd say something comforting, maybe even that I'd say something like I understood or I admired his protective spirit.

"May I ask..." he continued, then paused to clear his throat. "I know I have no right to ask you to keep this from Leigh Ann..."

I felt my hackles raise. "I can't promise that, Henri. I'm sorry."

"I'm not asking you to lie, Josie, just not to volunteer information."

"I guess I can do that," I said, thinking that sins of omission didn't seem as bad as sins of commission.

"Thank you, Josie. I am in your debt."

"No, you're not," I said, standing, wanting this conversation over. "I'm very uncomfortable with this situation, Henri."

He nodded. "It is bad in every way."

Back in the front office, Henri signed where Gretchen told him, slid his copy of the receipt into his inside pocket, then turned to face me.

"Merci, Josie. Merci."

I nodded but couldn't think of anything to say.

I STOOD BY the frost-edged front window watching Henri walk slowly to his van. Puffs of pale gray exhaust colored the air as Henri let the engine warm up. He backed out of the space and left the lot, turning right, toward the ocean.

Bad news in business was always discouraging, even if the loss was merely an extra contract you weren't counting on, even if you didn't need the money to put food on the table or pay the electric bill, but between yesterday's apparent despondency and today's request for my continuing silence, I wondered if the situation was worse than Henri was letting on. If he hadn't brought it up again, I wouldn't have thought anything about it. His motivation to keep the truth from Leigh Ann must be strong indeed to outweigh his desire to keep his business affairs private. I hoped I was wrong. I liked Leigh Ann and Henri enormously, and I admired their work. They were a wonderful addition to Rocky Point, and it would be a shame if their business failed and they had to leave.

SIX

"WHAT DID YOU decide was the best approach?" I asked Sasha.

She and Fred were standing at one of the worktables that ranged along the warehouse walls. Small, weighted glass cylinders held each of the four silent movie posters flat.

"We're still debating," Sasha told me. "I really think we need to authenticate them before we spend any time on valuation. They could be midcentury or even current repros, in which case, what's the point of identifying the artist and so on?"

"And I think we should find out what they're worth in a best-case scenario. If we find out that they're only worth two dollars each, who cares what material was used? Let's cut to the chase."

"There are loads of good tactics," I said, not so much to smooth over their differences as to avoid getting drawn into their debate. "Since you're working on the jewelry, Sasha, how about if Fred and I take on the menus and the posters? Fred, are you okay with taking a crack at the scrapbook? Maybe start with the menus while I see what I can find out about the posters, then we can decide on next steps?"

"Sure," Fred said, turning his laserlike focus toward the scrapbook.

I turned to Sasha. "Where are you with the jewelry?"

"I'm meeting Nate at two to drop it off," Sasha said,

lifting the antique watch she wore on a gold chain for a peek, "so I need to get going on inventorying everything."

I glanced at the clock. It was 12:38.

"Will you have time?" I asked.

She smiled. "Gretchen offered to help with the photos... so, yes."

"Great!" I held up crossed fingers. "Here's hoping!"

Fred took the scrapbook back to his desk, and I took photos of the four posters, then examined the originals under magnification seeking artists' signatures or makers' marks, but found nothing to indicate who designed, drafted, or painted them, or when. Gently sweeping the surface of each poster with my fingertips, I was able to confirm that none was a printed repro—I was touching paint, not ink. Which didn't mean they were original. Factories existed solely to churn out mass-produced painted pieces. Some of the processes were all machine driven; others were all or part hand-painted, in a paint-by-numbers sort of way. That none of these posters listed a company name or ordering information was encouraging, but not conclusive.

I decided to examine each poster again, this time using a grid pattern, dividing the space into inch-wide columns, beginning at the top left and working my way down. I kept alert for anything that might give a clue to the artist's identity or the poster's origin. Some artists, I knew, signed their work in print or script so tiny as to be nearly impossible to see unless you were specifically looking for it. Others signed their work in unconventional places, sideways, for instance, or near the top. Artists employed characteristic styles, too, and once you knew the "tell," you could identify the maker. Just as a savvy poker player learned to recognize a competitor's curled lip or foot-tapping as a precursor to a bluff, an artist's singular brush stroke or idiosyncratic paint-layering technique was often a dead giveaway to his or her identity.

I started with *The Clansman,* the poster showing a rearing horse bearing a man carrying fire. Peering through the loupe, I worked my way down through an unbroken expanse of twilight blue sky and black border until I came to the iron gray of the horse's hoof. I continued looking, moving from left to right, seeing nothing unexpected. The color transitions were consistently sharp, with nothing mottled or stippled; the brush strokes were consistent, too. I continued on, and there, hidden on an inside fold of the man's cape, was what appeared to be a cat's face.

I lowered the loupe and blinked, certain I was seeing some weird optical illusion. A cat in a cape? In a poster advertising a somber drama?

I eased the loupe into place and looked again. Now that I knew what to expect, the cat's face was evident. Woven into shadows, its eyes open, its expression cheerful, was a sweet-looking rendition of a playful cat.

I moved to the poster on my left, Charlie Chaplin's *The Gold Rush,* and began my meticulous examination, narrow column by narrow column. This poster featured a different color palette from the one used in *The Clansman.* Instead of blues and grays, the artist chose shades of brown, orange, and gold. The painting technique was different, too, the paint strokes broader and the application thicker, both indicators that I was dealing with two different artists, yet hidden in the folds of the blanket Chaplin grasped in his hands was the same cat's face.

"You're kidding me," I whispered.

I dashed to the Greta Garbo poster for *The Mysterious Lady.* This design was simpler than the other three, yet painted with more complex brush-stroke and coloration patterns. I looked in the folds of Garbo's veil, examining each flowery bit of the lace, without luck. I turned my attention to her hair, then her blacker-than-black outfit, thinking perhaps the artist had hidden the cat behind or in the text that ran over it. Nothing. I sighed, frustrated, then started at the beginning, the upper left, resuming my methodical approach. Fifteen minutes later, I would have sworn there was no cat.

Way Down East, starring Lillian Gish, was the last of the posters. A cursory examination showed that the colors were more pastel than jewel hued, the composition more detailed, and the paint strokes more delicate than in the other three posters. I started, as I had in *The Mysterious Lady,* with the veil, and this time, I found the cat right away. The same adorable cat face was hidden amid the flowing lace near her left ear.

I heard a rattle, then a mew. Hank dropped his favorite mouse, purple with white feathers and a long felt tail, at my feet. It was one of a set Gretchen had bought him to celebrate his two-year anniversary as Prescott's cat.

"Hi, Hank," I said. "What do you think, little boy? Did the artist's cat pose for him?"

Hank mewed again, louder.

"You know, Hank...this is very odd...don't you think so?"

He mewed again, this time with added urgency, and flipped the mouse toward me with his paw. I picked it up and shook it back and forth. He pranced forward a few steps, his eyes riveted on the mouse. I lobbed it as far as I could toward the back of the warehouse, and Hank tore down the aisle like a racehorse in the stretch.

I compared the placement of the three cat faces and noted certain commonalities. All three were hidden in folds of fabric, and all were roughly the size of my thumbnail.

I hurried across the cold expanse of warehouse to reach

the spiral staircase leading to my office, considering the implications.

Upstairs, I brought up one of the proprietary Web sites we subscribed to, the one with the largest database and most sophisticated search capabilities. Under the page devoted to artists' signatures, I typed "cat" in the search window. With my finger poised over the ENTER button on my keyboard, I told the monitor, "Talk to me." I tapped it and within half a second received a list of eighty-six artists whose signatures included the letters *Cat*. Three used Cat as their first name, all women. The others had the syllable in their last names. There was a Cathern, a Catursky, and the like. I went to the FAQ page to see if they addressed visual signatures, but they didn't.

I called their customer service number, punched through their interactive menu to get a human being, and asked if there was any way to search their database to identify an artist who used a cat face as his or her signature. The woman I spoke to was intrigued but unhelpful. They didn't have any listing like that because, she said, it was rare that an artist would use a symbol in lieu of his name. She'd never heard of one who used a cat, explaining that she was a Dutch-master-era gal and knew nothing about silent movie posters. She put me on hold to ask around the office, then came back to report that no one on staff could help.

"Darn," I said after I was off the line.

We had three books on authenticating artists' signatures and related identification tactics in our in-house library, but none listed any information about an artist who used a cat's face in lieu of a signature. I Googled every term I could think of, in every combination I could imagine, and came up empty.

"Dead end after dead end," I told the air.

I brought up the four photographs I'd just taken on a split-screen view and frowned at them, aware of my ignorance. Even assuming they were original to the period, I didn't know whether the movie studios created them, how many of each style were produced, which artists did what kind of work, or anything. In order to appraise them, I needed to do more than identify the artists and verify they were originals; I needed to get up to speed on how the silent movie advertising industry had worked.

I had just opened our photo-manipulation software, preparing to isolate the cat images, when Hank came bounding up the stairs. He didn't have the mouse.

"Oh, no...couldn't you find it, Hank?"

He sat down and gave me a dirty look, implying that it was my fault for throwing his mouse improperly. He meowed loudly.

"When I go downstairs, I'll look for it, okay? It probably skittered under a shelving unit."

He meowed again, wanting me to go now. Right now.

"I'm sorry, Hank, I can't. I've got to do some work."

He mewed, hitting a sour note, expressing displeasure, and waited for several seconds, expecting me to change my mind. When I didn't, he gave a little "oh, well" mew and jumped onto the love seat. He curled into a tight ball and closed his eyes, ready for a nap.

I zoomed in on the three areas hiding the cat's face, creating a separate image for each, then laid them over one another. Like any signature, they were the same, but different. In one, the whiskers were a touch longer; in another, the eyes were slightly more slanted; and in the third, the face was a bit wider, yet they were unmistakably drawn by the same hand.

I consulted another of the proprietary services we subscribed to. This one's focus was on ephemera, items designed to be useful or important for a limited time, like newspapers, pamphlets, and playbills—and movie posters. They had an entire section devoted to movie posters, but only about fifty of their examples dated from the silent film era, which, I learned, ran from 1894 to 1929. According to their database, *The Mysterious Lady* dated from 1928; *Way Down East* came out in 1920; *The Clansman,* later renamed *Birth of a Nation,* was first shown in 1915; and *The Gold Rush* dated from 1925. Only the *Mysterious Lady* poster was featured on the site.

I brought up the photo I'd just taken of *The Mysterious Lady* and lined it up side by side with the one posted on the Web site. For all intents and purposes, the colors were identical, but the color placement differed slightly, implying that I was looking at two hand-painted versions of the same design, a likely occurrence, if, for instance, the company commissioned more than one poster from the same artist.

Both posters featured a solid dark orange border with a thin white line delineating the inside area, but the thickness of the white line differed, not much, but enough to notice. Inside the border, the paint on both appeared textured as if a light orange squiggly pattern had been randomly stenciled or painted over a darker shade of orange. In both, the pattern was more stippled than lacy, but the overall pattern in Henri's poster was darker. Also in both, wavy violet lines dissected the entire background, as if bands of sunlight radiated from a source emanating from somewhere unseen in back of Greta Garbo. I read the description on the Web site. It seemed the poster we were appraising was a Batiste Madalena original. I clicked the link to bring up his profile.

From 1924 to 1928, Batiste Madalena had designed and painted nearly 1,500 movie posters for the Eastman Theater in Rochester, New York, using tempera on illustrator board. When the Eastman Theater changed hands, the new owners trashed all the old posters, literally putting them out on the curb. Luckily, Madalena saw what was happening in time to rescue a few hundred of them. What's unknown is how many, if any, of the remainder are extant. I looked over at Hank. He'd rolled onto his back, and was dead asleep.

"What do you think, Hank?" I asked. "Did the new marketing team take one or two or fifty for their records? How about the former boss's secretary? Did she take any? How about the trash pickup guys?"

Hank snuffled and flipped onto his side, wedging his back paws under a cushion.

I brought up another proprietary site, this one listing art and artifact auction prices worldwide. Because of Madalena's prestige—his work had been exhibited at the Museum of Modern Art in 2008, for example—and the scarcity of his posters, one in very good condition, like Henri's, if authenticated, might be worth as much as $100,000.

"Oh, Hank!" I said aloud, watching him sleep. "Timing isn't all, but it's a lot. Here Henri confides he's having business troubles, and what happens? Boom...the very next day, he finds silent film memorabilia worth a small fortune. Keep your paws crossed that the posters are genuine, my friend. Keep those gorgeous little paws of yours crossed."

I didn't want to get Henri's hopes up, but neither did I want to withhold news of a potential windfall of this size. For all I knew he might be about to implement some unpleasant cuts, and this news could enable him to delay the belt tightening. I glanced at the time display at the bottom of my monitor. It was nearly two. Time had zipped by. I dialed Henri's cell phone, and after six rings, it went to voice mail.

"Henri," I said to the machine, "it's too early in the appraisal process to give you any definitive news, but I wanted to give you a quick update on what I've learned thus far. Give me a call when you get a chance. And keep your fingers crossed that what I think might be true is!"

I turned back to the cat symbol, looking again at the three faces side by side. I stood up and starting pacing, thinking about what I should do next. Hank opened an eye as I passed him, then, when I didn't stop to pet him, closed it. I walked from the bookshelf to the cabinet that housed my rooster collection, then back again.

From what I'd learned on the Web sites, if a company decided to create movie posters, they hired commercial artists, men and women, although mostly men, who were used to providing work for hire. The artists did the job and took the pay and that was that. They didn't sign their names or receive public credit in any way. Some went on to enjoy fame designing or painting in other media, and their past work was therefore known, but most did not, their accomplishments lost in time.

Nothing came to me, no insights, no strategy, no ideas about new research options. With my stomach growling, I gave up. I couldn't even get a hint of who the other artist might be, and what I'd learned did not encourage me to think that any additional research on my part would bring me any closer to finding answers. I'd reached a locked door and needed an expert with a key. Luckily, I knew where to find one. To prepare, I uploaded all seven photos, the four showing the overall posters and the three showing close-ups of the cats, to our FTP site, then cut-and-pasted the log-in info into an e-mail I sent myself.

I called my old New York City pal, Shelley.

Shelley and I had worked together at Frisco's, a top-drawer antiques auction house. When the fraud mess hit the fan—I was the whistle-blower in a price-fixing scheme—Shelley was one of the few people who hadn't acted like I had a dread disease and was contagious. Pretty much everyone else had ostracized me. I was the one doing the right thing, yet I'd been penalized as if the conspiracy I'd brought to light had been my fault, proving the truth of the old maxim that metaphorically, at least, messengers are the ones who get shot. I still cringe recalling my naïveté. I'd been completely blindsided when the weenie acting-CEO told me that because I wasn't a team player, I had to go. When I'd been called into his office, I'd anticipated a hero's welcome, a thank-you for helping vanquish a scourge that threatened the integrity of the company, and thus its very survival. Instead, security was standing by to escort me out of the building then and there, parading me past colleagues' cubicles in an effort, I was certain, to humiliate me while presenting everyone else with a cautionary tale. Despite widespread anti-Josie sentiment and the consequent near-universal shunning, Shelley had stayed friendly, and we were still friends today.

"Josie!" Shelley said. "It's so great to hear from you! Are you all right? I heard on the news that New Hampshire has broken every weather record this winter. Have you frozen to death? Are you ready to come back to civilization?"

"I know you think I'm crazy," I said, swiveling to face my window, "but I love it up here—even in winter." Four-foot-high banks of snow encircled the parking lot, a testament to the plow driver's evenhanded work. Every tree and bush, from ancient hardwoods to the four-foot rhododendrons Eric had planted last spring, was covered in a thin layer of brittle snow glittering with a prismlike sheen under the midday sun. It truly was a winter wonderland.

I grabbed my smart phone, took a photo of the maples and oaks so Shelley could see the majesty for herself, and e-mailed it to her.

"You're right," she said. "I do think you're crazy."

I laughed. "I just sent you a photo of the view from my office window. When you see it, you're going to be on the first plane north, it's that spectacular."

"You are such a card, Josie. Always good for a laugh. So what can I do you for?"

"I'm trying to appraise four silent movie posters. They're painted, not printed. There's no type anywhere indicating they're repros. I've done no materials analysis, so I'm going on my gut when I tell you I think they're genuine. One seems to be a Batiste Madalena. The others all have a cat face hidden in a fold of fabric, which makes me think they were all painted by the same artist, but the styles are profoundly different from one another. I have no idea where to look for information about this cat thing or how to identify the artist. Is Lottie still in charge of film ephemera?"

"God, no. She left last summer for Hollywood. She's running her own shop out there, and doing very well, by all I hear. We have a new guy, very good—intuitive, you know? His name is Marshall. You got pics?"

"Yup. I've already placed them into an FTP site. I'll zip off the log-in info now." I tapped the keys and forwarded the e-mail. "All righty, you should have it any sec. Thanks, Shelley."

"No prob. I'm always glad to help, and Marshall will positively pant with pleasure. You'll see what I mean. He pants over things like silent movie posters. Hold on while I confirm receipt." She paused. "Got it...let me see if I can log in. Yesseree...one, two...all righty, all seven photos are accounted for. That cat's a sweetie, isn't she?"

"Very. I can't thank you enough, Shelley."

"You're welcome. Oh! Look what else is here...another e-mail, this one with an all-white photo attached. You must have misfired with that camera of yours, Josie—oh...wait...it's *not* all white. I see a couple of brown lines... oh, I get it! Those are tree trunks. That is so cute, Josie! And that's the view from your office. I don't know how you stand the excitement."

I laughed again. "You're missing a big chunk of the world, my friend. You need to get out and about more, Shelley."

"You're right, I do. Which is why a bunch of us are going line dancing tonight at that new place I told you about in SoHo. Want to come?"

"I'd love to, but I think you should come up here and give my favorite country dance place a whirl. Think about it, Shelley. There are lots of tall, handsome men in jeans and flannel shirts and they all know how to two-step."

"Oh! You got me with that one, Josie. Now I'm actually going to have to think about it."

"I hope you will. I miss you, Shelley."

"I miss you, too, Josie. But I gotta tell you...that photo of snow and brown sticks...that's no way to get a New Yorker to come for a visit."

I was still chuckling as I scooped up Hank and headed downstairs.

SEVEN

"WHAT'S THE LATEST on the storm?" I asked as I walked into the front office, cradling Hank like a baby.

"Let me check," Cara said, tapping into her computer.

Hank snuggled his head under my chin and wrapped his paw around my neck, hugging me. He was purring loudly.

"Scattered flurries starting tomorrow afternoon," Cara read, "becoming steadier and heavier, with increasing winds by nightfall. They're calling for eight inches to… oh, my…two feet or even more, saying the range is so wide because there are unpredictable winds at the upper levels of the atmosphere. The storm might blow out to sea early on or it might get stuck in place, in which case we're in for a nor'easter." She looked up and blinked. "I had no idea."

"It looks like CiCi's Uncle Willy was right," I said, repeating his prediction. "Has Sasha gone to meet Nate?"

"Yes," Cara said. "She expects to be back by three thirty or so." She glanced at her monitor. "About half an hour from now." She smiled. "She was very excited about the jewelry. And Gretchen is overseeing the tag sale setup until Eric gets back."

"That should be soon, too," I said. I turned to Fred. "Any early news on the two menus?"

"They look like the real deal," Fred said, "probably from the seventies, based on relative pricing. Since I have the prices from when the Four Seasons opened in 1959, and I know they've been at the top of the restaurant scene ever since, I can calculate the current dollar value of the prices and get a decent guess about when this menu was written. I'm waiting for a call back from someone at the restaurant and someone else at the New York Public Library to confirm it." He pushed his glasses up. "Did you know the library has one of the world's great menu collections? Tens of thousands of menus. The historical and scholarship value can't be overstated." He double knuckle-tapped the plastic-shrouded Four Seasons menu. "You had to be a real sport to afford this place. From what I can see, you're looking at about ninety-five dollars a couple for dinner and wine back when this menu was current."

"What's that in today's dollars?" I asked.

"If I'm right about the timing, about three hundred eighty. A little more."

I nodded. "About two hundred dollars a person. New York City prices for sure."

"How does anyone afford to live there?" Cara asked, looking up from her typing, her blue eyes round with astonishment.

"You don't eat at the Four Seasons every night," I said.

"You don't eat at the Four Seasons ever," Fred said.

Cara and I both laughed.

"Do you think the menu has any value?" I asked Fred.

"I don't know. Most menus don't unless there's something unusual about it or there's a nifty association."

Over the years, we'd learned that association, the connection between an object and someone of historical or popular importance, was one of the primary determinants of value.

Fred grinned and pushed up his glasses. "President Kennedy celebrated his forty-fifth birthday dinner at the Four Seasons. That was the day Marilyn Monroe sang 'Happy Birthday' to him at Madison Square Garden. Now *that* menu, maybe signed by the president and Marilyn Monroe even though she wasn't at the dinner, that would be worth something."

I grinned appreciatively. "Can you imagine?"

"Yes," he said, with a beatific look on his face. "I can indeed imagine."

I laughed again. "What about the other one? Delmonico's?"

"The restaurant is famous on a lot of fronts," Fred said. "They've been around since 1827, and in the same location since 1837. They were the first dining establishment to call themselves by the French word 'restaurant.' That's funny to think about, isn't it? Of their many firsts, my personal favorite is that they invented Eggs Benedict. Although the fact that they named Baked Alaska is pretty cool, too."

"That menu is also from the seventies?"

"That's my best guess. The prices are comparable. Delmonico's was the first place, by the way, to have written menus—period."

"It's a great restaurant. My dad used to take me there sometimes when he'd come in from Boston on business." A picture came to me of us walking down William Street, not far from Wall Street, toward the restaurant. My dad had been dead for more than a decade, and while the pain of that crushing loss no longer stabbed at me, thinking of the good times still brought on a wave of melancholy, half reflective, half debilitating. I shooed the memory aside, forcing myself back to the here and now, and grinned. "I'd like to get my hands on a copy of that first menu."

"Yeah," Fred said, "or even better, a collection of all of them."

Hank wiggled a little, waking up. He licked my chin and jumped down, stretching first his top half, then his bottom half, then ambled off to the warehouse door. He meowed imperiously, wanting in.

The phone rang, and Cara answered it. Someone was calling for directions to the tag sale. *Yay!* I thought as I opened the door for Hank—a new customer.

I waved good-bye to Fred and followed Hank into the warehouse. He headed left toward his domain. I walked to the right, toward the inside entrance to the tag sale venue.

When I'd first purchased the property, the room we used for the weekly tag sale was more like a shack than a sales room. I'd brought it up to code and winterized it but left it rustic in appearance. During last autumn's expansion, I'd integrated our vintage clothing shop into the space and added square footage, while maintaining the same simple decor. I glanced at the wall clock as I pushed open the door. It was 3:10. Gretchen stood near the front with her back to me helping two temporary workers arrange a collection of wooden boxes.

Before I could call to her, Eric walked in from the warehouse door.

"Hey, Eric!" I said. Noting his gloomy expression, I added, "Is everything all right?"

"Sorry it took me so long," Eric said. "I helped Henri load some stuff. I thought you wouldn't mind."

Eric was tall and thin, in his midtwenties. He was trustworthy and earnest, taking his responsibilities seriously, sometimes too seriously. He'd started at Prescott's as a part-timer while still in high school, went full-time as soon as he graduated, and was one of the cornerstones of my company's success.

"You thought right," I said, smiling. "Did you spot any good surprises as you were moving our things?"

"No—all I saw was bags and boxes. I put everything inside one of the roped-off areas. Section eighteen. It's too cold to leave things on the loading dock."

"Good thinking, Eric. I appreciate your initiative."

Eric flushed, discomfited yet pleased at hearing praise. Gretchen finished issuing her instructions to the temps and joined us, her emerald eyes bright.

"Those boxes are ingeniously crafted!" she said. "Did you see the one with the rosewood inlay? It slides open sideways so it doesn't mess up the pattern."

I agreed the collection was a terrific find, then asked for an update.

"We're on schedule," Gretchen said.

"Even ahead a little," Eric said, surveying the room with an experienced eye.

"I waited for you to decide about the decanters. How do you think we should display them?"

"I'll leave you to it," I said and hurried toward section 18.

Two hours later, after I'd sorted through a seemingly endless collection of no-name dishes and glassware, Cara's voice came over the PA system asking me to pick up the house phone.

"Sorry to disturb you, Josie," she said. "Everyone's left for the day except Fred and me, and we're leaving soon. Sasha said to tell you she has no news about the jewelry, and Leigh Ann Dubois is here asking to see you."

I thanked her, asked her to tell Leigh Ann I'd be right there, and headed for the front.

Leigh Ann stood next to a man about our age, maybe a year or two older. She looked sad or mad, I couldn't tell which. The man was taller than average and solidly built, like a weight lifter, with short, spiky graying hair. His expression was serious but not stern. He nodded at me, and I nodded back.

"This is Scott Richey, Josie," Leigh Ann said. "The old friend I told you was coming up from New York."

"Hi," I said, smiling in his direction, and he nodded

again but didn't return my smile. A dynamic was at work I didn't understand. I recognized trouble but couldn't imagine how I fit into the equation. "Would you like some coffee or—"

"Have you heard from Henri?" Leigh Ann asked, breaking in.

"He was here around noon. Is that what you mean?"

"When did he leave?"

"I don't know exactly. About quarter past, I guess. Why?"

"I'm worried that something's happened to him." She paused. "I know how I must sound—hysterical, right? The thing is... I know him. Henri was due back to the store by three, and I haven't heard from him. It's completely unlike him to be late and not call. Did he tell you where he was going?"

"Yes," I said, her worry communicating itself to me. She didn't sound hysterical. She sounded apprehensive for cause. "Back to the storage unit to finish clearing it out. I know he made it, because Eric helped him load the van. Maybe he found something he wanted to get appraised right away."

"Then he would have gone back to your place."

"Unless it was a specialty item. Like rare stamps or jewelry, objects we don't appraise in-house."

"In which case he would have called to tell me about it. Oh! Where is that man? Scott and I just came from Crawford's. The van isn't there, and the unit is locked up tight. I don't know what to do."

"Maybe he's just running some errands."

She was eager to believe good news; her eyes lit up. "Yes, that must be it. He's cooking one of his famous gourmet dinners tonight. He's probably ignoring his phone because he's talking to Al, the butcher, or Jonathan at the wine store."

I smiled. "That sounds exactly like him. Or Sal in the cheese shop. I bet he's stopping there, too."

"I'll call them right now."

"Let me get you the numbers," I said and asked Cara to look them up.

Leigh Ann sat at the guest table. With each "No, he hasn't been here" she reported, her shoulders drooped farther. She thanked Sal, her final call, and looked at me, her eyes moist, the flash of optimism gone.

"I don't know what to do, Josie," she said. "He's not answering his phone or responding to texts."

"It's only been a couple of hours," I said.

"He's never late. He always calls."

"What do you think happened?"

"I don't know...a car accident, maybe. The highways are cleared, but the back roads are still slick." She paused. "I'm just so afraid."

I glanced at Scott, but his eyes were on Leigh Ann, while hers remained on mine, a triangle of concern. I met her steady gaze, thinking that cell phones could be traced, but that there was no way a phone company would help a wife find her husband via his cell phone without police intervention.

"The van is new, isn't it?" I asked. "Because I think all new vehicles have GPS in them."

"That's a terrific idea, Josie," she said, buoyant again. "We bought the van up here after we moved. I'll ask the dealer. Thank you."

"Is the van in your name?" Scott asked, his voice strong yet warm.

"Oh!" Leigh Ann said, covering her mouth with her

hand, her spirits sinking. "No." She opened her eyes wide. "What should I do?"

"Let's stop at the dealer and ask how it works and whether we can access the info," Scott said. "No harm in asking."

She nodded. "Thank you, Scott." To me, she added, "I'm so upset…it helps to have something to do." She patted Scott's arm. "And someone to help me do it."

"Keep me posted, okay?" I asked.

She promised she would. Scott offered his hand and we shook, a good one, a real grip, but not a clench, and lasting just the right amount of time.

As soon as the door closed behind them, Cara put on her coat, preparing to leave.

"It's no wonder she's worried," Cara said.

"I would be, too," I agreed.

"What do you think is going on?" Fred asked.

I shrugged. "I have no idea. But I can tell you this— from what I know of Henri, Leigh Ann is right to be upset. One time, just before Christmas, we had an appointment to meet at CiCi's shop. He wanted my opinion on the value of a midcentury teak sofa he was considering purchasing for a client. He called to tell me he was running into more traffic than he expected and would be a little late. He called two more times to give me updates on his progress. Henri was not thoughtless. Just the opposite."

Cara shook her head. "Why would a man that thoughtful not call his wife?"

"Why do leopards ever change their spots?" Fred asked.

"They don't," I said. "Something happened. Maybe they had a fight earlier in the day."

"And weren't speaking," Fred said, pushing up his glasses. "That's logical…cause and effect."

"Or he can't call her," Cara said, her eyes clouding over

as she gave voice to her concern. "Leigh Ann is right. The back roads are slick, and in rural areas, there are so many of them that run alongside hills and cliffs."

"And plenty that don't have guardrails," Fred added.

"All true," I said. "We shouldn't let our imaginations go wild, though. Probably he's just talking to a new butcher, one he hasn't used before, someone Leigh Ann doesn't know about."

"Do you really think that's possible?" Cara asked.

I paused before answering, thinking about Henri and Leigh Ann and secrets. Fred leaned back, lacing his hands behind his head, elbows out, waiting for me to reply. Cara's intelligent blue eyes, guileless and attentive, stayed on my face.

"No," I said. "I left Henri a good-news voice mail about one of the silent movie posters around two—I think there's a better than even chance that it's valuable. If he could have called me back, he would have done so."

"Anyone would," Cara said, anxiety bubbling into her voice, her tone becoming tremulous. "Oh, my."

Fred shook his head. "Not calling back when you get a you've-got-money-honey message? That doesn't sound good."

"No," I agreed. "It really doesn't."

After Fred and Cara left for the day, I refreshed Hank's food and water, adding extra, just in case, layered up against the cold, and turned out the lights. I couldn't imagine how Leigh Ann must be feeling. I tried to think how I'd feel if Ty just vanished, if he went out for groceries and never came home. Heart-clenching terror, I thought. I'd be petrified, frozen into immobility, unable to breathe.

The entire time I was closing up, I tried to find a credible explanation for Henri's disappearance, but I couldn't. Something was very wrong.

EIGHT

THE *SEACOAST STAR* REPORTER, Wes Smith, called about nine. I thought of Wes as an adorable, yet annoying, younger brother. He was funny and hardworking and clever and honest, and he always seemed to know everything about everything. He was also as maddening as a mosquito.

I was sitting cross-legged on the long bench that ran under the windows next to my kitchen table watching Ty load dishes into the dishwasher and telling him about going to Delmonico's with my dad. I recognized Wes's number on the phone ID display and was tempted to let the call go to voice mail. Talking to Wes was work. I hadn't heard from Leigh Ann about Henri, though, and Wes never called about nothing, so I told Ty I needed to take the call.

"Wait till you hear my info-bomb," Wes said as soon as he heard my voice, skipping pleasantries, par for his course. Wes wasn't a bad guy; he was just rough around the edges.

"I'm fine, Wes. How about you?"

"Good, good, listen—I got major-league big-time news about a friend of yours. Henri Dubois. He's a friend, right?"

I sat forward, my nose for trouble signaling bad news was about to hit the airwaves. "What's happened?"

"Is he a friend?" Wes asked.

I understood his unspoken demand—if I didn't give him something, I'd get nothing. "Yes, and business colleague. What's going on, Wes?"

"He's missing."

"I know," I said.

"Fill me in," he demanded.

"I don't have any other information. I thought maybe you were calling to report that he'd been found. What do you know?"

"Just what I hear on the police scanner."

"The police scanner! Oh, my God, Wes! What happened!"

Ty paused, plate in hand. "What's wrong?" he asked in a low tone.

I looked at him, shock registering on my face, but I didn't reply. I was holding my breath, waiting for Wes's answer.

"His wife, Leigh Ann Dubois, reported him missing about an hour ago."

"What are they doing? Have they organized a search?"

"Not yet. The police won't declare an adult missing until he's been gone for twenty-four hours. So far, he's just late."

"This isn't good, Wes. He's been gone for hours, and he's not that sort of guy."

"That's what they all say. In any event, until he turns up, you're the hot potato!"

"What are you talking about?"

"You're the last person to see him today, which gives you all sorts of creds on this one. Talk to me. What do you know?"

Ty placed the plate in the rack, then took a step toward me. I raised my palm like a traffic cop, and he stopped walking, his eyes fixed on mine.

"I don't know anything! And I wasn't the last person to see him. Eric saw him later at the storage facility." As soon as I spoke the words, I realized that Wes had done it again. He had a gift for drawing me out, for getting me to tell him more than I'd planned. Talking openly to Wes wasn't necessarily a bad thing, because he always returned the favor, sharing information I'd have no other way of learning, and his fact-gathering tentacles reached far and deep, but I hated when it happened without my even being aware of it.

"When?" Wes asked.

"I don't know exactly...early afternoon sometime."

"Do you want to ask Eric about the timing yourself and call me back? Or do you want me to call him?"

"Neither," I said. "Let's not put the cart before the horse, Wes. There may well be some innocent explanation for Henri's disappearance."

"Like what? Leigh Ann told the police he was supposed to cook some fancy dinner. They have a guest staying with them."

"Maybe his van rolled into a ravine or something," I said, praying it wasn't true.

"We don't live in the middle of nowhere, Josie. He was driving from Crawford's on Route 1 to Rocky Point Village, to the wine shop and the butcher. There are no ravines en route."

"That's a good point, and really reassuring, Wes. Still, it's possible he was in an accident."

"I've checked with both hospitals in the area. No soap."

"You're scaring me."

"Well, it's pretty scary—a straight-arrow newlywed disappears in broad daylight. Great headline possibilities, though, huh? I could do 'Wed, Then Dead?' with a question mark, you know, to show it's speculation. Or 'Missing by Design?' again using a question mark. Pretty good, don't you think? Anyway...do you want to call Eric or shall I?"

"Leave Eric alone, Wes. Don't make me sorry I told you about him."

Wes sighed, signaling his disappointment. "Until to-morrow."

"In which case the police will be involved."

"That's why I need a head start." He paused, maybe ex-pecting me to cave. After several seconds, he sighed again, letting me know his disappointment had deepened. "Do you think Henri just vamoosed?"

"No," I said, hoping I was right, thinking that no mat-ter how bad business was, surely he wouldn't just pick up and go, leaving Leigh Ann holding the bag.

"Lots of guys do."

"I'm going to hang up now, Wes. I'll talk to you to-morrow."

"Don't hang up! I need background. I promise I won't use your name on anything you tell me unless I confirm it with someone else."

"You have to promise you won't use my name, period. Same as always."

"Josie," he whined, "you're not being reasonable."

"I'll talk to you tomorrow, Wes. Bye-bye."

I hung up and looked up at Ty. He resumed loading the dishwasher.

"Henri?" he asked.

"Wes thinks maybe he's gone AWOL."

"You don't?"

"Do guys really do that?"

"Sure. All the time."

"Jeesh! And you know this how?"

"From my years as Rocky Point's police chief investi-gating missing people. In a town this size, it didn't hap-pen all that often, but it happened more than a few times. Also, I keep current with Homeland Security's research about disenfranchised men, some of whom just disappear into the night to start a new life somewhere else and some of whom become terrorists. More men than you think just walk away."

"In today's technologically sophisticated world, why aren't they found in about a second and a half?"

"Sometimes no one cares enough to look. Sometimes they go off the grid, living on the land, joining a commune, disappearing into the bush in a distant country, that kind of thing. Sometimes they create a new fake identity."

He started the dishwasher, and it came to life with a muted whir.

"Do you ever think of leaving?" I asked. "Of just walking away?"

"No. Don't worry, sweetums." He gave me a knee-weakening smile. "I'm not going anywhere. Plus which, I don't fit the profile."

I smiled back. "I didn't know there was a profile."

"Most of the men who leave their families without a word and disappear have both a history of avoiding responsibility and difficulty handling setbacks. Some guys work very well in regimented situations, for instance, like the military, but can't cut it on their own. Other guys are fine as long as things go their way but collapse or freeze or go postal when trouble comes a-knockin'. I've always been a you-can-count-on-me sort of guy. Big into personal responsibility. And I'm of the 'trouble happens, move on' philosophical bent. Not to blow my own horn or anything."

I smiled again. "No wonder I fell for you."

Ty slid into the booth beside me, pulling me close.

"I love you," he said, nuzzling my ear.

"I love you, too," I whispered and kissed him, a long one, full of romance and caring.

I leaned my head against his shoulder, and we sat in

comfortable silence for several seconds while I thought about men who vanish.

"You're into personal responsibility," I said, "yet you thrived when you were in the army, and you're thriving now in a very big decentralized organization."

"The ability to work in a highly structured organization and valuing personal responsibility aren't mutually exclusive characteristics. If we're looking at it from a profile perspective, the key issue is fitting in. Men who leave don't fit in. They're physically, emotionally, or mentally isolated, and isolation is a reliable predictor of trouble."

"Of all sorts of trouble, right?" I asked. "From suicide to homicide."

"To just walking away—but nothing is black and white. Legions of people endure lifelong feelings of bitter isolation and don't kill themselves or others or disappear."

"'The mass of men lead lives of quiet desperation.'"

"Thoreau," he said. "He also said, 'It is characteristic of wisdom not to do desperate things.' Maybe Henri's not wise."

"I can't believe you just quoted Thoreau from memory."

"I'm a man of many facets."

"And very smart," I said.

"And lucky in love."

I looked deep into his eyes, feeling the familiar, irresistible pull of attraction, a visceral link that warmed me like fire. "So where's Henri?"

"I don't know."

"I'm upset."

He encircled me with his arms and held me close. "That means you need a hug."

As usual, he was right—I did need a hug.

At six thirty the next morning, just as I was about to

step into a steamy shower, the phone rang. I turned off the water and grabbed it.

"I'm sorry to call so early," Leigh Ann said, her tone frenetic, "but I need help. I know today is tag sale day, so I figured I'd better get you before you're tied up with business."

I shivered and clasped the lapels of my pink chenille bathrobe tightly around my throat.

"What can I do?" I asked.

"Ask Eric to meet me at Crawford's, at the storage unit, at noon. The police have agreed to open a missing person investigation then. As far as we know, Eric was the last person to have seen Henri, and since he saw him there, that's where they want to start the hunt. Can you do that?"

"Certainly. Do you want me to have Eric call the police now?"

"No. Because of that stupid rule—they won't do anything until Henri's been missing twenty-four hours—if they know someone saw him later than that, they'd delay starting the investigation. Once they officially open it, though, they have to continue. I've already hedged a little, calling it noon when you told me Eric saw him later than that."

"You haven't heard a word from him? Not a word?"

"No." She gulped, swallowing tears. "I've texted him a dozen times and called more often than that."

"Oh, God, Leigh Ann. This is so unbelievable. So frightening."

"I'm terrified, Josie. Just frightened beyond words." She gulped again, but this time it took her several seconds to regain her composure. "After we left your place yesterday, Scott and I drove every route I could think of from the storage facility back to the shop, trying to see if I could find the van…or if there was a broken guard rail or tire tracks disappearing down an embankment, anything like that. I didn't see any signs of an accident, and I didn't find the van. It's as if Henri just vanished into thin air."

"I'm so sorry, Leigh Ann. Did you contact the dealership?"

"Yes, and they can help, but they require a subpoena to let me access the records, and that requires the police to send a formal request to the attorney general, etcetera, etcetera. Nothing can happen until the investigation is officially opened. The van isn't fitted with LoJack or anything like it. There's an app called Find My Phone, but Henri never installed it. To use their own technology to find his phone, the phone company said the same thing as the dealer—they need a subpoena, too."

"You must be going insane with worry, Leigh Ann. Is there anything I can do at this point? Do you want company? Have you eaten anything?"

She sniffled, then swallowed loudly. "Thank you, Josie. I'm all right. As all right as I can be. Scott is here." She paused. "He'll drive me to the storage facility."

I ended the call with another offer to help, aware of spiky tension growing inside me at a feverish pace, tightening the muscles along my shoulders and upper back, pricking at my stomach and heart. I looked into the mirror hoping to see that I looked less panicky than I felt. Remnants of steam from the shower had created a moiré pattern on the mirror, and looking at my winter-pale skin and wide-eyed anxious expression through the cloudy, lacy weave suggested a fragility more in line with a character from a Victorian novel than the self-reliant woman I knew myself to be. Grasping my cuff to hold my sleeve in place, I used the chenille like a rag to clear the mist and was relieved to see that once again, with the glass clean,

I looked like myself. I found comfort in knowing that the emotions churning in me didn't show.

The time display on my phone told me Ty was an hour out of Rocky Point, with two hours still to drive to reach his training destination, Berlin. At five thirty, I'd barely been aware of his good-bye kiss. I pushed the speed dial button I'd assigned to him and got lucky. I caught him at a rest stop stirring milk into coffee.

"I have news," I said, "not good." I stared at the old-fashioned black and white hexagonal floor tiles, uncertain how to phrase the bad news. "It's Henri. Leigh Ann just called. There's still no word." I repeated what she told me, then said, "I wish you didn't have to work today."

"Me, too. I'm really sorry to hear this, Josie. I thought for sure she'd have heard from him by now."

"I know. This is the kind of thing that you read about, not the kind of thing that actually happens to people you know."

"How's she doing?"

"Better than I would be if you were the one who'd gone missing. She was actually formulating plans, like getting court orders and so on."

"You'd be doing just the same. You personify grace under pressure."

"Wow," I said, cheered up by his unexpected praise. "Thank you. Hurry home... Wait! What am I saying? Considering the storm they're predicting, drive slowly."

"I'm still hoping to make it back by late afternoon, but I got to tell you—the forecasts are growing more ominous by the minute. I may have to stay over."

I told him I understood and I loved him, and he told me he loved me, too, and then we hung up.

I turned the shower on again, and as I stepped under the hot, pulsing water, I thought that maybe when I'd tried to find a logical reason for Henri's disappearance, I'd been overcomplicating the issue. Maybe he'd left simply because he'd had enough.

I could see how a man who loved Paris and New York City might have found the unremitting quiet of a small New Hampshire town unendurable. Add in a dose of business disappointment, a wife he seemed certain would be unforgiving, and a forecast of yet another storm in a season of record-breaking snow, which along with the inhumane subzero temperatures we'd been enduring was certain to slow down commerce, and I could see how the prospect of starting a new life in a warmer climate might have appeal.

What if Henri found something valuable in his storage unit, something easy to sell and lucrative enough to fund a fresh start? Perhaps he tucked it in his pocket or tossed it in the van and headed for the interstate, instead of home. Route 95 was plowed clear and stretched all the way to Florida.

NINE

ERIC AND I arrived at Crawford's just before noon in separate vehicles, so when Eric was done he could make a delivery. He parked our company van off to the side. I drove my personal car and parked next to him. I waved to Leigh Ann, sitting in the passenger seat of her SUV, a white Ford Explorer. Scott was behind the wheel. The engine was running. Even from a hundred feet away, I could see that Leigh Ann's eyes were rimmed in red and her skin was blotchy, as if she'd spent the night crying. Scott's brow was deeply lined.

Police Chief Ellis Hunter stood with his back to Henri's storage unit. He wore a standard-issue police hat, heavy wool, with a fur lining. The ear flaps were down. The Rocky Point police medallion was embroidered on the front. His down coat was bulky. A dark red jagged scar ran along his right eye, the color muted in the dull light filtering through the thick clouds. Ellis was just shy of six feet, with regular features, and gray eyes that communicated both his sedulous approach to work and his genuine empathy. Ellis and I were friends. He'd taken Rocky Point's top cop job after retiring as a New York City homicide detective, and for just about the whole time he'd been here, close to three years, he'd been dating Zoë, my landlady, neighbor, and best friend. We spent a lot of time together as couples, all of it good. A younger police officer in uniform, a tall blonde named Officer F. Meade, stood beside him. She wore the same style of hat and a longer version of the down coat.

Scott kept his hand on Leigh Ann's elbow as they walked toward the locker. From the concerned glances he kept aiming in her direction, I had the sense he thought she might collapse. From her haggard appearance, I thought he might be right.

"Thanks for coming," Ellis told me as I approached.

Ellis looked at Eric, then back at me, his raised brows posing a question he didn't ask. He wanted to know why Eric was with me, but he didn't want to make a thing of it until he knew what was what.

"You remember Eric, right?" I asked.

"Sure." He looked at him. "Do you have information about Henri Dubois?"

"Is the investigation official yet?" I asked, jumping in before Eric could answer.

"No. Not until noon." He raised his jacket sleeve enough to see his watch. "Five minutes from now. That's the last time you saw him, right? Noon, yesterday?"

"About then, yes. I don't know the exact time."

Eric stood next to me, taking it in. Ellis focused on him. "What do you know, Eric?" he asked, his tone stern.

Eric looked at me, and I shook my head.

"Please," Leigh Ann said, her eyes on Ellis.

"I have noon straight up," Scott said.

I noted that he didn't look at his watch. Ellis did, and I followed his gaze. It was three minutes to twelve. Ellis didn't comment. He cast his eyes around the lot, then up at the sky. The clouds were solidly gray, and it smelled like snow. He waited another fifteen seconds or so, then turned toward Officer Meade.

"Please note that it's twelve. We're accepting a missing person report on Henri Dubois." He faced Eric. "What do you know?"

"I don't know anything," Eric said. "I mean, I saw Henri yesterday afternoon, here. I helped him load his van. He was fine."

"What time was that?"

"I've tried to think," Eric said, "but I just didn't notice the time."

"Can you figure it by working backward?" I asked. "You walked into the tag sale room about three ten or three fifteen. Call it three fifteen."

He nodded and bit his lip, concentrating. Leigh Ann clung to Scott's arm, her eyes steady on Eric's face, willing him to remember.

"It took me a good half hour to unload the van back at our place," Eric said. "That's two forty-five. And it's about a ten-minute drive from here. So I must have left here about two thirty-five. I swept out the unit, then got Vicki to okay it. She inspected it and gave me back our deposit. All told, that took about fifteen minutes. So that's two twenty. Before that, I loaded our van, and it took longer to load it than it did to unload it, because, you know how it is, you have to work it like a puzzle to get everything in...call it forty-five minutes...that's what? About one thirty-five. Maybe one thirty. I helped Henri just before that, and it took us, I don't know, about ten or fifteen minutes, not longer, so that would have been about one twenty, maybe one fifteen." He nodded. "Somewhere in there. That's when I saw him last. At the end of that time... about one thirty."

"Good," Ellis said. "How did you come to help him?"

"He asked. He came to where I was working and asked if I could help him load a couple of heavy items. I said sure, locked up our van and the unit, and walked with him over to his locker."

Ellis had him repeat their conversation as nearly as he could, and Eric did a good job, but I couldn't see how anyone could glean anything meaningful from their exchange. As far as I could tell, their discussion was both banal and innocuous. They made three trips to the van, lugging furniture and heavy boxes. Henri thanked him. Eric said he was glad to help. Henri starting carting more boxes on his own, and Eric walked back to our unit to finish loading our van. After he got the deposit back from Vicki, he left. He didn't notice if Henri was still working. He didn't notice if the van was still there. He was fretting about how long it took him to clean out the locker. He knew Gretchen was covering for him in the tag sale room, and he wanted to get back.

"How did Henri seem?" Ellis asked.

"Fine," Eric said.

"Same as always?"

"I guess."

"No sadness? No worry? No extra happiness?"

Eric looked bewildered. He wasn't a man used to considering people's emotional states.

"I don't know," he said. "He seemed fine."

Ellis thanked him again and asked him to come to the station house after making his delivery to repeat his statement on video. Eric, anxiety evident in his eyes, looked at me, and I nodded.

"Okay," Eric said.

Ellis told Officer Meade to alert Detective Brownley to expect Eric later. She nodded and tapped something into her smart phone.

"So Henri was last seen at one thirty," Leigh Ann said softly, trying to find hope, trying to find answers.

"Now we need to—" Ellis broke off as Vicki Crawford's clomping caught his attention.

We all turned and watched her cross the lot, her expression fierce.

"What's going on?" she demanded.

"I'm Police Chief Hunter," Ellis said, matching her tone. "And you are?"

"Vicki Crawford. I own this place."

"Good to meet you. We spoke earlier. As I explained, we're investigating the disappearance of one of your business associates."

"And I told you that I don't know anything about any disappearance."

"Did you see Henri Dubois here yesterday?"

"Sure, in the morning at the auction, and a couple of times during the afternoon, loading up his van."

"Can you pinpoint the last time you saw him?"

"I don't keep that close track. It was after lunch, so around twelve thirty. I eat early."

"Any altercations?"

"Altercations? Give me a break. This is a storage facility. Why would there be fights?"

"Did you notice anything unusual about Henri?" he asked.

"Like what?" Vicki asked, impatient and irritated.

"Like anything. Was he sad? Mad? Glad? Anything?"

"He was happy to have won the bid. He told me so when he paid for it."

"Anything else? Anything later?"

"This is a business. I don't ask about people's moods."

"Point taken." Ellis scanned the lot, his eyes coming to rest on Leigh Ann's statuelike face. My guess is that she was one rung away from hysteria, but to look at her, you'd never know it. She was totally self-contained. "Our next step, I think, is to open the storage room. Is this your lock?"

"No," Vicki said. "I presume it's his." Her lips thinned. "It isn't supposed to be here. The deal is you win the bid, you clear out the unit pronto, by the end of the day, which means he's forfeited his deposit."

"There may be extenuating circumstances," Ellis said. He turned to Leigh Ann. "Do you have a key?"

She shook her head. "Henri would have it."

Ellis turned to Vicki. "Do you have any shears we can use?"

"Forget it. No way can you break into a room just on your say-so."

"This is his wife," Ellis said, nodding in Leigh Ann's direction. "She's reported him missing. This is an official police investigation."

"I don't know anything about any of that. I don't know you. I don't know her. All I know is that the unit is registered in Henri Dubois's name, not his wife's, and if you want in, I need to see a piece of paper giving you the right."

Ellis didn't try to get her to change her mind. "I'll get the paperwork going. It shouldn't take long to get a court order."

"Whenever," Vicki said. "Let me know. I'll be in my office." She marched off.

I ran after her.

"Vicki!" I called, and she stopped. "Can we wait in your office? It's so cold, and it's, well, it's kind of an emergency."

She shrugged. "Sure."

I thanked her, but she waved it aside. Vicki wasn't wired for gratitude.

Leigh Ann, Scott, and I squeezed into Vicki's small office, standing around, taking turns sitting on the one guest

chair, talking quietly so as not to disturb her, working behind her desk, ignoring us. Out the window I could see
Ellis and Officer Meade sitting in his idling SUV, waiting.

At five after two, another police vehicle, this one
marked, pulled into the lot and rolled to a stop next to Ellis's. Two minutes later, the cruiser turned onto Route 1
and Officer Meade headed our way. She stepped inside the
office and handed Vicki a legal-sized document.

Vicki read it through and stood up. "Okay, then."

She brought out the shears, and we followed her as she
strode across the lot. Ellis used them, snapping Henri's
metal lock like a matchstick. He swung the door wide and
switched on his torch.

A jumble of broken objects littered the floor, chunks
of blue and white porcelain, maybe from a vase or garden stool, and shards of crystal. Before I had a coherent
thought about why trashed items would be in the locker,
Leigh Ann shrieked, a guttural sound that made me jump.
She stumbled backward two steps, then froze, her index
finger pointing toward the storage room. Her arm dropped,
her eyes fluttered, and she spiraled to the ground.

"Leigh Ann!" Scott exclaimed, lunging to catch her
as she fell.

I took a step to help, then stopped. Scott caught her before she hit the pavement. Holding her upright, he looked
around wildly, uncertain what to do, uncertain what was
happening. I peered into the unit and finally saw what
Leigh Ann had seen right away. Henri lay facedown on
the ground, half hidden by a stack of unlabeled cardboard
boxes.

I gasped. "Oh, my God!" I whispered, then covered my
mouth with my gloved hands.

Henri's arms were bent and his fingers curled as if he'd
braced himself to break his fall. His gold wedding band

glinted as Ellis's flashlight passed over his hand. Henri's head was turned to the right. His eyes were closed. Congealed blood dotted and striped his face and pooled alongside his head.

Without warning, Leigh Ann recovered from her faint, screamed like nothing I've ever heard, a wild animal shriek, and lurched forward, breaking from Scott's grip. She plunged into the storage unit and hurled herself on top of Henri's corpse, flailing. Her screams escalated into wails, echoing off the corrugated metal walls and ceiling, a death knell.

Ellis strode after her, reaching her in four paces. He grasped her under her arms and lifted her off Henri's body as if she weighed nothing. Dangling her in front of him, he backed out of the unit, her feet two feet off the ground. She thrashed, kicking air, kicking him, her wails now high-pitched screeches. He lowered her to the ground, then grasped her arms when she tried to rush back into the locker. Scott tried to subdue her, but she slapped and punched and kicked. She was hysterical, out of control.

I felt weak with horror and fear. I didn't know what to do. I couldn't think. I couldn't focus. Tiny gold dots flecked in front of my eyes, and I realized I was hyperventilating and if I didn't stop, I would faint. I leaned over, clutching my legs behind my knees, and took in a long, slow breath, exhaling through my mouth, and then took another deep, deep breath. The gold specks dissipated, and I grew calmer. I raised myself up, continuing my slow-breathing ritual until the phenomenon I called crisis-calm took hold.

In the frenzied period before crisis-calm kicks in and during the muddled confusion after a crisis has passed, I seem unable to put two coherent thoughts together. Yet from the day when I was eight and witnessed a car roll-over while walking to school, I've been able to maintain my composure during emergencies, no matter what. That day, I'd run to the nearest house, yelling, panicked. The grandmotherly woman who'd opened the door understood what was needed before I'd finished my first disjointed sentence. She called for an ambulance, then accompanied me back to the accident scene. Once there, she instructed me to keep passersby away from the injured driver. She sat on the ground next to the man, speaking slowly and softly, reassuring him that help was on the way. After he was released from the hospital, he told my parents how much he appreciated my quick action, that my running for help had probably saved his life. I knew that the EMTs' quick response mattered, but I thought it was that woman's poise and compassion more than anything that helped him hang on. From that experience, from that woman, I learned the value of calmness in the face of chaos. Today, watching Leigh Ann struggle, seeing how she seemed to not even hear Scott's repeated admonitions, "Calm down, Leigh Ann, calm down," I knew I might be able to help. I ran toward her.

"Henri! Henri!" she yelled, thrashing, screaming, "Let me go! Let me go!"

I touched her tear-stained cheek. "Leigh Ann," I said, inches from her face. "You've got to let the police work. We won't leave you alone. Scott is here. You won't be alone."

Leigh Ann didn't seem to hear me or to understand what was happening, and I wondered if Ellis would have to place her in handcuffs to quell her attack, to stop her from hurting herself or further corrupting the crime scene, when all at once, as if she'd used up all the energy she had available, she went limp and stopped hollering. Silent tears replaced shrieks. She hiccupped and closed her eyes, and Ellis let her go and stepped back. She swayed for a moment, then righted herself and grew still. She opened her eyes, blinking as if the light were too bright. She didn't speak. Scott slipped his arm around her shoulders, and Leigh Ann rested her head on his chest.

"Take her to the office," Ellis said.

Scott nodded, and they walked slowly across the lot.

Once she was out of earshot, Ellis asked, "Can you see enough of his face to identify him from here?"

Ellis's turbocharged torch cast an intense white light on Henri's head. He lay on concrete, his right profile in view.

"Yes," I whispered. "That's Henri Dubois."

Ellis thanked me, then began an inch-by-inch examination of the storage locker. Standing outside, he directed his flashlight along the concrete flooring, looking for I didn't know what. Officer Meade was on her phone. Two police vehicles drove into the lot, a cruiser and one from the medical examiner's office. *So fast,* I thought. I'd expected a delay of hours before the ME arrived, yet here she was within minutes. I stood unobtrusively off to one side. Two uniformed police officers, one I didn't recognize, and the other an older man named Griff, opened the patrol car's trunk and pulled out orange plastic cones and a large roll of yellow and black police tape. Officer Meade and Griff used the cones to create a secure zone about 150 by 50 feet, encompassing the entire locker frontage and a wide swath beyond.

"What do we have?" Dr. Graham, the medical examiner, asked as she got out of her car. I didn't know her, but I'd seen her on the news. She was petite and young and, from all reports, a stickler for details.

Griff moved the cone closest to the storage facility aside, and she stepped into the secure area. Ellis pointed into the unit, and she scanned it.

"The victim's widow was here when the corpse was

discovered," Ellis said. "She entered the unit and hugged the body."

"You're kidding, right?" Dr. Graham asked.

"No."

"Great. I can hear the defense lawyer now. 'How do you know that dirt you're saying matches dirt on my client's sneakers wasn't introduced by the widow?'"

"I know. I got her out quickly. It was all I could do."

She nodded. "Any more bad news?"

He shook his head. "That's it."

She opened her black bag and extracted plastic booties, two pairs, and handed one set to Ellis. She leaned against the outside wall to slip hers on, then entered the storage unit, stepping carefully. Once Ellis had his booties on, he picked his way across the rubble and joined her at the body. They squatted near Henri's head and began to talk, their voices too low for me to hear.

I shut my eyes, my breathing still too shallow, my shoulder muscles knotted. A dog barked. Cars rumbled along Route 1. A bird called out, one high chirp. I focused on my breathing, the only thing I could control, and stayed that way, unmoving and concentrated, until a vehicle, desperate for a new muffler, charged into the lot. I opened my eyes as it screeched to a stop with a jerk. It was Wes, driving his old clunker. He bolted out and ran toward me. Officer Meade, standing outside the secure area, threw out her arm to stop him.

"You need to back off," she told him.

"Why?" he demanded, sounding shocked.

"This is a crime scene."

"What's the crime?"

She folded her lips and didn't reply.

"What's going on, Josie?" Wes called to me.

I shut my eyes again and tuned out his shotgun-style

questioning. After a minute, he stopped. When I opened my eyes this time, I found him glaring at me. He raised his right index finger and thumb to his ear, miming holding a telephone receiver, then pointed his left index finger at my chest, and mouthed, "Call me." I glanced at the three police officers. Their eyes were on him, not me, so I nodded, one nod, then waggled my fingers at him, shooing him away. He turned his attention to the storage unit, pushing against the police tape to peer inside.

Dr. Graham and Ellis stepped out, still talking in near-whispers.

"I'll call you as soon as I have anything," Dr. Graham said.

Griff slid the cone out of the way, opening a narrow alley, just wide enough for her to pass through.

"What's the verdict, Doc?" Wes called, jogging to join her.

She acted like he wasn't there, got situated in her car, started the engine, and drove off. If Wes hadn't jumped out of the way, I think she would have hit him.

"Chief Hunter?" Wes yelled, unabashed. "What's going on?"

"Do you have a pen, Wes? I'm ready to give you an exclusive, my first statement regarding this situation."

"Great!" Wes said. He used his teeth to pull off his glove, dug into an inside jacket pocket, and extracted a ratty-looking lined piece of notebook paper and a pen. "I'm ready."

Ellis nodded. "The body of Henri Dubois, who'd been reported missing by his wife, Leigh Ann Dubois, has been found. Until the medical examiner determines the cause and manner of death, I will make no further comment about those issues. If anyone saw Mr. Dubois at any point yesterday afternoon, please contact our office. Anonymous tips are welcome. You have the number, right, Wes?"

"Yup. Off the record, is it murder?" Wes asked, sounding depressingly eager.

"Off the record, yes. He was bludgeoned to death by something smooth and fairly thin, like a section of pipe."

Wes's eyes lit up, and I knew him well enough to know that his excitement wasn't from hearing that Henri had been beaten to death, but from getting the news ahead of anyone else.

"Or a baseball bat?" Wes suggested.

"Could be, although that may be too wide and/or too rounded. The ME will let us know the dimensions and if there are any splinters in his scalp, something that would indicate whether the weapon was made of wood or iron or whatever."

Wes nodded. "Is there anything in the room that might be the weapon?"

"Early days to speculate."

"We're off the record, Chief."

"Same answer."

"What else can you tell me?" Wes asked.

"He's been dead for hours, although in this weather, it's hard to guess. More on that from the ME after the autopsy."

"So all you want me to publish now is the call for witnesses?"

"That's right. We need any and all information about this heinous crime, and witnesses can and often do play a crucial role in uncovering the truth."

"Good one, Chief! Got it."

Wes ran for his car and was gone. Knowing him, I bet he would call in his story while beelining for Leigh Ann's shop or house, hoping to win another exclusive.

Ellis turned to me. "I'm hoping you'll be able to help

me figure out what's broken and why and whether anything, collectibles and such, is missing."

"I'll do anything I can."

"It'll be a while before we can get inside. In the meantime, I want to get going on statements. I need to hang here for a few minutes, but there's no reason for you to stand around in the cold. You okay with letting Scott and Leigh Ann follow you to the station?"

I nodded. "Sure."

Ellis said something to Officer Meade, and she jogged to Vicki's office. Within seconds, Leigh Ann and Scott stepped outside. Leigh Ann looked awful, her skin pasty white, her gait a shuffle, her shoulders bowed. Scott stayed close to her, casting anxious glances in her direction every few seconds.

A black SUV drove up, and a man and a woman got out. The man pulled a black boxy case from the rear while the woman greeted Chief Hunter, then stepped over the crime scene tape. Moments later, an ambulance entered the lot, and we all turned to watch it back up to the tape barricade.

"We'll let you know when you can take the corpse," the woman called to the ambulance driver, a young man who'd stepped out of the cab to light a cigarette.

The driver nodded but didn't reply.

As I walked slowly toward my car, I watched the two techs begin their meticulous work, one video-recording the scene, the other photographing every inch. The man extracted a thick pile of plastic evidence bags and two pairs of tweezers.

I blinked away tears. *Poor Henri.* I felt weighed down by grief, rudderless and awash with sadness. Life as I knew it had changed forever. Life as Leigh Ann knew it was over.

TEN

WHILE I WAITED for Leigh Ann and Scott to pull up behind me at the parking lot exit, ready to follow me to the Rocky Point police station, I dug my phone out of my tote bag. I had three voice mails, two e-mails, and one text message—all, except one of the voice mails, from Wes. I didn't bother listening or reading his messages. I knew what he wanted, what he always wanted—information. *Later,* I thought. *I'll deal with Wes later.* Ty had called at two, just as Ellis was opening Henri's unit. I leaned back, the heat finally coming. I wiggled my feet, hoping they'd thaw soon, and glanced into the rearview mirror. Scott was backing out of his parking spot. I shut my eyes to listen to Ty's message in private.

"Hey, gorgeous," he said, and listening to the rich timbre of his voice, I felt my tension ease, just a bit. "Give me a call when you get a chance. Is it snowing there yet? It's coming down at a pretty good clip up here—there's already a couple of inches on the ground. Regardless, if the highways are open, I'll come home. If not, not. I've booked a room here just in case. Let me know if you decide to stay at my place so I'll know where to come home to. Love you, babe."

I hit the RETURN CALL button, and his phone went directly to voice mail.

"Hi, Ty," I said. "I got your message. I hate that you might not get home tonight, but of course I understand, and of course you shouldn't push it. It's not snowing yet, but it looks as if it may start any second. I was hoping to talk to you directly… I have news, terrible, terrible news." My throat closed, and I choked, then coughed. After a moment, I was able to continue. "Sorry. It's Henri, Ty. He's dead, murdered. I'll tell you everything later. Right now, I have to go to the police station. Don't worry… I'm okay. Leigh Ann… Leigh Ann isn't doing well…but why would she be, you know? Anyway…when I'm done with the police, I think I'll go to my place. Maybe Zoë will be around." I paused for a moment, thinking what else I wanted to say. "I love you, Ty."

Scott rolled to a stop in back of me. I met his eyes in the mirror and nodded. I slipped in my earpiece and called my office. Cara answered, and I told her I wouldn't be back to work. I didn't tell her about Henri. I didn't want to talk about it. Instead I asked about business, my default coping mechanism. I listened to her everything-is-fine news and felt the quaking world begin to right itself. Work has spared my soul more than once.

I drove slowly, signaling turns well in advance, and kept looking into the rearview mirror. Scott was a cautious driver, keeping pace without tailgating.

Cara reported that all the hearts and heart-themed collectibles Prescott's had gathered throughout the year had sold at the tag sale, creating a familiar tug of conflicting emotions—selling out was great news, but selling out meant missed opportunity; if only we'd had more inventory in stock, we might have sold more. She added that Gretchen and Eric would share closing-up duties and that she'd make certain that Hank was set up with extra food and water in case the coming storm was superbad and we couldn't get in on Monday. I had her confirm that the generators were all good to go, an insurance requirement to ensure that our security system was never compromised, and was reassured when she told me they all were fully gassed up.

I clicked off the phone, and as the reprieve that talking business had provided ended, my eyes filled. I swallowed heavily, willing myself not to cry. It worked. Instead of letting myself feel, I forced myself to think. I considered whether the bad-news call Henri took on Thursday was, in fact, the precipitating event that led to his murder, or whether it was not a cause but an effect, resulting from some other incident. Or maybe it was totally unrelated to his death. I had no way of knowing, which meant I needed to tell Ellis about it. I felt a momentary stab of resentment that Henri had put me in this position by making it clear that I was the only one he'd told about the call, followed by a longer, sharper stab of guilt that I would even for a moment resent the actions of a murdered man—worse, that I could in any way resent the actions of a murdered friend. I bit my lip, ashamed.

Flurries hit the windshield.

The heat was pumping, but it didn't warm me. I was cold to my bones and sad deeper than that.

The Rocky Point police station was set back from Ocean Avenue, across from the beach. The building that housed the police station had been designed to look like local cottages, with wood siding weathered to a light dove gray, shutters painted a dark forest green, and a mansard roof. On a sunny summer afternoon, the view from the parking lot included undulating near-white sand, seashell pink wild roses, and tall grasses waving in the soft breeze that almost always wafted in from the west. Now, all I saw was snow.

Wes stood off to the side of the building, partially hidden by a hedge, out of sight of the front door and large side windows, waiting and watching, his coat collar turned up, his ears and cheeks mottled red, chapped. Scott opened the car door for Leigh Ann, and she stepped out and walked beside him toward the station like an automaton. Her eyes were unfocused. No emotion showed on her face. It was as if she were sleepwalking. Scott's eyes never left her face, his hand hovering just above her elbow. I thought again how lucky she was to have him near. Scott held the door for her, then nodded at me, silently inviting me to precede him.

"Thanks," I said from ten feet away. I picked up my pace so he wouldn't have to stand there letting the cold stream into the building.

"Wait a sec, Josie," Wes called.

I glanced at Wes, then back at Scott. "I'll be right in," I told Scott.

Scott shot Wes a glance. "You need me," Scott said, "you shout, okay?"

"I will. Thanks."

Scott let the door swing shut and gave Wes a parting don't-mess-with-her glare. I waited until the door closed behind him, then joined Wes.

"That was nice of you," I said. "Not to bother them with questions."

"One look and you can tell he's a shoe breaker."

A shoe breaker, I repeated silently, wondering, not for the first time, where Wes got his colorful vocabulary. As near as I could tell, if he didn't know a word or term, he made one up.

"I'll get more info by waiting until Leigh Ann is on her own," he added, slapping his gloved hands together in a futile effort to gain some warmth. "Any news?"

"No," I said, thinking that it was just like me to assign a positive motive to Wes's action, and just like him to unabashedly tell the truth, even though doing so showcased his motive as practical and self-serving, not kind.

"Do you know if Henri was an American citizen?" he asked.

"Yes. He's not. He's French. Why?"

"Maybe there's an international angle."

"He's here legally, if that's what you mean."

"You never know," Wes said. "I'll contact the French consul and ask what's what. Can't do any harm. What did you see in the storage unit?"

I looked through the now steadily falling snow toward the snow-covered beach. "I saw blood," I whispered. "There was broken porcelain, some demolished wood. It was horrible, Wes. Unspeakable." I took in a deep breath. "I've got to go inside—they're expecting me."

"Why do they want to talk to you?"

"They think I might be able to help with antiques info. Also, I was with him the night before he died. We went to the Blue Dolphin...we had a great time...his last dinner."

"Did anything happen at the restaurant that gives you a hint about why he got killed?"

"No," I said, thinking of the phone call Henri had taken, the one he'd asked me to keep to myself, knowing I was splitting hairs about the timing.

"Why do you think he was killed?" Wes asked.

I listened to the waves for a moment, unseen behind the high dunes, the sound thunderous. Why are people killed? Lots of reasons, including money.

An image of the Dubois showroom came to me, filled to the rafters with high-end furnishings and accessories. I hadn't thought of their circumstances one way or the other, but considering the issue now, I realized the origin of their seed money was a mystery. Presumably it hadn't come from Leigh Ann. She'd told me that when she and Henri met, she'd been working a standard-issue retail job, which meant she earned barely enough to survive in New York City. My guess was that it hadn't come from Henri either, not on a midlevel salesman's salary, even though he'd worked for a company that manufactured high-end bed linens, the kind that sold for thousands of dollars. *Maybe one of them had family money,* I thought, then shook my head. Leigh Ann made no secret of her working-class roots. Henri had never mentioned his childhood, but Leigh Ann had.

Henri had been reared with cold formality by a distant cousin after his mother had been killed in a car accident when he was only seven. His father, Pierre, a doctor, couldn't keep Henri with him and continue his overseas work with Médecins sans Frontières, Doctors Without Borders. For the next ten years, Pierre came home only occasionally, and then only for short periods. Before Henri got into the rhythm of seeing his father, of having him near, Pierre was gone again, heading off to the next distant, desperate corner of the world.

Henri, Leigh Ann had confided, was as big a disappointment to his father as she was to her mother. Their parents had expected them to follow in their families' traditions, Henri becoming a doctor and Leigh Ann getting married and settling down in Thibodaux. Henri had entered medical school, then dropped out after one semester, explaining to his father that it simply wasn't for him, that his interest lay in art and artifacts. His father didn't talk to him for a year. Leigh Ann came to New York with visions of footlights shining in her head. Mostly, she waited tables. Her mother didn't speak to her for three years.

After leaving medical school, Henri tried to find a Paris-based interior design job, only to learn that the industry, while large, was well established and resistant to newcomers. He found the interior design world in New

York City equally impenetrable. It wasn't until he moved to Rocky Point that he discovered his ideal environment—in Rocky Point, he was the biggest fish in a right-sized pond.

I shivered in the bitter air. When I turned back to face Wes, I found him observing me closely, waiting, expecting information.

"It takes a lot of money to start a business," I said, "especially a business containing high-end furniture, like a showroom. I never really thought about it before...but how did they finance it all?"

Wes nodded. "Good question, Josie. I'll see what I can find out. What else?"

"Did Henri leave a will?"

"I don't know. Do you?"

"No." I sighed. "I'm sad, Wes. Really sad. I liked Henri. I like Leigh Ann. This is unfathomable, crushing, horrific."

He patted my arm, and I recalled why I liked him so much. Wes was aggressive and single-minded, but beneath his harsh exterior he was capable of great empathy.

After a moment, he asked, "Who was that guy with Leigh Ann just now?"

"A friend from New York. Scott Richey."

"Anything there?" he asked, nearly salivating at the thought.

"Wes! Of course not. He's a friend."

"Oh, paleeeze. Even you can't be that gullible."

"He was introduced to me as a friend," I said firmly, "and I have no reason to think anything else."

"What does he do?"

"I don't know."

"Was he Henri's friend? Or Leigh Ann's?"

"I think Leigh Ann's, but I'm not positive."

"What's he like?" Wes asked.

"I have no idea. I just met him."

"I'll check him out." He slapped his arms again. "Anything else?"

I shook my head. "No."

He opened the heavy door for me. "Talk soon," he said.

I stepped inside. Neither Scott nor Leigh Ann was in sight.

"Hi, Josie," Cathy, the civilian admin manning the counter, said. She was tall and heavyset, with golden hair and blue eyes. "Chief Hunter said you'd be coming in. You can have a seat. It won't be long."

"Thanks, Cathy."

I was too restless to sit, so I walked to the bulletin board and started reading notices; MOST WANTED posters were pinned next to announcements of church suppers and community board meetings. I was scanning a flyer advertising Rocky Point's upcoming ice carving competition, an all-invited contest cum skating party, when Detective Brownley called my name.

Her black hair was shorter than the last time I'd seen her, a little shaggy, with bangs. It suited her round face. Her eyes were as blue as ever, midnight blue. She led the way down a long hallway to a small room with a gold-tone numeral one on the door. I knew it well. A rectangular wooden table sat in the center surrounded by six ladder-back chairs. A human-sized cage was positioned in the corner. I'd never heard of anyone having to be placed inside it, and I hoped I never would. I sat with my back to it, facing one of two wall-mounted video cameras. A one-way glass panel, mirrored on my side, took up half the left wall. There was no window.

"Chief Hunter just called. He'll be here in a few minutes. He asked me to get you settled in, see if you'd like some coffee or anything."

I didn't know what I wanted. "Thanks," I said. "I'm okay."

She left, and to keep my mind off Henri, I checked my e-mail. Nothing.

Five minutes later, Ellis entered the room. He greeted me, turned on the video recorders, and stated our names, the date, and time and that he was conducting an interview with a potential witness.

"As soon as we're finished, I'm going to interview Leigh Ann," Ellis said, sitting across from me. "I wish I could wait to talk to her, to give her time to recover from the shock, but I can't. Since Leigh Ann says she has no idea why someone would want to kill Henri, I need to look for motives, and time truly is of the essence." He paused. "In a homicide, we always focus on questions of why now, why here, so I want to begin with what you know about his activities over the last couple of days. When did you last see Henri Dubois?"

Working backward, he took me through Henri's last forty-eight hours. I'd seen Henri three times on Thursday, at the auction in the morning, at his store in the afternoon, and at dinner in the evening. On Friday, I'd seen him twice, at the Crawford auction and when he'd brought the ephemera to my company around noon.

Ellis asked other questions, too, and my ignorance was patent. I didn't know of any animosity he'd felt toward anyone, nor any that someone might have felt toward him. He wasn't a fighter, a gambler, a drug user, or a thief. I'd never seen him drunk. He'd never made a pass at me or anyone I knew. He seemed devoted to his wife, engaged with his business, and as far as I could tell, he didn't want to live anywhere but Rocky Point.

"Let's talk antiques," Ellis said. "What did he find in that locker?"

"Some silent movie posters and a scrapbook. He brought them to my place so we could appraise them," I said. "He didn't mention anything else, which he probably would have if he'd found anything remarkable. After he went back to the unit…who knows what happened? Because you buy the units blind, there's no way to know what might be missing." I paused. "When I heard that Henri had disappeared, it crossed my mind that he might have found something valuable and easy to sell and just driven away."

"I thought you said he was content with his life in Rocky Point."

I looked at my hands resting on the table. I knew I needed to tell Ellis about Henri's difficult phone call and how he'd asked me to keep it quiet, but I didn't want to. I believed that confidences entrusted to a friend should survive the grave, but I couldn't convince myself that the call was definitely unrelated to his death. *Warring values,* I thought. I looked at Ellis, patiently waiting for me to speak.

"I promised Henri I wouldn't tell," I said.

"He'd release you from that promise if he could."

"How do you know that?" I asked.

"Murder victims want their killers caught."

I knew he was right, so with a sigh of resignation, I told him what I'd observed when Henri took the call and afterward, when he'd asked me not to mention it to Leigh Ann.

"Leigh Ann is my friend. It was bad enough that Henri asked me to keep the call secret from her. Now she's going to find out what I did and never speak to me again."

Ellis nodded thoughtfully. "I think we can keep it under our hats. His phone is missing, but we'll get his incoming-call log from the company. We've already applied for an emergency subpoena. As soon as we get the records, we'll find that call. Unless there's a good reason to do otherwise, I can let her think that's how we got the information."

"You're a good guy, Ellis."

"I try to be reasonable about things, but you do understand I can't promise anything, right?"

"Yes. That's fair." I sighed, bummed I'd had to tell, but also relieved that the burden of silence had been lifted off my shoulders. "I hate keeping secrets."

"Me, too."

"Do you think everyone has secrets?" I asked.

"Yes."

"Even you?"

"Especially me. I interview people about their darkest, most desperate thoughts and deeds for a living." He leaned back in his chair, tilting his head for a different perspective. "I'm not going to ask whether you have secrets, because it's none of my business, but I bet you do. Everyone does."

"Not all secrets are guilty secrets."

"Was Henri's?" he asked.

"I don't know. Maybe. The way he talked about it, it didn't sound like much of anything important. You bid on work, and sometimes you don't win the job. It happens to us all."

"Makes sense. On a different subject… I spoke briefly with Detective Brownley on my way in. Leigh Ann has asked that you sit in during her interview."

"Me?" I asked, surprised. "Why?"

"She's having a little trouble focusing, and Scott is still talking to us."

I nodded, understanding. Leigh Ann wanted support, a

friendly face, a caring friend, and since Scott wasn't available, I was her next-best option.

"Sure," I said.

"Thanks, Josie." He stood up. "I want to check on that subpoena application, then I'll get her. It shouldn't take me too long."

"Can I wait in the lobby?" I reached for my tote bag. "This room isn't exactly conducive to relaxation."

"Sure." He smiled, a small one. "The cage get you going?"

"I sit with my back to it," I said, "but I never forget it's there."

He brought me back to the front. Cathy was typing at her computer. Two uniformed police officers sat at nearby desks, one on the phone, the other reading from a yellow legal pad.

I sank onto one of the wooden benches, glad to have a few minutes to reflect on what I'd just learned. Henri's phone was missing, but not his wedding band. I didn't know what else might have been taken. Even if it was a botched robbery, why would someone rob that particular unit? Perhaps it was simply a random act of violence. A thief driving by seeing a lone van, a solitary man. An opportunist crime. Henri resisted, and he was struck, beaten to death. It was possible.

I leaned back and closed my eyes, willing myself to relax, wishing the steel-bandlike tension in my neck and shoulders would ease, knowing it wouldn't, not until I was home, warm and safe. I wished Ty would be there waiting for me when I arrived. I wanted to slip into a hot bath. I wanted to cook something comforting from the leather-bound handwritten cookbook my mother had created for me in the months before she'd died, and then sit down in my cozy kitchen and eat with Ty. I opened my eyes and looked toward the windows. Tiny snowflakes whirled up and around, then floated out of sight. The snow was falling faster than before, denser. I couldn't make out the beach through the white gossamer cloud of snow. The storm was gathering strength. I closed my eyes again and leaned my head against the unforgiving high wooden backrest. I felt somber and tearful and confused. "Don't ever fret," my dad used to say. "Act." I sighed, opened my eyes again, sat forward, found my phone, and called Zoë.

The call went to voice mail. "Hey, Zoë," I said into the machine. "I don't know if you heard the terrible news about Henri Dubois. If not, I'm sorry to be the one to tell you. He died…oh, Zoë, he was murdered." I took in a breath. "I'm at the police station now. I'm okay…actually, I'm really horrified. I'm so upset…anyway… Ty might not make it home tonight, what with the storm and all. I'm going to my place…will you be around? If so, want a French martini and dessert? Call me, okay?"

I slipped my phone back in my tote as the front door opened with a frigid whoosh. Vicki Crawford walked in, bringing a swirl of snowflakes with her. She stamped her feet on the gray entry rug, nodded at me, and marched to the counter.

"I got a call to come in," she announced. "I'm Vicki Crawford of Crawford Storage."

Cathy smiled and stood up. "I'll let the chief know you're here. You can have a seat."

Vicki plunked down beside me.

"Helluva thing," she said. "I don't know what the police think I can tell them."

"I know what you mean. It's unbelievable."

"I never saw him except at auctions. How about you? Did you know him?"

"Yeah…we were friends."

"Sorry, then."

"Thanks," I said. "It's hard." My throat tightened, and I focused on answering Vicki's rhetorical question about what the police expected to learn from her, hoping that using my brain would serve to keep my emotions at bay. "I bet the police want to know about your security."

Vicki snorted. "Security? Each to his own, that's my attitude. Locks are up to the renters, and I have a total of one camera. It's in my office, aimed at the door so I can track who comes in and catch anyone who tries to break in. That's it."

"I wonder if the office building next door might have any that include a view of your place."

She pushed out her lips, thinking. "Hard to say, but I don't suppose it matters. Henri's unit was on the far side of the building, so even if their cameras take in some of my place, it wouldn't include anything on that side of the parking lot."

"Good point." I thought about the property layout. I'd lived in Rocky Point for nearly a decade, yet there were whole sections of town I didn't know. "Where does that little street go? You know the one I mean, the one on the other side of your place from the office building. It runs from Route 1 somewhere."

"To Little Boston. Do you know it?"

"I've heard of it," I said, "but I've never been there. What's it like?"

"Well established. All residential. I think it was built as a development in the eighties. It's called Little Boston because all the street names are from Back Bay—the alphabet streets, you know? Arlington, Boylston, Clarendon, Dartmouth, Exeter, and so on."

"I gather it's not a gated community with a private security force or anything like that?"

"Hardly. I'd be surprised if any of those houses have

alarm systems or security cameras, let alone armed guards. It's quiet back there, and safe."

Safe, I thought. *Nowhere is safe.*

"Who was the new guy at the auction?" I asked. "The one wearing the Red Sox cap."

"Andrew Bruen. He just showed up, paid his deposit, same as everyone."

"A newbie. I wonder what his story is."

"I don't know anything about him but his name, and that he came back around four to get his refund."

"He sure looked upset when he lost out."

"Whatever," she said, shrugging.

"Whose unit was it, anyway?" I asked. "The one Henri won?"

"That I don't talk about. People expect privacy, even when they forfeit their lockers."

"That's another whole mystery, isn't it?" I asked. "I mean, why would someone just stop paying for a locker?"

"Beats me."

"Maybe they die and their heirs don't know about it."

"Not likely. I send notices and certified letters and so on, so even if the heirs didn't know about it when the person died, they'd learn about it soon enough. I send four letters. Three are required by my contract, but I send the fourth because I don't want anyone griping that I didn't try hard enough to notify them about losing their unit."

"Smart," I said. "You sound like a belt-and-suspenders sort of gal."

"You got that right."

"Me, too."

Ellis stepped into the lobby. "Ms. Crawford, thanks for coming in. Someone will be with you in just a couple more minutes. Josie, if you'll come with me."

"'Bye," I said to Vicki.

"See ya," she said.

I followed Ellis down the corridor that led to Room One. Inside, I took the same seat as before.

"The subpoena for the phone records has been issued, so we're all set on that front. I'll go get Leigh Ann." He headed for the door, pausing with his hand on the knob. "Don't be shy, Josie, okay? If you know something, pipe up. If you have a question, ask it."

I nodded, and the already tight muscles in my shoulders twisted yet another turn.

While I waited, I checked my voice mail. Zoë had called back offering sympathy and soup at Ellis's house.

"I'm so sorry, Josie, to hear about Henri," Zoë said, her voice rich and textured, her caring resonating with every word. "You must be beside yourself. I'm at Ellis's, though, for the duration of the storm, so I won't be around later. Too bad, because a French martini and dessert sound wonderful. The thing is, I figured you'd be at Ty's and I didn't want to risk being snowbound alone. Again. What a winter, right? So I wrapped the kids up and here we are, close enough to the beach to listen to the waves. Very cool. If you want to come over, I've made tomato soup. Jake's request, poor little fellow. His cold is better, but he still feels kind of punky. In any event, know you're welcome. Ellis has that extra guest room downstairs. Poor Leigh Ann. What a nightmare. If you think it's appropriate, please tell her how sorry I am. I can't even imagine how she must be feeling. You, too, my friend. Call when you can."

I clutched the phone to my chest for a moment, beyond grateful that I had a friend like Zoë in my life. The door opened, and I slipped the phone into my bag, bracing myself for unpleasantness. My only hope was that I would actually be of help to Ellis, and that when it was over, Leigh Ann would still be my friend.

ELEVEN

LEIGH ANN'S SKIN was sallow, and her eyes were dull. She looked decades older than she had the day before. She sat across from me, leaning heavily on her forearms, staring at the table. Officer Meade, the tall blonde, sat in a corner, keeping her eyes on Leigh Ann, holding an old-fashioned steno pad.

"I'm so sorry, Leigh Ann," I said.

"Thanks," she said, her voice all trembly and low.

Ellis placed a manila folder on the table in front of him, then used remote controls to activate the video recorders. I watched the tiny red lights flick on. When he stated the who-what-why information, he spoke to the camera. When he was done, he turned to face Leigh Ann.

"Leigh Ann," he said, waiting for her to raise her eyes, "as I'm sure you understand, the sooner we get facts, the better. Which is a long way of saying thank you for your cooperation."

Leigh Ann nodded.

"You asked for Josie to join us," he continued, "but I want you to know that if anything comes up that you'd prefer to talk about in private, all you have to do is say the word."

"I'm glad she's here," she said, glancing at me. She pressed the tips of her fingers into her forehead and rubbed. "I'm having trouble…" She lowered her hands and tried to smile, but her eyes filled with tears. "Maybe she can help me remember things."

"If you need anything," he said, "water, a break, whatever, just let me know." He waited for a moment, but she didn't respond. "Let's start with this list." He extracted three sheets of paper from his folder. He slid one across the table to Leigh Ann, handed me the second, and kept the third for himself. "This is a list of your husband's effects, those things found on his person. Is anything missing? Is anything a surprise?"

Leigh Ann took in a deep breath, girding herself for an ordeal, then picked up the list with a shaky hand. I looked down at my copy. The list wasn't long. They'd recovered his wedding band, a Montblanc pen I'd seen him use countless times, and $13.18; that was it. I looked at Ellis, then Leigh Ann. Lots of stuff was missing. Surely Ellis knew that, but from his neutral expression, you'd think he was asking nothing more provocative than if Henri's shopping list had been complete.

"Those are his things," Leigh Ann said, wiping tears away with the side of her hand. "He would have had more cash than that, though." She raised her eyes. "For the auction."

"He did," I said, following Ellis's instructions to speak up if I had something to say. "He had a wallet full of cash. I saw it when he paid for his unit. Although, as I think about it, I don't know how much cash he had left *after* he paid for the unit. It cost him two thousand two hundred and fifty dollars."

"Do you know how much money he took with him?" Ellis asked Leigh Ann.

"Five thousand dollars, or at least that's what he told me he planned to take. I didn't count it or anything."

Ellis nodded slowly, calculating. "Assuming he took five thousand as planned, twenty-seven fifty is missing."

He tapped his pen on the table, thinking. "Where did he get the cash from?"

"Our safe. We keep a lot of cash on hand. Henri stopped by the showroom this morning en route to the auction to get the money."

"Does the safe open with a key?" Ellis asked.

"No. There's a combination keypad, palm-print thing. You enter a four-digit number, then place your hand on the sensor."

"Who had access to it?" Ellis asked.

"Just us."

Ellis nodded and wrote a note. "What else did he carry in his wallet?"

"The regular stuff."

"Like...?"

Leigh Ann closed her eyes to concentrate. "Credit cards," she said, her eyes still closed. "He carried a MasterCard for personal charges and an American Express for the business. He had an emergency notification card with my contact info on it, his insurance card, a debit card, a grocery store discount card, and his driver's license." She pressed the heels of her hands into her eyes for a moment, then blinked. "I think that's it."

Ellis jotted notes as she called out the list, then asked, "What about his keys?"

Leigh Ann's eyes flew open. "Oh, my God—his keys! He carried a silver and turquoise key ring. Navajo...we went to Arizona on our honeymoon. The keys to his van and my car were on it. Plus one for the shop and two for home, one for the front door and one for the back. Someone has keys to our house!"

"We'll take care of it." He half-turned toward Officer Meade. She nodded and left the room. He swung back to face Leigh Ann. "So there are five keys total?"

"Yes," she said. "Plus he'd have the key for the padlock he used on the storage unit. Probably, though, he wouldn't put that on his ring because it's temporary. He'd just slip it in his pocket."

"Make a note," Ellis told Officer Meade as she walked back into the room. "Padlock key."

She nodded and picked up her pad.

"He wore a Patek Philippe watch, didn't he, Leigh Ann?" To Ellis, I added, "It was a real beauty."

"Yes," she said, her eyes and mouth opening wide. "He always wore it."

"Can you describe it?" Ellis asked.

"It's a split seconds chronograph, in platinum. I don't know the model number."

"Was it inscribed?" I asked.

She nodded. "Our initials and our wedding date are inscribed on the back. His father bought it for him as a wedding present. He bought me a gold and diamond bangle with the same inscription inside. So thoughtful. So generous." She gasped. "Oh, my God! Pierre... Henri's father! I can't believe I forgot...they were so close... I need to call him."

He asked Leigh Ann to confirm the initials, got their wedding date, then turned to Officer Meade. "Issue a BOLO for the watch." She left the room again. He turned to Leigh Ann. "A BOLO is shorthand for 'be on the lookout,' a notification that alerts police, pawnshops, and second-hand dealers that someone may try to sell stolen goods." He met my eyes. "Josie, will you notify antiques dealers?"

"Yes, right away." I reached for my phone and e-mailed Sasha, who would know which associations to call, how to upload photos, and so on. I typed instructions and hit SEND, then placed the phone on the table in front of me.

"Pierre is in Paris," Leigh Ann said. "What time is it?"

"It's close to five," Ellis said, glancing at the big wall-mounted clock over Leigh Ann's head. "Eleven in France. I'd like to talk to him, too. I can arrange an international call. It'll just take a few minutes to get it organized. As soon as Officer Meade gets back, she'll see to it. Pierre, your father-in-law...you said he's in Paris. What does he do?"

"He's a doctor. For many years, he worked with Doctors Without Borders traveling to places without proper medical care, war zones usually. Now he's with a hospital, a very important place. I forget its name. He consults with a television station there, too. You know, he's their on-air expert. He's a lovely man. Very supportive."

"How so?" Ellis asked.

Leigh Ann didn't answer right away, and when she did, her words seemed carefully chosen. "Pierre was very disappointed when Henri decided against becoming a doctor, and even more disappointed when Henri decided there was no place for him in Paris. They didn't speak for a year, but Pierre got over his anger, and they grew closer than ever. When Henri decided to marry me and make his move to America permanent, Pierre didn't try to convince him to return to France. That's pretty darn rare, I think. When I told my mama I was moving to New York, she said, 'If you leave, you're gone.' Pierre wasn't like that." She paused for a moment, then sighed. "He was kind to me, too."

"Thank you," Ellis said, glancing at the clock again. "I'm going to get that phone call figured out. There's no need to wait for the officer to get back. I won't be long."

He left the room. I noticed the video recorders were still running. Leigh Ann pulled her wallet from her purse, opened an inner flap, and flipped through a dozen or more plastic cards until she found what she was looking for, a folded piece of paper. She laid it on the table, smoothed out the wrinkles, then leaned back and closed her eyes. Neither of us had moved when Ellis stepped back inside, carrying a phone, its plastic-coated cords looped around the unit. He unraveled them, plugged one into the outlet and the other into a wall jack, then asked Leigh Ann for the number.

She opened her eyes and pushed the paper toward him.

Ellis dialed and put the call on speakerphone. In less than a second, a double-whir ring, an unmistakably European sound, filled the space.

A man answered, his voice deeper than Henri's.

Leigh Ann closed her eyes, gripping the tabletop so tightly her knuckles turned white, and said, "It's me, Pierre... Leigh Ann." Her voice cracked and she began to cry.

I pulled a tissue from the minipack I kept in my bag and pressed it into her hand. She didn't know it was there, and it fluttered to the table.

"Leigh Ann?" Pierre said. "What is it? Tell me."

"It's Henri," she managed. She spoke through tears. "He's dead. Oh, my God, Pierre. He's dead."

"Qu'est-ce qui s'est passé? Mon Dieu!"

What happened? My God, I translated, my high school French barely adequate to the task.

Leigh Ann collapsed onto the table, weeping, unable to continue.

Ellis eased the phone from her grasp and said, "Docteur Dubois? Est-ce que vous parlez anglais?"

"Un peu. Some."

"I speak almost no French—I will try to be clear. I am Rocky Point Police Chief Ellis Hunter. I'm terribly sorry for your loss, Docteur Dubois. As you can imagine, Ms. Dubois is too distraught to continue. She's here at the police station helping us try to understand what's happened.

So far, all that's known is that your son, Henri, was attacked in a storage unit he won at an auction. His wallet, phone, keys, and watch are missing."

"Merci, monsieur. Forgive me...my English...it is not as good as I need. Are you saying my son was killed during a... I do not know the word...a steal?"

"A robbery. I don't know. It's possible. We're looking into it. We're notifying everyone—other police departments and stores—about the stolen watch."

"My poor Henri."

"I'm sorry to have to bother you with questions at a time like this, but do you know of anyone who might have wanted to hurt your son?"

"Non. Mon Dieu! He was a good man. A gentle man."

"When did you speak to him last?" Ellis asked Pierre.

"I do not know...two, maybe three days ago. We had a short conversation. I am a doctor, and my time is not always as much my own as I would like. My poor Henri."

"Is there anything you can think of that might help us?"

"Non. Not now. I will think more."

"Thank you, Docteur Dubois. Please do."

I touched Leigh Ann's shoulder, and she sat up, her tears still flowing, her cheeks wet, her nose red. I pointed to the phone, then at her chest. She shook her head.

Ellis gave Pierre his contact information, and Pierre gave Ellis his office number, and then he was gone. A green light flashed on my phone, signaling that I had an e-mail. Sasha replied to my request with one word, "Done." I told Ellis and Leigh Ann.

Officer Meade stepped into the room. Leigh Ann had stopped crying, but she looked miserable, broken.

"Are you able to continue?" Ellis asked.

"Yes," she whispered. "I'll try."

"May I ask you to take another look at the list? Can you think of anything else that might be missing?"

She stared at it, the skin surrounding her eyes puffy. "I don't know. I don't think so."

"Josie?"

"Nothing occurs to me."

"All right, then. What about the broken things in the unit?" He extracted some Polaroid snapshots from his folder and lined them up so Leigh Ann and I could both see them. They were close-ups of the damaged objects. "Do either of you recognize anything?"

"I didn't notice anything but Henri," Leigh Ann said, staring at the photos.

"This appears to be an Asian vase," I said, "or maybe a garden stool. The blue and white porcelain is distinctive. From this photo, there's no way of telling if it's an antique or a reproduction. These pieces of wood could be from anything—a bookcase, for instance, or a shelf." I looked up at Ellis. "When we were bidding on the unit, nothing like either object showed. Which doesn't mean anything. Maybe the bookcase was hidden by the stacks of boxes. It's certainly not unusual that Henri opened boxes right away. We want to see what we bought."

"That takes care of that, then. I have a few personal questions to ask you, Leigh Ann. Would it be all right if I talked to you one-on-one?"

"Of course," Leigh Ann said.

"Josie, Officer Meade will escort you to the lobby."

"I'll hang around until you're done," I told her, swinging my tote bag onto my shoulder and standing up. "If you want me to come back in, you just let me know, okay?"

She nodded. "Thank you."

Officer Meade led the way back to the entry area. Cathy was still busy at her computer, and the two uniformed officers were talking to one another, their voices muted. I sat on the hard wooden bench and stared at nothing. Witnessing Leigh Ann's despondency had darkened my mood.

Detective Brownley brought Scott into the lobby and thanked him. He nodded at me, then walked to one of the double-wide windows overlooking the front parking lot and stood, watching the snow.

Wes once told me that when I tried to analyze situations or find logical reasons to understand nonrational behaviors, I was wrong a lot, and he was right. I was—but I was right a lot, too. Now, though, I was neither right nor wrong because I didn't have a clue. I looked at Scott. Wes had chortled at the idea that Scott and Leigh Ann were just friends. Perhaps he was right. Maybe Henri's murder wasn't random after all.

TWELVE

"HOW ARE YOU DOING?" I asked Scott.

He looked at me over his shoulder. "I've been better. You?"

"Same."

He nodded, then turned back to watch the snow. "Now, that's a storm."

I joined him at the window. Windswept drifts made it hard to tell for sure, but it looked as if four or five inches had already accumulated. The dark-colored cars parked along the side appeared veiled in white; the white ones were nearly invisible.

"It sure is," I agreed.

"What's the forecast?" he asked. "Do you know?"

"Unpredictable. The weatherman says it depends on upper-level winds or something. From an old-timer in the know, I hear two feet."

"Two feet—that's no joke. I can't remember if I've ever been in a storm that dropped two feet of snow."

"Where are you from?"

"New York—the city. We get plenty of snow, but if anything like this happened... I don't know...maybe I was out of town."

"I lived in New York for a few years. It's the buildings, I think, and the subway. Most of the time, they keep the sidewalks and roads warm enough to limit accumulation."

"Plus, in Rocky Point, we're more than three hundred miles farther north."

"That, too," I agreed. The wind shifted and flakes spun sideways, peppering the window. "Driving isn't going to be any fun tonight."

"Thanks for the warning." He flexed his back muscles. "So much for a quiet country weekend." He shook his head. "How long have you been up here?"

"Nine years, going on ten."

"Quite a difference from New York."

"Yeah. I love it here." I smiled a little. "But I love the city, too. Chocolate and vanilla, both good."

"Leigh Ann's the same. She loves both places." He looked around, then turned back to the window. "They've been talking to her a long time now. Do you know what about?"

"I was with her for a while, then they wanted to ask her questions privately. Personal stuff, I gather."

He nodded. "They asked me plenty of personal questions, and I never even met the guy."

"Were you able to tell them anything helpful?"

"Who knows? Mostly I said 'I don't know.' I don't know who wanted to kill him. I don't know if they were having money problems. I don't know if their marriage was on the rocks."

"Really?" I asked. "I thought you and Leigh Ann were close. I would have expected her to have confided in you."

His eyes remained on the blowing snow. "Sure, we talk. But you know how that goes. You only know what someone chooses to tell you, right? It can feel like they're confiding in you until you figure out they're toeing the party line, not telling you how they really feel." He shrugged. "Case in point: I just told you that Leigh Ann loves it here. Maybe she does. Or maybe she just wants me to think she loves it here. Pride, you know?"

"Sounds like you guys have some history."

He turned toward me and grinned, a frisky one. "You might say that. We were married for ten years."

"What?" I gawked, then laughed, enjoying a rare moment of genuine surprise. I expected to hear a tale of star-crossed lovers, not that they'd been married. "Well, you just proved your point, didn't you. You never can tell. I had no idea Leigh Ann was married before. When did you guys divorce?"

"About three years ago." He turned back to the window. "I was the stupid one—I fell for a leggy blonde named Natasha, just like in the movies. Whoever said, 'There's no fool like an old fool,' had me in mind, except I wasn't all that old. Thirty-two at the time, to be exact."

"John Heywood. My dad changed it a bit. 'There's no fool like an old fool except a young one.'"

"That's funny. And true. Who's John Heywood?"

"A sixteenth-century playwright who married well. He was employed through four royal courts, which is quite an accomplishment in any circumstances, and downright extraordinary when you think that he was a devout and vocal Catholic and one of the four monarchs he served under was King Henry VIII. I've always wondered why King Henry didn't have him beheaded."

"Maybe he liked his plays and didn't care about his religious beliefs."

"Probably. Did you marry her? The leggy blonde named Natasha?"

"Of course. Didn't I mention I was a fool? The marriage lasted about twenty minutes. Fifteen, really, but we were stuck in traffic leaving the chapel, so I call it twenty."

I laughed. "I'm sorry. I don't mean to laugh at you."

"Feel free. I'm laughing at myself."

"At least you realized you'd made a mistake and fixed it."

"You're kind to say so, but you're off the mark. My

foolishness ran far deeper than you know... I lied to Leigh Ann for two years." His left hand formed a fist and he softly pounded the window frame. "I was embarrassed to admit what a screwup I'd been, so I told her everything was hunky-dory. Let's repeat that quote again, this time in unison—I'll take the role of the fatally flawed hero if you play the Greek chorus. 'There's no fool...'" He shrugged.

"So then, after you found the courage to tell her the truth, you discovered she'd married Henri."

"God loves irony."

"And she may be lying to you about how happy she was," I said, thinking aloud. "How did you come to be up here?"

"Leigh Ann thought we could be friends. She told me that I'd like Henri and that he'd like me." He paused for a moment, and his expression shifted from self-deprecating to reflective. "It's sort of like wiggling a loose tooth with your tongue. You know it's going to hurt like hell, but you do it anyway."

"You still love her."

"When I married Natasha I thought I was in love with her, that Leigh Ann and I had grown apart...you know, that it was over. I was wrong. Turns out, I just succumbed to momentary lust while in the throes of temporary insanity. Not to sound like a dude out of a romance novel or anything, but my heart belongs to Leigh Ann, always did."

We stood side by side for a few minutes, neither of us talking, both of us watching the snow and thinking private thoughts. I liked Scott. He was funny and outgoing and open. He also had one heck of a motive for murder.

"Did the police check your alibi?" I asked.

"Yeah. I have none. I got up here early and drove around. The police asked me to try to re-create my route. I asked if they were kidding me. I wouldn't know one town's Ocean Avenue from another town's Ocean Street. They all look exactly the same. Nice cottages on the left. Snow-covered dunes on the right. All I could tell them was that I stayed on the road closest to the ocean except when I saw a sign for some town's village green or business section, then I drove inland until I found it. Once there, I took streets whichever way my mood took me, checking out the central areas, then heading back to the coast, meandering north. A perfect nonalibi. How about you? Did they ask you?"

"No...but I'm due for one more go-around as soon as they're done with Leigh Ann. If they ask, though, I'm covered. I was at work with lots of people around."

"Go ahead, rub it in."

I smiled at him. "You sure have a good attitude about it."

"What's a man to do? It is what it is, right? I didn't kill Henri, if that's your next question."

"Sorry... I didn't mean to be inquisitive."

"Don't worry about it. I don't blame you. I've got motive up the kazoo. From what I hear, the murder weapon is a pipelike thing. They found metal flakes embedded in Henri's scalp."

"Oh, my God!" I said, closing my eyes for a moment. "I hadn't heard."

"Yeah...it's bad. It's also easily available. If you're going to be cold-blooded about it, stop at any hardware store and pick up a length of metal piping. If the murder wasn't premeditated, you can assume the killer found something in the storage room. Maybe a screw-in wrought-iron table leg, something like that, or a cane. The problem they have with me is opportunity. It's true I don't have an alibi, but that doesn't figure into the equation. I had no idea Henri was at Crawford's."

"Maybe Leigh Ann told you," I said.

"So now we're in it together?"

"I'm just following your logic. Plus, it doesn't have to be a conspiracy. She could have mentioned it in passing."

He turned to face me, all trace of joking gone. His brown eyes looked straight into mine. "I didn't kill him. I wouldn't kill him. I had no need to kill him. I'm a believer in divorce."

"What if he refused?" I asked.

"You can't refuse. Them days is gone forever. No one has to stay married."

"Did Leigh Ann want a divorce?"

"I never got the chance to ask her."

A marked patrol car pulled into the lot and parked near the entrance. An officer I didn't recognize stepped out and hurried toward the door.

"What do you do?" I asked. "If I may ask."

He smiled. "You know everything else about me—why not that, too? I'm a landlord. I own apartment buildings. And you're an antiques dealer."

"Sort of," I said. "We run monthly high-end antiques auctions and a weekly tag sale of vintage collectibles. We also appraise antiques for clients who don't plan on selling."

"Like for insurance purposes?"

"Exactly. Or estate planning. Or because they're considering a purchase and want an objective assessment of value. Or they want to know how much Granddaddy's humidor is worth in today's market, even though they have no intention of selling it. Etcetera. Etcetera."

"Sounds fascinating, actually."

I smiled. "It is. I'm very fortunate."

"Excuse me," Ellis said from the corridor.

Scott and I both turned.

"With Henri's keys missing, Leigh Ann's decided that it makes sense to change all the locks," he said, speaking to Scott. "At her request, I've called a locksmith. He's going to meet her at the shop at six thirty." Ellis looked at his watch. "Half an hour from now. Officer Meade is going to escort you to both places, the store and her house, just to be certain everything is all right." He glanced out the window. "You okay driving in snow?"

"I'll be fine," Scott said. "How's Leigh Ann?"

Ellis didn't answer right away, and when he did, his tone was so measured I wondered what he wasn't saying. "About how you'd expect. She'll be out in a minute. She's on the phone talking brand choices with the locksmith."

Scott nodded, retrieved his coat from where he'd tossed it on the bench, and said, "Is there anything you can tell me? Do you have any leads?"

"We're looking at a lot of issues from a lot of angles," Ellis said, revealing nothing.

"You don't think it was a thief, do you?"

"We haven't ruled anything out."

"Scott," Leigh Ann said, entering the reception area ahead of Officer Meade.

Leigh Ann clutched her coat to her chest like armor. She looked better, exhausted, but more controlled, less befuddled. Scott stepped forward and took her coat, holding it for her to put on. She wrapped her scarf around her neck and dug a wool hat out of her pocket.

"I'm so sorry," I told her again.

She nodded. "Mama always said to look for the sun behind the clouds, which on a day like today is not the easiest thing to do. Still and all, today could have been worse, believe it or not. Henri could have been killed on a day when Scott wasn't here to help me cope." She smiled at him, barely. "Thank God for Scott."

He touched her shoulder and said, "Let's go."

"Thank you to you, too," she said as she headed out.

"Of course. Anything I can do, I'm glad to."

"I'm going to see you home," Ellis said to me once they were gone.

"That's very sweet, Ellis," I said, getting into my coat, "but not the least bit necessary."

"It's on my way. Zoë asked me to ask you whether you're sure you don't want to bunk with us tonight."

I smiled. "Thanks, but no thanks. I'm so looking forward to a hot bath in my own bathtub and cooking in my own kitchen. I'll be fine. You know I'm not nervous alone. Plus, Ty may make it back. I haven't heard from him yet."

"I doubt it. They've closed sections of 95. The plows can't keep up."

"Darn!" I smiled. "Still...my bath is calling me."

"Will you park down the hill?" he asked, referring to the Meyers' farm stand lot. Al and Dawn Meyer were nice enough to make it available to local folks on nights like this, when driving up Ellison Road might be treacherous.

"That's my plan."

"I'll drive you home from there. My SUV can take that hill with no problem."

I grinned. "Now that's an offer I'll accept. It's funny how a quarter-mile hike feels like a mile in weather like this."

As I drove through wind-whipped snow, I wondered if Ellis would soon be asking me whether I had an alibi. I couldn't see why he'd think I was involved, but Scott's prosaic analysis of the murderer's ways and means had spooked me a little. It was all fine and dandy to be matter-of-fact about issues, but not when the issue at hand was murder. I began to suspect that there was more to Scott's seemingly casual conversation than I'd first thought. It was almost as if he were laying the groundwork for reasonable doubt.

THIRTEEN

I FORAGED FOR ingredients and, using one of my mom's favorite recipes, made a hearty beef stew.

While it simmered, I took my bath, lying neck deep in the lilac-scented water until it cooled, then showered off the bubbles under a steamy hot spray. Afterward, wrapped in my fuzzy warm pink robe and matching slippers, I lit two tall white tapers I kept at the ready in my mother's sterling silver candleholders and sat at the round table in my kitchen to eat. As I dipped pieces of buttery garlic bread into the gravy to sop up all the yummy bits, I watched the storm raging outside my safe haven. *There's no place like home,* I thought.

I got into bed around eleven and called Ty.

"I'm glad I came home," I said. "I wish you were here."

"Me, too. I'll be on the road the first minute I can."

"I'll make you a wonderful breakfast."

"What if I don't get home until lunch?"

"You'll have breakfast for lunch," I said.

"Good." He paused for a moment. "Are you okay, Josie?"

I thought for a moment, uncertain how I was feeling besides relieved to be in my own bed, to be home, and safe, and warm. "More or less," I said. "You know."

"Yeah. Will you be able to sleep?"

"Probably not."

"I hope you can."

"I love you, Ty."

"I love you, too, Josie."

I READ FOR more than an hour, waiting for sleep to come, then gave up, turning out the light, telling myself that I would rest my eyes, that's all, just rest my eyes. As I was crossing from that dreamy spot between weary consciousness into the cocoon of sleep, the familiar snick of a door latch catching catapulted me awake. In a spasm of panic, I shot up like a jack-in-the-box. The wind-up alarm clock with the eerie green luminescent numbers, a relic from my childhood that I kept on my bedside table, read 1:18.

I waited, listening to silence, certain I'd heard a door close, the back one, I thought. Perhaps Ty had decided to come home after all. As the seconds ticked by and I heard no other sounds, doubt crept in, and I began to second-guess myself. I could have been in the grip of a nightmare so vivid, so lifelike, it felt real. *That's it,* I thought, preparing to lie back down. *Much ado about nothing.*

If it was Ty, he'd be upstairs by now.

I caught myself twisting the duvet into a tight little screw and stopped, sitting instead in frozen silence. I was breathing hard, and my heart was pounding against my ribs so hard it hurt.

A quiet shush of hushed footsteps dragged me fully awake.

It was real and it wasn't Ty.

Don't jump to conclusions, I warned myself. If Ty had driven home through a blizzard in the middle of the night, he might be so tired, he'd drag his feet. Except Ty and I had spoken at eleven. Ty had been in his hotel in Berlin, three hours north. Even if he'd left right after we spoke, he couldn't be home yet.

Someone, not Ty, was downstairs.

I flung the covers aside and rolled to the far side of the bed, dropping to the ground as quietly as I could, crouching on the thick Oriental rug. I held my breath to listen. Nothing. I stretched out flat, my right cheek pressed against the rug so I could see under the bed into the hall. The night was cloudless, and my blinds and drapes were drawn. No drop of moonlight counteracted the near-black darkness. The only light came from the residual glow from the neon green numbers of my old clock. I couldn't see anything more than wiggly green shapes.

Perhaps Ty decided to surprise me, I thought, hope spiking as denial set in. Who else could it be? Who'd break into my house in the middle of a blizzard, risking being caught outside in killing cold? Ty's vehicle was designed for rough travel, and I'd probably miscalculated the time.

Ty never parked at Meyer's farm stand. His SUV could get through quagmirelike mud and over stones and jutting tree roots. Knee-deep snow, even thigh-deep snow, was nothing—it wouldn't even slow him down. He must have set out despite the storm, navigating south on secondary roads. I crawled to the window, lifted the drape, and eased the blind aside expecting, praying, that Ty's vehicle would be in the driveway. The darkness was so dense, I could barely make out the snow hitting the window right in front of me. I pressed my forehead against the frost-laden glass and cupped my eyes. The glass was as cold as the martini glasses I kept in the freezer, and my forehead instantly went numb and I pulled my head back a little. I used the heel of my hand to clear the condensation, and for a second, not more, I was able to discern the shape of the driveway, the empty driveway.

I heard more muffled steps, pushed my hands against my mouth to keep myself from gasping aloud, and fell backward onto the rug, rocked by the realization that a stranger was creeping through my house. Worse, he must have disabled my alarm system. If someone had broken in, the security company would have called, asking for the safe word, "tomatoes," to confirm the alarm had sounded in error.

Unless I hadn't set it.

A strangled moan escaped my throat. No one would have heard it, but to my own ears it sounded as loud as bells tolling from the rafters.

I shook my head. I always set it, just like I always used my key to turn the dead-bolt locks and gave the doors a little tug, just to check. Like I told Vicki, I was a belt-and-suspenders kind of gal. I didn't recall setting the alarm and locking the doors. Still, I knew I had. I always did. My heart was hammering against my ribs so hard, it felt as if my ribs might break.

I peeked under the bed again, and again I saw nothing but luminous green reflections.

I heard another stealthy step, then another.

I was having trouble breathing. The tiny hairs on the back of my neck rose and a shiver slithered up, then down, my spine.

The footsteps stopped, and I heard a soft whoosh and a rustle. I didn't recognize the sounds. More silence. Footsteps again, retreating, and then, seconds later, another snick.

According to the clock, it was 1:21. Three minutes had elapsed. I forced myself to count slowly to 120, two minutes more, listening, waiting. I heard nothing. Satisfied I was alone, I crawled across the bed to reach my tote bag and grabbed my phone.

The alarm hadn't sounded because my power was off. According to Ellis, wind gusts topping sixty-five miles per hour had snapped off tree limbs, bringing down power lines all over town. Whoever had broken in got lucky. The intruder got lucky with footprints, too. I hadn't heard a car, so I figured he must have hiked or snowshoed in. With the storm so blustery, all trace of his route would have been obscured within moments.

"What a risk," I said to Ellis after we'd completed our walk-through by the light of his supersized torch and my standard household flashlight.

"You think so?" he asked. "Unless there happened to be a patrol car in the neighborhood for some reason, it would take the police five to six minutes to get here on a sunny day with no traffic. On a night like this—in near white-out conditions with roads blocked by fallen trees and live electric lines—they couldn't make it any sooner than fif-teen or twenty minutes. You said the intruder was inside for how long? Three minutes? If he thought it through and did the math, he'd reach the same conclusion. He could get in, do whatever he came here to do, and get out in three, four minutes, tops. He'd be in the woods, out of sight of the street in another minute or two." He shrugged. "Not so risky."

"You're right—and I bet he thought I wasn't home be-cause my car wasn't here and the house was dark."

I scanned the living room again, sweeping my light along the furniture. I saw only my own possessions, noth-ing out of place, nothing unexpected. I owned and dis-played valuable antiques, yet nothing had been taken. My father's proudest find, a seventeenth-century oil painting he'd purchased on a business trip in London nearly twenty years earlier, hung undisturbed on the study wall. It was called *A River Crossing with a Ferry* and was attributed to Jan Brueghel the Younger. To update my insurance policy, I'd hired a Boston-based antiques expert who'd appraised it at $425,000 three months ago.

A thief wouldn't necessarily know the value of the painting, but surely he would find my mother's sterling silver candlesticks irresistible. They were small enough to fit in any satchel and sat out in the open on the round kitchen table next to the eighteenth-century Waterford cut crystal bowl I'd purchased for myself to celebrate my first year in business. The rare books that lined the shelves in the study were intact, too, as were the framed antique maps on the walls. In the living room, antique Chinese vases decorated tabletops. I owned electronics, too, and sterling silver flatware, and other objects that would be easy to carry and quick to pawn.

"Nothing is missing," I said, closing the hutch drawer, confirming that my sterling silver wine caddy was untouched.

"Do you have a safe?" Ellis asked.

"No."

"How about a stash of cash?"

"Upstairs, next to my passport."

"Let's take one more look, room by room, then let's get you packed up for the night. I left Zoë making up the guest room."

"Do you believe me?" I asked. "Do you believe that someone was here, walking around?"

"Yes," he said without hesitation.

I exhaled, and only then did I realize that I'd been holding my breath. Without corroboration, it would be easy to dismiss my claims as the product of an overly active imagination.

"How did he get in?" I asked. "There's no sign of a break-in, and the lock is a dead bolt."

"Which wasn't in place," Ellis noted.

"It was when I went to bed. I always check to be certain. Just like I always set the alarm."

"Routine is dangerous, Josie, you know that. Anyone observing you can learn your habits, which lets them have the upper hand. Besides, there's no way to confirm you actually did something. You just assume you did because you always have in the past."

"You're right. I can't say with a hundred percent certainty that I did either thing—I simply have no recollection…but I'm such a nut about safety, Ellis, I just don't believe I would have skipped either step. It would be like forgetting to brush my teeth. Which means either I'm wrong, which would be one heck of a fortuitous coincidence from the intruder's perspective, or he somehow managed to unlock a dead-bolt lock without a key."

"You use the same key for both doors, right, front and back?"

"Yes. There are four copies, total. Ty, Zoë, and I each have one. A spare is locked in my desk at work, and I'm the only person who has that key. I keep it hidden in a hollowed-out chunk of rock I use as a paperweight. My house key is on my key ring, which attaches to a little hook in an inner zippered pocket in my tote bag. The ring is always handy, and I never lose my keys."

Ellis asked me to show him the key ring, and I ran upstairs to get my bag. The ring was in its place. My key was intact.

"We'll need to confirm that all of the others are accounted for, but assuming they are, we have a more complex situation. Someone picked a dead bolt."

"I thought it couldn't be done."

"Oh, it can be done, all right. It's not actually all that hard. The issue is that it takes minutes, not seconds, of delicate finessing to pull it off. It would take a hardy soul to attempt it on a night like this where they'd have to worry about frostbite and where they'd have no way of knowing that the alarm system was deactivated. The intruder counted on gaining access in two, call it three minutes, or less."

"So what you're saying is that someone copied my key."

"Or Ty's. Or Zoë's. Or your spare."

"I don't believe it."

"Then you tell me. How did he get in?"

I met his eyes. "I have no idea."

"We'll check with locksmiths. If someone had a copy made locally, he may remember it. A Hotchkins isn't an everyday lock."

"Oh, my God, Ellis! I just thought of something." I paused to take a breath. "I'm sure everything is fine, because I haven't heard from my security company—but if the intruder copied one key, maybe he copied them all. Keys to my building, Ty's house, and my car are all on that one ring. Even if the power went off at my business, I have generators. Ty does, too. But I should call anyway, just to be sure."

Ellis nodded. "Good idea."

"Ty uses the same security company I do, and I'm registered on his account, so I can check on his place when I call about mine."

The man who answered the phone spoke with a slight accent, a lilt I couldn't place. He sounded young. From his tone, not bored exactly, but as if my request were routine, I got the impression I wasn't the first customer he was taking to during this blizzard.

He had me answer two security questions to prove I was who I said I was, then told me no intrusions had been recorded at either my business or Ty's residence.

I thanked him, hung up, and told Ellis, "That's a relief."

"I want to take a good look at that lock," Ellis said and led the way into the kitchen.

"Can we stop by Meyer's farm stand on our way to your place, just to be certain my car is where I left it?" I asked as I followed along.

"Sure," he said.

Two steps into the kitchen, I froze, gasping.

"Ellis," I said, pointing to the floor, my heart skipping a beat. Droplets of water dotted the hardwood flooring near the door, the one that led from the kitchen into the little entryway I called a mudroom. I looked up, half-expecting to spot a damp spot on the ceiling, a leak. The ceiling was dry. "How come we didn't notice that before?"

"That's why investigations take time. You can't notice everything at once." He squatted near the moisture, leaning in close. "There's no discoloration. No mud, dirt, or debris is visible. Were you carrying a glass of water when you locked up?"

"No. I didn't wash the floor, either."

"Let's see what's in here." He stepped into the mudroom and did another close-in inspection, this one of the coir mat abutting the outside door and the inexpensive carpet runner that ran the length of the room. "Nothing. I'll have the lab take a look, but I doubt we'll find anything." He stood and opened the back door, his torch aimed at the lock.

Snow blew into the mudroom, and I shivered and returned to the kitchen. I shone my flashlight into corners, through doorways, and along walls. Nothing anywhere was disturbed. No windows were unlocked or broken. If I hadn't known better, I'd wonder if I'd imagined everything. Except that the dead-bolt lock on the back door wasn't engaged and there were a few drops of water on the kitchen floor.

"I don't see anything on the lock or housing," Ellis said. "No scratches or jimmy marks." He locked the door. "You okay going upstairs alone to pack?"

"Yes," I said. "I'll only be a sec."

Tucking my flashlight under my arm so I'd have both hands free to pack, I tossed a few sundries and miscellaneous supplies into the bag, added a few work projects in case I couldn't sleep, and placed clothes chosen solely for warmth on top. Everything looked odd, misshapen in the wavering light. I slung the bag onto my shoulder, doubting that I'd ever feel warm again.

Downstairs, I turned the thermostat down to sixty, high enough so the pipes wouldn't freeze.

"I'm lucky I have gas heat," I said, thinking that I was also lucky the intruder hadn't ventured upstairs, hating it that my safety might depend on luck.

When we got to Meyer's, I was relieved to see that my car was parked in the same spot, buried under a thick blanket of snow as if it were snuggled in for the night.

As we drove through the gusty storm toward Ellis's house, I kept glancing into the sideview mirror, unable to shake off a sense of foreboding. It was as if a poltergeist had materialized in my home, completed some dangerous or malevolent or mischievous act I hadn't yet discovered, then vaporized. I wouldn't have been the least bit surprised to see lights glimmering in back of us, but the only thing I saw was snow.

"Make yourself at home," Zoë said, opening the door to the guest room. The walls were painted light blue with darker blue trim. The curtains were dark blue and maroon plaid. Oval maroon rag rugs covered most of the hardwood floor. "There's lots of food in the fridge and a carrot cake, a cherry pie, and brownies on the counter. Help yourself."

"You are a baking machine," I said.

"I am. Baking is my go-to stress reducer. Just between you and me and the rag rug, Jake is driving me a little crazy. He's better, but when he's sick, he gets fussy." She shook her head, sending her luxurious black hair swinging. "What an unnatural mother I am. My son is sick and I feel sorry for myself."

"You're a wonderful mother, not the least bit unnatural." I patted her arm. Even in the middle of the night, wearing a bathrobe and without makeup, Zoë was striking, with sculpted cheekbones and expressive brown eyes. "How about if I babysit for a while tomorrow, so you can sneak away for some private time?"

She smiled at me, the kind of smile Helen must have used to launch ships. "Want a pie?" Zoë said. "I bake to order."

I laughed, and my tension eased a notch, maybe two. There is no substitute for girlfriends. "Next time we have dinner, I'll place an order for my favorite. Boston cream."

"Done. In the meantime, try to get some sleep, okay?"

She hugged me, then closed the door softly. The sound of the latch clicking home was exactly the same noise I'd heard earlier—*snick*. I stared at the door for a moment, reliving the confusion and fear that had gripped me during those long minutes while someone had been in my house. I still felt afraid, more so than before, because as I unbuttoned my sweater and pulled off my jeans, I knew it wasn't a nightmare or my imagination. I knew that something evil was at work.

FOURTEEN

It was nearly four when I got undressed and slipped between the soft flannel sheets in Ellis's guest room. Despite feeling physically exhausted and emotionally drained, I was certain I wouldn't be able to sleep, and I was right. I tried. I forced myself to lie still, to think of the Bahamas, to recall the sun-scorched beach and turquoise water where Ty and I had last vacationed, a place where soft breezes blew through palm fronds and my only task was to unwind, but my mind wouldn't cooperate. Instead of the gentle lapping of a Caribbean tide and the unfamiliar caws and chirps of native birds, I kept hearing the muted sound of stealthy footsteps. I clutched a pillow to my chest and rolled onto my side, then flipped the other way. I couldn't seem to find a comfortable spot, and the more I tried, the more restless I became. It felt as if tiny jolts of electricity kept sparking inside my veins. I flopped onto my stomach, then twisted sideways, then lay still again, growing more and more anxious with every failed attempt to find a comfortable position and drift off to sleep. Finally, I gave up. I switched on the bedside light and stared at the ceiling, seeing nothing. I felt too tense and fretful to rest or read, so I did what I always do when I'm upset: I worked.

I threw on my jeans and heavy wool socks and a fisherman-knit sweater, made the bed, stacking pillows against the headboard for a comfortable backrest, and drew back the curtains. Sometime during the last hour or so since I'd arrived, the storm had ended. Looking west, the sky was clear. Instead of impenetrable darkness, a three-quarters moon illuminated the bare trees that circled Ellis's property. Stars twinkled across the western sky. To the east, the clouds had thinned. The storm had nearly blown itself out to sea.

"All right, then," I said aloud, feeling my mood lighten along with the sky. "Let's do it to it."

I extracted a folder containing catalogue copy for the upcoming music objects auction that Fred had asked me to review, work I'd brought along for just this contingency. The auction, scheduled for June, featured rare musical instruments, sheet music, and music-related furnishings and decorative objects. I got settled on the bed, reading his informative and engaging descriptions, impressed, as always, with his ability to interpret meaning while describing details.

Just before seven, I noticed oblongs of pale light running along the wood floor. The sun was rising. I set aside the pages and called Ty. I'd expected to wake him; instead I learned he was more than halfway home.

"I woke up around five," he said, "and saw the storm was over. I was out of there in about two minutes. How come you're up so early?"

"I'm at Ellis's," I said, looking out the window. Opalescent pink and yellow stripes of light marked the sun's progress. "I'm fine. Everything's fine, but, well, someone broke into my house while I was home, asleep."

"I'm pulling over. Hold on." A few seconds later, he added, "All right, I'm set. You sure know how to get a man's attention. What happened?"

I explained what I'd heard and done. "I can't understand it, Ty. Nothing looked disturbed. That someone would break in and do nothing...well, that's why I'm superscared. There seems to be no rhyme or reason for it."

"There's always a motive."

There's always a motive, I repeated silently, not reassured at all.

Ty told me he loved me, that he'd be there soon, and I told him I loved him, too, and couldn't wait to see him, then I flopped over, and unexpectedly fell heavily asleep. Just after eight, I awakened to the homey sounds of Zoë puttering around with the kids. Pots and pans and glasses clinked and clattered. Laughter peaked, then quieted, then rose again. Emma squealed. I rolled out of bed, glad the night was over and the day officially under way.

"Have a coffee," Zoë said, handing me a steaming mug. "How did you sleep?"

"As expected." I cupped the mug, its warmth a comfort. "Are those mangoes?"

"Yes. I was thinking about making mango tarts. Why?"

I told her Ty would arrive shortly, and when he did, I'd make us all French toast with my mom's killer Mango Surprise Syrup and bacon.

Ty pulled into the driveway around 8:30 and stopped to talk to Ellis. I could guess what their conversation was about. I served the kids first, and by 9:30 they'd finished and were settled in the living room, watching cartoons. At 10:00, the four adults sat down to eat.

"You need to be a houseguest more often," Zoë said. "This mango thing is to die for."

"Thanks. Not many people in this part of the world happen to have mangoes on hand in February. I thought I'd take advantage of the bounty."

"I have blueberries, too. Want to make pancakes for lunch?"

I laughed. "Next time."

"You called it Mango Surprise Syrup," she said. "What's the surprise?"

"Pineapple."

"Pineapple? That's a surprise!"

"See?"

While Ty helped Ellis clear the front path and driveway, I gave Zoë a mommy break by playing a rousing round of Pictionary with twelve-year-old Jake, still under the weather but improving, and nine-year-old Emma, determined to win. She did. Zoë stayed upstairs, listening to Vivaldi's *Four Seasons* and writing in her journal.

Just before one, Ty and I drove to the Meyers' lot to retrieve my car.

"I need a generator," I said. "I feel stupid about it. I made sure to have backup systems at work—why wouldn't I do the same thing at home?"

"You didn't think of it, that's all."

"That's what brains are for, to think of things."

"Don't be so hard on yourself, Josie. You're human, not a thinking machine."

I smiled and stroked his arm. "You're very sweet," I said.

He patted my hand as we passed utility workers finishing a repair, then pulled into Meyer's lot. The open areas had been plowed, but thigh-high drifts surrounded each vehicle. Ty reached into the back for a snow brush and shovel and waded through the fluffy snow to reach my car.

"If you clear the trunk first," I said, "I'll get my shovel. Then we'll both be able to work."

He swept the snow that covered the trunk aside, then pushed his way through to the front. I used my clicker to open the trunk. Next to a tub of emergency supplies, next to the shovel, lay a tire iron I'd never seen before. I gasped. Under the dim yellow light cast by the small bulb, I saw dark crusty bits at one end. I was looking at the murder weapon. It had to be.

Whoever came into my house had opened my car, not to take something, but to leave the tire iron. God only knew what they'd hidden in my house. Panicky shivers raced up my spine. My first thought was to get rid of it, to fling it aside, to deny I'd ever seen it. I stared at it, feeling weak with impotent rage. I wouldn't fling it aside. I would do the right thing, the only thing. I'd call the police and submit to their relentless questions. I'd endure the media's unremitting innuendo. It had to be done. As molten anger replaced frozen panic, the tire iron's black hue reddened—I was seeing it through a red haze as fury took hold of my soul.

"Ty?" I said, my voice hoarse.

"What?" he called from the front.

"Come look."

He trudged to the rear, followed my gaze, and said, "You don't own a tire iron."

Ellis explained that he'd call for the flatbed to transport my car to the police garage on his cell phone to keep it off the police scanner, to keep it from the media, if he could. I thanked him, knowing it was a lost cause; too many people, from the tow truck driver to the lab techs, would know what was up.

Ty drove me to the police station and waited in the lobby while I gave a formal statement. It didn't take long since I had no information, no ideas, no suggestions. I told Ellis I'd never seen the tire iron before. I had no idea how it got into my trunk. I didn't have a clue how someone could have got my keys, since only Ty and I had keys to my car, and neither one was missing. I said that I'd never bought or owned a tire iron, that I wouldn't know what to do with one.

He thanked me and turned off the video recorder.

"Once the lab finishes testing the tire iron, we'll probably have more questions," he added, his tone empathetic.

Just after three, Ty parked by the old stone wall across from my house, next to a six-foot-high bank of snow.

"It's going to be all over the media," I said.

"Not necessarily."

"I didn't do it, Ty."

"I know that. So does Ellis."

"I feel powerless, as if I'm caught in a maelstrom and can't swim clear."

"An apt description of chaos," he said. "Let's get this snow cleared and get you a rental car, then go back to my place. I'll make you a fire."

"And a sandwich?"

"And a salad."

"What a guy."

Ty used Zoë's snow blower to clear our driveways, and I shoveled our walkways and porch steps. I was exhausted and fretful, and the sun and exercise brought a welcome burst of energy.

The electricity was still out, and walking into my home felt strange, as if the house had been abandoned long ago or I were opening up a summer cottage after a long winter. It was bone-chillingly cold. The silence was omnipresent and ominous.

"I hate the quiet," I said, looking around, seeing familiar things that seemed foreign. "I'm scared, Ty. Worse even than last night. Someone snuck what is probably the murder weapon into my car. Someone is framing me for murder."

"Trying to, it looks like. They won't succeed. You won't let them. I won't let them."

I leaned my head against his arm for a moment, then said, "Let's do what we came for and get out of here."

We stepped into the long hall that led to the front door and began our survey. We stayed together, retracing the path I'd walked with Ellis. I examined every flat surface, every wall, and every inch of flooring. Ty did the same using his government-issued high-powered torch. This time I also looked behind and under furniture, in drawers, even in the refrigerator.

"You didn't hear a vehicle approaching or leaving?"

"No, but if someone had parked at Meyer's and hiked or showshoed in, I wouldn't."

"Not with the snow muffling sounds," he agreed.

"I wondered about footprints, but with the way the snow was blowing, there's no way we could spot any."

"The rational part of me needs to ask...there's no chance you forgot that you bought a tire iron and tossed it in the trunk, is there? Or that you imagined those footsteps? Spilled the water yourself?"

"Zero, unless I've started hallucinating for the first time in my life."

He nodded. "When you realized you were hearing footsteps, what came into your mind?"

"I thought it was you because who else could it be? The whole time, though, I knew it wasn't."

"Why?"

"The timing. You couldn't possibly have covered that distance in that time." I paused, remembering. "One thing...at first I was certain the noises started from near the back door...but now I'm not so sure. I know how sounds reverberate and bounce off walls and so on." I shrugged. "Although the intruder probably entered through the back, since the dead bolt wasn't in place. We checked the front door lock, and it was set." I turned and looked at the door. "Ellis said he'll send someone over to check for prints, but he wasn't optimistic. Ditto examining the mat and rug for evidence."

Ty squatted to inspect the lock and keyhole, then stood

up. "You can pick a dead bolt," he said, "without leaving any marks."

"Doesn't the idea that someone would set out to pick a lock in the middle of the night during a blizzard stretch credibility?"

"Depends how badly they wanted in."

My mouth opened, then closed, then I said, "That's a terrifying thought."

"Yeah," he agreed. He stood and opened his arms. "Come here, gorgeous."

I walked into his embrace. His arms enveloped me, and I closed my eyes, feeling secure and loved and, for the moment, at least, safe. After a minute, maybe longer, I leaned back and traced his jawline with my finger.

"I could stay like this forever," I said.

He kissed me. "Me, too."

"Ellis said I needed to confirm the keys hadn't been lost or stolen. You have yours, right?"

"Yes. Right here." He patted his pants pocket, setting his keys jangling. "I already checked."

"And I have mine. I'll make sure my extra one is in my desk at work, but I'm certain it is. Let's run over to Zoë's now. She said that as far as she knows, the spare is in her kitchen catchall drawer, same as always, but we should look."

I used the spare key Zoë had given me, and we entered her kitchen. Zoë's house was bigger than mine but similar in layout. When they'd been built, mine had been designed as a fancy in-law abode, a sort of dower house.

My key was in the back of the drawer, on an Empire State Building souvenir key ring.

Trudging through mounds of snow back to my house, I thought about what Ty had said—there was always a motive. I believed that to be true. Sometimes, motives were obvious and evident; other times, they were hidden or disguised. Just because I didn't know the motive for the break-in didn't mean none existed.

"Let's blow this pop stand," I said as I turned the dead bolt. "Let's go somewhere safe."

I spent the rest of Sunday on Ty's couch, dozing and sleeping and listening to the crackle and pop of the fire. He brought me a salad at seven, a turkey sandwich at eight, and a cup of tea at ten. I did my best not to think, and more or less, it worked. I was able to relax and let information and impressions and intimations simmer just below the surface. By the time I arose from the sofa, as the last tiny embers glowed red, I knew I would sleep. I also knew the first thing I would do in the morning—call Wes.

FIFTEEN

"WHATCHA GOT?" WES ASKED.

"Questions," I replied, adding a thimbleful of milk to my tea.

We sat at a small table near the window in the Portsmouth Diner early the next morning, Monday. I ordered my regular, tea, a fruit salad, and an English muffin, dry with jam. Wes ordered his regular, too, a double side of bacon and a Coke.

"Shoot," he said.

That Wes hadn't jumped in with questions about the break-in and finding the tire iron was a relief. So far, it looked like Ellis had succeeded in keeping the news off Wes's radar. Since Wes listened to the police scanner religiously and seemed to have sources in every corner of the police department, I was both surprised and appreciative. The last thing I wanted was publicity that my house contained valuable antiques and was easy to access. Even less did I want to announce to the world that someone was out to frame me for murder.

"The initial shock of Henri's murder has worn off, but I'm still stunned, Wes. I just can't believe he's dead. I can't fathom that someone wanted to kill him." I shook my head and looked out the window, taking in the sun-streaked snowbanks and the salt-covered asphalt. The red SUV I'd chosen from the rental options stood out among the rows of vehicles—it was the only shiny car in the lot. "So all I have is questions."

"It's all there is," Wes said. "It's all there ever is. Questions and answers. And questions without answers."

"You might be right... I don't know." I sighed. "Have you learned anything about Dubois Interior Designs' financing or Henri's will?"

"A little about the financing and everything about the will. The business is in Henri's name only. So are their house and their cars. They paid for everything in cash—no line of credit, no loans, no net-thirty credit terms, nada."

"Wow. That's not something you hear about every day, not for first-time business owners. That means they must have had..." I paused and mentally tallied the cost of the furniture they had on display, guesstimating the rent they must be paying at their prime village green location, and throwing in an extra percentage to cover all the other expenses I knew they must have incurred, from signage to insurance and from utilities to office supplies. "Double wow, Wes. You're talking about Leigh Ann and Henri's having had close to five hundred thousand dollars in cash."

"That's big buckeroonies, but not unique in Rocky Point start-ups. You did, too, when you opened up. Even more than that when you add in the cost of your building and the renovations you made—all of which you paid for in cash. It happens."

"How on earth do you know how much I spent opening my business, or that I paid for things in cash?"

He grinned. "I like knowing stuff. Questions and answers... I told you, it's all there is."

"Don't be evasive, Wes. How do you know anything about my company's financing?"

"Confidential source," he said as he dismissed my question with an airy wave and picked up a piece of bacon.

"Wes, if my banker or accountant is telling you about

my private affairs, I need to know it. I will not talk to you ever again until you tell me how you know."

"Simmer down, Josie! No one betrayed you! You told me yourself."

"What are you talking about? I did no such thing!"

"Sure you did—just now." He grinned again. "Don't fly off the handle. All I did was float a trial balloon. I said you paid your start-up costs with cash, just like Henri and Leigh Ann, and you confirmed it for me." He leaned back and faux-shot me with his index finger. "Gotcha!"

I stared at him, speechless. Fury at Wes and mortification at my own naïveté churned inside me. He'd conned me like a pro, and I'd fallen for his ploy like an amateur.

"Where'd you get all that money anyway?" he asked shamelessly. "Rob a bank or two?"

My dad died. I used the money from his estate and insurance. "There is no force on earth that could possibly make me answer that question, Wes."

"Don't you want to know what I learned about where Leigh Ann and Henri got the money?"

"Yes, but there's no quid pro quo here. None."

"Okay, okay," he said with an irritating chuckle. "Especially since I have no idea where their money came from. When they moved here, they didn't open up a new bank account—they just changed branches from New York City to Rocky Point. They had nearly six hundred thousand dollars in the account. Since then, their balance has never dropped below the high five figures, and sometimes it's been up in the low six figures. That's a lot of moola in the coola, no matter how you cut it. I have inquiries out, checking where the money came from in the first place, but so far, no dice."

"How long has the account been open?" I asked.

"Since last August thirty-first."

"Shortly after they married, then," I said.

"Looks that way. As to his will, he left everything to his father, Pierre Dubois."

"Maybe his father put up the financing for the business, and part of the deal was that he would be Henri's heir."

"That's what I think," Wes said. "The father's some top-dog doctor in Paris. I checked. What do you know about how Leigh Ann and Henri met?"

"They met at a huge annual expo, the gift show. Do you know it, Wes? It's held every year in New York City. Specialty manufacturers from candle makers to cabinet-makers and artisans like potters and sculptors rent booths so that gift shop owners and department store buyers can see what's available and place orders. Henri worked in sales for a French fine-linen company and was manning their booth. When Leigh Ann first moved to New York, she planned to be an actress, but I guess it didn't work out. She went back to school to become an interior designer, and that wasn't going so well, either. When they met, she was working for a big-box store helping customers choose tiles and fixtures for their do-it-yourself projects. She hated it—she called it soul-annihilating work, where all anyone cared about was speed, ease of installation, and cost, where concepts like beauty and style were secondary at best. So there Leigh Ann is in Henri's company's booth admiring the linens, and they ended up having one of those unexpected conversations, you know the sort of thing I mean, don't you, Wes? You're on an airplane or a bus or at a conference and you end up having a deep conversation with a complete stranger. Leigh Ann and Henri spent an hour discussing the true meaning of quality."

Wes chomped bacon, unimpressed. "His boss must have loved that."

"That conversation led to their meeting later that day

for coffee," I continued, ignoring Wes's interjection, "then the next for lunch, then dinners each evening, and then Henri had to return to France. Ten days later, Leigh Ann spent what she called a halcyon week with him in Paris. A week after that, Henri returned to New York, and their fates were sealed."

"Yawn," Wes said.

"It's a wonderful story, Wes. Romantic."

"No wonder I'm single, huh? What happened next?"

"Henri applied for and received a fiancé visa, and they were married in August. By November, they'd relocated to Rocky Point and opened their business. They seemed perfect together." I sighed. "It's so sad."

"Sounds kind of, I don't know, gooey."

"You won't think it's gooey when it happens to you. Do you know when Henri signed the will?"

"Why?" Wes demanded, catching a scent of a fresh angle.

"I'm curious," I said, thinking that figuring out how to handle money as a couple represented a pivotal moment in any relationship. If the process went smoothly, the couple would grow closer, aligned and allied. If it didn't, even if the couple managed to stay together, resentment and ill will would invariably follow, gnawing away at trust and contentment as subtly and surely as a termite destroys wood.

"He signed it a few days before they moved to Rocky Point. After they were married. What do you think it means?"

"That our guess is probably right—Henri's dad financed their move to Rocky Point."

Wes chuckled. "Since Leigh Ann isn't in Henri's will, it looks like she didn't kill her husband for money."

I ignored his mordant humor. "Does she have an alibi?"

"I don't know. I'll check. You think she might have killed him for real? If not for money, for why?"

"I don't know," I fibbed, thinking of Scott.

"Is she screwing around?" Wes asked as if he could read my mind.

"Wes! Of course not! She was a newlywed."

He chuckled again. "Right, right…that never happens," he said, dripping sarcasm.

I stared at him, shocked that such a young man would sound so jaded, would be so jaded, until I realized I'd had the same thoughts, and then I felt amused and guilty and embarrassed, all at once.

"If so, I have no information about it. Everything I know argues against it. Leigh Ann and Henri seemed to care deeply about one another."

"God, Josie, got any more pap you want to spew?"

"When did you become Mr. Hardnose?"

"What are you talking about?" Wes asked. "I've always been Mr. Hardnose."

"You said you were going to find out about Scott," I said, rolling my eyes, eager to change the subject.

"All I know so far is that he owns a company called SRR, whatever that means, and he's divorced. How about you?"

I couldn't see any reason not to tell him that Scott and Leigh Ann had been married and divorced, and that Scott's company's initials probably stood for Scott Richey Realty, since Scott had told me he owned apartment buildings.

"I heard a few things," I said and told him what I knew about Scott and Leigh Ann.

"Rocket science, Josie!" he exclaimed when I was done. "You're the bomb."

I rolled my eyes again and asked, "Any news from the French consul?"

"The consul is just a local lawyer, did you know that? He's hired by the French government to represent their interests in the area. Interesting, huh? Anyway, Henri was here legally, just like you told me. No surprises on that front. They called him a French national in good standing." He pushed his empty plate aside and drank some Coke through a straw that bent at the top. "The police got Henri's call logs. They're focusing on one call in particular, a call he received Thursday afternoon—it's the last call he made or received before he died. It came from an unlisted number in the nine-one-seven exchange, New York City. They don't know who it belongs to. The reverse directory, you know, the thing that lets you look up phone numbers to get the name and address—nothing. It's a pretty reliable tool for landlines, not so much for cell phones. Do you know anything about that call, who Henri was talking to?"

"Why don't the police just call it?" I asked, using a trick I'd learned from Wes years earlier—if you don't want to answer a question, ask one instead.

"They did. The guy won't talk to them. He won't even give his name."

"Really?" I asked. "That's strange, isn't it?"

"Very. The service provider for that phone won't give out any info without a subpoena. Which the police received, natch, but getting the log still takes time. Back in the day, you'd get a buddy at the phone company to look up numbers for you on the q.t., but now any research an employee does on, let us say, an informal basis leaves a computerized e-trail, and if someone catches on and tries to see who leaked the goods, bam, they get nabbed dead to rights."

"You said it takes time to get the log," I said, skipping over Wes's wistful discussion of how hard it was to breach security today compared to the good old days. "How long are we talking? Days? Weeks? Months?"

"At least a couple of days. As soon as the subpoena is received by the company, they forward it to their legal department for review, blah, blah, blah."

I nodded. Bureaucratic wheels often turned slowly, and sometimes they ground to a halt.

"What do you know about Andrew Bruen?" I asked.

"Who's he?"

"A stranger who bid against Henri for the storage locker and was really upset that he lost out. I mean, really, really upset."

"You think he might be the killer?" Wes asked, his eyes fiery bright.

"I have no idea," I said, "but when you consider the circumstances, well, it seems suspicious. Andrew Bruen bid on one and only one locker...he's outbid and is visibly upset...the winning bidder is murdered within hours, and his body is found in that very storage unit. I'm not suggesting a causal relationship here. I'm saying it's enough of a coincidence that I want to know more about him."

"This is bonzo, Josie! Totally bonzo! You rock! Tell me what you know about him. What does he look like?"

"He's about my age. Ordinary looking. You know, nice enough, but nothing remarkable. He was wearing a Red Sox baseball cap and a blue parka."

"He sounds like a thousand other guys."

"That's what I thought, too. His cap and jacket...they were dirty, you know, greasy."

"Like he's a sloppy eater?"

"It's possible," I said, thinking about it, "but I don't think so. I'm talking tiny spots. I'm talking smears."

Wes nodded, taking it in. "What was he driving?"

"An old model, silver. A Camry, I think."

"I'll see what I can find out. What else you got?"

I stared at him, debating whether to reveal how Henri had asked me not to tell about the call. I decided yes. It couldn't do any harm and might do good.

"I'll tell you what I know with my usual condition—you can't ever quote me."

"Josie!" he whined.

I shook my head and closed my lips. Wes fussed with his usual vigor, then gave in. I don't know why he even bothered. I always demanded the same level of anonymity, and he always agreed.

"What do you think it means?" he asked after I'd filled him in.

"I think Henri told me the truth, that he got some bad business news—news he didn't want to reveal to Leigh Ann."

Wes nodded. "More to think about," he said. "What else you got?"

"Nothing," I said.

"All right, then," he said. He double-tapped the table, then stood up. "Catch ya later."

I watched through the plate glass window as he charged toward his old car, filled with purpose. His confident stride reminded me of my dad.

An hour later, I thanked Tim of Rocky Point Home Services Company for installing the generator, tested the automatic turn-on/turn-off feature, set the alarm, and left. News reports said the power should be fully restored by the end of the day.

"Oh, Josie," Cara said, her eyes moist. "I heard about Henri on the news. Are you all right?"

I nodded. "More or less."

"I made chocolate chip cookies," she said. "Your favorites. I couldn't think of anything else to do to help."

"You're wonderful, Cara," I said, touched. "Thank you."

"Any news?" Gretchen asked, her eyes clouded with concern.

I shook my head. "Not yet."

"Poor Leigh Ann," Cara said, and Sasha echoed her sentiments.

Fred's eyes stayed on mine, his concern apparent.

"It's so awful," Gretchen said. "They haven't even been married a year."

"Have the police made any progress?" Fred asked.

"I don't know," I said. "I wish I had news, but I don't." I unwrapped the plastic platter piled high with Cara's luscious cookies. "Anyone but me want one?"

Everyone did. I had two. They were as tasty as all Cara's cookies, maybe more so because of the caring she'd baked in.

The key to my desk was in its hidey-hole, as expected. My spare house key was in the drawer, also as expected. I didn't know whether to be relieved or not. I was thankful that no one had stolen my spare key, but the question about how the intruder had gained access to my house and car remained unanswered, and that was beyond alarming; it was terrifying.

I called Leigh Ann about ten, and Scott answered the phone.

"I wanted to check in," I said, "to see how Leigh Ann is doing."

"She's sleeping," Scott said. "She was up most of the night, finally fell asleep around four."

"That you know the timing means you were awake, too."

"That's true."

"How is she?" I asked.

"The same."

"Tell her I was thinking of her, okay?"

"Will do. How about you? You all right?"

"No. Not really."

"Yeah."

"I have Nate Blackmore on the phone," Sasha said just before eleven. "I think you'd like to hear what he has to say."

"Come on up," I said.

Two minutes later, with Sasha settled on the guest chair in my office, I activated the speakerphone and greeted him.

"Hey, Josie," he said, and I could hear the smile in his voice. "I'm the bearer of good news. While most of the jewelry in the collection is costume, good costume, but not particularly valuable, with no piece worth more than a couple of hundred dollars, the wrapped heart is a different can of beans all together. The jewels are real. The materials that look like eighteen-karat gold and platinum are. From the design and craftsmanship, I think it's a Verdura, but only they can authenticate it."

"You sure know how to put a smile on a gal's face," I said. "Two gals. I think Sasha's smile is broader than mine. But before I do my happy dance—and I gotta tell you, my friend, you have not lived until you've seen my happy dance—you didn't mention a signature. Is there one?"

"I didn't find any additional marks besides the one you spotted, which may be significant, or not. Signing jewelry wasn't as common back then as it is now. I can usually smell a fake, you know? And this one smells like the real deal."

I knew what he meant. Experienced appraisers, like experts in all fields, get so familiar with their areas of expertise, it's almost as if they can sniff out a real deal amid a slew of fakes.

"That's very encouraging, Nate," I said. "Do you have any sense of value?"

"You're going to love me—although I'm tempted to tell you in person so I can witness the happy dance."

"I promise a reprise."

"Well, then, okay...based on gem quality alone, you're looking at a hundred thousand dollars, plus. If the brooch can be authenticated as a Verdura, add a hundred thousand more. If there are any interesting associations, well, you'll go up from there. As you know, Verdura designed for high society, so there's a chance you've got something unique, something with a wonderful story behind it."

"Oh, Nate!" I exclaimed, awed. "This is *such* great news. Do you have a name for us at Verdura's?"

"Adèle Bové," he said. "I worked with her on a project a year or so ago. You'll like her. Say hey for me."

I said we would, thanked him again, and told him we'd be in touch when we'd arranged for a courier service to transport the brooch to New York.

I looked at Sasha. Her eyes were big with excitement.

"Wow," I said.

Sasha nodded. "Wow."

"Double wow."

She smiled and stood up, tucking her hair behind her ears. "I'll call Malca-Amit," she said, naming one of the world's top jewelry and art courier companies. "Do you want to call Ms. Bové?"

"Let's do it together," I said. "Let's do it now."

She sat back down, and I got the phone number for the Fifth Avenue–based salon. When Adèle Bové came on the line I introduced myself and Sasha, extended Nate's regards, and explained why we were calling.

"A wrapped heart," Adèle said. "I love those."

"Are they marked in some way somewhere we can't see?" I asked.

"You won't find a signature, but each piece has a unique scratch number—that's what we call them. It's a code, etched into the metal. For a brooch, the mark will start with *C*."

"Why *C*?"

"*B* is for bracelet."

"Got it. We looked and saw C-136. Does that mean it's real?"

"Not necessarily. Someone might have copied an original—including the scratch mark."

"How can you authenticate it?"

"If we can find the original drawing, we'll know it's a Verdura design. Some pieces were made in quantity, but most were not. The wrapped hearts, for example, were all custom designs. That means there's a very good chance we can find the original drawing, and from that, we can identify the original buyer."

"I can't believe you have all those records," I said.

"It's something, isn't it? We have boxes and boxes of paper, all the records since the company was founded in 1939. We're slowly computerizing everything. In the meantime, we search manually."

"Impressive," I said, holding crossed fingers in the air. "You can't see it, but my fingers are crossed that you're able to find the drawing for this heart."

"We'll do our best," she said. "It's amazing that you found it in a storage locker. Who did the locker belong to?"

"We don't know," I said, knowing Vicki would never tell. "We never know, and we can't find out."

As Sasha discussed the logistics with Adèle, I considered our next steps.

Assuming the heart was a genuine Verdura, once we

had the original buyer's name, we could begin our detective work. Using auction records, letters, bills of sale, and other written and oral evidence, we would attempt to track the brooch from its first owner to the storage locker, proving clear title, showing that each owner along the way had the right to possess it.

I felt my pulse quicken with a familiar burst of exhilarating anticipation. I loved every aspect of my job, but my favorite part was the hunt.

"Guess whose meeting tomorrow morning got canceled?" Ty asked.

"I can't imagine," I said, smiling. "Whose?"

"Mine. Guess which restaurant has added your favorite fish prepared your favorite way to its menu?"

"You're kidding! Sole Veronique?"

"Yes, indeed. Suzanne, the manager of the Blue Dolphin, was just interviewed in the Newcomers segment on the radio. She's very good, by the way, articulate and genuine sounding. So having heard this momentous news, guess what I did?"

"You went for an early lunch?" I asked, glancing at my computer monitor. It was 11:45.

"No. I made a reservation. For two. At seven tonight."

"Yay! You are so wonderful! My mouth is watering already."

We decided to meet at the restaurant at seven, and I'd just resumed reading my accountant's updated revenue report when Cara's voice crackled over the intercom. "Chief Hunter on line two, Josie. He says it's urgent."

I picked up the line.

After we exchanged quick hellos, he said, "I need some antiques help, Josie." I heard loud background noises, some grinding, metal on metal, and men's voices. "I'm at the police garage on Turler Street. Do you know it?"

"I think so. It's off Baylor, right?"

"Right. First block in, on the right. Can you come now?"
A clatter sounded, like a tool hitting the ground with a
bang, not a thud. "We found Henri's van."

SIXTEEN

THE POLICE GARAGE was housed in a one-story concrete building that took up most of the block. Triple-wide access doors opened to a cavernous space filled with vehicles, mostly patrol cars. Henri's van was in the middle bay, high on a hydraulic lift. Electric heaters were spaced every ten feet or so, creating a zone warm enough to work in.

"You can bring it down," Ellis called to a young man in a green jumpsuit. The hydraulic lift lowered smoothly. His eyes on the van, Ellis added, "I expect Leigh Ann here shortly." He turned toward me. "She's coming from Dixon's Funeral Home. The burial will take place in France, and she's making the arrangements."

"It must be horrible, sickening, to have to plan your husband's funeral," I said, then wished I hadn't spoken. Ellis's wife, a dancer, had died not that many years ago. Her death was one of the reasons he'd relocated to Rocky Point. *So many of us came here to get away from memories of loss, to start over,* I thought.

"Yeah," he said. The van's tires hit the ground. He walked closer to it. "The van is packed with boxes and tubs and crates. The techs have cleared it for you to go through. I don't even know the questions to ask, Josie. Is it all junk? Is anything worth killing over? Can you tell if anything is missing?"

"When we do an appraisal, we video-record everything we see, talking about it as we go. We create an annotated record. I'm thinking we should do the same thing here.

Placement may be relevant down the road. I have a camera in the trunk. If you want, I can get it."

"Good idea. But let me get one of our recorders. It's a chain of custody thing, if and when it ever comes up. I'll send someone for a setup."

He used his phone to call in the request. "They'll be here in about ten minutes."

I nodded.

"I sent a team to try for prints on your back door this morning," he said. "Nothing."

"Implying someone wiped it clear?"

"Or you're a really good housekeeper."

"Trust me, that means it was wiped." I paused. "So there's nothing more to do."

"We're canvassing the neighborhood, checking security cameras, considering other lines of investigation. We're not giving up."

"Thank you," I said. "Where did you find the van?"

"In Little Boston. Buried under a snowdrift on Dartmouth Street. An officer on routine patrol spotted it."

"Any idea how long it had been there?"

"Since before it started to snow. Several nearby residents noticed it, but no one saw who drove it in."

"Do you think Henri left it there and walked back to Crawford's?"

"Why would he?" Ellis asked.

"I don't know. Why would anyone?" I paused, then answered my own question. "To make you think he left voluntarily, which would delay your investigation."

"Why would someone do that?"

"To make it harder for the ME to determine the time of death."

"Maybe. They're pretty good at taking environmental

factors into account, but, of course, it's possible the killer doesn't know that."

"So why?"

"You tell me," Ellis said, using a ploy I recognized, designed to get me talking.

It worked. I thought about his question for a minute. "If the killer's alibi is dicey, any ambiguity regarding the time of death works in his favor."

Ellis nodded. "That's logical."

"Has the ME given an opinion yet about when Henri died?"

"Yes. Between noon and 3:00 P.M. on Friday."

"That's about what we expected."

"Don't sound so disappointed," he said. "Confirmation is a good thing."

"Always," I acknowledged. "You were going to check whether any local locksmiths made a duplicate of my door key, the Hotchkins."

"We did. They didn't. Nor did someone try to replicate your car key. The lab didn't find anything notable on your floor mat or rug, either. I'll drop them off next time I'm by."

I nodded, let down but not surprised.

"There were metal splinters in Henri's scalp," Ellis said, confirming what I'd learned from Scott. "Not painted. Something narrow and rounded, roughly five-eighths of an inch in circumference."

"Like the tire iron," I said, horrified.

"Looks that way. Your fingerprints aren't on it, by the way."

"Are anyone's?"

"No. They're still testing it, but the blood is a match, and the shape of the wounds is consistent with that weapon. That's an official term—consistent."

"Which means the murderer could have used another weapon, then doctored the tire iron to implicate it."

"Theoretically."

"Why would someone do that?" I asked.

"I don't think they would. I think the tire iron is the murder weapon."

"But it could be something else, like a fireplace poker. Or a golf club."

He nodded toward the van. "It'll be interesting to see if there's an old set of fireplace tools or golf clubs in there, especially if one piece is missing."

"Did you look in the storage unit?"

"Not yet. I'm hoping you'll go through that stuff next." He glanced at his watch. "The techs tell me they'll be done there by one."

The van was packed with Rubik's Cube–like precision. We video-recorded the entire load, then each piece of furniture, box, or tub as we removed and examined or unpacked it. From what I could tell, there was nothing remarkable, nothing that would have caught Henri's attention.

Everything appeared to be the remnants of someone's house, the kind of things that we regularly sell at the tag sale but that the Dubois would never be able to use, repurpose, or sell. The teak furniture, two triangular side tables and a low chest, was all midcentury Danish modern, without marks or signatures. At the tag sale, we'd price each piece at just over a hundred dollars. There was a nice but undistinguished cocktail set; reading copies of novels from the 1970s to the early 2000s; six framed 1890-era fashion plates, attractive and collectible, but not worth more than fifty dollars each; boxes of decent quality, no-name dishes, pots and pans, flatware, and glasses, all lovingly wrapped in newsprint; and stacks of *National Geographic* maga-

zines in pristine condition, but with no market value. My
guess was that Henri had planned on driving the entire
load to my place for sale or consignment.

Leigh Ann and Scott drove up in her SUV just as I was
finishing. Concerned about how Leigh Ann was coping,
I watched her step out of the passenger's seat. To my surprise, she looked better than I'd expected, more rested, less
wan. Scott looked the same as he had when we chatted at
the police station, kind, caring, and worried.

Leigh Ann's eyes fixed on the van, and she walked forward as if she were in a trance. Just before Scott swung
his door closed, I saw a copper-colored, Rorschach-style
stain running down the side of the seat. I knew the color—
it looked like dried blood. My stomach clenched and the
muscles along my upper back and shoulders tightened in a
spasm of empathetic grief as the memory of Leigh Ann's
collapse on Henri's bloody corpse came to me as vividly
as a snapshot. How dreadful for her to have to see it each
time she slipped behind the wheel, a constant reminder of
her devastating loss. I hoped Scott would think to get the
upholstery cleaned.

"I can't believe it was parked so close to Crawford's the
whole time," Leigh Ann murmured.

"Why would anyone leave it nearby?" Scott asked Ellis,
joining Leigh Ann on her inexorable, stupefied march.
"Wouldn't that make it more conspicuous, not less?"

"You see a van with a reputable interior design company logo on it," Ellis said, "I'd assume a neighbor was
doing a renovation, wouldn't you?"

"Sure…but a day later? On a Sunday? No one would
think that's normal."

"'Normal' is a moving target," Ellis said, and I knew he
was right. "After a day or so, especially since there was a
blizzard, no one even noticed the van. It became part of

the scenery. It became 'normal.'" He turned to Leigh Ann. "We've already removed some items we found in the glove box. I'm hoping you can identify them."

He reached into his vehicle's backseat and extracted five clear-plastic sealed evidence bags, which he held up for her to view, one at a time. The first contained a black tri-fold wallet, closed. The material, which looked like leather from where I stood, was scratched and rubbed.

Leigh Ann gasped and covered her mouth with her hand. She nodded. "That looks like Henri's wallet." She looked at Ellis. "Is anything inside missing?"

"We haven't examined it to that level of detail yet. It contains various credit cards and so on, but no cash."

He held up the second bag, this one containing several keys on a silver and turquoise key ring.

"That's it," she said.

"You said he carried five keys. I know you can't be certain without trying them, but from what you can see, are these them?" Ellis asked.

She leaned in for a closer look, then nodded. "Yes."

The third bag contained a single gold key.

"That's the style of key that goes with the padlocks we buy," Leigh Ann said. She stared for a moment, then nodded. "A Maswell, yes."

The fourth bag held a silver-colored men's watch. Leigh Ann's eyes filled, and she looked away. "That's Henri's," she whispered.

The last bag held a smart phone.

She nodded again. "That looks like his." She brushed away tears. "Henri...how could someone do this to him?"

"It's a tragedy," Ellis said, using a stock line, the sort of comment that filled space without committing the speaker to an opinion or plan of action. "A crime and a tragedy."

"Do you have any theories yet?" Scott asked.

"We're looking into several possible explanations," Ellis said, giving his typical nonanswer.

I wondered once again if the explanation might be as simple as a straightforward theft and an attempt to delay the investigation. What I'd told Ellis was true: If there had been something in the unit worth stealing, how could we know? We only knew what was there, not what might be missing. It was possible that someone, Andrew Bruen, for instance, knew the unit contained something valuable, something he was determined to get his hands on. When he lost the bidding war, he stormed off. Maybe he came back. Leigh Ann said Henri left in the morning with $5,000 cash. After winning the bid on the storage unit, he would have had $2,750 left, money now missing. Perhaps Andrew took it, thinking of it as a bonus. Leaving the watch behind was smart. It had value but was inscribed, and as such, it would be simple to trace. Anyone could have driven the van away from Crawford's without attracting notice. Vicki was in her office, busy with her work. Eric was on the other side of the facility, loading our van, or sweeping up, or en route back to the office. No one else would have noticed. Vehicles came and went all the time, anonymously, privately. If Andrew Bruen left his own car at the office building next to Crawford's or at one of the scores of shops or restaurants along Route 1, he could have walked out of Little Boston and been on his way in minutes. Maybe he stopped somewhere for a late lunch, then returned to Crawford's at four to pick up his deposit.

Ellis turned toward Leigh Ann. "I understand that today is another tough one for you," he said, "and I hate to ask you to take on more stress, but I'm hoping you'll be able to take a look around inside the van, to see if the contents of the glove box and center console are the same as you remember. I need you to let me know if anything that should be there isn't, and if anything unexpected has been introduced."

"I can do this," she said, her tone sounding more like a pep talk to herself than a statement to Ellis.

She walked to the open passenger-side door and hoisted herself up onto the seat. Scott came and stood beside me. Together, from ten feet away, we watched Leigh Ann unlatch the glove compartment.

She peeked in, then methodically extracted a car manual, a few napkins, and a document-sized, blue plastic case, probably containing their car registration and insurance cards. They stored their toll pass in the center console, along with more napkins.

"How about you, Josie?" Scott asked me, keeping his eyes on Leigh Ann. "You holding up all right?"

"Yes. Sort of. I wish I understood…but how can anyone ever understand murder?" I shook my head to dispel encroaching sadness. "How's Leigh Ann really doing?"

"Pretty well, all things considered. Henri's father asked for his body back, and Leigh Ann agreed."

"Will she go there for the funeral?"

"Maybe. She's not sure about anything yet."

Leigh Ann swiveled to talk through the open door.

"I think everything is here," she said, still composed, although tearful. "I don't see anything unexpected."

Scott helped her down.

"We had to be certain," Ellis said. "Thank you for coming. I appreciate it."

"What about all those boxes?" Leigh Ann asked.

"Josie's just gone through everything for us. So far, nothing stood out as significant, but we've just begun our analysis. I've asked her to go through the contents of the storage room, too. We're going there shortly. Do you want to join us?"

"I can't. I just can't."

"I understand," Ellis said.

She turned to me and reached out a gloved hand. I took it in my own. "Thank you, Josie," she said.

Scott touched her elbow and led her slowly toward her vehicle. Ellis and I stood and watched, and as I did, I wondered if Leigh Ann would go to France, and if so, if Scott would go with her.

APPROACHING HENRI'S STORAGE ROOM, it was easy to picture him as I'd last seen him, focused, exhilarated, his attention fully engaged. My eyes were drawn along the concrete floor to the back of the room, to the coffee-colored streaks, his blood, so much blood. My eyes began to fill, and to stop myself from crying, I raised them to the boxes, to the work at hand.

Going through the storage room was harder than going through the contents of the van. Nothing was organized. Several boxes were opened, and some were half empty, presumably because Henri had found things that he wanted to look at right away, or that he'd repacked into other boxes or tubs for safety's or organization's sake. It was also a more difficult work environment, too small and too cold for comfort. Squatting to video-record disparate objects in such a cramped space quickly became impractical. The sun was bright, and the temperature hovered around freezing, but it was still cold enough to require gloves, and working in gloves slowed me down, adding to my discomfort and frustration.

"How about moving everything to my place?" I asked Ellis after about ten minutes. "I could go a lot quicker if I wasn't wearing gloves, and I could concentrate better if I wasn't frozen stiff."

Ellis nodded. "We can do that. The techs have given a complete all clear. I'll call some guys."

I gave a mental *whew* and said, "I'll let Eric know so he can prepare the space."

Ellis and I took a couple of steps away from one another and made our separate phone calls.

"We'll be there in an hour," he told me when we were done.

"We'll be waiting for you," I said.

I turned back to the storage unit, reliving the moment Henri won the bid. He'd been so hopeful, so excited. I could almost feel his presence, but I recognized that sensation for what it was: wishful thinking.

When I got back to work around 1:30 P.M. I found a voice mail waiting.

"Hey, Josie," Shelley said. "Marshall White, that movie memorabilia expert I told you about—he's ready to give you his assessment of your posters. You're gonna be happy, my friend!"

I IM'd her, and we set a time to talk in thirty minutes. I swiveled to look out my window, past the old maple and the new rhododendrons, to the church. I was pleased, ecstatic, really, to learn that evidently, from Shelley's teasing message, Henri's posters had value, but I felt beyond sad, closer to dejected, that he wasn't here to share the good news.

SEVENTEEN

WHILE I WAITED for Shelley's call and the police truck containing the contents of Henri's locker, I created a bulleted list of relevant facts. I planned to ask Fred to handle the Batiste Madalena poster authentication, while I stayed focused on confirming its provenance.

- Madalena immigrated from Italy. Full name = Batiste F. Madalena
- Graduated from the Mechanics Institute (later, the Rochester Institute of Technology)
- Hired as commercial artist by the Eastman Theater, Rochester, New York, 1924
- Produced seven posters, each at least somewhat different from the others, for each movie shown at the theater. All 22" × 44".
- Worked from 1924–1928, produced 1,400+ posters, 225 known to be extant, saved by the artist when the new theater owner threw them in the trash.
- The artist's collection (all 225 posters) was sold to Los Angeles–based documentary filmmaker Steven Katten.
- If Steven Katten bought the entire collection, how did one poster get into the storage unit owner's hands?
- Do other Madalena posters exist in any museum or private collections?
- Check with MoMA exhibit curators re 2008 show.

- Do the materials match one another? Are they consistent with his known work?
- What else?

I nodded. With that level of detail, Fred could get a running start on his part of the appraisal.

I e-mailed him the list, explaining the division of duties between us, and headed downstairs.

I carried the silent movie posters across the warehouse to the worktable nearest Hank's area, so I'd have company during my call with Marshall. Hank sat nearby, mewing, and I squatted to pet him.

"How's my boy?" I asked, scratching under his chin.

He mewed again and nuzzled my hand. I gathered him up and kissed the top of his head. He placed his paw on my arm, and we stood like that, hugging one another, until the call came in. Cara's voice came over the speakers. Shelley was on line two.

"All right, Hank," I said, placing him in his basket, "I've got to go to work now." I got my headphone in place so I'd have my hands free.

Meow, Hank said, his tone gruff, his disapproval clear. His meows were way different from his mews, more imperative, less tolerant, making no secret of when he was disappointed in me. I understood; he wanted more attention. I picked him up again, settling him on my shoulder, and he began purring.

"Josie, meet Marshall. Marshall is our resident film guru."

"I don't know about that," Marshall said, giving an awkward guffaw.

I greeted him, still petting Hank. "Thanks for taking a look at the posters."

I surveyed them as I spoke. All four were beautifully

designed and executed, yet each was as different from the others as yin from yang. Their chief commonality was that they each communicated intrigue through emotion.

"It was pretty exciting," he said, sounding enthused. "Of course, I can't confirm anything without examining the originals, but based on these photographs and your belief that they're not modern-era reproductions, I can give you encouraging news. First, some background. Early movie posters were all originals, produced by each theater, if they chose, not by the movie studios."

In other words, I thought, *Henri's posters could have been produced anywhere in the country.*

Marshall continued. "When a movie went out of circulation, most of the posters, which were well worn from use by that time, were thrown away, thus increasing the value of any extant examples."

Supply and demand, yet again.

"I agree with your analysis of the Garbo poster," he added. "In all probability, it was painted by Batiste Madalena. We'll be glad to authenticate it for you, and handle the sale, if you'd like."

He paused, and when he continued, he was breathing so heavily, I heard exactly what Shelley meant by saying he panted.

"I'm confident that several major museums will be interested in acquiring it," he stated, "and with our well-established relationships with both the curators and directors, we could help facilitate the process, ensuring your seller enjoys the most favorable terms possible."

"Thanks," I said, skipping it, not bothering to mention that I, too, had well-established relationships with museum curators and directors. Hank squirmed a little, then jumped down and sauntered away a few steps, then sat down and began licking his flank.

"Of course, we'll be glad to arrange transport," he said.

He wanted my business, big-time. "What about the other three, the ones with the cat?" I asked.

"A. P. Markham," he said, not letting my dismissal ruffle his feathers, "known as Al Markham. He painted in tempera on colored poster board for the Ioka Theater in Exeter, New Hampshire, and was known for using multiple styles—he was a commercial artist by training, which meant he was expert in adaptation. Markham didn't sign his work-for-hire pieces, thinking of them as ephemera, which is to say, as throw-aways, not art. This idiosyncrasy, combined with his chameleonlike talent, makes his unsigned work significantly harder to validate than his signed work—except for the cat's face. Everything he painted, signed and unsigned, featured that cat."

"What sort of work did he sign?" I asked.

"Portraits, some in tempera, others in oil. During the 1920s, he was the go-to portrait artist for families and corporate executives in New Hampshire. He also has a solid reputation in the 'works on paper' arm of the art world. One of his signed lithographs recently sold at auction for twelve thousand five hundred dollars."

"Interesting," I said. "What do you think the Markham posters are worth?"

"I don't know," Marshall said, his breathless excitement mounting, "but I think it may be a fair amount, perhaps as much as forty or fifty thousand dollars each. They're so scarce. I'd love to get a look at them."

Shelley chimed in, laughing. "Forget it, Marshall," she said. "I know Josie. Think barnacle. No way is she letting those posters out of her sight."

"I might," I said. "You never know. If I need more help, I'll know who to call, that's for sure!" I thanked them both again, told Shelley I'd be in touch, and promised to keep them updated.

With the artist's name in hand, my research path was clear. I removed my headphone, told Hank I'd talk to him later, and ran for the stairs. Settled in my office, I called Fred to pass on the good news about Madalena and asked if he had any questions about my e-mail, the one containing the bulleted list. He didn't.

I went to the large proprietary Web site and searched for "A. P. Markham."

"Yay!" I said aloud as a bio appeared on my screen alongside a photograph.

The photo showed a distinguished-looking middle-aged man, around sixty, holding a pipe. An artist's easel stood in the background, partially hidden by his torso. His expression was thoughtful, communicating that he was a serious man, a serious artist.

Markham had lived and died in Manchester, New Hampshire. Born in 1885, he'd been eighty-three when he'd died in 1968. He'd married Rose G. Odell in 1922. They had two children, Katrina, born in 1930, and Lester, born in 1932. Markham had learned commercial art during a stint in the U.S. Army, serving as a publications specialist, and by the time he married he was a well-established freelancer working with local ad agencies and small businesses throughout the Manchester area. He also dabbled in fine art, experimenting with materials, subjects, and styles. He was known for his versatility.

So far, so good. It looked like we'd identified our artist.

Now I needed to demonstrate that these posters were originals and that they could be sold with clear title. I e-mailed Sasha explaining what I'd discovered and asking her to take charge of the Markham posters' authentication process, explaining that I'd assigned the Madalena to Fred and adding that I'd take a crack at confirming provenance.

We had two options: We could trace the posters from the artists' hands forward or we could trace them from the storage locker backward. The latter approach was the best hope, but there was a glitch. I didn't know who'd owned the storage locker where Henri had found the posters, and Vicki had made it clear she'd never tell me. I pursed my lips, thinking. Ellis would have needed to know the owner's name as part of his murder investigation, and if he'd had to get a court order to get the information, he would have done so.

Cara's voice came over the loudspeaker. "Josie, pick up line one, please."

When I had her on the phone, she added, "Chief Hunter is here with some men in a truck. Eric is meeting them at the loading dock."

Perfect timing, I thought.

EIGHTEEN

ELLIS AND I stood near the roped-off area Eric had set up to receive the contents of Henri's storage unit watching Eric and the two police helpers wheel in dollies and rolling flatbeds of boxes, furniture, bags, and tubs. The area was about triple the size of the storage unit, which would allow ample room to maneuver. He'd labeled this section number 31, writing the numerals on one of the dozens of standing whiteboards we used for the purpose.

"You know how you asked me to let you know if I identified anything that might be worth killing for?" I asked, keeping my voice low. "I think maybe I just did."

"Tell me," he said, matching my tone.

I explained about the posters, describing why I needed to know who'd owned the unit.

"We've already submitted paperwork to compel Vicki Crawford to provide that info. You've just given me a good reason to turn up the heat."

Once everything was unloaded, Ellis sent his men back to the police station and turned to me.

"Now what happens?" he asked.

I glanced at the wall clock. It was just after four.

"Now we record everything, then begin our object-by-object review."

"Good. Call me on my cell if there's anything I should know."

I promised I would and escorted him out. In the front office, I asked Sasha to join me at section 31.

"Bring a camera," I said, "and ask Fred to join us, too." I noted his empty desk. "Is he in the warehouse?"

"Fred stepped out. He said he wouldn't be back until seven or so. Do you want me to call his cell?"

"No," I said. "No prob." I wasn't concerned about Fred's absence. Unless a meeting or conference call required Fred's or Sasha's presence at a certain time, they were free to set their own schedules, and Fred, I knew, was a consummate night owl, often starting his day at noon and working well into the evening. I turned to Gretchen. "You're drafted. Get Eric and a second camera. This is an all-hands-on-deck situation." To Cara I added, "You're in charge of holding down the fort."

Cara gave a two-finger mock salute. "Will do."

I considered how best to proceed as I scanned the stacks of boxes and tubs and the piles of bags. Gretchen and Eric could work the cameras, but our protocol required that only antiques experts could provide the narration, naming objects and describing any markings, nicks, mars, or dents we observed.

"Gretchen and I will start on this side," I said, pointing to the left. "You guys work from the other end, and we'll meet in the middle. I know it's late. Let's see how much we can get done in an hour."

We dug in.

Box after box, tub after tub, and bag after bag revealed more of the same sorts of things I'd discovered in Henri's van. We unpacked serving dishes; kitchen utensils; a nice collection of sterling silver booze labels, the kind that hang around cut-glass decanters on silver chains; and men's clothing, pants sized 38/32, and sweaters, sized large.

Just after five, Cara came in to tell me she was leaving. I asked Gretchen, Sasha, and Eric if they could stay for another hour or so, and they all could. No one needed to call anyone. No one needed a break. Gretchen and I were three boxes from running into Eric and Sasha when I spotted a tightly rolled paper cylinder wrapped in a red and cream-colored crocheted afghan.

"Look at what I found," I said, waving it in the air like a trophy. "Anyone want to bet on what it is?"

Sasha and Eric stepped closer to watch as I slid the rubber band off and unfurled it, revealing a silent movie poster advertising *Johanna Enlists,* starring Mary Pickford. The painting showed the young beauty, her skin flawless, her cheeks rose-petal pink, striding toward something on the left, her gait and demeanor evoking a soldier marching in formation. She wore a long-sleeved white dress.

"I want to look for the cat's face," I said and headed for the nearest worktable.

"What's that?" Gretchen asked.

"A tell," I said, explaining about the artist's visual signature. "I'm betting this is another Markham."

With Eric and Gretchen standing on my left and Sasha on my right, I switched on the overhead work lamp, placed glass weights on the corners to keep the poster flat, grabbed a loupe, and started examining the folds of Mary Pickford's white dress.

Nestled in the shadows of the collar was a delicately rendered cat's face.

I set aside the last empty box and glanced at the clock; it was nearly six.

"That's it," I said. "Thanks, everyone, for staying late. You all go on ahead. I'll close up."

They offered to stay, and I told them there was no need, and they left.

I transferred all the empty containers to the far end of the roped-off area—nothing would be discarded until the police investigation was completed—then went to my office to call Ellis.

"What do you do now?" Ellis asked me as soon as I'd reported on our initial assessment: We'd identified another potentially valuable silent movie poster and hadn't found any fireplace tools or golf clubs, nor anything else that could have been the murder weapon.

"Hope you're able to get the name from Vicki Crawford and that it helps me trace the Markham posters."

"I should know more in the morning. You going to be there for a while? I want to ask you something."

"What?"

"It's a show-and-tell thing. I'm ten minutes away."

The time display on my monitor read 6:17. "I have half an hour."

"I'll see you in ten."

Downstairs, I changed Hank's water and added food, getting him set up for the night. He was in his basket, napping.

"What do you think Ellis wants?" I asked him.

He opened one eye, then closed it.

"I don't know either. Good night, little fellow. Be a good boy." I leaned in to kiss his furry cheek, then went to the front to greet Ellis.

Ellis stepped into the office, setting the wind chimes jangling. I offered him a cookie from the batch of chocolate chips Cara had made for me and a drink, and he said no to the cookies, a masterful example of self-control, and yes to a lemonade.

"You going to your place tonight?" he asked.

"I don't know. Why?"

"We checked security cameras in the area. There aren't many, but there is one at the end of your street. Rocky Point Community Bank has cameras mounted on its light poles. One unit caught a partial of a car passing at 12:50 A.M., the only vehicle on the road in either direction after a police patrol car went by at one minute after twelve. Nothing else passed until a snowplow at one fifteen. Twelve fifty is twenty-eight minutes before you say you were awakened by the break-in. That sounds like about the right amount of time to get from the bank to that farm stand, park, and hike the rest of the way to your place, doesn't it?"

My throat closed and my eyes opened wide. I'd known Ellis was investigating. I'd hoped he'd find evidence. Yet here I was, astonished.

"Sorry to come at you with this without warning," he said, "but you need to know. I need your help."

"I'm okay," I said, managing to smile. "I just wasn't expecting news so soon. I'm impressed. What else can you tell me?"

He eased a black-and-white photograph from an inside pocket and handed it to me. The photo showed a sliver of car, the left side, a sedan, not a van, SUV, or truck. It was driving north, toward my street. The storm was in full force. I tried to look through the white haze, but whirling streams of snowflakes distorted the view, and I couldn't see much beyond vague shapes.

"Do you recognize it?" he asked.

I shook my head. "No, but it's such a small image, and it's so hard to see through the snow..." My voice trailed off.

"We have enough to identify the car model, at least I think we do. I have a man on it now."

"The license plate isn't visible."

"True," he acknowledged.

"What color is the car, do you think?"

He looked down, frowning, his lips pushed together. "Hard to say...not white...not dark colored...metallic, maybe."

"Silver is the most common car color, I think."

"Know anyone who drives a silver car?"

"Sure," I said. "Lots of people, including Zoë. Can the tech guys use Photoshop or something to enhance the driver's face?"

"They're working on it, but they told me they weren't optimistic. It's not the highest-quality photo to start with."

"Can I keep this?" I asked. "I'd like to show it to Ty."

"Yes." He tilted his glass high, finishing the last drops of lemonade, then slid the glass onto the table. "Nothing wrong with letting lots of people see it. Just 'cause you and I don't recognize the car doesn't mean someone else won't. It's pretty unusual to be out driving at that hour in the middle of a blizzard. Someone might have remarked it."

I looked at him, surprised. "Are you releasing it to the media?"

"No. That would be inappropriate at this point in the investigation. No one knows your place was broken into, and I don't want to call attention to it. It's one thing to ask your neighbors if they heard a car or saw someone walking in the area. We can be discreet when it's one-on-one. But this... I can't release it without telling reporters why. You could, though."

"What would I say?"

He reached into his pocket again and extracted a single sheet of paper. "I took the liberty," he said, "of jotting down a few thoughts." He glanced at it, then handed it over.

I gave him a sideways glance to let him know he wasn't pulling any wool over my eyes, that I understood he was orchestrating our conversation like a puppeteer manipulates a marionette. I read his paragraph-long suggested statement.

When conducting antiques appraisals, you never know where your research will lead. In this case, I have reason to believe that the driver of this car can help me appraise a valuable nineteenth-century painting. If any of your readers know who was out late at night during this past weekend's blizzard, please ask them to contact me.

"This is a lie," I said, looking up, meeting his eyes.

"How do you know? Maybe the person who broke in was after that painting you told me about, the Jan Brueghel the Younger. It's possible he knows something about it that you don't know."

I stared at him for several seconds trying to figure out his agenda. "Do you think the break-in is related to Henri's murder?" I asked.

"Let's just say that I mistrust anything that looks like a coincidence."

I nodded. "I'm grateful, Ellis, for the seriousness with which you're taking this." I reread his statement. "When you talked about releasing the photo, you specified 'readers.' Does that mean you don't want me to contact the broadcast media?"

"Do you have a buddy on TV?"

"No." A lightbulb in my head flashed on. "Oh…you're thinking of Wes."

"Wes Smith? Good idea, Josie. He does a solid job. As far as I can tell, he's an honest man."

"You don't really think this will work, do you?"

"You never know what will work until you try it." He picked up his coat. "I'll e-mail you the photo so you can forward it on. Save it to your computer, will you, so when you send it to him, it will come from you, not me?"

"Will do. What do I say when Wes asks where I got it from?"

"A security camera."

"He'll ask which one and how I got it," I said.

"Tell him he's not the only one with sources."

"You're devilishly clever, Ellis."

He stood up and shook out his pant leg. "Just doing my job, ma'am."

I smiled, relaxing a bit. Ellis wouldn't joke about it if he thought I was in danger.

I downloaded the photo to my shared folder, renamed it "mystery car," and called Wes. He was tickled that I'd contacted him and cooperative, promising to highlight the reader challenge both in tomorrow's printed paper and on the newspaper's Web site starting now.

I checked the time on Gretchen's Mickey Mouse clock. It was 6:48, time to go. I gave Hank a goodbye cuddle, turned out the lights, set the security alarm, and headed out to meet Ty for dinner.

As I pulled open the Blue Dolphin's heavy oak door, Fred was just leaving, shrugging into his coat as he walked, and we nearly collided.

"Sorry," he said, pushing his glasses up.

"Great minds, right?" I said, smiling. "Did you have an early dinner?"

He didn't blush, not exactly. The color that flooded his cheeks resembled a pale pink flush of surprise more than the deep red of mortification, but it was enough for my gossip antennae to whip up and begin vibrating. I had the sense that I'd just caught Fred with his pants down.

"Yeah," he said, with impressive aplomb, "I did. It was great. I'm heading back to work now. Is there anything I should know?"

I was tempted to drag him into the lounge and, under the guise of filling him in about Markham, elicit answers that would quench my gossip thirst, but I didn't. What Fred did on his own time was none of my business. It took discipline, but I managed to swallow my curiosity.

"Just the e-mail I sent you about Madalena," I said, waving good-bye. "You might be able to get a start on your part of the appraisal. Regardless, I'll see you tomorrow."

Suzanne was hovering near the hostess stand. She looked as lovely as she had before, but her mood was different, distressed.

"Hi, Josie," she said. "Ty's already here, in the lounge. He told me to set aside a Sole Veronique for you." As I handed over my coat, accepting a pink claim check in return, she added, "Do you have a minute?"

"Of course," I said.

Suzanne led me to the back corner of the entry room, out of traffic.

"Are the police close to naming a suspect in Henri's murder?" she asked, her voice low.

"I have no idea," I said, wondering why she would have thought I did. "I'm sorry."

She sighed and stared into the middle distance for a moment. "I feel so horrible. Really, I'm just beside myself. I don't know what to do."

I murmured something soothing, nonwords intended to convey empathy.

"Have you heard anything?" she asked, her tone plaintive.

"I know the police are pursuing many leads, but if they're making progress, I don't know it." I thought that I knew both too much and too little. I had plenty of facts, but no conclusions. "I know how vague that sounds."

She sighed again, and her eyes moistened. "Do you know about funeral plans? I'd like to attend."

"I think the burial will be in France. I don't know if Leigh Ann plans a local memorial service. I hope so—I'd like to go, too."

She nodded and touched my arm again. "Thank you,

Josie. Please keep me updated. I'd like to know what's going on...what the police learn...please let me know anything you hear, anything at all."

I promised I would, and as I headed into the lounge, I wondered whether Suzanne's interest was related more to the manner in which Henri died than it was to the man himself, like the voyeuristic fascination people feel driving past a car wreck where their attention is riveted to the carnage not by concern but by curiosity. I stopped myself. Just because she'd only met Henri a couple of months ago didn't mean their friendship wasn't genuine or meaningful, or that her grief wasn't authentic. I gave myself a small mental slap, ashamed at the cynicism that led me to question her motivation.

Ty stood as I approached, and as I looked at him, I felt myself begin to glow. No matter how wearing the day, no matter how upset I might be, Ty was an elixir.

"Boy, oh boy," I said as I settled into the banquette by the window, "are you a sight for sore eyes."

"Why are your eyes sore?" Ty asked.

Jimmy came over, and I ordered a French martini before answering. "Because of this."

I placed the photo showing the snow-shrouded bit of car on the table. Ty looked at it, then up at me.

"Ellis thinks that if this driver and the person who broke into my house aren't one and the same," I said, "it's one heck of a coincidence."

He picked up the photo and tilted it under the light, reviewing it with care, then placing it alongside his beer. He tapped the border with his index finger.

"I know this car," he said.

I smiled. "I'm not the least bit surprised. Pretty much, you know everything, huh?"

He laughed. "Hardly. The guy I worked with in Berlin

was driving one just like it—a Malibu. He'd rented one and loved it, so he went out and bought his own."

Ty texted Ellis to let him know he thought the car was a Malibu, while I texted Wes the same message.

Our phones tucked away, Ty proposed a toast, using what he knew was my favorite, my dad's favorite, passed down to me.

"Here's to silver light in the dark of night," he said, touching my glass with his own.

I sipped my martini. "What will Ellis do now?"

"Start looking for a metallic-colored Malibu."

"That sounds impossible, like looking for a needle in a haystack."

"Time-consuming, yes. Impossible, no. This wasn't a stranger, Josie, randomly picking a house to break into. This was someone who knows you, which means someone you know drives a Malibu."

My heart plummeted, then leaped into my throat. I stared into Ty's brown eyes, seeing not his concern or love but a slide show of cars. Ty was wrong: No one I knew drove a Malibu.

"I don't know anyone who drives a Malibu," I said, then, realizing that I did, in fact, know someone who drove a Malibu, I gasped and pressed my fingers against my lips. "Scott. He's driving a rental car. I'm pretty sure it looks just like this one."

I couldn't believe Scott was involved in the break-in at my house. I just couldn't. It made no sense, but I reminded myself that if nothing makes sense, it's not that sense can't be made; it's that you lack information. In an antiques appraisal, you either are able to determine value or you aren't, and if you aren't, you dig deeper, talk to more people, investigate details you'd previously dismissed as irrelevant.

All research shared that pattern. The only cure for ambiguity was knowledge.

"What do I do?" I asked.

"Call Ellis."

I called Ellis. Our conversation lasted about ten seconds.

"You probably have already thought of this, but Scott, Leigh Ann's friend, is driving a rental. Lots of rental fleets include Malibus. It's a popular car."

"Thanks, Josie," he said. "All tips are welcome."

I hit the END CALL button, then sipped some martini.

"You know," I remarked to Ty, "Ellis is better at playing his cards close to his vest than anyone I know."

"Except maybe me," Ty said, cocking his head sideways. "When I had his job, I was pretty good at the no-news two-step."

"So true. You still are. How's security at private airfields?"

"It's one of many issues Homeland Security is looking into."

"See?" I reached across the table to touch his cheek. "You're a wonderful man, Ty."

He took my hand in his and kissed my palm. "You're a wonderful woman, Josie."

"We're very lucky," I said, feeling the familiar, welcome pull of attraction, of love.

"And we know it."

Frieda approached, ready to seat us for dinner.

Walking into the dining room beside Ty, my hand tucked in his, I felt a rush of gratitude. It might have been blind luck that Ty and I found one another, but whether it was luck or fate or serendipity, I never took our love for granted.

Picking up the menu, I wondered whether Ellis would call Scott and ask about his rental vehicle or whether he'd drive by Leigh Ann's house to see the car for himself. Ellis would go in person, I decided, because he wouldn't want to alert Scott to the possibility that he was a suspect in the murder of his ex-wife's husband. Half of me wanted to rush to Leigh Ann's house to watch the police at work. The other half was eager to stay away, to eat Sole Veronique and listen to Ty talk about his day.

I hoped that Wes's article would work, that someone would recognize the car and come forward, and that with this new information, chaos would resolve into order.

NINETEEN

BECAUSE I SUBSCRIBE to both the online and paper editions of the *Seacoast Star,* I was able to check the paper's news flashes before I went to bed. Knowing Wes's predilection for listening to his police scanner, I wasn't surprised to see Scott mentioned. I was pleased my name didn't appear.

MURDER VICTIM'S WIFE'S FRIEND
TAKEN IN FOR QUESTIONING

Scott Richey was brought to police headquarters at 8:45 P.M. last evening and is still being questioned regarding his whereabouts during the overnight hours of last weekend's blizzard. According to Rocky Point Police Chief Ellis Hunter, "There's no reason to think this issue is related to the murder of Henri Dubois." When asked to clarify what "this issue" refers to, he declined to provide details at this point. More information will be posted on this site as it becomes available.

If I were Scott, I'd be furious. Every fact Wes included was true, yet the article itself insinuated something I doubted was true, and the word for that was sophistry. Without evidence, implying Scott was guilty of a crime and, worse, suggesting he was somehow connected to Henri's murder was more than wrong; it was dastardly.

I fired off an e-mail to Wes.

Low blow, Wes, implying Scott has some evil association to Henri and is guilty of some unspecified crime. I'm seriously not impressed.

I was so riled up I expected to toss and turn all night, but I didn't. I slept dreamlessly and long. When I finally awoke, it was after eight, and Ty was long gone. He left a "see you later" note on the mirror. I smiled at how he'd signed it "xxo." I would tease him later, asking why I only got one kiss.

Before I went into work, I looked for an update about Scott on the *Seacoast Star* Web site and read Wes's article about the car photograph. I also checked my e-mail. Wes's reply to my earlier message was classic Wes.

Lighten up. Jeez, Josie.

In spite of myself, I smiled.

Wes had updated the article about Scott, adding that he had left the police station at 3:10 A.M.

I couldn't imagine what the police had found to discuss that could have filled six hours. After asking if he'd driven around in the blizzard and whether he had broken into my house and planted the murder weapon in my car, then what?

I thought Wes did a great job on the other article, the one about the car photograph. He managed to convey gravitas, mystery, and urgency all at once. His headline read:

DO YOU KNOW THIS CAR?
*Driver Might Hold Answers in
Rocky Point Antiques Mystery*

His article used the paragraph Ellis had written, adding a Q&A with me.

Q: What's the mystery?
A: There may not be one—that's why I need to ask the driver some questions. The antique is a valuable painting, nineteenth-century, European. I can't reveal any more about it, but I can say this—one of the key aspects of an antiques appraisal is provenance, proving that the object has an unbroken, legal chain of ownership. The driver of this car may be able to help confirm provenance.

Q: How?
A: I'd like to thank anyone who helps identify the driver in advance, and assure them they'll be doing society a world of good. Yes…society. Finding the driver is that important.

Wes listed my contact information at the bottom and in the photo caption.

I sent him a follow-up e-mail. This one read:

Maybe you're right about me needing to lighten up. In any event, "Do You Know This Car?" gets two thumbs up. Well done, Wes.

Ellis got the court order compelling Vicki Crawford to disclose any and all information about the owner of the storage locker Henri won at auction first thing Tuesday morning.

He called at nine to put me on alert. "I'm en route to hand-deliver it, and I plan to wait for the information. I'll come directly to your place afterwards."

He showed up at 9:50 A.M., and we went upstairs to my private office. I sat on one of the wing chairs. Ellis sat across from me on the love seat.

He placed a manila folder on the cushion next to him and tapped it. "This folder contains the information you need. I'm willing to tell you everything—names, addresses, bank account numbers, the works, but I have a condition." He paused, his eyes unwavering. "You can't reveal the name to the media. I need to tell you as part of an active investigation. I understand that you may need to mention it in the course of your appraisal, but there is no need to know that goes beyond that. We simply don't know what ships loose lips might sink."

"I'm good at keeping secrets," I said.

"I know," he said.

I wondered which secret he was referring to, the one I'd kept for Henri or the many secrets Zoë had entrusted to me, late-night confessions about how much she loved him; how fearful she was that theirs was a rebound relationship, his first serious romance since his wife's death, and wouldn't last; or how anxious she felt about her children bonding to a man who might simply walk out the door at any moment and disappear from their lives.

I met his gaze but didn't comment.

"You okay with that?" he asked.

"Yes," I said.

He nodded, satisfied. "I don't know if or how this will help you, but here's the deal. The unit was leased five years ago to a man named Gael Patrick," Ellis said. "Gael is spelled G-A-E-L. Vicki doesn't remember a thing about him except that it was, in fact, a man who rented it. She thinks he was older but isn't sure. As she explained it, she has nearly a hundred units, most rented short-term, which means she has scores of people coming and going, and this was five years ago." He smiled. "She says she pays attention to their paperwork, not their faces."

"What about her security camera? She told me she has one in the office."

"She only went digital a few months ago. Photos from back then no longer exist. Gael Patrick has been delinquent for the last five months. Vicki mailed a certified letter as required by their contract warning him that she was going to repossess the unit and sell the contents at auction unless all back rent and late fees were paid by a certain date, but it was returned as undeliverable. In case the post office messed up somehow, she sent an additional certified letter. It, too, was returned as undeliverable. The New York City address Gael Patrick provided was a fake. It's 454 West Thirty-fifth Street. Do you know the West Side at all?"

"Yes. In fact, I know that address. It's a beautiful brownstone."

"Right. It's privately owned. There are four residents, all men, and they've all lived there longer than five years. I checked with all four, but no one had ever heard of Gael Patrick. So I checked out both 445 and 544 West Thirty-fifth Street, in case Mr. Patrick accidentally transposed numbers. From the satellite view, those two buildings look identical, indistinguishable from any of the dozens of new high-rises popping up everywhere in that area. Both buildings' property managers told me the same thing—they'd never had a Gael Patrick on their rent rolls."

"Yet another dead end," I said.

"Looks that way. The phone number he listed at Crawford's is a dud, too. When I called, the phone was answered by a Spanish-speaking woman who doesn't speak or understand a word of English. She'd never heard of Gael Patrick. Using my very rough Spanish, I learned that the number was assigned to her when she moved to New York two years earlier."

"I didn't know you spoke Spanish."

He grinned. "I don't think anyone would call what I speak Spanish. I picked up a few words while I was on the job in the city, enough to get by." Ellis leaned back and crossed his legs at the ankle. "Until Patrick fell behind at Crawford's, all the payments were made on time by automatic debit from an account at Rocky Point Community Bank. The account was closed five months ago. I spoke to the branch manager, and she wouldn't tell me anything. I need another subpoena, which is in the works."

"Do you think Gael Patrick died?"

"No. I asked the bank manager specifically, and she said that if an account is closed because the owner died, they keep the death certificate on file, and she doesn't have one in this case." Ellis shook his head. "Gael Patrick doesn't have a current phone number, utility account, or voter registration record, and he isn't listed on any tax roll in either New York or any New England state. Any other ideas how I can find him?"

I thought about it. "He lived in New York and moved his possessions to New Hampshire, but not into his own place, into storage. Could he be in an assisted living facility?"

"Not in Rocky Point. We've called them all. We're continuing to check facilities in a continuously expanding geographic area. We're already into Maine. What else?"

"Maybe he moved in with one of his children."

He nodded. "And if it's a daughter who changed her name when she got married, we're screwed. How would you go about finding him?"

I looked out the window into golden rays of sun. The snow coating my maple's limbs was melting. I turned back to Ellis. "Through his doctor."

He nodded again. "We're making those calls, too."

I smiled, pleased that Ellis was consulting me, pleased that I was coming up with smart ideas. "Ask the media to publicize it?"

"It's too early in the investigation to show our cards."

"What if it's a fake name?"

"Could be. There's lots of reasons someone might not want to use his real name when renting a storage unit."

"Like if he's storing stolen goods or a pornography collection," I said.

"Nothing like that was found in the unit, so unless the killer stole those kinds of objects, those reasons don't apply."

"Maybe he's a privacy fiend or a conspiracy nut afraid the government is out to get him and he needs a place to store his canned goods and guns for when the revolution starts."

"You have a great imagination, Josie. Impressive. Except we didn't find canned goods or guns in his unit, either."

"I have no idea why someone would use a fake ID to store ordinary household goods."

"Me, either," he said. "Will knowing his name—or rather, the name he used—help with the appraisal?"

"If we can't find him, no. I need to know how he acquired the posters. If his identity is an invention..." I stopped talking and shrugged. There was no point in stating the obvious. "Never say never. Onward and upward. Fight to the end."

Ellis smiled. "Any other clichés you want to drop in my lap?"

"No, that should do for now."

"So what's your next step?" he asked.

"Find someone who knows about the posters."

"How do you do that?" he asked.

"I have no idea."

"That's what I was afraid you'd say."

I walked Ellis downstairs, discouraged. *Nothing,* I thought peevishly, *was easy.*

I WATCHED ELLIS stride across the parking lot, then turned and surveyed the office. Cara and Gretchen were on the phone. Sasha was reading from her computer monitor. Fred was flipping through a stack of papers on his desk. A printout of *Mysterious Lady* was on top.

"Any early news?" I asked Fred, pointing to the photo.

"Nothing surprising. So far I've been researching past auction records. The news about sales of Madalenas is uniformly good, and since his popularity is growing, our timing is excellent. For provenance purposes, we need to demonstrate how the poster got into that storage unit, though. There's no record of any extant posters other than those included in the Katten collection."

"How about if you look into the materials of the Madalena? I'm trying to nail down how all the posters got into the locker, including that Madalena, and there's no point in our duplicating work."

"Sounds good," Fred said.

I turned and asked Sasha if she had any news about the Verdura wrapped heart.

Sasha started and blinked a few times, switching gears from her focused reading to me.

"I spoke to Adèle," she said. "The heart arrived intact. She'll let us know as soon as she has any information."

"Excellent." Hank mewed loudly and rubbed his jowl against my calf. I scooped him up. "Do you want to help me do some research, Hank?"

Upstairs, I got Hank settled on my lap, but he lost interest once I started tapping into my computer and stopped petting him. After mewing a few times, he jumped down.

"I'll play with you later, Hank, all right?"

He loped out the door without replying, and I turned my attention to my monitor.

Because Markham was less well known than Madalena, there were fewer sources of information available. He'd never had a museum or gallery exhibition; he hadn't taught at a university; and he hadn't been favored by a rich patron or a famous collector. From what Marshall had told me, he was a working commercial artist, a man who earned most of his living by producing art on demand. Just for the heck of it, I checked whether the name used by the owner of the storage unit, Gael Patrick, had a listing on any of the Web sites we used for research, but he didn't. There was nothing left to check.

Deciding to take a break from research, I called Leigh Ann and got her.

"I just wanted to let you know I was thinking of you," I said.

"I'm glad you did," she said. She sounded weak, as if she were just out of bed after a bad case of flu. "I've been so overwhelmed that I haven't thanked you for all your help...looking through that locker...talking to the police... everything. Thank you."

"Please, Leigh Ann, don't even think about it. I wish I could do more. Can I do anything for you now? I could stop at a grocery store and bring you some supplies."

"That's nice of you to offer, Josie, but I'm fine. Scott is out shopping now."

"How's he doing? I heard he had a night of it."

"Oh, Josie! The police kept him half the night. As if anyone could think that Scott was involved in anything criminal...why, it's just absurd."

"What crime?" I asked, holding my breath.

"We don't know! The police wouldn't tell him. Something about his being out during the blizzard, which, of course, he wasn't. I'm telling you it's ridiculous! I mean, even if he was driving around that night, driving isn't a crime!"

"I wonder what they're thinking. On the face of it, it makes no sense."

"Nothing about this nightmare makes sense, Josie. Nothing."

"I'm so sorry that you're having to deal with all of this, Leigh Ann. Are you certain there's nothing I can do?"

"Not at this point. Thank you, Josie. For everything. You're a true friend."

She agreed to let me know if there was anything else I could do, and I told her I'd check in with her again soon.

I leaned back, closed my eyes, and after a minute of wishing I could do more to help, I turned my attention to research options. How could I learn more about Markham? Since I was stymied going backward from the locker, it made sense to try going forward from the artist. Markham was dead, but he had two children, both of whom might still be alive.

If Markham's daughter, Katrina, was living, she'd be eighty-three. Lester, his son, would be eighty-one. There was no phone listing for either of them in any New England state, but that didn't mean they didn't live in the area. Lots of people had gotten rid of their landlines, using a cell phone as their only phone. If that's what Lester did, I was out of luck. There was a chance, however, that I hadn't located Katrina's number because she had changed her name when she'd married, as most women of her generation had.

I called the Manchester city vital records clerk and spoke to a woman named Lara.

"I need to find out if a woman got married," I said, "and if so, to whom. I only know her maiden name. This probably would have occurred, if it happened at all, in the late 1950s. Is that info online?"

"No," Lara said. "Our marriage records weren't computerized until 1995, but we can look things up manually. It'll take a while, that's all."

"Thank you," I said and gave her Katrina's name and year of birth.

Lara promised to call me as soon as she had news. In the meantime, I decided to do some manual checking of my own. The Manchester *Union Leader*'s online archives only went back to 1989, but a quick call to the Rocky Point library confirmed that they had copies on microfiche dating back to the early 1900s.

I told Cara where I was going, said I'd be back in a couple of hours, and headed out.

The Rocky Point library sits on a large hill across from South Mill Pond. It was an idyllic location with lush landscaping and a clear view of the pond.

The microfiche machines looked as unexpected as dinosaurs, artifacts from a bygone age. The librarian, a tall woman with short brown hair, named Phyllis Straw, got me set up at the workstation, and I began the laborious task of checking the marriage notices in each Sunday's newspaper, starting in 1950, when Katrina would have been eighteen. Nearly an hour later, I found the notice, dated September 6, 1952. Katrina Mayhew Markham had married Edwin Mark Greeley in Manchester. In another ten minutes, I'd located Mrs. Greeley's phone number and called her from my car.

"You want to talk about Dad," she said after I explained that I was calling for information about his silent movie posters. "How nice! Would you like to come for coffee? I make a mean scone."

I accepted with pleasure, got her address, called Lara at the Manchester records bureau to cancel my request, and headed south, smiling.

Ty called as I was driving to Mrs. Greeley's house in Rye to tell me he had to go to D.C. for an early-morning strategy meeting.

I slipped in my earpiece and asked, "Anything juicy?"

He chuckled. "Dry, not juicy. The analytics are in. Good news—I can now confirm that training works, so we need to talk about next steps."

"Umm...wouldn't that be obvious...schedule more training?"

"Don't be sassy. Not all training is equal. We need to see which programs are working and roll them out and which aren't and retool them."

"I'll miss you."

"I'll miss you, too," he said. "Why don't you stay at my place tonight? Make a fire and curl up with a good book."

"I think I will," I said, sighing. "At this point, I'm not keen on staying at my house alone. The thought of it gives me creepy jeepies, and that makes me mad enough to spit. I hate feeling all wiggly squiggly."

"Wiggly squiggly?"

"You know—it's the flip side of nervous and jerky."

"Oh, of course. That clears it right up."

"When do you leave?" I asked.

"Now. I'm en route home to pack. I should be able to make the 5:35 train out of South Station. How about you? Besides the wiggly squiggly thing, how's your day going?"

"I'm making good progress on the appraisal," I told him. I recounted what I'd been doing and what I'd learned, adding, "I sure hope the artist's daughter can give me a lead. Otherwise, I'm out of ideas."

"Nah. You'll just go on to plan C or D or whatever letter you're up to. I've never seen anyone as persistent and thorough as you. It's what makes you such a good appraiser. It's what makes you such a good businesswoman."

"Thanks," I said, pleased at the tribute. Curiosity was a fact of my life. Not knowing things was like an itch I couldn't scratch, a pebble in my shoe. "Wish me luck with Mrs. Greeley."

"You don't need luck…but good luck."

We agreed to talk before bed, and I smiled the whole drive to Rye, thinking about Ty.

TWENTY

KATRINA GREELEY LIVED in a bungalow overlooking the ocean in Rye. I parked on the shoulder and climbed a snow-covered dune. Watching the ebb and flow of the ocean always helped me relax, my pulse slowing to match the rhythm of the tide.

Gold sun-tipped flecks of light danced along the bottle green ocean surface. The ocean was calm. The sun was blinding. A cargo ship, far out to sea, steamed north. The snow was pristine here, unmarked by animal or bird tracks, unsullied by soot. To the north, the bungalow next to Mrs. Greeley's was boarded up for winter. To the south, smoke streamed from one of the house's three chimneys. The breeze was cold, and I raised my coat's collar. The water rolled farther toward me—the tide was coming in. I watched a while longer, then slid-walked down the dune, stomped my feet to rid my boots of clumps of snow, brushed stray flakes from my slacks, and walked the twenty paces to Mrs. Greeley's shoveled path.

Mrs. Greeley's bungalow was expansive, a one-story sprawling home with a wraparound porch designed to capture the view. I rang the bell and waited. The woman who answered the door looked like more like a latter-day hippie than the grandmotherly type I'd expected, and I wondered if she was a friend or hired companion.

"Mrs. Greeley?" I asked.

"That's me," she said, grinning, "but please call me Trina. Everyone does. Come on in! I was just lighting the fire. I love chatting in front of a fire, don't you? I think it must evoke my primitive self, back when my foremothers were done with their day's work and knew they were safe for the night." She pointed to a cushy red velvet couch positioned to face a fieldstone fireplace large enough to hold six-foot logs. "Have a seat. I'll just get this started."

I'd assumed that Mrs. Greeley would look her age. I'd expected that her face would be lined with wrinkles and dotted with dark sun spots, that her hair would be white and crimped in an old-lady style, and that she'd wear warm, but shapeless, clothing. Instead Trina looked about seventy. Her creamy white skin was smooth, with only a few crinkly lines near her needle-sharp eyes and full lips. Her gray hair hung to her waist in a loose braid. She wore a stylish, belted, hip-length burnt orange sweater over a to-the-ankle India-print paisley skirt and henna Birkenstock shoes. Bead-and-feather earrings dangled from her ears.

"That's a beautiful fireplace," I said as she struck a long match and held the yellow flame to the kindling. "Don't tell me you lifted that log yourself?"

"Not even when I was your age!" she said, laughing. "I have a young man who comes in to help. He does all the shoveling and heavy lifting and so on." She stood watching the fire until she confirmed that it was spreading nicely. "I have a tray ready. I'll be right back."

"Can I do anything?"

She laughed again. "No, thanks."

She pushed through a swinging door, leaving me alone in the living room. The decor matched her appearance, from the red and purple psychedelic prints to an orange lava lamp sitting on a corner table. The furniture was an eclectic mix of oak and mahogany covered in red velvet and purple corduroy. Nothing matched, but everything seemed to mesh perfectly. Pepper red flames licked at splinters of bark as the fire caught and grew. The door swung wide and she was back, a gleaming silver tray in hand. She placed it on the mosaic coffee table and sat on a purple chair.

"So," she said, pouring coffee from an ornate silver pot, "have a scone and fire away. What can I tell you about my dad?"

I smiled as I settled in. Most of my research required me to crawl under furniture in dank cellars or stuffy attics, sort through reams of useless papers in the hopes of finding one pertinent document, and bother busy, uninterested people. Sitting in Trina's cozy living room, sipping strong coffee, and nibbling the scone she had every right to be proud of baking felt a little bit like I was playing hooky.

"As I explained on the phone," I said, "a film memorabilia expert is confident that the silent movie posters I'm trying to appraise were designed and painted by your father, A. P. Markham. I have several questions, and I can't thank you enough for taking this time to talk to me. If it's all right with you, I'd like to start with the artwork itself." I reached into my tote bag and extracted a miniportfolio I'd put together showing printouts of the four posters.

Trina placed her mug on the coffee table and picked up the portfolio. Her eyes brightened and her smile broadened as she flipped through the pages.

"Will you look at these. I didn't know anyone outside the family had any of them." She raised her eyes to my face. "Where did you get them?"

"From a storage unit rented to a man named Gael Patrick. Gael is spelled G-A-E-L."

"Gael Patrick," she whispered, her eyes reflective.

She looked over my shoulder, out the French doors. I skewed around and followed her gaze. Past the covered porch railing, past the snow-shrouded dunes, white froth riffled across the smooth sheen of ocean surface as the water pumped toward shore. I turned back to face her. She was remembering something, a private memory, a good memory. Her smile was wistful but not sad. I waited for her to explain. A full minute passed before she spoke again.

"It might be nothing," she said, meeting my eyes, "just one of those strange coincidences that happen sometimes... but my mother's full name was Rose Gail Odell, and my father's was Albert Patrick Markham. Gael Patrick."

"Wow," I said, the implications ricocheting through my brain like pinballs at a video arcade.

"I know. It's probably nothing...but still. I wonder if my brother might have rented it. He moved to Rocky Point a few years ago. He died last summer."

"It might be," I said, thinking it had to be; it was a logical conclusion. "Let me tell you about some of the other things we found in the unit and see if anything rings a bell."

I rattled off a list of the unusual or distinctive objects we'd found in the unit, including the Four Seasons and Delmonico's menus and the Batiste Madalena silent movie poster. When I was done, she shook her head and handed me the portfolio.

"I have no idea," she said. "I'm sorry."

"Not a problem," I said, smiling again. "Do you have any of your dad's posters I could get a look at?"

She waved toward the boldly colored abstract prints on the wall in back of her. "I loved my dad to death, but my taste runs in a different direction. A few years ago, I crated everything up and sent it to my boys. I have two sons." She laughed a little, not loudly. "Once I turned eighty, finding good homes for my unwanted but much-loved possessions became a priority, even a preoccupation." She looked at the coffee service. "This coffee service, for instance. It's getting so I resent having to polish it, but I can't stand seeing it tarnished." She shook her head, her expression rueful. "I have the whole shebang—the coffeepot, teapot, sugar bowl, creamer, even sugar tongs that match." She sighed. "You don't know anyone who'd want the set, who'd love it, do you?"

"Yes."

Startled, Trina's eyes opened wide. "Really?"

"On one level, that's exactly what I do. I find loving homes for worthy antiques."

"I never thought of your business that way."

"I may be romanticizing the process a bit," I said, smiling. "I do, after all, run a business. I don't run a wholesale business, though—I don't sell to dealers. I sell to end users. The only people who buy sterling silver sets as magnificent as yours are people who want them very much, who love them very much."

She nodded, her expression thoughtful. "I may just be in touch about that."

"Any time," I said. I tucked the portfolio back into my tote bag and smiled again. "Do you think your sons might be willing to let me examine a few of your dad's posters? By comparing materials and craftsmanship, we can often make headway on authenticating objects."

"I'm certain they'd be glad to help. Before you leave, I'll give you their phone numbers. Hal is a lawyer in New York City. Bert teaches science at Andover, a private school outside of Boston."

"Thank you. Might either one have rented a storage unit in Rocky Point?"

"I can't imagine why. Growing up, whenever they wanted to store something, they put it in the spare room. Now, of course, they own their own houses and put things in their own spare rooms!"

I smiled. "Am I correct that your father never signed his posters?"

"In a manner of speaking he did. My dad didn't like the name Katrina. He didn't like Trina any better, but my mom wanted to name me after *her* mom, Katrina, and she won." Trina laughed, a cheery sound, and raised her hand as if she were about to swear an oath, communicating, "whatever...no matter...not relevant," as clearly as if she'd spoken those words. "The point is that she declared that her first daughter would be named Katrina soon after they married. He never called me anything but Kitty, and he planned it out right from the start. He painted a little cat's face in every poster, in every painting, years before I was born, even before he and Mom married. Like the *Playboy* bunny. You know what I mean, don't you? How they hide bunny ears somewhere on every cover of the magazine?"

"Yes," I said. "Al Hirschfeld, too. He hid his daughter's name in every one of his drawings. Sometimes he put a number near his signature, letting people know how many times Nina's name appeared in that drawing. Did your dad ever insert more than one cat's face per painting?"

"No." She smiled again. "It's sweet, isn't it? Fathers who love their daughters."

"Very," I said, thinking how special my dad was, how much I missed him, how close we'd been. "Your dad signed some things with his actual name, right?"

"Yes," she said. "It wasn't that he thought commercial art was beneath him so much as he thought signing it was inappropriate. He didn't think of it as his work. He thought of it as his client's work. Work for hire, they called it. Still do, I think."

"What can you tell me about his materials and techniques?" I asked.

She paused before answering, and I could almost hear the wheels of memory turning.

"Tempera," she said. "That's what he used for posters. He liked both its flexibility and durability." She smiled, this one impish. "He had a shortcut—even though all his silent movie work happened before I was born, he made me promise not to tell. Isn't that funny?" She looked at the ceiling. "I'm telling on you, Dad!" She lowered her eyes to my face and smiled at me. "I don't mind telling you— Dad would be so thrilled that you thought his work was worth appraising! Anyway, Dad painted on colored poster boards to save him from having to paint the background. That's clever, isn't it? That was his big secret." She shook her head. "As to his brushes…he used all sorts, and palette knives and sponges, too. Anything that would create the effect he was trying for, like stencils for lacy patterns, that kind of thing. My dad was above all else a pragmatist."

"How did he decide what the posters should look like?" I asked. "Did he design them himself? Did he need approval from a committee?"

She laughed. "He came up with the idea himself based on what he'd been told was his number one job: Keep it simple. The movie studios sent still shots and promo copy, but the man he worked for didn't care about that. He wanted customers to be able to read the posters from twenty feet away, driving by in a car or walking on the other side of the street. Dad's assignment was to ensure that the film's title and main star's name were visible— those elements and one key graphic image were all that was allowed. The dates and times were always in a smaller font and were placed at the bottom. The posters weren't designed to be informational pieces—they were to attract attention, to create a mood." She smiled again, a big one this time. "I know all this because my dad loved his work and talked about it."

I nodded and smiled. "My dad was the same. It's how I learned to love business."

"What did your dad do?" Trina asked.

"He was a partner in a management consulting firm. He helped small businesses thrive."

"From your voice I can tell you were close to him."

I smiled. "We're two lucky women," I said. "We had great dads."

"That's the truth if I've ever heard it. Even though he thought I was from another planet most of the time, he loved me unconditionally."

"That's a great gift to give a child," I said, then finished my coffee and scone and told Trina that it was the best scone I'd ever eaten.

She thanked me and said the secret was vanilla, wrote out her sons' phone numbers, and wished me luck.

"Imagine Les having a storage room and never saying a word about it," she said, shaking her head. "It makes you realize that even the people you're closest to, the ones you think you know the best, have secrets."

Everyone has secrets, Ellis had said. *Everyone.*

I promised to let her know if I was able to confirm that her brother was Gael Patrick, then left. On the drive back to my office, I found myself wondering what my life would be like when I was eighty-three. Would I be ready to wind down, to give possessions away, to lighten the load? Or would I still be in acquisition mode? Regardless of which way it went, I hoped I'd look as good, feel as confident, and be as gracious as Trina.

TWENTY-ONE

As soon as I got back to work I called Hal Greeley. I glanced at my computer monitor—it was 3:04 P.M.

An officious-sounding man named Mr. Peterson answered the phone and wouldn't even tell me if his boss was in the office. From his supercilious tone and stodgy diction, I wouldn't have been surprised to learn he was an actor working a day job.

"I'm sorry, Ms. Prescott," Mr. Peterson said, "but without an appointment it's very difficult to arrange for you to talk directly to Mr. Greeley. If you care to tell me what your call is regarding, I will be certain to convey the message."

"Certainly," I said, adding an extra measure of sugar to my tone. "Please tell him his mother suggested that I call. If it's inconvenient for him to talk now, I'll call Mrs. Greeley and let her know."

Hal Greeley came right on the line.

"Josie Prescott?" he asked in a resonating baritone. "I read about your company a few years back in *Antiques Insights*. You were nipping at the big boys' heels and they didn't like it much. How you doing now?"

"We're doing fine, thanks. I'll tell you why I'm calling. I just spent a delightful hour with your mother, and she thought you might be able to help me. I have a few questions about your grandfather's silent movie posters. Is now a good time to talk?"

"Totally," he said. "I love those posters."

"Thank you. My first question may sound pretty random, but I promise it's relevant. Have you ever rented a storage unit in Rocky Point, New Hampshire?"

He guffawed. "Anything to be mysterious—us experts are all the same. No, I've never rented a storage unit in Rocky Point, New Hampshire."

"Do you know anyone who has?"

"No. I sure hope you're going to tell me what a storage unit has to do with my grandfather's posters."

"We're trying to appraise some items, including his posters, that were found in a storage unit. It had been rented by a man named Gael—spelled G-A-E-L—Patrick. Does that name mean anything to you?"

His jocular manner vanished. "Maybe. What does he look like?"

"I don't know. The facility owner doesn't remember him—it's been five years since the unit was first rented—and any photos they might have had through their security system are long gone. The renter gave a nonworking New York City phone number and a private residence on West Thirty-fifth Street where he never lived as his address. Who do you think it is?"

"Uncle Les, my mom's brother. Gail and Patrick were my grandparents' middle names."

I nodded, glad for the confirmation. That mother and son both reached the same conclusion was encouraging.

"What can you tell me about him?" I asked.

"He was a great guy. A perfect uncle. He's dead now, and I've got to tell you, I miss him...a lot. My brother, Bert, and I were just talking about that, about him. When we were kids, in college, you know, and just starting out in our careers, he'd swoop down and take us and a bunch of our buddies out for dinner and a show. I was at law school in Denver when he took me to see Dave Brubeck, and that began my lifelong love affair with jazz. He was a real bon vivant, Uncle Les was, with boundless energy and an independent spirit. He was an art history professor at NYU, a real gentleman."

"People like that are so rare," I said.

"You got that right."

"When did he move to New Hampshire?"

"About five, six years ago, He entered the Belle Mer assisted living facility in Rocky Point after a fall—he broke his hip and had a difficult recovery. I can't understand why he put stuff in a storage facility, but nothing else makes sense, not with that name and the timing. I visited him and my mom a couple, three times a year, and he never mentioned it. I assumed he'd taken my advice to sell off his possessions to help pay for his care. Now you're telling me he kept everything in storage all these years." He paused. "Years ago, Uncle Les told me he never left his apartment without a thousand dollars hidden in his belt, sometimes more, and his passport in his pocket. He called it the adult equivalent of bus money. If push came to shove, and he wanted to get out of Dodge, or had to, he could walk into any airport and buy a ticket to somewhere he'd rather be." Another pause. "I can absolutely see him thinking that if the nursing facility was unacceptable, he'd get his buddy to drive to New Hampshire, pick him and his possessions up, and head home to New York."

"I see what you're saying. An independent man not ready to give up his independence, hedging his bets, in a sense...but why would he use a fake name?"

"Probably to avoid a scene with me," he said, his tone severe. "God...this is not a recollection I'm proud of. Talk about insensitive. I told him not to be silly, that he was never going to live on his own again. Jesus. What was I thinking? Here was Uncle Les secretly hoping his stint was temporary and planning an escape route in case it was un-endurable, and there I was telling him that this was his last stop." He sighed. "One question, though. If Uncle Les had everything in storage, and was current with his bill when he died, how did he pay for it? He was on a fixed income, an income that went to Belle Mer directly."

"Good question," I said. "He never recovered from his fall?"

"His hip got better...then he was diagnosed with sun-downer's syndrome—a form of early-stage dementia that kicks in when the sun goes down. It went downhill from there."

"Who helped him move from New York?" I asked.

"His best friend, Brock Wood. I have his number here somewhere. I called him after Uncle Les died. He told me they'd been friends for more than fifty years."

"Fifty years," I said, hoping that Zoë and I would be celebrating that anniversary when we were in our eight-ies. "If Les thought his stint in rehab was temporary, why did he come to New Hampshire at all?"

"I asked the same question when he first got there. He knew it was going to be months, not days or weeks, and he thought he might as well be near the beach. He spent all his summers up in New Hampshire with us when I was a kid, and he loved the area, loved the ocean. Plus, he and my mom were close, and he said it was a good excuse to spend some time with her."

"Did he leave a will?" I asked.

"No. I didn't think anything of it at the time because it seemed he didn't have anything worth bequeathing. The facility refunded some of his money—I assumed it was the unused portion of his bank balance. Really, I didn't look into things much because it never occurred to me that anything might be missing or improper. Les led a comfortable life, but he wasn't a rich man. He never owned real estate—he lived in a rental apartment his entire adult life—and he lived well. I called him a bon vivant, and that's exactly what he was. He never missed a Broadway show. He traveled to Europe a couple of times a year. He dressed nicely. I simply assumed he spent what he earned, but now you've got me wondering."

"Did you know he owned some of your granddad's silent movie posters?"

"Not specifically, no."

"There was a Batiste Madalena silent movie poster in the storage unit, too. Would you have any idea if he owned that?"

"I've never heard of that artist…so, no."

"What about your brother? Might he have any additional information?"

"I doubt it. Although we went up together when Uncle Les died, the responsibility for closing up his affairs fell primarily on me, not him. I don't mean to suggest he shirked his duty or anything. I'm a lawyer, so it was easier for me, that's all. You're welcome to talk to him directly." His voice grew quieter. "To tell you the truth, I'm a little dazed. Uncle Les having a storage unit…it seems so damn improbable. But that name, Gael Patrick—what are the odds that it's a coincidence?"

"Maybe Mr. Wood will be able to shed some light on the situation."

"Let me give you his number."

"You've been very helpful," I said, meaning it, thinking how direct and frank Hal was, how he'd shifted from blustery at the start of our call to reflective and quiet at the end, perhaps a testimony to how much he loved his Uncle Les. "Your mom gave me your brother's number, so I'm all set there. If you have a contact at Belle Mer, I'll take that information, too. Your uncle might have mentioned something about the storage unit to someone there."

He gave me Brock's number, then said, "Good idea about Belle Mer. In fact, let me put you on hold and see if the woman in charge, Tabatha Solomon, is available to talk to us here and now."

I agreed, then heard clicks, followed by a long silence, then a woman's voice.

"This is Tabatha Solomon. Mr. Greeley, is that you?"

"Yes, with Josie Prescott on the line. Josie?"

I had started to explain why we were calling when Ms. Solomon interrupted me. "Excuse me. Let me stop you there. I can't talk about a patient's private affairs without written permission. Period. No exceptions."

Hal said he understood. He asked if a letter from Les's sister, his next of kin, would serve, and Ms. Solomon said it would. He thanked her for her time and ended the call.

"What's your fax number, Josie?" he asked. "I'll get it organized immediately. Inquiring minds want to know, right?"

I gave him my fax number, saying that I'd be glad to stop by his mom's house and pick it up if that was easier for her, adding that if she had any questions, I'd be glad to explain what we were up to. He said that would be perfect, that he'd ask his mom to have it ready by eight the next morning and would call me if there was a delay.

"I'm thinking that once I have it in hand," I said, "I'll call Ms. Solomon to schedule an appointment. She might be able to direct me to someone your Uncle Les knew at Belle Mer, someone who could confirm that he used Gael Patrick's name as his own."

Without that connection nailed down, all we could do was speculate that Lester Markham had the right to own the posters. To command top dollar, I needed more than conjecture and logic—I needed proof. I felt a trill of anticipation ripple through my veins. I had two new viable leads. It was not a stretch to expect that either or both Brock Woods and Tabatha Solomon might know more than a nephew Uncle Les had apparently perceived as unsympathetic.

"One last question," I said. "Your mom told me she passed along your granddad's posters to you and your brother. May I borrow a few of yours? Comparing a painting to a known original is one of the best ways to authenticate it."

He paused. "Let me think on it a little. With some sort of surety, I would probably be okay with it."

"My company, Prescott's, is fully bonded and insured, and, of course, we'd arrange safe transport with what's called 'nail to nail' security. One other thing—while I'm examining the posters, I'll be glad to provide formal appraisals. That will help you determine your own insurance needs, do estate planning, decide whether to sell them, that kind of thing."

"Thank you," Hal said, warming to the prospect. "That's a great offer. Especially with a daughter in medical school. Selling a few might be smart. Don't get me started about the cost of college tuition. All right, you're on. How many posters would you like?"

We discussed which ones he should select. I asked for a representative sample of different styles, designs, and painting techniques.

"I'll get them packaged up tonight," he said.

I made suggestions about safe-packing techniques, thanked him for his cooperation, and gave him Gretchen's name and number, explaining that she would be the person arranging the courier transport. We ended the call, me with a list of follow-up tasks, him to continue his soul-searching, I suspected, reliving how he'd treated his much-loved Uncle Les when he'd entered Belle Mer. *So many things in life,* I thought, *offered no opportunity for do-overs.*

I called Tabatha Solomon, the Belle Mer administrator, back and explained about Hal's plan for me to pick up his mom's letter of authorization. Based on that, she was happy to give me an appointment at 8:30 A.M.

IT WAS NEARLY five before I reached Bert Greeley. A bevy of kids shrieked in the background, the happy high-pitched sounds of children at play.

"Sorry," he said, laughing. "I'm babysitting my grandkids—four-year-old twins."

"Really," I said, grinning, "it sounds more like half a dozen."

"It feels like half a dozen, too. What can I do for you?"

"I'll try to be quick. I have a few questions about your Uncle Les relating to some collectibles I'm trying to appraise."

"You should call my brother. Hal took the lead in handling Uncle Les's affairs."

"I already spoke to him. I'm on a hunt for confirmation. As I said, I'll be quick. Did your Uncle Les ever mention silent movie posters to you?"

"Sure. My granddad painted them, and Les thought they were great. We all did."

"Did Uncle Les own any?"

"Yeah. One summer—God, this is a lot of years ago. Hal was at college, I remember, and I was a senior in high school. I remember because I was a lifeguard that summer and I'd just come in from the beach. Uncle Les was so excited, he couldn't wait to show me. Dad gave him a bunch of his posters. Four if I'm recalling right."

I smiled, thrilled that I'd just edged one step closer to my goal.

"Do you remember which ones?"

"You're really putting me to the test today. There was a Charlie Chaplin one, and one for a movie starring Mary Pickford…hold on…let me think… I can see them in my mind's eye, the way Uncle Les held them up one at a time, but I remember seeing them in his apartment, too, in New York, years later… Lillian Gish, she was in one, and there was one more…oh, yeah. *Birth of a Nation*. I can't believe I remembered."

"Me, either. I'm dazzled. Thank you so much."

"Did I get it right?" he asked.

"You did indeed."

I now knew how Uncle Les got possession of the posters. All that remained was to confirm that Uncle Les had used the name Gael Patrick. I asked Bert if the name meant anything to him, but it didn't. I thanked him again and ended the call. The last sounds I heard before placing the receiver in the cradle were Bert calling out, "Who wants to play Go Fish?" followed by gleeful shouts.

Brock Wood's phone rang and rang and rang. No machine picked up. I tried every half hour or so, until nine, without luck. For all I knew Uncle Les's good friend was on a round-the-world cruise.

My best hope to connect the storage unit with Les Markham lay with Tabatha Solomon.

TWENTY-TWO

TRINA GREELEY HAD no questions. As I climbed the porch steps at eight the next morning, I saw a standard #10 envelope with my name on it taped to her front door. Inside I found a typed letter addressed "To Whom It May Concern," authorizing me to ask questions about Lester Markham on behalf of the Greeley family, with an oversized pink Post-it Note attached.

Thank you, Josie. Hal tells me you're hot on the trail of those posters. Let me know if I can provide additional help.

Best, Trina

I stopped at Rocky Point Pharmacy, where they had a small photocopier you could use for twenty-five cents a copy, and made four copies of Trina's letter and two of her Post-it Note, just in case.

Belle Mer looked more like a Mediterranean mansion than an assisted living facility. Positioned at the top of Strawberry Hill on Rocky's Point's northern border, the building was oriented to capture an unfettered ocean view on three sides.

Tabatha Solomon's ground-floor office was smaller than I would have expected and overlooked the parking lot. If I were considering placing a relative in the facility, I would have been impressed. Clearly, Ms. Solomon saved the best views for the residents.

She was about five feet tall and stout, with curly brown hair cut short and reading glasses hanging from a black cord around her neck. She looked to be about sixty. I handed her the letter, and she read it through, then placed it on her desk.

"How can I help?" she asked, all business.

"A couple of things. First, how did Mr. Markham pay for his care?"

"His pension and Social Security checks came directly to us. At his request, a hundred dollars was transferred into a bank account each month." She smiled. "Les called it his walking-around money. As far as I know, he never used it, but it meant the world to him to have it available."

"It represented independence," I said, nodding.

"And hope."

"That he'd be able to leave the facility?" I asked.

She nodded. "Yes. I assumed his nephew, Hal Greeley, closed the account. Didn't he?"

"I don't think he knew about it."

She tilted her head, thinking. "I suppose he might not have. Les once bragged that he was able to check his balance online—no paper statements. We have wireless Internet available throughout the facility. Les had his own computer and was quite facile in using it. If Mr. Greeley hadn't known about the account, I suppose he wouldn't have thought to look for one or ask about it."

"What happened to the computer?"

"Mr. Greeley arranged with our IT fellow to wipe the hard drive; then he gave it to Zach. Zach Moore, Les's primary aide. The computer was quite old, but still, it was a nice gesture. Zach was glad to get it."

"You said that Les's retirement payments came directly to you. How do your financial arrangements work?"

"Most residents make a cash payment when they move in, then pay a small monthly fee. Mr. Markham opted for our month-to-month plan instead. I don't think he planned on staying as long as he did. His monthly fee was just shy of four thousand dollars."

"Was there a balance in his account when he died?"

"Yes, about five thousand dollars. Mr. Markham died intestate, so a check was issued to his sister, Katrina Greeley."

"Change of subject," I said. "Did Mr. Markham ever mention silent movie posters?"

"No. Why?"

"I'm an antiques appraiser trying to assess some artwork," I said, smiling. "You mentioned Zach Moore. Might Les have spoken to him about something like artwork?"

"Let's find out." She used her phone and directed someone named Pam to send Zach in.

Zach Moore came into Tabatha's office with the cautious tread of a frightened man. His lips were pressed tightly together, his eyes round with worry. He stood with his hands clenched in front of him, waiting for bad news. He was tall, with strawberry blond hair, and thin. I put him in his midtwenties. He wore an all white uniform, pants and shirt, with ZACH stitched on his chest pocket.

Tabatha smiled, and when she spoke, her voice was low and soothing.

"Thanks for joining us, Zach. This is Ms. Prescott. She has some questions about Les Markham, and, of course, I thought of you. You knew him better than any of us."

He nodded, still reticent and timid.

"Have a seat," Tabatha said, pointing to the chair next to mine.

He slid into it, keeping his eyes on her face. Ms. Solomon looked at me, smiled, and nodded.

I smiled at Zach. "I appreciate your talking to me, Zach. I understand you knew Les Markham well."

"Pretty well."

"He was here five years and you were his aide the whole time, is that right?"

"I have other guys, too, not just him," he said as if I'd accused him of something.

"Did Mr. Markham ever talk to you about art?" I asked, keeping my tone friendly.

"I don't know."

"How about a storage unit he rented?"

"I don't know nothing about any storage units," he said, agitated.

"How about movie posters?" Lines appeared on Zach's brow. When he didn't reply, I clarified my question. "Did he ever mention that his dad painted silent movie posters?"

Zach looked at his feet and wiped his hands on the sides of his pants. He was growing ever more nervous, and I couldn't understand why.

"I don't know nothing about nothing," he said.

I turned to Tabatha, silently asking for help.

"It's important, Zach," she said, her tone softer than before. "Les would want you to help."

He shook his head. "I don't owe Les nothing. That's what my brother says, and I think that's right."

"What is it your brother says, Zach?"

He folded his lips together and shook his head. "I promised I wouldn't tell," he said, still staring at the ground, "and I won't."

He wouldn't tell us what his promise involved or to whom he'd made it. He wouldn't say another word about Les. When Tabatha or I asked a question, Zach shook his head. We'd hit a brick wall. Finally, Tabatha thanked him for coming in to talk to her and told him he could return to work.

"That's one for the books," she said once we were alone. "I've never seen Zach like this."

"What do you think that promise is all about?" I asked.

"I have no idea. Our aides aren't paid privately by our residents, yet he sounded as if he thought Les owed him something."

"Do residents often leave aides something in their wills?"

"It happens, but it's not typical by any means. Zach getting a computer was above and beyond the norm."

I thought about Zach and promises. I told Henri I wouldn't tell anyone about the phone call he received the day before he died, and Ellis had persuaded me to reveal it, because he'd said that murder victims want their killers caught, and I'd believed him. I wondered what it would take to persuade Zach to break his promise.

"Secrets imply knowledge," I said. "A man named Henri Dubois was killed in a storage room locker that might have belonged to Lester Markham. If there's even a small chance that Zach knows something... I think we need to tell the police."

"Let me talk to him first."

She left me in the lobby. The receptionist, a pleasant-looking woman with a tan so dark I wondered if she was just back from a beach vacation, offered me a coffee. I declined with thanks. I didn't want a coffee. I wanted answers. Too itchy to sit, I got up and paced.

The lobby was attractive in a don't-offend-anyone sort of way. Blond wood furniture was arranged in small clusters, four chairs and a low square table. The chairs had armrests and were upholstered with a blue nubby fabric.

Stacks of lifestyle and craft-themed magazines sat on each of the tables. Framed museum exhibition posters advertising shows of impressionist paintings were placed at eye level along the longest wall. Well-tended plants sat on tables and in big pots in the room's corners. The receptionist sat behind a chest-high partition. A brass plaque said her name was Karla.

I walked to the window and looked out over the snowy fields to the dark ocean beyond.

I hated waiting. I was impatient all the time, but when I was waiting for someone else to do something that affected me, it was worse.

"Ms. Prescott?" Karla said. I turned in time to see her hang up the phone. "Ms. Solomon is ready for you now."

"Zach is quite upset," Ms. Solomon told me once we'd settled back in her office. "He says he doesn't know the name Henri Dubois, and I believe him."

She began fussing with an old-fashioned Pink Pearl eraser, the kind we kept in stock to remove pencil marks from rare books and dirt from pottery, flipping it over and over. I wondered why she had an eraser on her desk, whether she was an artist or wrote in longhand. She raised her eyes to mine and held them.

"I believe him because with Zach, what you see is what you get. He's reliable and hardworking, but I doubt he watches the news or reads the paper."

She was saying he was slow. She paused again, waiting for a comment, perhaps, but I didn't have anything to say, so I stayed quiet.

"Zach is a truthful man, and guileless. The eyes are a window to the soul, right?"

"The French say the eyes are the mirror of the soul. Both are true, I think, or not."

"In Zach's case, they're both true. When he assured me that he knows nothing about any murder, I believed him."

"What's his secret?"

"I don't know, but it's not related to the murder."

"You can't know that," I said.

"I know Zach."

Wes said that I'm wrong about people as often as I'm right, and maybe oftener. I had no reason to think Ms. Solomon was any better at it than I was.

"We need to tell the police about Zach's secret," I said. "It might be nothing, but it might be something."

"No."

"I'm sorry."

"You don't know how this will hurt him. He's come so far."

"I'm sorry," I said again.

Ellis's work and cell phones went to voice mail. When I called the police station's main number, Cathy said Ellis was in a meeting and couldn't be disturbed. She offered to put me through to his voice mail, and I agreed.

"Ellis," I said to the machine, "this is Josie. I just met with Tabatha Solomon, the director of Belle Mer, where a man named Lester Markham lived for the last five years. I think he rented the locker under the name Gael Patrick. I can fill you in about that later. The thing is, Mr. Markham died about six months ago, and his chief aide at Belle Mer, a fellow named Zach Moore, knows something. I have no idea what it is or if it's relevant to Henri's murder. I just know he knows something he won't tell either Ms. Solomon or me. He keeps repeating that he promised he wouldn't tell, and he won't. Ms. Solomon and I agree there's something there, but I've got to tell you, she's pretty upset that I'm calling you. Zach is, well, he thinks about things at his own pace. You should talk to her before you talk to him." I gave him Ms. Solomon's direct phone number, then added, "I can fill you in on what I've learned about Lester Markham and the locker whenever you're available."

I wondered how long it would take for Ellis to call me back. Not long, I thought, if I knew him half as well as I thought I did.

Ellis called as I was about to back out of my parking spot at Belle Mer. I put the car in park and answered the phone.

"I got your message about Zach Moore," he said. "Thanks for the lead. You also said you had some info about the locker. I'm ready."

I recounted my conversations with the Greeleys, explaining how and why I reached the conclusion that the storage unit where Henri died had been rented by Lester Markham.

"This is all very helpful, Josie," he said, and something in his tone, a hint of formality or distance, got my attention, and my worry meter zipped into action. "Can you stop by? I have some other questions."

"Sure," I said, glancing at the dash clock. It was just shy of ten. "How's one? I haven't been in to work yet, and I should."

"Now would be better," he said, his tone clipped.

With my worry meter spiking, my pulse started pumping faster, too fast for comfort. "What's wrong, Ellis?"

A long pause. "I'll explain when you get here."

I laughed, an awkward sound. I couldn't think of how to reply.

"When can I expect you?" Ellis asked.

"I'll come now," I said.

I sat a while longer, staring at the phone. I didn't know

what I was in for, but I knew the sound of trouble when I heard it.

Wes called just as I was finishing a call to my office, telling Gretchen that I didn't know when I'd be in, asking about everyone's work, hearing that all was well.

"I've got a shockeroonie or three or four," he said. "You know how you told me that Scott and Leigh Ann used to be married?"

"Yes," I said, uncertain where he was heading.

"It looks like Scott wants her back. He's told lots of people he was a fool to let her go. That's one heck of a motive."

"Even if he did regret the divorce, that doesn't mean he's a killer. Lots of exes stay close, even those who regret being apart, and it doesn't imply anything other than maturity."

"You think?" he asked, shifting from tough-guy reporter to kid brother in a heartbeat. "Are you still in touch with any ex-boyfriends?"

"No. But I wish I were—or rather, I wish my last relationship hadn't ended badly, that we'd simply parted company instead of descending into ugly. How about you and that girl who moved to Florida? There was no nastiness, was there?"

"No, but no way am I going down to Jacksonville for a weekend hi-di-hi-ho if she's living with some new guy."

"Good point."

"Here's the kicker—are you ready? Neither Leigh Ann nor Scott has an alibi for when Henri was murdered. Leigh Ann says she was at Suzanne Dyre's condo helping her select paint colors, but the ME can't narrow down the time of death down close enough to clear her for sure, plus Suzanne was late. She got caught up in reading a report on food costs and lost track of time. Can you believe that? A real page turner, huh? And Scott is completely open."

"I think you're making a mountain out of flat land, Wes. Having a perfect alibi is more suspicious than being unable to account for every second of your day. Scott told me he was driving around, checking out the area, and Leigh Ann—jeesh! She was meeting with a client. Both of them were doing normal things."

"'Normal' is one of those words, right? What I call normal, you call whacked. Have you had any more ideas about that Andrew Bruen guy? No one can find him, not under that name."

"Really?" I asked, intrigued. "Interesting. All deposits at Crawford's are in cash, and you don't need to show ID to register. So I guess it could be a made-up name."

"Why would someone use a fake name to bid on an abandoned storage unit?" he asked.

"Because you don't want your interest in the unit known."

"Why not?"

"I don't know," I said, "but it sure sounds suspicious to me."

"How would you find him?"

I remembered the list Ellis rattled off when we were talking about finding Gael Patrick. He'd searched various databases from taxpayers to voting rolls. I repeated the options.

When I was done Wes said, "Yeah, they've done all that. Makes you wonder, huh? Are you ready for another news flash? I got the goods on that phone call Henri got Thursday afternoon. The number goes to a smart phone used by...wait for it...a lawyer."

"How on God's earth did you find this out, Wes? You told me anyone at a phone company would leave an e-trail, so they couldn't give you info anymore."

Wes got haughty. "If a person is conducting a legitimate

inquiry for someone like a police officer, there's nothing that says they can't tell me, too."

"Yes, there is."

"Never mind that. What do you think it means that Henri's last phone call came from a lawyer?"

"I don't know," I said slowly, thinking. "Maybe there was a snafu with his immigration situation."

"Like what?"

"Like he didn't fill out the paperwork right. The government is very cautious. All your t's have to be crossed and your i's dotted just right. You know that, Wes."

"True. Maybe. I don't know... I still think it's Scott, don't you? Don't you think he seems guilty as dirt?"

"What's guilt got to do with dirt, Wes? You're making no sense."

He laughed. "Jeez, Josie, can't you fill in the blanks? Obviously I meant that he seems as guilty as a little boy who's caught playing in a mud pile while wearing his Sunday best. It's a truncated metaphor, Josie, not a literal reference."

"And I'm to know this how?"

"'Cause you know me."

I rolled my eyes. "Do you have any real news, Wes?"

"What about Scott? Do you think he's guilty?"

Of what? I wondered. *Of killing Henri? Of breaking into my house? Of framing me for murder?* "I don't know. Is there any evidence? Regretting a divorce isn't evidence. Lots of people regret getting divorced. Not having an alibi isn't evidence, either. Lots of people lack alibis...like me."

"Good one, Josie! Catch ya later!"

I parked as close to the Rocky Point police station's front door as I could, backing into the space. I didn't plan on staying long, and I wanted to be able to make a quick getaway.

TWENTY-THREE

CATHY TOLD ME Ellis wouldn't be long. I sat on the wooden bench and shut my eyes, trying to figure out why Ellis had sounded so stiff, as if he were mad at me, as if he'd caught me in a lie. Ellis had no reason to sound stern. I was one of the good guys.

Ellis stepped out of his office, his expression grave. "Josie?"

I stood up.

"This way," he said.

I felt Cathy's eyes on me as I followed Ellis down the long corridor to Interview Room One. From his stiff stride and ongoing silence I knew something had happened, something that involved me, not in a good way. I couldn't imagine what he'd learned, but my heart began thumping wildly nonetheless. I felt guilty for no reason.

A police officer I'd met before was fussing with the video camera remote controls, pushing different buttons and watching what happened. His name was Darrell. He was young, new to the force, and eager. I sat in the same place as I had the last time I was in the room, with my back to the cage, facing one of the two cameras. Ellis sat across from me.

"Before we turn on the video recorders," Ellis said, "I want to say something to you semi off the record. The officer will listen in, but it won't be part of our official conversation. We're friends, Josie, you know that, right?"

"Of course," I said, shooting a look at Darrell. He was listening, but his eyes showed no emotion.

"That we're friends has no effect on how I do my job. If you did something, I'll find out about it, and I'll see that you're charged for the crime."

"What are you talking about, Ellis?"

"I will ensure you're treated fairly."

"If you think I'm understanding you," I said, "you're wrong."

"Turn on the video recorders, Darrell," Ellis said, his eyes on my face.

"We're recording, Chief," Darrell said a moment later.

"Thank you, Darrell." Ellis looked into the camera mounted over my head straight-on. "This is an interview conducted by me, Police Chief Ellis Hunter, with Josie Prescott." He gave Darrell's name and the date and time, then said, "This is an official interview, Josie. I'm going to ask you some questions, and we're going to record your answers. First, though, I want to read you your rights."

"What's going on, Ellis?"

He slid a single sheet of paper across the table as he rattled off the Miranda warning. "Please sign at the bottom indicating that you understand these rights."

I stared at the document but didn't see it. Instead, I saw my father's face. I was twelve, and I'd been about to sign a form he'd handed me when he stopped me.

"Never sign anything you haven't read, Josie. Never."

I laughed. "But you gave it to me, Dad. I trust you."

"And you can. Someday someone's going to ask you to sign something you shouldn't, though, and it may well be someone you trust."

"Jeez, Dad…that's dark."

"It's real. After you read the document, if you have any questions, any at all, refuse to sign it until you've consulted a lawyer. Don't be intimidated. Don't get defensive. Don't feel any need to explain or justify your decision. Take your time. Think things through."

I looked up and saw Ellis's poker face watching me, and the memory of my dad faded away. I read the pro forma document. I was familiar with it. I'd signed one just like it before. Ellis was waiting, patiently. The lights on both video cameras shone with pinprick-sized red dots.

I pushed the paper away. "I want a lawyer," I said.

AN HOUR LATER, Max Bixby, the lawyer I called when only a lawyer would do, sat beside me at the wooden table. Over the years, his counsel had saved me money, time, and angst. The world always seemed less chaotic and frightening with him by my side. He was a rock of support, a fount of knowledge, and an ally in times of strife.

Max was tall and thin and wore tweed jackets with leather patches on the elbows and bow ties. Today's jacket was green with brown nubs. His tie was brown with green dots.

He extracted a legal pad and squared it up to the table edge. He placed his pen, a brown and gold StarWalker, on the diagonal.

"What do you know?" he asked me.

"Nothing." I blinked away an unexpected tear. "That's why I called you. I asked, and Ellis didn't answer. Up till now, he's been all friendly and chatty, asking for my help. Now he's acting like I'm his chief suspect."

"Let's find out what's up," he said.

He opened the door and nodded to someone in the corridor, then returned to his seat and patted my hand. I smiled at him in response and felt my lip tremble. Every nerve was hypersensitive, braced for bad news.

Ellis and Darrell came in and resumed their places,

Ellis across from us, Darrell manning the cameras, off to the side. Ellis laid a manila file on the table.

Darrell announced the camera was rolling. Ellis repeated the information about who was present, adding that Max was with us, and stating the date and time. He asked me to sign the Miranda form, Max nodded his okay, and I did.

"Thank you, Josie, for coming in today," Ellis said, declaring my volunteer status for the record, a courtesy I noted and appreciated.

"You're welcome. I'm glad to help in any way I can."

"The lab has finished testing the tire iron found in your trunk. I told you earlier that it looked like it was the murder weapon—that's now been confirmed. I wanted to offer you another opportunity to explain how it got in your car."

I opened my mouth to answer, but before I could get a word out, Max held up his hand.

"Excuse us a moment," he said to Ellis. He moved his mouth so close to my ear I could feel his breath. "What is he referring to?"

In hushed tones, I recounted the break-in, described my shock at seeing the tire iron in my trunk, and told him how I'd previously given a statement explaining that I had no idea how it got in my vehicle, adding that I still didn't.

"What else did you tell him?" Max asked.

"Nothing."

"Say you have nothing to add to your previous statement. I'm going to request a copy of your initial interview and the lab report. Remember that short, responsive answers are best. One-word answers are best of all."

I nodded at him, then turned to face Ellis.

"I understand from Josie you've already discussed this issue," Max said. "I'd like a copy of that recording."

"Certainly," Ellis said.

"And the lab report."

"All right." He turned to me. "Josie?"

"I have nothing to add to my previous statement," I said.

"Josie, it's the murder weapon. We found it in your car. You have to know something."

"I found it in my car; you didn't. And I immediately called you."

Max patted my hand. *Calm down,* the pat communicated. *Chill.*

"I have nothing to add," I repeated.

"The lab report indicates that the tire iron was placed in the trunk at some point after the crime was committed, after the organic matter dried. The only related material found in your vehicle appears to be bits that fell or rubbed off naturally."

"That's great news, Ellis!" I said. "That's consistent with someone sneaking it in the night of the break-in."

He shrugged. "Or you could have moved it yourself for some reason."

I leaned back, deflated. I didn't speak. Words escaped me. I couldn't think of how to reply, of how to explain that he was wrong, that he had to know he was wrong, that I didn't do it.

Ellis pursed his lips, thinking. "Please tell me about your relationship with Henri Dubois," he said.

Max held up his hand and leaned into my ear again. "Is there anything about your relationship I should know?" he asked.

"No."

He nodded, indicating that I could continue.

"Henri and I were friends and business associates," I told Ellis.

"What kind of friends?" Ellis asked, and from his oh-so-casual tone, I perceived quicksand looming in front of me.

"Ty and I hung out with him and Leigh Ann. Not a lot. Sometimes."

"What sort of business association did you have?"

"Henri and I were frequent friendly competitors at abandoned-storage-room auctions. I conducted several appraisals of antiques and collectibles on his behalf. I bought antiques and collectibles from him. He consigned objects to us as well."

"Did you ever spend time just with him?"

"What are you talking about?" I asked, perplexed.

"Did you and Henri ever hang out, just the two of you?"

Red warning lights flashed in my head. "No."

"Not even for coffee after an auction?"

"No."

"Were you ever alone with him?"

"Sure."

"Like when?" Ellis asked.

"Like when Henri took me to the back room to show me an art book. Like when we visited one another's storage units to see what the other guy got. Lots of times."

"I'm sorry, Josie, but I have to ask...were you and Henri having an affair?"

"What?" I exclaimed, shocked to my booties, stunned nearly speechless. "Ellis!"

"Were you?" he asked again.

I stared into his eyes. Ellis knew me well. He knew I was over the moon about Ty. He knew I was honest to my toenails. I saw wisdom and empathy in his gaze. He thought my goose was cooked, that he had unassailable evidence against me. I recalled something else, a conversation Zoë and I had a few months back about love and romance. Ty and Ellis had been interested observers. Zoë thought philanderers should be summarily shot, whereas I thought there were sometimes extenuating circumstances. *No one is exempt,* I'd said that night, *no one. When Cupid's arrow strikes, you're a goner.* I believed it. I could hear Ellis's thoughts as clearly as if he were speaking them aloud. He was remembering that conversation, too. He'd thought then that I was talking theoretically. Now he thought I'd been reporting on myself.

Max touched my arm. "Were you?" he whispered.

"No," I said, turning to face him, my tone hushed. "God, no."

"Answer his question, then," Max told me.

I met Ellis's eyes. "No," I said. "I wasn't involved in a romantic relationship with Henri."

"We have the e-mails, Josie."

"I don't know what you're talking about."

"We found Henri's phone in the van, remember? You were there. We've reviewed his e-mails over the last three months. Henri maintained three e-mail accounts, one for business, one for personal, and one that he only used with you."

I felt my brow furrow. "I don't think I've ever had an e-mail from him. When we arranged a time to meet or something, we spoke on the phone."

"We've got them, Josie. They were sent to your account."

"That's impossible."

"Let's take a look at your phone."

"No," Max said, smiling.

Ellis shot Max a look that left no doubt what he thought of lawyers refusing what he perceived to be a reasonable request.

"Here's a printout," he said. "An example."

He opened a manila file folder, extracted a single sheet

of paper, and pushed it toward me. Max fingered it toward himself, and we read it together. As I read, indignation fired from my heart and brain, and my blood began to boil. The messages comprised an e-mail thread allegedly exchanged between Henri and me, both issued from Gmail accounts, using e-mail addresses I'd never seen. Henri's e-mail address listed his full name followed by 1746; mine was JosieAntiques, followed by 194. Henri's e-mail began:

Ma cherie, we must meet and soon.

Now?

Before I could say a word, Max whispered into my ear. "What do you know about this?"

"Nothing," I whispered back.

"Is this your e-mail account?"

"No."

"Is this his?"

"If so, I don't know it."

He pursed his lips. "We need to examine your phone, see if this account is on it." To Ellis, he said, "Would you excuse us for a moment?"

"You want to examine the phone, right?" Ellis asked.

"Right," Max said.

"Let's do it together."

"No. We won't be letting you look at the phone until we've had sufficient time to examine it ourselves."

"Is this e-mail account on your phone?" Ellis asked me.

Max raised a palm to stop him. "I've instructed Josie not to answer any questions about what may or may not be on the phone."

"We have an expert standing by," Ellis said.

"Sorry."

"I can't let you walk out of here with that phone. I can't risk evidence being destroyed or tampered with."

"You can't force us to hand over the phone, Ellis. We're here voluntarily, remember?"

"Detective Brownley is before a judge seeking an emergency court order. We need her phone, Max."

Max stood up and touched my arm. "Let's go, Josie. We're done here."

"Turn off the video, Darrell," Ellis said, standing.

Darrell tapped buttons, and the red lights disappeared.

"I can arrest her as a material witness, Max," Ellis said. "Don't make me do that."

I felt my mouth fall open.

Max leaned in close to my ear. "I think they'll get their court order. We'll score some minor points by cooperating, so I think we should. Let's offer to let them search your place, for evidence of this alleged affair, too. Save him the need to get a search warrant. More points."

"I don't want them searching my place!" I whispered.

"Why not?"

"Would you want the police pawing through your stuff?"

"No, of course not. We need to be realistic, Josie. I don't think we have a lot of options at this point. Let me try to negotiate an arrangement by which we get to observe them. My gut tells me that's the best I'm going to be able to get."

"All right," I said through gritted teeth, outraged.

"You don't have anything illicit, do you? Illegal drugs? Unregistered weapons? Child pornography? Anything like that?"

"Of course not!" I said, feeling the world spin out of control.

As Max and Ellis began their negotiation, I plunked down in my chair, more angry than offended. I hated everything about what was happening, and I was enraged thinking about the how and why of the situation. I was here enduring this affront because someone decided I was an easy mark.

TWENTY-FOUR

The Rocky Point Police Department's go-to technology guru was a beautiful blonde named Katie. She was younger than me by a lot and seemed both knowledgeable and articulate—a killer combination in an IT expert.

Before I handed over my phone, I tapped the screen and brought up the Messaging folder. I showed Katie the two icons, one labeled text messaging and the other listing my Prescott's e-mail address.

"See?" I said, pointing to the screen. "This is my only e-mail account. I use Prescott's for everything."

She took the phone, slid her index finger across the screen, then tapped it and nodded.

"Here it is," she said. "It's in the App folder. Let me see something else." She slid her finger and tapped the screen several times. "Yup. Someone installed remote access software."

"What?" I exclaimed. "That can't be!"

She looked at Ellis, her boss. "This program was installed directly on the device, not remotely, which means subsequent permission to access it isn't required. Someone remoting in has to use a password, that's all."

"How hard would it be to install that software?" Ellis asked.

"Easy as pie. Bring up a browser, go to the software company's Web site, and download it. Soup to nuts, you're looking at ten to fifteen minutes. Keep in mind, this product is used in business all the time. Like if you have a sales force out on the road, you need your IT folks to be able to fix problems with their smart phones then and there. Say some guy's phone is stolen. He can buy a replacement anywhere, and by installing the remote access software his company uses, the home office people can reload all his data and documents within minutes. My point is this is not an unusual app."

"Couldn't I tell if someone was remoting in?" I asked.

"Yes. The background changes color."

"I never saw that."

"Were any of the e-mails sent late at night?" Max asked.

"Several were sent during overnight hours," Ellis said, nodding his understanding, "when someone might expect that Josie would be asleep. Not all of them. More than a few were sent during business hours or early evening."

I shook my head, mystified. "Is the remote access software on Henri's phone, too?"

"Yes," Ellis said. "Installed earlier on the same day as yours."

"Which was when?"

"January twenty-sixth at 8:26 P.M. Henri's was set up at 4:20 P.M. So the question is, who had access to your phone at 8:26 P.M. that evening?"

I reached into my tote bag for my calendar and flipped back to the January pages.

"That was the Winter Festival. I was at the Community Center, along with half of Rocky Point."

"And you went to the buffet line, leaving your tote bag behind, leaving your phone behind."

"Three times. Once for dinner, then for dessert, and third for another helping of Mimie's Whiskey Bundt Cake. You're right that theoretically someone could have scooped my phone away, then slipped it back in—but what a risk!"

"Not if you take it to the restroom and do your setup there."

"Who had Henri's phone at 4:20 P.M.?"

"Leigh Ann doesn't know. She doesn't know exactly where he was. Leigh Ann's online calendar has her at a potential client's house—the deal is still pending. The client confirms the appointment was kept that afternoon, but neither of them recalls the exact time they met."

"And you have no way of knowing where Henri was," I said.

"I have no way of verifying he was where his schedule said he was, which was out canvassing interior design stores along the Maine coast, all the way up to Kennebunkport, looking over the competition, sussing out vendors, and so on. None of the shop owners remember him, but it was a while ago, and we can assume he made a point of calling as little attention to himself as possible. We can also infer that he completed at least some of his trip, because he sent out a spate of e-mails the next day asking vendors for catalogues."

"Excuse me for interrupting," Katie said, "but I have a meeting. Anything else for me at this point?"

Ellis told her no and thanked her.

Katie placed my phone in a plastic evidence bag and sealed it. Seeing my expression, she said, "Sorry. I'll need to keep it for the time being."

"Why?" I asked, upset.

Max placed his hand on my forearm and shook his head at me.

"Routine," Ellis said.

My phone in hand, Katie left the room. I wanted to run after her, to stop her, to get it back.

A memory came to me. I'd been about ten. My mom's car had to go into the shop for service, and the whole time it was gone, she'd been crabby, explaining that she felt lost without it, that to her, it represented freedom. That's how I felt now. *Don't be absurd,* I told myself. *It's just a phone. You'll get it back or you'll get a new one.* Yet even as I tried to quash my feelings of powerlessness and isolation, I knew that while my reaction might be absurd, it was real. To my mother, a car represented autonomy and personal power. Without my phone, I felt vulnerable and alone.

"As a working hypothesis," Ellis said to Max, "let's assume Josie is telling the truth."

I frowned. I wondered if I was supposed to feel grateful that he was willing to assume that I wasn't a liar, that I hadn't been screwing around on Ty, that I hadn't killed Henri.

"That's a smart idea," Max said dryly.

Ellis ignored Max's tone, maintaining his normal all-business attitude.

"Maybe some of the messages weren't sent remotely," Ellis said. "Maybe someone sent them directly from your phone, which leads to the question, who has access to your phone?"

I looked at Max, and he nodded.

"No one," I said. "It's with me all the time."

"How about at work? Your phone is in your tote bag, right? Do you keep it under lock and key?"

"No, of course not. It stays beside my desk all day."

"Which means everyone who works for you knows your habit and has access to the bag."

I thought of my full-time staff, Eric and Cara, Gretchen and Sasha, and Fred.

"It's easy to say that anything is possible," I said, "but that's absurd. The thought that one of them would betray me, would try to frame me for murder, is ludicrous, beyond reason. It is not possible. Every single one of them is loyal and honest."

"Maybe. What do you know about them? Really?"

I felt as if I'd stepped through Alice's looking glass. "Curiosity often leads to trouble," Lewis Carroll wrote. *Did I somehow bring this on myself?* I wondered, aghast at the thought. *Have I unintentionally pricked someone's ego? Spoiled their plans? Crossed them? Who hated me enough to try to frame me for murder?* I shook my head. *I know my staff well. I've worked with them for years.*

"I can't imagine that any one of them is involved. As to their backgrounds, they're all bonded."

"If need be, we can dig deeper," Ellis said, seemingly unimpressed with my confidence. He jotted a note on his pad.

I had a harrowing thought. Had Henri been killed not because of something he did, but rather because someone wanted to get rid of me? Had Henri been sacrificed so the killer could reach his or her primary goal—convincing the police to arrest me? Someone who couldn't simply murder me because he or she would be the primary suspect? Who did I know who hated me or feared me or would benefit by my death? Who would have no compunction in killing an innocent man? *Think,* I told myself. *Work the logic.*

The only people close enough to be automatic suspects were Ty, Zoë, and my staff. That one of them did it simply wasn't credible. All things are not possible.

I nodded and took in a deep breath. *Good,* I thought. *This is progress.*

I could assume that Henri was the intended victim, not me. What I didn't know, and couldn't see how to figure out, was whether Henri had been killed because of something connected to the storage room locker or whether his being murdered in the storage room was an accident of timing.

"Who else has access to your tote bag?" Ellis asked.

"No one," I said, refocusing on Ellis.

"How about Ty?"

"Of course, but come on, Ellis! That's ridiculous. I hang with Zoë a lot, too." I waved it aside. "I understand you have to consider every possibility, but these simply aren't possible. There's another answer. There's something we're missing."

"What?" Ellis asked.

"I don't know."

"What's next?" Max asked.

"A few more questions," Ellis replied, "then we'll go to Josie's place for the search. Thank you again for your cooperation."

Max nodded, then Ellis turned to me. "While I personally believe that you didn't kill Henri, and the remote access software lends credence to that belief, strictly speaking, these e-mails provide evidence of an illicit romance, the sort of relationship that might go sour and bring up emotions that lead to murder—and that's motive." He held up a hand. "I understand you're denying the e-mails' veracity. That's on the record. We have the murder weapon in hand, a weapon Josie could easily have acquired and one that was found in her vehicle, and based on my knowledge of Josie's level of fitness—I've seen her ice-skate and snowshoe and swim, for instance—I know she would be strong enough to wield it. Which leaves opportunity. I need to ask, Josie: Where were you last Friday between 1:00 and 3:00 P.M.?"

Max leaned into me and whispered, "Where were you?"

"At my office."

"With people?"

"Not every minute."

"Can you retrace your steps? Phone calls, conversations with staff, anything like that?"

"Yes…maybe… I can come close. No way will the gaps between meetings be big enough for me to have driven to Crawford's, killed Henri, and gotten back."

Max nodded. "Good." He looked at Ellis. "Josie was at her place of business during those hours. She was in meetings, took some phone calls, made others, and so on. It was a regular business day. She doesn't know how completely she can account for all her time during those hours, but is confident there won't be enough unallocated time for her to be considered a viable suspect. Would you like her to document those meetings as closely as possible?"

Ellis smiled. "That would be very helpful."

"She'll do it today and send it to me. I'll ensure you get a copy." Max pushed back his chair, preparing to stand. "Anything else?"

Elli stood. "Let's get that search out of the way."

Inside my house, I turned up the heat and switched on lights. Ellis, Max, and I stood in the kitchen.

"Given those e-mails," Ellis said, "I'm betting that if we find anything incriminating, it will be love notes." He glanced around. "If someone snuck some into your house, they'd place them in a logical spot. If you kept love notes, where would they be?"

"I do keep love notes—Ty's love notes—in a hatbox on a shelf in my bedroom closet."

Ellis's face registered surprise. "Why a hatbox?"

"It's pretty."

"Oh." He waved an arm. "Lead the way."

I mounted the steps, embarrassed. I hadn't made the bed when I'd fled my house for Ellis's guest room, and I hadn't been upstairs since.

"The room's a mess," I said with an awkward laugh.

"We don't remember messiness," Ellis said. "I promise."

I pointed to the round floral-printed antique hatbox sitting on the top shelf. Ellis put on plastic gloves, then dragged it closer by the strap, catching it as it tottered and lowering it to the rug. I hated the idea that anyone but me would read Ty's lovingly inscribed greeting cards and the sweet messages he'd scrawled on scraps of paper, sticky notes, and cocktail napkins.

Ellis removed the snugly fitting lid, revealing disorganized heaps of envelopes and cards and bits of paper, a mishmash.

I stood off to the side, blushing as I recalled how personal some of the messages were, realizing that while Ty signed his cards, he didn't sign his notes, so Ellis would need to read them.

"I hate this," I said.

He removed items, one by one, scanning them, then placing them off to the side. Some notes were romantic, testaments to our love. Others were practical, making plans or assigning tasks, homey peeks into our private world. Some were intimate, intended for no one's eyes but ours.

"Can I leave?" I asked. "Watching you go through my most private correspondence is up there with moments I don't want to experience. Words like mortifying and humiliating come to mind."

"I'm only looking at the handwriting, Josie," Ellis said, "not the words."

"That's nice of you to say. Why don't I make us some tea?"

"Sorry. I need to keep you in sight."

I turned my back, closed my eyes, and leaned my head against the wall. Max patted my shoulder empathetically. A few minutes later, Ellis announced that he was done, that I could put everything away.

"Where else do you keep letters?" Ellis asked.

"Nowhere. Except for Ty's, I don't keep any."

"Do you have a staging area? You know, a place you keep them until you have time to get the hatbox down from the shelf?"

"Sometimes I'll leave them on the kitchen counter."

"Where else?"

"My tote bag."

"Let's take a look."

Downstairs, he emptied the bag onto the kitchen table, flipped through my notebook, examined every nook and cranny in my wallet, and peered into zippered compartments.

"Any place else you can think of?" he asked as I put everything back in place.

"No."

"Who knows about the hatbox?"

"Ty. Zoë." I shrugged. "That's it."

"Let's think like a killer," Ellis said. "If I were trying to frame you, and didn't know about your hatbox, where would I put a note I wanted someone to find."

"Here," Max said. "In plain sight."

"It wouldn't be out in the open," Ellis said, scanning the countertops. "Josie would find it right away and either destroy it or tell us about it."

"In a drawer," I said. "In my study."

I led the way to my tiny study. The room was attached to the dining room, closed off by French doors. My desk sat kitty-corner to the window, allowing me to have the money view, the meadow, as I worked.

Ellis opened the slender center drawer, the only drawer on my antique ladies' writing desk, an eighteenth-century mahogany beauty. He moved a pad of notepaper, and there was an ivory-colored sheet of heavy-weight paper. I saw handwriting I didn't recognize. When Ty and I had toured my house on Sunday, I'd opened this drawer, but I hadn't moved the notepad. This note had been there all this time. Ellis grasped it by the corner and tugged. Max and I read over his shoulder.

Ma Cherie,

Life is not so funny when it plays tricks on us with timing and love. I only find you now, when it is so difficult. Don't give up on me. Love conquers all.

Your Henri

"This wasn't written to me," I said.

"I'm going to need to do a more thorough job," Ellis said. "I'm going to ask Detective Brownley to oversee a complete search."

"I've never seen that note. I wasn't having an affair. I didn't kill him."

"Josie," Max said. "Let's go."

"She'll be available for questions?" Ellis asked.

"Of course."

"Have you spoken to Zach?" I asked. "Zach Moore, the Belle Mer aide?"

"No. Not yet. Why?"

"Because he has a secret."

"We'll be talking to him," Ellis said.

"Check that note for fingerprints," I called over my shoulder, as Max shushed me and led me away. "I never touched it."

Outside, standing by my car in the bright midday sun, Max said, "Don't be scared, Josie. An investigation is a process. There's an arc to it. I don't think you're guilty of anything, and I don't think Ellis does either. All we can do now is wait. Let them find whatever there is to find, and we'll deal with it as a total package."

I thanked Max for his time and headed out, back to Belle Mer. To me, Ellis's response to my question about Zach sounded like a blow-off, a cavalier dismissal. I would not stand by passively and wait for another go-around in Room One, not if there was an alternative. If Zach's secret was related to Lester Markham and his storage room, perhaps through that seemingly tenuous relationship, I'd find a connection to Henri's murder.

The worst that could happen was that I'd get nowhere, but getting nowhere was better than doing nothing. Max might be all right with waiting, but I wasn't, not when someone was setting me up to take a fall for murder.

TWENTY-FIVE

I DROVE STRAIGHT to the phone store and bought a stripped-down cash-and-carry smart phone with a whole new number. I could use it right away and always, refilling it when the balance got low. My first call was to Ty. I got his voice mail and left my new number, telling him I'd explain later. I got Zoë's voice mail, too, and left the same message. I reached Max's secretary in person and asked her to give the number to Max.

I felt inordinately pleased to have a phone, especially one with a number so few people knew.

I toyed with calling Zach to see if I could schedule a meeting during his lunch hour but voted against it. It was already after two, and if Zach worked the seven-to-three or eight-to-four shift, his break was long over. I also considered calling Ms. Solomon and asking for her support, but I didn't do that either. Since I'd refused her request to keep Zach's secret from the police, the chances of her helping me open him up were, I suspected, somewhere between zero and nil. As I sat in the parking lot, eating an unexpectedly tasty fast-food grilled chicken salad, it occurred to me that given how skittish Zach was during my last visit, taking him by surprise would probably work to my advantage.

"Hi!" I said, greeting Karla, Belle Mer's receptionist, with a bright smile. "I'm here to see Zach again. Zach Moore."

She glanced at her computer monitor, checking the time,

and said, "Oh, no…it's after two. Shower time. Zach is overseeing his patients' showers. He can't be disturbed."

"Darn! I was really hoping to see him. Do you know when he might be available?"

"The aides are pretty busy. Did you want to talk to Ms. Solomon?"

"Thanks, but I don't need to disturb her. When does Zach's shift end?"

"Four."

I smiled again, thanked her, and left. I didn't bother to ask for Zach's home address. I couldn't imagine Belle Mer allowing Karla access to that information, let alone authorizing her to release it. Plus, it was twelve minutes to three, and with a plan in hand, I didn't mind waiting.

I used the time until I expected to see Zach emerge from the staff entrance to write down my schedule for the day Henri died. I found some information in my old-style pocket calendar, but the situation required more than the basics, and for that I needed Cara.

"It's me," I said, in response to her standard welcoming greeting.

"Oh!" she exclaimed, flustered. "I didn't recognize the number on the display."

"This is a new phone." I laughed awkwardly, then stopped, embarrassed. "Don't give out the number, okay?"

"All right," she said, and from her hushed tone, I could tell she was worried about me, or wary about what I was about to say, or both.

"So," I said, "I'm in a kind of a situation here, and I need your help."

"Of course, Josie. Anything."

"The thing is that I need to be able to account for my time the afternoon Henri was killed, and for that I need your phone log."

"Oh, my."

"Yeah, well…let's start at noon."

Between my online calendar and Cara's detailed phone log, I was able to account for something within every fifteen-minute window. I smiled. No way could I be considered a suspect. A normal workday's busy schedule would, I hoped, provide an effective counterpoint to the efforts someone was expending to implicate me in Henri's murder. I typed it out on my netbook and used Belle Mer's free wireless to e-mail it to Max.

With the remaining time, I called Ty, hoping to get lucky and reach him, but the call went to voice mail immediately. I didn't leave a message beyond saying I loved him. I couldn't think of any quick way to tell him all that had transpired. I wanted to fill him in completely, or not at all.

From my position high above the beach, I had a clear view of the gold flecks twinkling on the midnight blue ocean surface. Ellis would ask Leigh Ann about the love letter, maybe reserving where he'd found it, maybe not. She'd conclude the husband she adored had been cheating on her. I could almost feel her heart breaking. There was nothing I could do to reassure her, to comfort her, to let her know that as far as I knew, Henri had cherished her and no one else.

I sighed, then turned my gaze back to my phone and called work again. Cara told me Sasha had astonishing news from Adèle Bové at Verdura.

"I'll transfer you, but what would you like me to tell her about the number you're calling from?" Cara whispered.

I could picture my entire staff turning toward Cara like synchronized dancers, wondering why she was whispering.

"Nothing," I said. "Don't mention it."

Sasha reported that Ms. Bové had found the sales record

of the gold-wrapped heart. It had originally been sold in 1945 to an oil tycoon as a gift for his wife. Her children sold it back to Verdura after her death in 1985.

"Later that year," Sasha said, her voice rippling with barely contained enthusiasm, "Averell Harriman bought it for his wife, Pamela Harriman, who later became the American ambassador to France. It was sold to an anonymous buyer at auction in 1994. Apparently Ms. Harriman needed cash to settle a family lawsuit."

"And then?" I asked, rapt.

"And then, nothing until it appeared in our storage room locker."

"Which auction house sold it?"

"Are you sitting down?" Sasha asked. "Frisco's."

I smiled. "I'll make the call," I said. "This is really something, Sasha."

"I know. It's quite a story. Do you know about Pamela Harriman? I've always admired her. I'm so shy…" Sasha said, her voice trailing off for a moment. "When I think of all that she experienced, well, I guess that's what an outgoing personality gets you. Life, you know?"

"Some people would credit her success more to her ambition than her personality, but I always thought those comments came more from jealousy or chauvinism. Very successful women get some people's goat."

"Not mine," Sasha said.

"Or mine." I laughed. "I can already hear my friend Shelley telling me they can't release anonymous bidders' names. I'll ask her to contact the buyer on our behalf."

After we were done, she put Fred on.

"I've gone through Henri's scrapbook. There's nothing worth anything. Even those two menus have no value to speak of."

"Too bad," I said. "Still, the appraisal had to be done."

Those silent movie posters offer the best hope of value,
I thought as I dialed Shelley's number.

Shelley was her usual peppy self until I explained what
I wanted.

"Josie, Josie, Josie," she said. "You want the keys to
Fort Knox next? You know I can't give you that name."

"Of course," I said, laughing. "I was wondering if you'd
contact the winning bidder on my behalf. Ask him or her
whether he'd be willing to talk to me. All I want to know
is what happened to the wrapped heart. Did he sell it? Give
it away? Lose it? You know the questions I need to ask.
If he doesn't want to talk to me, maybe he'll talk to you."

Intrigued, she agreed to try. "You're always full of sass,
Josie. Of course, my boss won't mind my doing research
for a competitor. No prob."

"You scratch my back, etcetera, etcetera."

"You're so cute. Frisco's would love the idea that your
sweet little company has something we need or want."

"Ha, ha. One of the top five small antiques auction
houses, according to *Antiques Insights* magazine, baby.
Your bosses are just jealous of our explosive growth."

"Speaking of which, I heard a rumor you're working
on a music-themed auction. We have an antique violin we
might be interested in consigning to you."

I paused, recognizing that our friendly banter had just
morphed into a serious business negotiation. Someone at
Frisco's had noticed that we were buying up stellar music-
related objects and called on Shelley to ensure they could
get in on the action. I was beyond flattered. For an auction
house of Frisco's stature to want to ally with us was tan-
tamount to an endorsement spelled out in flashing neon
on a billboard in Times Square.

"When were you planning on asking me?" I kept my
tone casual.

"Later today."

"Very cool, Shelley. We'd love to include your violin. I'll tell Fred to contact you. It might require your in-person participation, though."

She chuckled. "You drive a hard bargain, my friend, but let's work to keep the terms realistic, okay?"

I laughed, and we chatted for a minute longer. Shelley promised to contact the anonymous bidder on my behalf ASAP.

I was still smiling as I dialed Brock Wood's number yet again.

This time, Mr. Wood answered with a chipper "Hi-ho!"

I introduced myself, explained how I got his number, then asked, "Hal Greeley said that you helped his Uncle Les, Lester Markham, relocate to Rocky Point. Is that correct?"

"Yes, that's right. That was five years ago—how time flies."

"Did Mr. Markham rent a storage locker in New Hampshire?"

"That was our first stop," he said, "but he'd hate you calling him mister. Call him Les. Call me Brock. Les told me he wanted to know where his stuff was, and that it was safe and sound and ready to go."

"Do you remember the name of the storage facility?"

"Cambridge, maybe? Coleford?"

"Crawford?" I prompted, my fingers crossed.

"That's it!" He laughed, a rolling low rumble. "I knew it would come to me."

I smiled. Buck's memory would serve as testimony that Uncle Les had rented the storage room. I decided to dig a little deeper. "Do you know the name he used to rent it?"

"The name? His own, I guess. Didn't he?"

"Were you in the office with him while he rented it?" I asked, skipping answering his question.

"No. I stayed with the U-Haul. Les had called to book the room and arrange for some movers. What with his bum hip and my bad back, we couldn't do it ourselves. What name did he use?"

"Gael Patrick."

"I wonder why."

"His nephew Hal thought it might be to keep it a secret from him. Hal was pushing him to sell everything."

"Young whippersnapper. Les talked about that. Resented it, too."

"Do you know anything about Les's silent movie posters?"

"I know he had some from his dad, is that what you mean?"

"That, and another. A Batiste Madalena."

"That would be the one he bought from that girl, right?"

"I don't know. What girl?"

"It was years ago. One of his students…what was her name?" He paused, thinking. "She was a beauty, that I can tell you. It'll come to me… I can't remember squat about what happened this morning, but I'm sharp as a razor about things that happened thirty years ago, which is about when he would have bought that poster. She wanted to study in Italy but didn't have the money. Les had mentioned his father's silent movie posters in a class, so she consulted him about selling a Batiste Madalena silent movie poster she owned. I haven't thought about that poster in many years… let me think, now…her name will come, see if it doesn't."

"How did she happen to own it, do you know?"

"Her great-grandfather had been a maintenance man at the Eastman Theater in Rochester, New York. When the theater sold, the new owners said to get rid of all the old stuff, posters included. He kept one of his favorites, *Mysterious Lady* it was. Wait! Hilary Reise! That was her name. I knew I'd remember. Les liked the poster and he liked the girl. He got the poster appraised for her, then bought it for full price."

"That was awfully nice of him, wasn't it?"

"That was Les, one helluva nice guy. He was my best friend for more than fifty years."

"It must be so hard, losing him."

"You've got that right, young lady. It was bad when he moved away. It was worse hearing he died."

I asked some follow-up questions, but I'd reached the end of Brock's knowledge. He had no current information about Hilary Reise, but we didn't need it. I'd just received reliable, disinterested testimony explaining how the poster got from the Rochester Theater into Les Markham's possession. I'd just confirmed provenance. Now all we needed to do was assess value.

I called Sasha back to pass on the two bits of good news, about Frisco's violin and Brock's confirmation, and asked her to tell Fred abut the violin and take charge of the appraisal of the silent movie posters. I'd just hung up when Zach came out of Belle Mer. According to the dash clock, it was 4:16. I watched him get settled behind the wheel of a dark red old Honda. He came to a full stop at the exit, then turned south.

There was almost no traffic, and I kept far back. Once we hit Route 101, though, we picked up plenty of company, and I had to work to keep him in sight. He was a fast driver, and I didn't want to get too close. I nearly lost him when he passed a slow-moving truck, and I was trapped behind it for two miles, but I saw him, far ahead, still in the passing lane, still driving fast. He finally slowed down once he turned south on Brown Avenue. Three miles down, he turned left onto a small unmarked road. As I sailed on by I saw the street was a dead end, a cul-de-sac. I passed a convenience store and a fried chicken drive-through and dashed into a body shop's parking lot and turned around. I drove back slowly, pulled off to the side at the entrance to the dead-end street, and turned on my flashers. The rear-view mirror told me the road was wide enough for cars to give me a pass-by without a problem; then I looked for Zach's car.

The Honda was parked in a driveway three houses down on the right. Zach stood by the porch steps talking to some-one out of sight around the side of the house.

I couldn't hear any words, but I could see his mouth and head move. No, he said, then no again, then okay. He shrugged and nodded, climbed the porch stairs, and used a key to enter.

I eased forward, prepared to drive closer. I could pic-ture the next five minutes. I'd park. I'd knock on the door. I'd say, "Hey, Zach. Got a minute?" Before I could frame Zach's imaginary reply, a man laden with firewood came onto the porch from the back, and I gasped. I bounced backward, knocking my head against the headrest, causing the car to jerk forward. I slammed my foot on the brake.

"Oh, my God!" I whispered, mesmerized.

The man wore a blue parka and a Red Sox baseball cap, and his expression was fully as surly as it had been that day at Crawford's. He lowered his arms, and the logs rolled into a messy pile near the front door. He retraced his steps. I sat in a haze of stupefaction, unable to believe my eyes, unable to deny what I was seeing. I'd just found Andrew Bruen.

He reappeared with another armful of logs.

I didn't know what to do.

My first instinct, which lasted about a second and a half,

was to call Ellis. *Ellis,* I thought, fuming, *who at this moment is probably rummaging through my underwear looking for evidence he knows full well doesn't exist.*

Andrew left again, no doubt off for a third load. Two minutes later, he reappeared, huffing a little, the wood stacked higher this time, and I wondered why Zach wasn't helping, when all at once, Zach came around the corner carrying a few logs, two per hand, an inefficient approach. Zach had wanted to wash up after work, to change his clothes before helping carry wood. Four minutes and two more loads later, I realized that I needed guidance.

Talking to Zach was no longer an option.

Talking to Andrew Bruen wasn't even a possibility.

I couldn't sit on a busy thoroughfare indefinitely.

I had to act, but I still didn't know what to do, so I did what I always did when a situation arose with legal and moral implications too complex for me to sort through on my own: I called Max.

TWENTY-SIX

"I'LL CALL ELLIS," Max said after he heard me out, "and tell him that as part of appraising the silent movie posters, you planned to talk to Zach Moore. As soon as you saw him talking to the mystery bidder, Andrew Bruen, you asked me to contact him. I'll call you back as soon as I reach him."

"Thanks, Max," I said, relieved to transfer the responsibility of calling in the news. I wasn't in the mood to talk to Ellis.

"Are you still in that neighborhood?" Max asked.

"Yes, down the block. I'm watching them cart loads of firewood from somewhere in the back onto the front porch."

"You should leave," Max said.

"I want to see what happens."

"The police are going to come and talk to both men. Probably they'll go inside. There will be nothing for you to see."

"Maybe Andrew will run," I said. My throat closed for a moment. "Maybe he's the killer."

"Another good reason for you to leave. Don't put yourself in harm's way, Josie."

"I won't," I said. "Call me as soon as you know something, okay?"

He said he would, and I decided to stay but find a better, less conspicuous viewing spot. I was sensibly cautious and circumspect, but I was also relentlessly curious.

I would never put myself in danger—just the opposite, in fact. I thought of myself as a safety queen. In this case, I couldn't see how my hunkering down out of sight was risky. I began scoping out options. If I wanted to keep an eye on the action without getting noticed, I needed a different, more discreet vantage spot.

With the snow pushed into high banks on both sides of the road, there was no room to maneuver a U-turn, so I drove forward into the convenience store, then drove back to the chicken place, choosing a parking slot with a direct sightline to the no-name road, and settled in to wait.

I didn't have long. Max called three minutes later.

"I reached Ellis. He thanked you for the information and has asked to see us again. They've found something else, Josie. Something he wants to show you. He wouldn't say what…but from something in his tone…well, I don't like the sound of it."

Max and I were in Ellis's private office, seated at the round ash guest table, not in an interrogation room. He'd offered coffee and shaken hands. He was smiling. Max was adept at reading moods, so something must have happened in the twenty minutes it took me to get here, but I didn't know what.

"First, I'm pleased to report that you are no longer a person of interest in the murder of Henri Dubois." Ellis slid a color photograph across the table. "Take a gander at this puppy."

The photo showed me and Henri standing side by side, our torsos touching, an intimate position, as false as it was suggestive. I was on the left wearing a green cotton sweater, a denim skirt, and my favorite green lizard cowboy boots. Henri wore a suit, blue pinstripes, with a blue oxford shirt and a maroon tie.

"Someone's good with Photoshop," I said. "If I didn't

know better, I'd think this was pretty damning evidence against me."

"My thought exactly," Ellis said. "When Detective Brownley called that they'd found it, I was, as you might imagine, concerned." He looked at Max. "That's when I asked you and Josie to come in." He smiled in my direction. "When I saw the photo, well, I was no longer the least bit concerned."

"Why not?" Max asked.

"This photo of me was taken New Year's Eve at the Diamond Cowboy Bar and Grill," I explained. "I know because it was the first time I wore that sweater, and the only time I've worn it with those boots." I grinned. "Ellis took this shot. He and Zoë joined Ty and me to welcome in the new year with a raucous evening of burgers and line dancing. In the original photo I was standing next to Zoë. Someone replaced her with Henri."

"That's reprehensible," Max said, appalled. "Who had access to the photo?"

"The world. Zoë posted it on Facebook." I looked at Ellis. "Did you compare it to the original?"

"Yup. It's identical."

"Can you imagine wearing a pinstripe suit to the Diamond Cowboy?" I asked.

"You'd be laughed out of the place," Ellis said. He looked at Henri's face. "Do you have any idea where his photo was taken?"

I shook my head. "No."

"Where did you find it?" Max asked.

"Tucked in between two pages of a notebook in the same desk drawer where we found the love note. Someone did a one-stop delivery, dropping off that note and this photo."

"I'm no longer mad at you," I said.

"You're not off the hook yet. Your fingerprints are all over the love note. Smudged, just the way they would be if you picked it up several times, folded it, and so on. So are Henri's. No one else's. Just you two."

"That's impossible."

"No, it's not," he said. "It's true."

Max held up his hand and leaned into my ear. "You have to tell me the truth, Josie. Now. How did your prints get on that note?"

"I have no idea. None."

He nodded, then spoke to Ellis. "Josie has nothing to add to her previous statements on the subject."

"We need to account for the fingerprints," Ellis said.

"Whoever is trying to frame me put them there," I said. "How could someone get my prints on that paper?"

Ellis rubbed the side of his nose. "There are two options. Either the note was written on paper you'd touched or someone transferred your fingerprints. Have you ever touched paper like that note—white card stock?"

"I suppose. I touch all sorts of paper all the time. We use card stock for promotional postcards and produce them in-house. Except I don't generally touch the raw material. I delegate."

He nodded. "Transferring fingerprints is called 'spoofing.' You roll a receptor material over the prints to pick them up, then roll it again over the receiver."

"What's a receptor material?" I asked.

"Play-Doh. Paraffin wax. A hard-boiled egg."

"You're saying someone rolled a hard-boiled egg over my fingerprints, then took that egg and rolled it over the love note?" I asked, incredulous.

"Something like that, assuming you're telling the truth."

"Unbelievable," Max said.

"How can fingerprint evidence ever be admitted in court?" I asked.

"You don't convict someone on fingerprints alone." He leaned forward, his eyes peering into mine with such ferocity it was as if he were trying to see inside me. "So... since it now seems evident that someone is, in fact, trying to frame you...who is it?"

I paused, my mind tangled by conflicting emotions, unable to sort through what was real and what I only thought was true. I felt as if I'd been dumped into the middle of a stormy sea on a starless night and told to swim for shore. Ellis and Max were waiting, monitoring my expression, alert for clues that I'd recognized the handiwork of a devil.

"What makes you think it's personal?" I asked, mortified. "Maybe I'm just a convenient target."

"Who would think you're a convenient target?"

"No one I know."

"It has to be someone you know."

"Why?"

"How else could they have gotten your prints?" he asked.

"That's true, isn't it?" I asked, skeevied out. "It's disgusting. Literally, I feel sick."

"Think, Josie. Who?"

"I don't know."

"Keep thinking about it," Ellis said. "Someone set you up. We need to know who." He turned to Max. "I'm going to ask Josie to help with an interview. Do you need anything else from me to wrap up this part of the investigation?"

"No, assuming I have your assurance that you won't ask her any further questions outside my presence."

"You have it," Ellis said. He turned to me and smiled. "Will you help me, Josie?"

I looked at Max.

"It's up to you, Josie. Ellis can't ask you anything else unless I'm with you. As a citizen, if you can help him, you should."

I turned to Ellis, still reeling, still raw with mingled fear and relief. "All right."

Ellis thanked me and said he'd be back shortly, meanwhile, I could wait in his office. Max stood up and patted my shoulder. I stayed seated while Ellis escorted him out, reminding myself to breathe slowly, to calm down.

Someone took Play-Doh or wax or an egg and captured my fingerprints. Someone hated me. Or considered me expendable.

I took in a to-my-toenails breath and exhaled slowly. Instead of asking unanswerable questions, I focused instead on thinking about something that offered the promise of providing useful information. I tried to recall more about the Winter Festival, about who might have taken my phone.

Specific moments stood out. A funny remark from Ty. Mimie's spectacular bundt cake. Seeing Suzanne for the first time. Thinking how beautiful Gretchen looked in green, how it brought out the emerald sparkle in her eyes, matched her creamy complexion, and complemented her red hair. Laughing at a joke Zoë told, I couldn't remember what, and a myriad of other moments, the small pleasures of an evening out among friends. Other details had slipped away, leaving in their wake nothing more than an overall impression. I'd had fun, and that was that. No way would I ever be able to remember who'd been near my bag.

When Ellis returned, his mood had changed again. He'd put on his let's-get-it-done hat, informing me that Zach Moore and Andrew Bruen had been picked up for questioning. He was ready, he said, to interview Andrew Bruen, and was hoping I would help.

Ellis's plan was to approach Andrew Bruen as an ally in the murder investigation, not a suspect.

"I've already set the groundwork," he said, "getting him comfortable in the interview room, letting him know about the videotape, and so on. Darrell is with him now. He goes by Drew, so that's what I'll be calling him."

"Was he angry?" I asked.

"Frightened more than angry, I think. You know how it is. Some people, men especially, when they get scared, they get loud. I think he's pretty calm at this point, but we'll see. I told him I need his help with some antiques questions. Zach is with Detective Brownley. I know they haven't been talking long, but so far, he still won't say a word about that secret. What I'm hoping you'll do is get Drew talking about the contents of that storage room. I want to know why he was bidding on it in particular. So far he's not answering. He's just saying he wanted to give abandoned-storage-room auctions a whirl and that one looked good. Which we might have believed until you connected him to Zach."

"It might actually be a coincidence," I said. "Maybe Zach mentioned that one of his patients had a storage room locker, and it got Andrew thinking."

"It's possible." He shrugged. "Let's find out."

Ellis and I walked into Interview Room Two together. I nodded at Darrell, took my customary chair with my back to the cage, and smiled at Drew. Ellis asked Darrell to activate the video recorders and stated who was present for the record.

"I don't think you've ever met Josie Prescott, have you, Drew? You saw her, though, at Crawford's."

"Hi, Drew," I said.

"Josie is an antiques expert," Ellis explained, "an appraiser. I asked her to join us to help me figure out whether the locker Henri Dubois won is somehow related to his murder. Since you were bidding on it, I figure you must know something about the contents." He held up his hand, anticipating Drew's objection. "I know you said you bid on it because it looked good, and that's it, but I'm thinking there must have been something you saw that got you interested. Maybe you'd heard something and forgot to tell me." Ellis smiled, man to man. "Happens to me all the time." He turned to me. "Josie, how about you? What did you think about that locker?"

"I saw that mahogany table and I was hooked." I turned to Drew and smiled. "What made you decide to bid on it?"

"I don't know."

"Are you a collector?" I asked.

"Just cars."

"Oh, yeah? What kind?"

"Mustangs. I like vintage Mustangs."

"My dad had a red 1966 convertible," I said. "I loved that car."

"Did he rebuild it?" Drew asked.

"No. He bought it from a guy like you."

He nodded. "I sell about two or three a year."

"Is that your primary job?"

"Yeah. Sort of. I do body work at Best Bodies over on Ipswich Drive. He lets me use his tools and stuff and keep my parts there. It works out."

That explains the grease stains, I thought. *Drew's a car guy.* "Sounds perfect for you. Were you thinking of adding a little income by buying abandoned storage lockers?"

"No," he said, then reconsidered his answer. "Maybe."

"Have you bought any others?" Ellis asked.

"No."

"Did you know that unit had belonged to Lester Markham?" Ellis asked.

"I'd heard something about it."

Ellis nodded. "From Zach."

"I guess."

"When we ask him about Les Markham, he won't say a word. He'll only say that he promised he wouldn't tell. Did you make him promise something?"

Drew shrugged and looked down.

"What was it?"

"I don't know what you're talking about."

"It's time to release him from the promise."

Drew didn't reply. He kept his eyes on the table. From his expression, he could have been considering anything from ways to avoid war to whether he felt like pizza for dinner.

"You guys live together?" Ellis asked, changing the subject.

"Sure. With our mom, too, until she died about a year ago. Now it's just us."

"Oh, I hadn't realized you were brothers."

Drew shrugged again. "My dad died at Heartbreak Ridge on Grenada was when I was three. He was in the army. My mom married again a couple of years later, and that's Zach's dad. It didn't work out. He walked when Zach was one."

"I hear Zach's a real good worker," Ellis said, changing the subject again.

"The best. Never late. Never skips a shift. Takes everything seriously."

"And I bet he doesn't get half the appreciation he should," Ellis said.

"You got that right. They pay him squat for doing what's got to be one of the worst jobs in the world, taking care of those old guys. I mean, he changes their diapers, you know? I couldn't do it. I wouldn't do it. But he likes it. He likes his patients."

"From what I hear, they appreciate him a lot."

"Management does, I guess. I mean, the pay isn't great, but he gets regular raises, you know? Vacation pay, health insurance, everything. It's the patients that are the problem."

"Lester Markham didn't appreciate him?" Ellis asked.

"Five years Zach took care of him, and what did Zach get when he died? Besides an old computer, more like a paperweight, if you ask me, a big fat goose egg."

Ellis shook his head sympathetically.

"It's not like I'm greedy," Drew said. "It's not like we're stealing."

It wasn't a glib answer, but he had the words ready. I got the impression we were hearing his side of an argument he'd had with Zach, probably more than once.

"You're just trying to get what's due," Ellis said, nodding empathetically.

"Zach will never say a word, that's just not his way. If I don't stand up for him, no one will, and he'll be taken advantage of forever."

"You're a good brother."

Drew looked down. "I promised Mom I'd look after him."

"And when Lester talked about how much stuff he had in his locker, it only seemed right that Zach get something for all his trouble."

Drew met Ellis's eyes for a three-count, then nodded. "Yeah. We didn't do anything wrong. I tried to buy it, that's all."

"It just sold for more you expected."

"Exactly." He lowered his eyes again. "I let Zach down. I took all the money we had."

"You did the best you could," Ellis agreed, "which is more than a lot of people do. Was it the posters that you were hoping to get?"

"Yeah. Old movie posters. Les told Zach that one of his dad's posters sold for fifteen thousand dollars just a few years ago. Zach was real impressed that his dad drew paintings that sold for that much money. Les said he had four of them and one from some other artist. He got that one, according to Zach, from a student of his, and it was worth even more. I figured if his dad's posters were worth fifteen thousand dollars each a few years ago, they had to be worth at least that much now. That's sixty thousand dollars. The other one was worth more, I figured maybe as much as twenty thousand dollars. I was looking at eighty thousand dollars, a fortune." He shook his head. "It was worth a shot."

"How did you know about the auction?"

Drew opened his mouth, then closed it. "I kept my eye out for notices."

"Zach knew Les's locker was at Crawford's," Ellis said. "He knew the room number."

"Sure. Les mentioned it a couple of times. When the newspaper ad came out last week, well, there it was."

"After Les died, you closed his bank account, didn't you?"

Drew's eyes opened wide and he froze.

"The bank has security cameras," Ellis said.

He didn't mention that he hadn't seen them, and wouldn't be able to until the subpoena came through.

"It was for Zach," Drew whispered.

"That's what I figured," Ellis said, his tone communicating interest and understanding. "How much did you get?"

"About eighteen hundred."

"Where is it now?"

"Mom set up a retirement account for Zach. An IRA, it's called. I put it in there."

"Why did you close the account? Why not just empty it out?"

"If it's closed, they don't send statements."

"Got it. That way, no one would be alerted that an account existed."

Ellis looked at me and raised his eyebrows, silently asking if I had any other questions. I shook my head.

"You've been very helpful, Drew."

"Can we go now?" he asked.

"Soon. We'll need to talk some more about that eighteen hundred dollars."

He nodded, resigned. "I want to see Zach."

"Let me see what I can do." Ellis stood up. "Josie, you can come with me. Darrell, you can turn off the machines. You want a soda or something, Drew?"

"Yeah...thanks." Looking like a puppy who'd chewed his master's shoes and knew he was in trouble, Drew repeated, "I did it for Zach."

"Does Drew have an alibi for Henri's murder?" I asked Ellis as we headed to the lobby.

"You know I can't discuss an ongoing investigation with you, Josie."

"Does he?"

"Josie!"

"I bet he was working on a car. He got mad at losing the locker, went and blew off some steam by working, then went back for his deposit. Other people would have seen him working."

"Lots of guys coming and going at a body shop like that. Regulars who might notice whether Drew was there or not."

"Am I right?" I asked. "He's got a good alibi?"

"What's your point, Josie?"

"You didn't ask him about the murder, so he must be out of it."

"Maybe I just didn't ask him yet."

I shook my head. "Drew is safe…what about Zach? He must have an alibi, too. You heard what Drew said. Zach never misses a shift."

"And that sort of alibi is easy to confirm," Ellis said. "He clocks in and out; he's with half a dozen patients; he's seen by nurses and other aides; it's about as good an alibi as you can get."

"So, they both are okay?"

"You're a piece of work, my friend."

I smiled and play-punched his arm. "Do you think Zach's secret is that he knew Drew took money from Les's account?"

"That would be a logical assumption, but until he tells, we have no way of knowing."

"He'll never tell."

"Probably not."

"What's going to happen to Drew?"

"My guess is that it will depend on the family. If they want to prosecute, we've got a confession."

"You should let it go."

"He stole money from a dead man."

"For his brother."

"You've spoken to Markham's relatives, his sister and nephews. How do you think they'll feel?"

"Empathetic."

"I'll talk to the prosecutor. I suspect that if he returns the money and apologizes, he might walk away from this one."

"Give him a break, Ellis. Zach needs him. Let him offer

to return the money. It's all in how you broach the subject. I think they'll follow your lead."

"I've said it before and I'll say it again—you're a good egg, Josie."

TWENTY-SEVEN

I WAS STARVING. I stopped at a sub shop en route to my office and picked up a turkey sandwich.

The wind chimes jingled as I stepped into the front office, surprised to see Cara at her desk.

"Wow!" I exclaimed. "It's almost seven...what are you doing here?"

"Welcome back!" Cara said with her comforting and familiar smile. "I'm writing a letter to my cousin and thought I'd finish it here, in case you needed me for something."

My eyes filled and I closed them tightly for a moment. "Thank you," I managed, then turned to Fred, reading something on his monitor. "Hi, Fred. Everything under control?"

"You bet," he said, flashing a quick grin. "Smooth sailing on all fronts."

"How are you holding up?" Cara asked me.

"Medium to good. Are there any cookies left? That would definitely give me a much-needed boost."

Cara smiled. "I made a fresh batch."

"You're an angel," I said.

She removed the lid from a blue plastic tub. The aroma, rich chocolate, with a hint of spice, nutmeg, maybe, brought me back to my childhood, to the days when I'd come bounding in from school, and milk and fresh-baked cookies would be waiting for me in the kitchen. I took a cookie.

"Thanks, Cara. These smell unbelievably delicious."

"You know my theory—cookies cure all."

"A theory we've proven to be true for years now. Thanks again, Cara. I'll be upstairs."

I hurried toward the spiral stairs and had just started up the steps when Hank came skittering across the concrete, meowing imperatively, clearly asking why I hadn't called for him, why I hadn't let him know I was back.

"Hi, Hank," I said. "I'm having a hard day."

He rubbed my leg as we climbed the steps.

"Thank you, baby. I love you, too."

I sat at my desk, relieved as always that my staff was able to work independently. Nothing required my immediate attention, which meant I was able to sit quietly and eat and think. Hank asked for, then demanded, a cuddle.

"In a minute, Hank," I said.

He meowed, *Now. Now. Now.*

Once I was situated, I invited him into my lap. I did face petties with my left hand while eating with my right, and he began to purr.

Ty called, and as soon as I heard his voice, I felt a sense of calm come over me, as if I'd been steering a ship through rough waters and had finally reached safe harbor.

"I am soooo glad to hear your voice," I said.

"I hear trouble. Are you okay?"

"Yes...sort of...not really. Oh, Ty, Ellis found a love note from Henri in my desk at home. It wasn't addressed to me or anything, but isn't that completely creepy? Someone snuck in my house and slipped a love note into my desk drawer."

"At least now we know why someone broke in, to hide it."

"True," I said, thinking how fortunate I was that Ty was confident in my love. No smoke without fire, some men might think or say. Not Ty. Never for a moment did he doubt me. "There's more." I could barely get the words out. I sipped some water, then told him about the photo, and was about to describe locating Andrew Bruen when he interrupted me.

"This is crazy, Josie. I'm coming home."

"Thank you, Ty, but there's no need. I'm no longer a suspect. The attempt to frame me failed. There's nothing either of us can do at this point." I took a breath. "I don't want to talk about the ugly anymore. I'll fill you in about the rest later. Tell me about you instead. What's going on there? Is it going well?"

"Very. They want me to stay at least one more day, maybe two."

I swallowed disappointment. "Because of good news or bad news?"

"Good news. The initial assessment is done, and we know which programs we're going to focus on. Now we need to plan the hows and wherefores and so on. The head of training has asked me to be on the roll-out committee. Since getting these programs into the field is top priority, the committee starts meeting tomorrow."

"Ty, that's wonderful! What an opportunity."

"Yeah," he said, and I could hear the smile in his voice. "I'm pretty pleased. Except I hate being away from you. Especially now."

"Me, too," I said. "You know that if I needed you here, I'd say so."

"And you know that if you did, I'd be on the first plane out of here. I love you, Josie."

"I love you, too, Ty."

We agreed to talk before bedtime, and when the call was over, I pressed the unit to my chest, keeping Ty close for just a moment longer.

With Ty out of town, there was no reason to hurry

home. I tried to put the murder out of my mind, to think about work, but my thoughts kept sliding back to Henri. I picked up the last-minute additions to Fred's music catalogue copy, including the 1861 Jean-Baptiste Vuillaume violin we'd be auctioning off for Frisco's, and realized a minute later that I'd just read the first paragraph three times over without a word registering.

All I could think about was whether the murder was related to Lester Markham's storage unit, and why someone would pick on me. Facts and impressions came in seemingly arbitrary order. I was privy to countless details about both investigations, but nothing I knew seemed to gel. Out of ideas, I decided to write down everything I knew about the situation. Without worrying about order of importance, chronology, or any other variable, I made a list, jotting down anything that might be relevant. When I was done I read it over.

1. The five silent movie posters in Henri's storage room were valuable, maybe worth as much as $250,000 or more. Drew thought they were worth $80,000, but his information was out of date. Everything was relative, though, since to Drew, $80,000 was a fortune. Robbery was a possible motive.

2. Nothing else in the locker had anything close to that level of value.

3. Someone stole my phone at the Winter Festival and set up the fake Gmail account and downloaded a remote access app. That meant that whoever did those things attended the festival.

4. Essentially everyone I knew from Rocky Point was at the festival, but people came and went.

Some people ate and ran. Others lingered late into the evening.

5. Leigh Ann and Henri had plenty of money, cash, to start their business. No one knew where the cash came from, or if they did, they weren't talking.

6. Henri left everything to his father, Pierre.

7. The day before he died, Henri spoke to a lawyer.

8. Henri said the call from the lawyer was urgent.

9. Henri pledged me to secrecy because I'd witnessed his reaction to the call. Henri said he didn't want Leigh Ann to know the caller had conveyed bad business news.

10. Scott adored Leigh Ann.

11. Leigh Ann adored Henri.

12. Leigh Ann wanted to be friends with Scott.

13. Someone tried to frame me for Henri's murder, breaking into my house, planting a phony love note and doctored photograph in my desk, and placing the murder weapon in my car.

14. Whoever broke into my house used a key.

15. That person drove a silver car, a silver Malibu, or a similarly shaped car.

16. Whoever tried to frame me knew how to use photo-manipulation software, which meant everyone who worked at a computer, or most everyone.

I reread the list considering whether each entry was, in fact, true. No one knows what anyone else feels. You can't. We rely on what people say and do to assess how they feel, and behaviors can be faked to create a certain perception. People do it all the time.

No patterns emerged.

No entry stuck out as especially meaningful, or not.

I reread the list yet again, this time from the bottom up, and still nothing occurred to me.

I had no epiphany. I felt no clarity at all.

Forget the list, I told myself. *Consider only motive, means, and opportunity.* I nodded, eager to see how the facts fit into those three buckets.

The motive was unknown. Why do people kill? Lust, love, jealousy. Revenge, hate, humiliation. Greed, envy, pride. Any one of those emotions could be building inside someone, festering without anyone else knowing about it. Then when the killer explodes in murderous rage people express astonishment, saying they had no clue. Often there were plenty of clues, if only people knew where to look.

Means was all too vividly known. Anyone could buy a tire iron at any one of a hundred stores in a twenty-mile radius. Pay cash and no one would remember the transaction.

A bird chirped, a high-pitched, urgent sound, and Hank looked up. I swiveled to face the window, but I couldn't locate it. The sun was low and the tree limbs were shimmying. It looked cold. Hank considered getting up to investigate further; instead, he resettled in my lap.

Motive...unknown. Means...known, but knowing didn't lead to the killer. Regarding opportunity, there were four times to consider—the January afternoon when the e-mail and remote access had been set up on Henri's phone, and later when it had been set up on mine; the February afternoon when Henri had been murdered; and the overnight hours when my house had been broken into and the tire iron secreted in my car.

Since the car Scott drove matched the color and model of car seen in the bank's security film, I started with him.

Scott hadn't been in Rocky Point the day of the Winter Festival. Or had he? I'd known, at least by sight, almost everyone at the Winter Festival. I had no way of knowing if I simply hadn't noticed Scott or if he hadn't been there.

I'd gotten the impression from Leigh Ann that Scott's weekend visit was his first trip to New Hampshire since she'd moved to Rocky Point, but maybe my impression was wrong. Scott said he didn't know the area, which is why he'd been driving around while Henri was being killed, but not knowing the area was different than never having set foot in a place. Regardless, Scott had no alibi for Henri's murder.

Scott could have left Leigh Ann asleep and driven to my house during the overnight blizzard. He'd been the one to tell me Leigh Ann hadn't slept, not her. I considered the logistics. Scott was a landlord, so it wasn't a stretch to think he knew his way around locks and keys, at least enough to jury-rig keys. Hank licked my hand.

"You're wondering whether Henri might have held a different view of divorce from Scott's it's no-biggy attitude, aren't you, Hank? Perhaps he had religious objections. How can I find out? It's not a question you can ask a widow."

Hank jumped down and walked toward the door. Three paces short, he sat down and began grooming, licking his flank with long, sweeping motions of his tongue, as if he had a sudden itch and couldn't wait to scratch it.

"Well, answer me this, young man. Don't you agree that I can make anyone look guilty simply by focusing on certain facts and excluding others?" Hank looked up, made a soft mewing noise, then returned to the task at hand. "I agree. It's why it's crucial that in thinking things through, I try to determine not only who's guilty but who's innocent." Hank raised his leg like a Rockette and began cleaning his inner thigh. "In fact, I think it's innocence that matters most."

Scott might not be the only person who knows his way around locks and keys, I thought. *Suzanne might, too.* I recalled her saying that to do her job, she had to know how to wield a screwdriver. I wondered just how handy she was.

An image of her came to mind. Her delicate features. Her designer clothes. Her seemingly innate warmth and graciousness. When Suzanne had greeted Henri at their shop and at the Blue Dolphin, she'd welcomed him with familiar delight, her eyes twinkling, her hands outstretched. Maybe Suzanne decided to stay in Rocky Point not because we were all such nice people but because she'd fallen in love with Henri. It couldn't be; it just couldn't. Not after the nightmare that led to the Blue Dolphin closing in the first place.* *Don't be silly,* I thought, telling myself I was imagining things. Sparkling eyes didn't prove a woman was in love. If she had loved Henri, though, and their connection was, to her, a relationship laden with significance, not a tawdry affair, and if she discovered that to Henri their relationship wasn't meaningful at all, that it was about sex, not love, she might have lost it.

I could picture them in the storage room. Henri tells her it's over. She begs him to leave Leigh Ann, to be with her. He refuses. She turns to leave, sees the tire iron in a box of miscellany, grabs it, and beats him senseless, killing him. Crimes of passion happened.

The saga I'd just constructed was woven out of factual threads, but that didn't make it whole cloth. If I assigned too much meaning to a fact, or if I interpreted one improperly, the thread it represented wouldn't hold and the fabric would unravel. Maybe Suzanne's eyes lit up because she'd just heard she'd been promoted. Perhaps she won at

---

* Please see *Deadly Threads.*

bingo. Maybe she was just a happy gal, and her eyes always sparkled.

Guilt stabbed at me, then receded. I had nothing against Suzanne. My faux-indictment wasn't personal. I could perform this same exercise with anyone, with everyone. Or at least with everyone who'd attended the Winter Festival.

Like Suzanne.

That night, she could have taken my phone from my tote bag, added the software and e-mail account, and slipped it back into the bag. She could have approached the chair where the bag sat, leaned over, perhaps to see if the winter berries in the centerpiece had a scent, and while there, scooped out the phone. Five seconds, maybe less, was all it would take.

The morning Henri was murdered, Suzanne sat at my guest table with easy access to my tote bag. Sasha and I went to the warehouse to gather up the wall art. Suzanne wouldn't have been able to photocopy my keys or scan them, not with Cara sitting there. She could have pressed each key into putty, creating exact outlines of the shapes. Cara was on the phone and almost certainly wouldn't have noticed. Later that day, Suzanne was late for her paint color consultation.

She could have driven to my house during the overnight hours. Suzanne, I recalled, with a sharp intake of breath, drove a silver car, a Mercedes. *Maybe Ty was wrong,* I thought, *and the car barely visible in the bank security camera photo wasn't a Malibu.* A Mercedes sedan has a similar shape.

I laughed, embarrassed. "Well, that proves my point," I told the air. "I can convict anyone of anything."

I needed to stop speculating and find the truth, not indict people in a make-believe kangaroo court.

I couldn't just walk away. I needed to know who tried

to frame me for murder. I felt violated. I'd been violated. I needed more information, and I would get it. I had a vested interest in the outcome, two vested interests, as I thought of it, one personal and one professional. I wanted to know, I needed to know, who'd been dastardly enough to try to convince the police that I was involved in Henri's murder. For my appraisal, I needed to know if the silent movie posters could be sold with clear title.

From what Wes had told me, everything the couple owned was registered in Henri's name, and he'd left everything to his father. I didn't know why Leigh Ann wasn't a party to the business or his heir, and I needed to. Decisions had been made, and I couldn't imagine that the reasons behind them had died with Henri, which meant that someone else knew. Leigh Ann, certainly.

I thought about Leigh Ann, bubbly usually, yet with an undercurrent of something, I didn't know what. Discontent? Worry? I had no way of knowing. I couldn't ask her why Henri excluded her from the business, why he cut her out of his will. I could, however, ask his dad, or maybe I could, if I could think of a business need and come up with appropriately businesslike language. If Henri had confided in anyone, it would have been his father.

I glanced at my computer monitor. It was nearly 8:00, 2:00 A.M. in Paris, too late to call. Neither my French nor his English was good enough to talk to him about issues requiring specific vocabulary anyway, issues like whether he wanted to consign the silent movie posters for sale or have them shipped to him in France, issues like love and passion. I needed a translator.

I reached for the phone, then paused, wondering if I needed to tell Ellis that I planned to call Pierre. Yes, I was calling because of my personal interest, but so what? I wasn't breaking any laws. I was also calling as an antiques appraiser, and no matter what he thought of my personal motive, there was nothing improper about that.

I dialed Fred's extension.

"Do you still use Dr. Bounard for French translations?" I asked, referring to a New York City–based art historian.

"Sometimes. It depends on the project. For general translations, I've been using Yvonne Linten, a grad student at Hitchens. She's very nice, and, of course, she's local."

I took Yvonne's number and dialed, getting her voice mail. *Darn!* I thought.

"Hi, Yvonne," I told the machine. "This is Josie Prescott. Fred, one of my antiques appraisers, tells me you're terrific at French translation. I need to make a call to a French speaker in Paris. It's already too late to call there, so I guess we'll need to wait until tomorrow. Would you call me back so we can set something up?" I gave her my contact information and ended with "It's pretty important, so the sooner I hear from you, the better."

I hate delays. I took my time making decisions, but once the decision was made, I wanted to act. I might not be able to reach Pierre tonight, but that didn't mean I couldn't talk to other people. Suzanne, for instance.

Obviously, I couldn't ask Suzanne if she'd been having an affair with Henri, but there were plenty of other questions I could ask, questions that might help me understand why someone chose me to frame, why she might have thought that I was an appealing or easy target.

Dinner service at the Blue Dolphin would be well underway, so she might be available to chat.

TWENTY-EIGHT

SUZANNE WAS STANDING in her usual spot by the Blue Dolphin's hostess stand, and she greeted me with a big smile, yet her manner seemed subdued. She was warm, but not open. Her eyes weren't sparkling.

"Do you have a reservation, Josie?" Frieda asked, casting her eyes down to the reservation book.

"No, not tonight," I said. I looked at Suzanne. "I was wondering if you had a moment to talk."

"Of course," Suzanne said, covering her surprise with another smile. "Come to the lounge and I'll buy you a drink."

Walking toward the lounge, I glanced into the dining room. Leigh Ann and Scott sat at a small table near the window, near the fire.

"Leigh Ann's here," I said.

"Yes. Scott called this afternoon for a reservation. He told me he thought she needed to get out of the house. He seems genuinely concerned about her, doesn't he?"

I agreed and followed her to a round table by the window. Jimmy came out from behind the bar, and I ordered a French martini.

"I'm on duty," Suzanne said to me and asked for hot tea.

Before I sat, I asked, "Would you mind if I take a minute and say hello to them?"

"Of course not. I'll be right here."

Scott saw me as I approached, said something to Leigh Ann, and stood up.

I nodded at Scott, then said, "Hi, Leigh Ann." I leaned over to kiss her cheek. "I'm so glad to see you. You look great."

She did, too. Her skin had regained its color. Her eyes were clear.

"Thank you, Josie. It's day by day, but once the shock wears off, well, then it's just about keeping on keeping on, you know?"

"I can't even imagine, Leigh Ann. It's so horrible."

"It is, but I keep reminding myself what Mama always says about times like this…it's awful…it's awful…and then it's over. That's how I'm feeling now. Like I'm still in the awful part, but it's not as awful as it was even as recently as yesterday. Today, I know the awful will be over and I'll be able to move forward. Yesterday, I wasn't so sure."

"Will you join us?" Scott asked, sitting. "We haven't even ordered yet."

"Thanks, no. I'm meeting someone for a drink, so I only have a minute." I turned to Leigh Ann. "I just wanted to tell you I was thinking of you. Let's get together soon."

"I'd like that. I was going to call you tomorrow. It looks like I'm leaving for France on Saturday. I think it will be Saturday. It depends on when they release Henri's body. Pierre, Henri's father, you remember, Josie, he wants Henri buried in Paris, next to his mother."

"Are you okay with that?" I asked, wondering how she could bear to let him go. If it were Ty—I broke off the thought. If it were Ty, I'd die.

"I have mixed feelings, but I think it's what Henri would want. At heart, he was a Frenchman." She shrugged, a delicate gesture. "Why I planned on calling… I'm hoping you'll sell those silent movie posters, and everything from the locker—" She paused, then took in a breath and looked at me, her eyes distant, distracted. "Would you take

the art book, too? On consignment? You know the one I
mean…with all those insects and things."

"Of course," I said, wondering if she had the right to
make a deal with me or anyone. With Henri dead, Pierre
owned the business, not her. I thought about asking directly, then decided it would be better, more sensible, more
circumspect, to act as if I didn't know anything about her
affairs; I could get clarification from Pierre in the morning. "You want me to frame them individually and sell
them as art prints?"

"Would you?" she asked.

"I'd be glad to. Our usual arrangement for everything?"

"Yes. Thank you. There's an antique plant stand, too,
that Henri didn't get to show you. It came from a locker
he bought last week. He was going to ask you to appraise
it. Would you sell it, too?"

"Of course."

She looked away, then back at me. "I have to go to the
funeral home tomorrow at ten to finalize the arrangements.
If it works with your schedule, Scott could drop me off
there, then open up the shop for you." She pressed her fingers against her temples. "I need to put a sign up, telling
people we're closed. I've written it… Scott can tape it up
while you get the book and plant stand."

"Are you closing for good?" I asked, surprised.

"I hope not. I don't know." She paused and swallowed,
and when she looked at me again, her eyes were moist. "I
don't know if I can run it alone."

"It's so hard," I said, thinking that my words were
meaningless, that I didn't know what to say.

"A little light shining in the darkness is finding Scott
again." She smiled at him. "He's a rock. A complete rock."

"I'm glad," I said, then turned to Scott. "I'll see you at
the shop about ten fifteen, is that good?"

"Perfect," he said.

"Let me get a look at everything," I told Leigh Ann, "and we can go from there."

"Thank you, Josie," she said.

We said our good-byes, and as I headed back to the lounge, I wondered how long it would be before they remarried, then wondered what I thought about that. I thought I was happy for them, but I wasn't sure. The emotional wound of Henri's murder felt too fresh, too raw for me to feel unadulterated happiness yet. That would come later, after the healing.

Suzanne was looking across the Piscataqua River into Maine. As I approached, I followed her gaze. Shimmering sparks of light glimmered on the deceptively calm surface of the river. The water was fast moving and ice cold, but in the dark, under the undulating lights, it looked inviting. Each summer two or three people drowned, jumping in for an innocent frolic, unprepared for the river's constant and roiling current, unable to withstand its frigid temperature.

I sat across from her and took a sip of French martini, trying to decide how to begin. Suzanne was waiting for me to speak, her demeanor serene and patient. I decided on the truth.

"Leigh Ann seems to be coping well," I said. "Better than I would, I think."

"You never know how you'd react to something like this until it happens."

"That's true." I shook my head. "I'm still so upset about Henri."

She nodded. "I've never known someone who was murdered. Besides the grief and fear, it's... I don't know how to express it...it's like standing on shaky ground."

"Instead of stability, everything feels precarious."

"Exactly."

"So sad...you've been interviewed by the police, right? Did you pick up any information?"

"Me? No. I'm completely out of the loop. The police talked to me briefly because I'd been one of Henri's clients, but I couldn't tell them much. I don't know much. I didn't know Henri well."

"You seemed so fond of one another."

"Yes," she said and looked again toward Maine. "We were, and given time, we might have become friends. I'm fond of Leigh Ann, too."

"So much in life is timing, right?" More lights came on in the houses that lined the Maine shoreline. On the river's surface, in the spots where the glimmers and shimmers overlapped, there was enough light to see the water rushing by. I turned toward Suzanne. She was staring into her teacup. "Was it happenstance that brought you to Rocky Point?"

She shook her head, then looked up. "Sort of." She shrugged, her expression philosophical. "Everyone has a story, right? Mine is short and not so sweet. I loved a man. He left me. I was heartbroken. Everywhere I looked reminded me of him, our favorite restaurants, the stores where we shopped, even things like my condo's extra parking space, how pathetic is that. After a few months of glumping around, I said, forget this, and put in for a transfer. So, yes, my being here is a happy fluke." She shrugged again. "How about you? You're not a native, are you?"

"Not hardly. Mine is a similar story. Within a few weeks' span of time, I lost everything I cared about—my family, my job, my boyfriend. It was bad." I shook off the memory. "My dad always said that when you feel as if you're at the end of your rope, tie a knot and hang on, and if you can't hang on, move on." I shrugged. "It took me longer than you to realize it was time to move on. I hung around for more than a year."

"Look how wonderfully you've settled in," Suzanne said.

"That also took me forever. Years. I envy you your ability to assimilate."

When I first moved to Rocky Point, I'd struggled with searing loneliness, whereas Suzanne seemed to have found her sea legs effortlessly. I tried to account for the difference. Maybe it was as simple as Suzanne being more outgoing than me. I wasn't shy, but I was reserved. I shook my head. True, I'd been absorbed by business, so I'd had no time to seek out new friends, but neither had she. Setting up a business allowed you to meet plenty of people, potential employees, vendors, contractors, and service providers, like accountants and graphic designers. My encounters had been uniformly pleasant and businesslike, but not especially warm. Probably everyone had taken their cues from me. I wasn't feeling warm, so why would they? During my first few years in New Hampshire, I'd focused on coping, not making friends.

"I had help," she said, breaking into my thoughts. She laughed and looked down, then up. "I never thought I'd fall in love again, let alone so quickly."

"May I ask?" I was trying to keep my surprise from showing on my face, unable to keep my curiosity in check.

"Sure. You know him… Fred."

"Fred? My Fred?"

"Why are you so surprised?" she asked, laughing again. "Does he have a wife and family stashed away somewhere?"

"No…of course not!" I laughed, then reached across the table and touched her hand. "I'm delighted, Suzanne. Fred is a wonderful man."

"I never knew how easy love could be. God, the years I've wasted trying to make relationships work."

"I know exactly what you mean. When it's right, you just fit."

"And it's such a relief to put all the anguish aside."

"How did you meet?" I laughed. "I don't mean to be overly inquisitive, but I'm curious."

She smiled, and I recognized the gleam in her eye: She was glad to talk about Fred, could do it all day.

"We met the old-fashioned way, in person, through mutual acquaintances. Fred is friends with our executive chef, Ray. He came in to meet him for a drink shortly after I got here, right when we were beginning to plan our reopening." She paused, remembering. "Not to sound silly, but it truly was a case of our eyes meeting across a crowded room."

"Fabulous! I can see how much you must have in common, both of you city folks, both of you transplants."

"I think that's all true. Certainly, we share tastes and interests, even hobbies." She grinned. "Here's an example. We both love visiting museums, so we each made a list of the ones we want to visit before we die. I can't tell you how much fun we're having merging and prioritizing our lists. My first choice is the Albertina in Vienna."

"Drawings, right?" I asked, hoping I was remembering right.

"You know it? Have you been?"

"No, I've only heard of it. It's supposed to be fabulous."

"Fred is holding out for the Louvre. We've both been there, though, so I don't think that's fair. I think our list should only include places neither of us has visited. He's offering a two-for-one deal if I agree to revisit the Louve." She smiled and her eyes lit up. "I'm holding out for three."

I laughed. "It sounds heavenly. I'm happy for you both."

"Thank you. But I shouldn't mislead you. I didn't fall in love with him because of shared interests or styles." She smiled again. "One kiss and I was a goner."

"A soul kiss," I said, thinking of Ty, how he looked into my eyes and I'd melt. How he seemed able to see deep into my soul when he leaned in to kiss me. "Once experienced, never forgotten." I finished my drink and stood up. "Thank you, Suzanne. Next time, how about lunch? Have you ever been to Ellie's? She makes crepes like you've never tasted."

"I'd love it, Josie."

As I hurried to my car, I remembered the day Suzanne came in to buy the wall art. She said that Fred had told her we had some in stock. Cara had said it was good to see her again. I'd completely missed the implication that, duh, she knew Fred and Cara. It made me wonder what else I'd missed.

Around ten, as I was squatting in front of Ty's fireplace placing an applewood log on top of smoldering embers, Yvonne called. She sounded young.

"Hi," she said, her voice low and appealing. "I was so glad to hear from you. I hope I'm not calling too late."

"Not at all. I appreciate your getting back to me. Do you have any time tomorrow to help me with that call?"

She said yes. We decided that she'd come to my office at eight. I thanked her again, then pushed the OFF button, tossed the phone on the rug, and stretched out on top of one of Ty's suede-covered body-sized pillows to watch the flickering flames. After a while, I picked up my latest book, Rex Stout's *Three for the Chair,* and settled in to read.

Ty called a few minutes later. We talked for more than an hour, describing our days, detailing key events, comparing notes. I smiled when I heard his good news: His last meeting was scheduled to end by noon the next day; with any luck, he'd be home for dinner.

"Yay!" I said.

I read another chapter, then closed my eyes and listened to the crackle and sizzle of sap exploding, some of my favorite sounds.

I woke up to ash and fog. I'd fallen asleep on the body pillow and had no sense of time. I sat up, crinked and befuzzled. A thin layer of tan-gray ash had filtered through the fireplace screen and settled on the hearth. The fire was out. A faint aroma of burned wood and dried apples lingered in the stale air. Outside, thick fog obscured the deck, the railing, the snow-covered lawn, and the trees beyond. I reached for my phone. It was 6:45, but it looked more like dusk than dawn. I tapped some keys on my phone to find the weather. It was forty-two and it was predicted to reach fifty by noon, sixty-three by sunset, a veritable heat wave for New Hampshire in mid-February. The roads would be wet by nine. Low ground would be flooded by two. I, along with everyone I knew, would be talking about our chances for an early spring.

I lay back, thinking I might doze for another few minutes, but sleep eluded me. I stretched and turned to look out the window. Staring into the fog, I had a sense of shapes but not objects. Wispy tendrils of low clouds swirled over and around the woods. I rolled over, anticipating my day. First up, Yvonne. I needed to reach Pierre, to talk to him, to understand.

I smiled, thinking that whatever else the day might bring, the day would end well—Ty was coming home.

TWENTY-NINE

I FOUND DR. PIERRE DUBOIS'S office number on the Internet and was ready for Yvonne when she arrived. I watched her dial, talk, listen, wait, then talk some more. She pushed the HOLD button and reported that according to his receptionist, Dr. Dubois wouldn't be available to talk to me until six, Paris time. He was eager, however, to talk to me then.

"That's noon our time," I said. "Can you come back?"

She said she could and firmed up the date with the woman on the other end of the line.

I saw Yvonne out and headed back upstairs. Hank came to keep me company. With Hank purring on my lap, I clicked on Dr. Dubois's office's Web site. His photograph was a standard business head shot, taken by someone good with a camera, probably, but not a professional. The lighting wasn't ideal. Father and son didn't much resemble one another, except perhaps for their smiles and the shape of their strong jaws.

I closed my eyes for a moment, petting Hank, thinking of loving fathers and of Paris.

Dubois Interior Designs smelled empty.

"You know where that book is?" Scott asked.

"Yes. In the back."

"Leigh Ann said the plant stand was in the back, too. She said it was light, but if you need help carrying it, let me know."

"Thanks," I said and waited until he'd flipped on all the overhead lights before venturing into the back.

The book was in the same spot as when I'd last seen it. The plant stand stood off to the side. I'd brought a large plastic sleeve for the book, and I slipped it in. I carried both objects back inside.

Scott was taping the sign to the door.

"Need any help?" I asked.

"Two more pieces of Scotch tape would be great."

I placed the book on Leigh Ann's desk and brought them over, then read the sign. Leigh Ann had used a font that looked like human handwriting. She'd positioned their logo at the top and surrounded the text with a plain gold border, simple enhancements that added style.

I'm sorry to have missed your visit.

She asked for e-mail messages, and ended with:

I hope to see you soon.

"If you can give me five minutes," I said, "I'd like to take a few photos of the book and plant stand, notate any markings, that sort of thing. I'd been thinking I'd do everything back at my place, but I'd prefer to do it here, and in your presence. An excess-of-caution sort of thing."

"Sure," he said, his eyes signaling that he got it, that he was in business, too. "Leigh Ann asked me to adjust the automatic timer for the lights. I'll do that while you take your photos."

He slid open the right panel on the credenza. "She said she keeps the timer gizmo in here." He poked around both sides, then dragged out the wicker box of tools where Leigh Ann had found the loupe and slid it onto the desk. "Maybe it's in here." He pawed through the miscellany, then paused to hold up what looked to be a square piece of a flattened

Pepsi can with a ragged edge running down one side. He dropped it back in the box and returned the box to the credenza. "Aha! Here it is, on its own, in the back."

He sat in her chair to set the timer, and I turned the plant stand upside down.

The piece was made of oak, with no obvious markings or signatures. The top wiggled a little. There were no embellishments or decorative elements worth noting. I took photos of both objects and e-mailed them to Gretchen, along with my notes and instructions to prepare a consignment agreement for my review.

"I'm done," I said.

"Me, too. May I walk you to your car? I'll carry your book bag."

"I accept with pleasure."

He locked up and walked beside me the half block to my car.

"I don't know that I'll be seeing you again," he said, placing the book on my backseat and helping me position the plant stand in the trunk. "I'm leaving this afternoon."

I couldn't think of what to say or ask. "Oh."

He offered a hand, and we shook. "Nice meeting you."

"You, too."

Just like that, Scott was gone.

Shelley called at twenty minutes to twelve.

"You're not going to be happy," she said.

"I'm sitting down," I said, "and braced."

"The sale of that Verdura wrapped heart went through the buyer's lawyer, so that's who I called. I spoke to him myself. He refused to put me in touch with the buyer, but as you know, my friend, I can be persistent, so I was able to get a smidge of information. The buyer died ten years ago. He was in retail, very rich, but not a household name. That's all I could get about him, and I was lucky to get that. The lawyer wouldn't tell me where the man was from, which means we could be dealing with someone from New York or Paris or Dubai or wherever. The heart was purchased in this circuitous way as a gift for the buyer's mistress. At my request, the lawyer called her to ask if she would talk to me. She died eight years ago. The lawyer refused to question her heirs, and I can't say I blame him. In other words, the trail stops there."

"You're right—I'm not happy. I hate half a story."

"You and me both, my friend. To say nothing of screwing up provenance. What will you do now?"

"Cry."

"Pass the hankies," she said. "Then what?"

"Figure out how to position it. I got it from an abandoned storage locker. They auction them off at between three and six months after nonpayment, depending on the contract. If the mistress died eight years ago, well, in all probability, it wasn't her locker, so probably she sold it at some point after her lover's death. Maybe I'll put out a call for sightings."

"Don't mention my name."

"Never in a million years, Shelley, would I do that. You know me. You know you can trust me with the family jewels."

"You're right, I do. If I didn't I wouldn't have made the phone call."

I sighed. "You know what's hardest about this, Shelley? Coming to terms with the fact that not all questions have answers."

I told Sasha the bad news about the wrapped heart and asked her to prepare a request for sightings, a notice asking dealers worldwide to contact us if they had any information about the heart. We could specify a window of time, but not much else. I also asked her to place ads in all the local and regional newspapers, in both their printed and online editions, offering a cash reward for information leading to our locating the former owner of the storage unit. Both tactics were long shots, but I'd discovered over the years that sometimes long shots paid off.

Yvonne sat on one side of the desk, and I sat on the other. Once Dr. Dubois came on the line, we placed the phone on speaker, and Yvonne explained who she was.

"Please tell him that I'm Josie Prescott. I run an antiques appraisal company, and I worked with his son, Henri. Please tell him how sorry I am for his loss."

She did so, and he thanked me, then commented that Henri had mentioned my name more than once, that he had been very fond of me.

The unexpected compliment brought tears to my eyes, and it took me a moment to regain my poise.

"Thank you," I replied. "I was very fond of him, too."

"Perhaps when I come to New Hampshire," he said, through Yvonne, "which I hope will be soon, we can meet. I would like to hear your stories about my son. I would like to see where he was…where it happened. To see for myself. To talk to the police. To help them." He paused. The sound of his breathing echoed over the phone lines. I knew the sound, heavy, raspy, wet with unshed tears. I knew the rhythm, jagged, pained. "My time…my operating schedule is challenging." Another pause. More husky breathing. More staccato catches of breath. When he spoke again, he said, "My secretary told me you had questions about Henri's business and some other questions, too. Did she understand you right?"

"Yes," I said, appreciative that he was encouraging me to be direct. "I know your son has only been dead a few days. Are you sure you're all right to talk about business so soon afterward?"

"Yes. Thank you for your courtesy. Please…begin."

"Leigh Ann has asked me to sell some objects, but I understand you're the owner. Is that correct?"

"Yes. That was our agreement. I was their backer in opening the business. What objects does she want to sell?"

I told him, and he asked about the estimated value, then said, "Yes. Please do sell them."

"Since you're the owner, you'll need to sign the consignment agreement. May I e-mail it to you?" I asked, adding, "The form I'll send is the same one I've used for many other consignments with Henri."

"That will be fine. Once I sign it, I'll have it scanned in and e-mail it back."

He gave me his e-mail address, and I sent a test message, which he replied to.

"Hearing your American accent—" Dr. Dubois said in English. He broke off abruptly. After several seconds, he continued in French.

"Dr. Dubois apologizes for his poor English," Yvonne said. "He wanted to say that hearing your American accent reminded him how much Henri loved America, how content he felt in Rocky Point."

"That's great to hear," I replied. "Henri seemed very happy here, very happy in his business."

"Yes," Dr. Dubois said, "he felt comfortable there, more so, perhaps, than in France, where the business climate is so competitive." He cleared his throat. "It is possible that his father, that would be me, of course, unintentionally cast a long shadow, and for a man as creative and sensitive as Henri, that might have been difficult. I am grateful I learned my mistake in time to have a good relationship, to be close to him, to help him succeed in his chosen career. Henri was determined to be in America, to find a community that would welcome him, and he did." A pause. "Leigh Ann was a very good friend to Henri. Very understanding."

I closed my eyes, stricken. I'd listened hard to discern whether Henri's father was communicating an unspoken message, one that held the answers I sought to the questions I couldn't bear to ask, and he was. From what he said and all he didn't say, I knew who killed Henri, and why.

I had one last question, but Dr. Dubois wouldn't know the answer. For that, I needed Wes.

Yvonne was gone. From the look on her face as she left, I had the impression she thought Pierre and I had just spent fifteen minutes speaking in code.

I reached Wes on my first try.

"Whatcha got?" he asked.

"That lawyer, the one who called Henri on the day before he died, what's his name?"

"No idea. If the police know, they're not saying, even on the q.t."

"How can they not know?" I asked.

"The cell phone he was using is one of eighty-three issued to his firm. The police know the firm's name, but not which person was assigned which phone."

"Which firm is it?"

"Why? You got something?"

"No. Which firm?"

"Bailey, Haines, Lockwood, and Pirelli. They're located on Seventh Avenue in New York, the fashion district. Come on, Josie. Give."

I had him spell the name, and as he did, I typed it into Google. Within seconds, I confirmed my worst fears. Bailey, Haines, Lockwood, and Pirelli was a full-service law firm with divisions specializing in estate planning, personal injuries, and family law...and immigration.

"Come on, Josie. You wouldn't be asking if you didn't have something."

"I'll call you later, Wes. Thanks."

I heard him sputtering in protest as I replaced the receiver.

I did another Google search, this one seeking out ways and means of picking locks, and within three minutes determined how the intruder got into my house and car. I knew the how and why, and I could prove it. I reached for the phone to call Ellis. Before I could lift it to dial out, Cara's voice came over the intercom.

"Josie," she said, "Chief Hunter is on the phone. He says it's urgent."

THIRTY

"I NEED YOUR HELP," Ellis said. "If you agree, I'll coordinate with Max to make sure you're covered, no potential liability, etcetera."

"Sure," I said, then backtracked, thinking that only a fool agrees to something blindly. "I mean, probably. What do you need?"

"I need you to wear a wire. I think there's a decent chance you can get a confession."

"Me?" I asked, flabbergasted. "Are you kidding?"

He wasn't kidding.

I sat across from Ellis at the round ash table in his office. Cathy had brought us cups of tea.

"I want to tell you something in confidence."

"All right," I said warily.

"Not to be repeated," he said. "Ever."

"Okay."

"I spoke to Henri's father, Dr. Dubois, Pierre. He called to tell me what you and he discussed."

My pulse sped up, then slowed. Neither of us was telling what we knew.

"Scott left Rocky Point today," I said, keeping my eyes on Ellis's face, alert for subtle changes in his expression. I didn't see any reaction at all. "Did you know that?"

"Did you talk to him?" he asked.

"I should have realized what was going on as soon as Scott told me he was leaving, but I didn't." I shook my head. "There were so many clues, but I missed them all."

"You know, then," he said.

"I do now, yes."

"Scott came and talked to us on his way out of town, doing the right thing."

"He's a brave man. Or righteous."

"Maybe. Or covering himself."

"Which do you think?"

"I think he's an honest man, doing the right thing."

"Me, too." I looked out the window. A small stand of birch lined the parking lot. Glistening drips of melting snow dribbled from the trees' limbs, puddling on the asphalt below. Drifts were shrinking, almost in front of my eyes, melting, shriveling into themselves. "What is it you want me to do?"

He told me, listing talking points, explaining the attitude he wanted me to adopt, promising we'd rehearse until I was comfortable, then added, "You can understand why I need your help, can't you? No way could a police officer have this conversation."

"You think I can do it because we're friends."

"Yes."

"I hate this, Ellis."

"Anyone would," he said.

"Did you ask Scott?"

"Yes."

"Why wouldn't he do it?" I asked, wondering if Scott knew something I didn't.

Ellis didn't speak for several seconds. "His reasons are personal and shouldn't be taken as an indictment of my plan. He liked the plan."

I didn't want to do it. I hated everything about it. Even thinking about the conversation Ellis was proposing left me feeling achy and hollow, similar to the way I'd felt the day after I'd been shown the door at Frisco's when I'd awakened at my regular time and realized I had nowhere to go. I'd felt sick, like I was coming down with the flu, and empty, because I had no one to take care of me.

"You won't be alone," Ellis added. "We'll pick some restaurant. There'll be a two-man backup inside with you. I'll be in the van, listening in. Will you do it?"

"When?"

"Now."

"I want to talk to Max."

"I'll call him," he said. "We can hash it out together."

"I want to think about it."

"Let's get Max down here, then."

Within the hour, I'd agreed to Ellis's plan.

While Max and Ellis fussed about the wording on the letter of agreement, I called Ty. The call went to voice mail. I left an "I love you" message, wishing it were evening already so he'd be home, then hating myself for wishing time away, knowing time was all we had. *Except for Wes's questions and answers,* I thought. There were too many questions that had no answers. No answers I could discover, anyway, and most of them started with "why."

I tried Zoë and got her in the frozen food aisle at the grocery store.

"I need some advice," I said. "Ellis wants me to wear a wire to try to win a confession from a murder suspect. I've agreed, but now I'm having second thoughts."

"What's your hesitation?"

Good question, I thought. *What is my hesitation?* Nothing came to mind. You can't betray a betrayer.

"Thanks, Zoë. As always, your advice is spot on."

"I didn't give you any."

"Yes, you did," I said. "Talk to you later."

I sat on a banquette in the Blue Dolphin lounge twirling a cinnamon stick through hot cider. Steam rose and swirled, then dissipated. I took a sip, then another. The cider was rich with spice and warming. Miles Davis's jazz classic "So What?" was playing softly in the background. The apple-cinnamon aroma took me back to my childhood, to autumns when my mom and dad and I would go pumpkin picking, then stop at a country tea shop for hot mulled cider.

The two-man backup was really a woman and a man, both on loan from the Portsmouth police force. I knew Dawn from when she'd helped me prepare to deliver the ransom after Eric was kidnapped, almost two years ago.* She was short and stocky, with shaggy brown hair, a wig, she'd told me, dark brown eyes, and freckles sprinkled across her cheeks and nose. Last year, she'd dressed in jeans and leather. Today, she wore a navy blue pantsuit with a peach and blue flowered blouse, very corporate. She was reading the *Seacoast Star,* and from her demeanor, it seemed the article fascinated her. Her partner, a man named Matt, sat a few tables away. He wore a red sweater and black jeans and was reading something on his smart phone. Both were in profile, their earpieces hidden from view.

I knew the recording system worked because we tested it twice, first at the police station when the technicians had taped the microphones to my torso, and again once we were situated in the lounge. Someone on the force had arranged which tables we should use in advance. When I'd arrived, Dawn and Matt were already in place, and Suzanne led me straight to a table midway between them. A brass stand reading RESERVED stood on top. Four other tables were occupied, all by groups or couples. No one seemed to notice us.

---

* Please see *Dolled Up for Murder.*

"Jimmy will be right over to take your order," Suzanne said, removing the sign.

I thanked her, and my voice sounded gruff. I was dry. I cleared my throat, feeling self-conscious, knowing people were listening in. I closed my eyes and mentally rehearsed the key points Ellis wanted me to cover. Since all I had to do was tell the truth and ask questions, Max had okayed everything. When I'd been seven, I'd been secretly desperate to be an actress. Stage fright kept that dream under wraps. Now was my chance to shine by playing the lead in an epic tragedy. I didn't feel pumped up, though. I felt heartbroken.

Suzanne entered the lounge, the corners of her mouth pointing to the floor. Dawn raised her eyes for half a second, then lowered them back to her paper. Matt glanced in Suzanne's direction, then back at his phone. *Look happy, Suzanne,* I thought, *or you'll blow our cover.* As if she could read my mind, she smiled. Leigh Ann trailed along behind her.

"There she is," Suzanne said to Leigh Ann, pointing to my table.

Leigh Ann thanked her, and Suzanne left the lounge, her part over.

"That smells wonderful," Leigh Ann said, her eyes on my mug as she slid into a chair across from me.

"Hot cider. It tastes great, too."

Jimmy came over, and she ordered one, then said, "Thanks for asking me to join you, Josie. I'm feeling a little down pin, as Mama would say."

She looked down pin, too, her skin gray-white and splotchy, her eyes moist and red, redder even than after Henri died. Her nose and upper lip appeared chafed.

"Scott told me he was leaving," I said, jumping in, wanting this conversation over, remembering Ellis's instruction to push, to take control and keep it, to steer to the pain.

She turned her head to the side, averting her eyes, and I saw the muscles in her neck tighten.

"It was a surprise," she whispered.

"Yeah. Pretty tough break, his looking through that wicker box."

She faced me, opening her eyes wide, communicating innocence and surprise. "What box?"

"The one in your credenza. I think it was the piece of flattened Pepsi can that got him. That ragged cutout. He knew what it meant."

She blinked at me, then gave an awkward laugh. "There's no mystery about it. I have too much time on my hands." She laughed again, more convincingly this time. "One February, ten, maybe twelve years ago, Scott and I drove out to the North Fork, you know, on Long Island. A vineyard was open, so we thought, why not take a tour? The tour guide was the owner, a nice man, glad for company. In the tasting room, he showed off his cork covers, cute little crocheted animals designed to snuggle right over the tops of wine bottles. I asked him whatever for, and he told me it's strange what ideas come to you in February, what with the snow and cold and isolation. He crocheted cork caps. I flatten Pepsi cans and cut out designs to use as stencils."

"Where are they? Those designs to use as stencils?"

She laughed again, confident now. "It seems I'm not as deedy as I'd always flattered myself. None came out in any usable fashion. Not one." She fluttered a hand. "I'm hopeless."

"I saw the YouTube video," I said. I'd watched two of them, lock-picking manifestos. "You used the aluminum to fabricate keys to my back door and car, then a tension wrench to turn them. The tension wrench is in the box, too."

"What are you talking about?" she asked, feigning innocence, not well. Her narrowed eyes and guarded expression betrayed her.

Jimmy brought her cider, but she didn't seem to see it.

"You got your hands on my keys on Thursday," I said, "the day before Henri was killed. I went into the back room with him to look at the Merian book. You took my keys from my tote bag, easy enough, since I always keep them attached to that little ring in the inner zippered compartment, and you've seen me access them for months now. You scanned in their images. I only have a few keys, so you could do them all at once, spacing them out on the glass. It wouldn't take you longer than a minute or two, not with the scanner right there by your desk. There's lots of Pepsi cans around. From there, it was easy—meticulous, but easy. You print out a scan, precisely cut out each key's shape, trace it on a piece of the flattened aluminum, then cut it out, and voilà, you have a metal key. Pretty clever, if you ask me."

"You're raving, Josie," she said, her tone earnest. "You're making no sense."

"How did you know how to do it? Probably you just Googled some key words and watched some how-to videos. You're good with Photoshop, too, and that transferring-fingerprints trick—yowzi—that bit was beyond clever."

Leigh Ann scanned the room, seeking out signs that this was a trap, perhaps, knowing she needed to let me finish, to discover how much I knew and what I planned to do with the information. She had to be worried that I was laying the groundwork for blackmail. "Don't ease up," Ellis had told me. "Keep the pressure on."

"I don't know what you're talking about," Leigh Ann said.

"I'd invited you and Henri to dinner that night at my place. I was going to make a winter clambake, remember?

If you'd been there, it would have been easy to sneak the love note and photo into that drawer. The Blue Dolphin's reopening messed that up for you, didn't it? I canceled dinner at my place and invited you here instead, so you had to risk a break-in. In a blizzard. It worked out to your advantage, though. Since you waited until after you'd murdered Henri, you were able to kill two birds with one stone. Two drop-offs, one in my house and the other in my car trunk, and you set me up with a motive and means. Pretty slick. You were smart enough not to drive your own car, too. For a while, the police thought it was Scott who did it, but it was you."

Leigh Ann cupped her mug, seeking warmth, perhaps. "I didn't kill Henri."

"I was in and out of your shop all the time," I continued. "How long in advance did you plan the murder? I bet you captured my fingerprints that same day you copied my keys. Did you use some I left by touching your desk? No, then the wood grain would have shown in my prints during the police inspection of the love note. The glass mug, I'm thinking…a nice smooth surface…that's where you got them. I wondered for a while if you had me touch the paper itself, the card stock, before you wrote the note, but no, then your prints would have been on it, or if you'd wiped it clear, you would have removed mine, too. Ditto for the glossy photo paper. It had to be a transfer. Plus, you didn't write it. You used an actual love note Henri wrote to you. Dark, Leigh Ann. Very dark."

Leigh Ann sat forward, concentrating, trying, I assumed, to calculate the odds. Should she flee? Stick around to hear what else I had to say? Attack my logic? She was breathing fast, too fast. Emotionally, she had to be all done in.

"Did you use a hard-boiled egg for the fingerprint transfer?" I asked. "Or wax? That's why Henri wasn't wearing gloves when we found his corpse, wasn't it? I didn't realize at the time... I didn't think it meant anything... but of course it did. You took the love note and wiped it clean. You had to because it had your prints on it. You rolled mine on first, I suppose, then pressed his on after you killed him."

"No."

"Oh...did you do his first?"

"Nothing you're saying is true."

"It's easy to remove gloves from a dead man, or at least, it's easier than putting them back on. Did you try? Or were you so focused on getting out of there, you took them with you by mistake? Did you even try to put them back on his hands?"

She looked at me as if she thought I was crazy. She was doing well, I thought, holding it together. "Push," Ellis told me. "Push."

"That love note was beautiful," I continued, "romantic. 'Love conquers all.' Virgil, right? What was the difficulty Henri referred to in that note? My guess is money. It had to cost him something to approach his father. You did a good job on that negotiation. Impressive. Of course, it didn't work out as planned. You changed your mind. You asked Henri for a divorce, right?"

She raised her chin defiantly. "There's nothing illegal about wanting a divorce. Henri was a nice man, just not my soul mate."

"That was Scott."

"Always."

"Henri said no," I said.

She didn't reply.

"Because of his green card," I said. "He couldn't get

permanent resident status if you didn't stay married at least two years, isn't that right?"

"I'm not a lawyer," she said.

"That was the bad news Henri got that day. He spoke to his immigration lawyer. Not only would a divorce preclude his getting his green card now, it would make his getting it in the future all that much harder. His solution was simple—let's stay married."

"I couldn't."

"Because Scott was back," I said, nodding, aiming for a sympathetic tone. "I understand wanting to be with Scott, but why did you have to divorce Henri? Why not just stay married long enough to fulfill your end of the bargain? His father funded the business, and once Henri got his green card, the business would be turned over to you, right?"

"And the house and cars."

"Did you have a prenup?" I asked. "Was that the issue?"

"We couldn't. We worried that it would smack of the unsavory to connect financial gain to getting a green card."

"I can see that. It's probably illegal to boot."

"I cared about Henri," she said, her tone defensive now.

"So why not stay married for a couple of years?"

Her eyes opened wide. "You've met Scott. What odds would you give that he'll still be single in eighteen months? Some cutie will snap him up faster than a lightning bug can flare."

Such is the course of true love, I thought.

"Did Scott get your car seats cleaned?" I asked, hoping my quick shift of topic would surprise her into revealing guilty knowledge.

"No...my God! Who's had time to think of that?" she asked.

"True. Still, it would seem pretty darn urgent to me. You know you got Henri's blood on the driver's side, don't you? When we found Henri's body, you collapsed—that was very affecting, by the way—then got in the passenger side of your car. So the bloodstains there can be explained away. This is different. How did his blood get on the other side, on the *driver's* side?"

Her gray pallor whitened.

"I noticed it at the police garage," I added, "but didn't realize its significance until later. You weren't careful enough, Leigh Ann. You left a boatload of loose ends, and the police are going to find them all."

"Stop it, Josie," Leigh Ann said.

"Are the scanned images of my keys still on your computer? The police will find them. And the flattened aluminum in the wicker box in your credenza. And the tension wrench. How about the wax or putty or whatever you used to transfer the fingerprints? Where are Henri's gloves?"

She pushed aside the mug and stood up. "I don't know why you're doing this to me."

"You're not going to your shop, are you? The police are inside already. They have the evidence. Pierre gave them permission. He owns the business now, remember?"

She sank back down and covered her mouth with her fingers.

"It's over, Leigh Ann," I said softly. "Your best bet now is to tell the truth."

She stood up again, and this time, she walked out.

"Sorry," I said to the wire, aware I didn't get a confession, certain I'd ruined everything. "Oh, my God... I'm sorry."

THIRTY-ONE

DAWN AND MATT left the lounge on Leigh Ann's heels. I followed, reaching the front door in time to see Leigh Ann marching up Bow Street. Ellis, standing near a row house, stepped in front of her and said something I couldn't hear.

I stepped outside and shivered in the chilly air.

Leigh Ann spun away, dashed across the street without looking at traffic, and disappeared into the alley that ran behind the shops facing Market Street. Two cars slammed on their brakes, skidding on the slick roadway. Horns blared. Ellis started after her, shouting something to Dawn and Matt and pointing right, then left. Dawn veered right and flew down the sidewalk along Market Street. Matt raced up Bow Street, following its left-curving route.

"What's happening?" Suzanne asked, standing beside me under the copper overhang. She patted her upper arms for warmth, huddling into herself.

Droplets of melting snow from the roof pinged the metal before rolling off and hitting the sidewalk.

"I don't know," I said. "Leigh Ann ran away."

We stood and waited. A car honked for no reason that I could see. A woman wheeling a baby carriage passed by, heading south. Two older women walked by laughing so hard they couldn't talk. A man in a suit, carrying a briefcase, looked worried.

Ellis appeared on Market Street heading toward us. He kept two fingers on Leigh Ann's elbow. Her hands were cuffed. Tears streamed down her cheeks. Dawn walked on her other side. A patrol car drove up, stopping in the middle of the intersection. Starkly iridescent abstract shapes spun up and sideways on the wet black roadway, reflections from the car's spinning blue and red lights.

Dawn opened the back door. Ellis said something to Leigh Ann. She didn't reply. She didn't move. She didn't react in any way. Ellis spoke again, and still she didn't respond. He took a step toward her, closing in.

Leigh Ann raised her eyes and looked straight at me, standing in stoic silence. I met her gaze and returned it, thinking I was in the presence of evil, that it took a certain breed of devil to kill a man solely because he was inconveniencing you. Henri had expected Leigh Ann to live up to her end of a lucrative bargain. Instead, she killed him, then set out to frame me, her friend.

Dawn and Ellis maneuvered Leigh Ann into the back, and still she kept her eyes on mine. Suzanne and I stood side by side, our shoulders nearly touching, until the patrol car drove away.

THIRTY-TWO

"I'M SORRY," I told Ellis.

The team had removed the microphones. Detective Brownley had taken my official statement, which amounted to nothing more than that I'd done my best, that I hadn't tried to communicate with Leigh Ann about anything off-wire, and that I understood I might be called to testify.

"You have nothing to apologize for. Based on her testimony, we have her breaking immigration laws, selling herself in marriage so Henri could get his green card. That gives us the leverage we need to hold her." He leaned back, relaxed, grinning. "Katie, our IT gal, just called. She found those key scans on Leigh Ann's computer, plus—and this I love—the original photo of you and Zoë." His grin faded. "The receipt for the tire iron, the murder weapon, was in her desk drawer. Unbelievable. If she'd murdered him with something she found in the storage room, she might have been able to argue she did it in the heat of passion. That line of defense is gone. She entered the room armed with a deadly weapon. That's premeditation."

My throat closed, and for several seconds I couldn't speak. "She went out to buy something to kill him with," I said.

"She didn't even clean it," he said, shaking his head.

"She didn't have time. She had to hurry to get to her appointment at Suzanne's condo, then Scott arrived. It takes time to clean blood away so there's no residue, longer to find a spot to leave it." I paused. "A junkyard would be the perfect spot, but this time of year all their piles of miscellaneous parts are covered in snow. If you dumped a tire iron on a mound of snow, it would stand out, black on white."

"That's what I figure, too. She thought it was safer to lay low for a while. Her car was in Henri's name, too, so we could search it. His gloves were in the trunk. They're covered with blood."

"She's a fool," I said.

"She's not stupid," Ellis said.

"I don't know that I agree with that. I think she's wicked."

"So do I," he said. "Just because you're wicked doesn't mean you're not smart. She planned things well."

"I hate her. She tried to frame me. I can't forgive her. Ever."

"I'm not in the forgiveness business," Ellis said. "My job is catching criminals and gathering evidence. Someone else can worry about sinners and forgiveness. As far as I'm concerned, if you don't want to forgive her...don't."

"She betrayed me. We were friends. I liked her, Ellis. I really liked her. I trusted her. I feel so stupid."

"There's nothing stupid about trusting people, Josie."

"Sure there is. You can't just trust. Leigh Ann took advantage of my openness. There's a lesson there for me."

"What? To be less open?"

I met his gaze. "I don't know."

"You have good instincts, Josie. This time it got away from you. You're only human, just like the rest of us. Leigh Ann was smart about things, that's all."

"Maybe." I sighed, ready to think about something else, to skip wallowing in futile anger and dismay. "Did you ever find out why Les used a fake address?"

"He didn't. You know how I thought it might have been a transcription error, that instead of 454 West Thirty-fifth

Street, maybe it was 445 or 544? I was right, but wrong—it wasn't the house address that was transcribed, it was the street itself. Lester Markham's last New York City apartment was located at 454 West Fifty-third Street. The phone number was his, too, back when he lived in New York."

"And it got reassigned to that Spanish-speaking woman after a few years' hiatus."

"Exactly," Ellis said.

"What about the night Leigh Ann broke into my place? Scott said he was awake."

"Funny how that works. You think you're awake but you're not. Turns out, Scott was wrong. He's come to realize he was deeply asleep and only dreaming about Leigh Ann."

"What did the DA decide about Drew Bruen and Zach Moore?" I asked.

"They're in the clear. Their alibis checked out, not that it matters at this point, and Drew gave the money back to Les Markham's family. He told the DA how he took it for his brother but never felt right about it. He said he's really sorry."

"You coached him."

"I made a few suggestions, that's all."

"And the DA declined to press charges?" I asked.

"At the family's request."

"That's great." I smiled, pleased, then laughed. "I just realized something about Leigh Ann. What you said...that she was smart...maybe...but you know what? All things considered, I was smarter."

THIRTY-THREE

FRED WAS STILL at work when I got there about six. I was stopping by just to turn off my computer and say good night to Hank before heading home. To my home. Where I would be able to cook for Ty in my own kitchen without fear.

"Hey, Fred," I said, smiling. "Anything going on I need to know about?"

"Hey, Josie." He pushed up his glasses and grinned. "That guy from Frisco's, Marshall White, called to speak to you. I took the call. He's eager to get his hands on those silent movie posters. I told him they'd be available for inspection for several days before the auction, and by appointment anytime."

I laughed. "You must have broken his heart. What did he say?"

"That he wanted to talk to you."

"I bet. We have to decide how to market them. What would you think of avoiding the obvious—not marketing them as movie ephemera or commercial art, instead as part of a larger concept...hidden messages?"

He pushed up his glasses again. "Interesting. Tools of cryptography, that sort of thing?"

"We still have that Jefferson letter, you know the one I mean, referencing the artichoke code he used in the Lewis and Clark expedition."

"Very cool idea."

"I haven't decided yet, but it's worth considering. It

might be more trouble than it's worth, marketing to all the separate subgroups, movie buffs, Jefferson collectors, and so on. Do you know if Sasha got any hits about the wrapped heart?"

"Yes. She didn't."

I nodded, resigned. "We'll keep the notices up and run ads periodically until we're ready to sell it, but I'm not hopeful. There goes fifty percent of the value. C'est la vie. We're still looking at the low six figures, which isn't hay, but it sure would have been nice to pop into the mid-six figures."

"Words to live by," Fred said. "'It sure would have been nice.' Think of everything that applies to."

"My height for starters. It sure would have been nice to be five-seven."

He laughed. "You're perfect just the way you are."

"Thanks!" I said, then walked toward the warehouse, pausing at the door. I looked back, aware my eyes were twinkling. "I had a fun conversation with Suzanne."

Fred laced his hands behind his head and grinned. "So I heard. Don't tell her, but if you're okay with my taking the time off, I'm planning a ten-day jaunt in April, before tourist season slams the Blue Dolphin—and us. Our first stop will be Paris for the Louvre, then Austria for the Albertina, then two more stops to be determined based on her finalizing her priority list."

"She gets her three-fer," I said, smiling. "April in Paris. Perfect. Have you ever been during the spring?"

"No. Have you?"

I shook my head. "I always wanted to, though." I smiled, as pleased for Suzanne as if I were the one getting the surprise, not her. "Your vacation is approved. Tell Gretchen so she can get the dates into the master schedule, okay?"

"Will do," he said. "Thanks, Josie."

I pushed open the door, then paused again to ask, "Did you know right away that Suzanne was the one? The first time you saw her?"

He sat forward, grinning again, broader this time. "I knew she was drop-dead gorgeous the first time I saw her, but it wasn't until we talked for a while that she knocked my socks off. It took a good two, three minutes for me to realize she had brains and heart in addition to good looks."

I laughed. "That's how it was with me and Ty, too."

Upstairs, before shutting down my computer, I scanned through my e-mails. One from Sasha got my attention. The Markham silent movie posters Hal Greeley sent had arrived. Sasha was excited. She reported he'd sent eight posters, all painted in different styles, all featuring the artist's signature, a hidden cat face.

"Yay!" I said aloud and picked up the phone to call Hal Greeley.

"You got me with my coat half on and one foot out the door," he said, his tone jovial.

"I won't keep you," I said. "I just wanted to thank you again for letting us examine some of your grandfather's posters and let you know they arrived safely."

"Good, good!"

"Also, I wanted to tell you that the posters we're appraising, the ones from the storage unit, the owner plans on selling them."

"How does it work?"

"In all probability, we'll build an auction around them, adding in other related ephemera and decorative objects. Once we have that organized, we market the auction extensively, trying to build advance buzz. I contact museum curators and collectors, for instance. We'll send out news releases and try to get media coverage. I think we'll attract some attention and command good prices."

"That's wonderful news, Josie—on a lot of fronts. It's terrific that the world will learn about my grandfather's work. It's great to think the posters are worth paying good money for, and it's beyond great to think that some of the posters might end up in museums. I'll tell my mom and brother. They'll be thrilled to know Granddad's work is getting the royal treatment. When do you think you'll schedule the auction?"

"Next winter, probably."

"I'll let my brother know. We each might want to consign some posters. We'll decide after we see that appraisal you're working up."

"I hope to have information for you soon," I said, then asked that he give my regards to his mom and assure her I'd always be available for questions.

He promised he would, then thanked me again, and we agreed to talk again soon.

I finished closing up for the night, stretched, and headed downstairs to say good night to Hank. I found him in his basket, asleep. His water had recently been refreshed. His food bowls were full. Life was good.

Ty came out to greet me as soon as I pulled into the driveway. He stood under the golden porch light in the soft blue twilight, smiling, waiting for me to join him.

"Hey, gorgeous," he said.

"Hey, handsome."

He smiled, and I felt my breath catch. I loved everything about him, his looks, how he treated me, how seriously he took his responsibilities, how I could talk to him about anything. I trusted him with my life, with my heart. He was kind and tender and competent and as strong as steel. I adored him.

"You okay?" he asked.

"If you're here," I said, climbing the porch stairs and stepping into his embrace, "I'm okay."

Wes called as I was driving to work the next morning, and I pulled over to talk.

"I can't believe you didn't call me," he said, sounding hurt, not angry.

"Everything happened so fast, Wes. Even if it had occurred to me, there wasn't time."

"Tell me now. Let's meet."

"I can't. I have to get to work."

"Please?" he asked. "Give me ten minutes."

I agreed to meet him at the Portsmouth Diner, not because I thought I knew anything he hadn't already learned from his other, better-connected sources, but because he might know details I lacked.

He was already settled in a booth when I arrived, using standard household scissors to cut a wiggly line in a piece of flattened aluminum can.

"This is hard," he said. "I don't know how she did it."

"Probably she used shears designed to cut metal."

He pushed the aluminum sheet away from him, placing the scissors on top of it.

"So," he said, "did you get any photos?"

"No!" I said, wondering why I was shocked at Wes's question. He was always outrageous.

He sighed, Wesian for disappointment. "How did she look? Pugnacious? Defensive?"

"Haggard. Terrified. Cagey."

"Good ones, Josie! When did you know Leigh Ann was the killer?"

"Yesterday morning, as soon as Scott said he was leaving. The only possible explanation for his sudden decision to leave was that he realized Leigh Ann was the killer. Then other memories came to me, like the bloodstain on the driver's side of her car, like the aluminum square with the ragged edge in her credenza, other things." I sighed. "Do you know if she's cooperating with the police?"

"No way! She's holed up with her lawyer. The police think they're in the catbird seat. The DA says she confessed to what they expect will add up to conspiracy to commit immigration fraud, an element of racketeering. They anticipate indicting her on that charge, maybe as soon as today. They have a lot of circumstantial evidence against her for the murder, including physical evidence, but nothing that can't be explained away somehow."

"Explained away? How can she explain away buying the murder weapon in advance?"

"She says the tire iron she bought is missing. It's not like they have serial numbers on them or anything. There aren't any fingerprints on the tool itself. No one can prove the tire iron she bought was the same one used to kill Henri."

"Is she trying to implicate Scott?" I asked, astonished.

"Maybe."

"What does she say about Henri's blood on the driver's side of her car?"

"That Henri borrowed her car and had a bloody nose." Wes took in my shocked expression and said, "What did you expect, Josie? That she'd just roll over? She's scrappy as all get-out."

"Do you think she'll get away with it?"

"No way, but I think there's a better than even chance that it will go to trial. You know how it works. The DA will dredge up every charge they can think of to try to get her to cop a plea. The DA and her lawyer will dicker back and forth, and if Leigh Ann is stubborn enough, or if she thinks a jury will find it impossible to believe a pretty woman like her could be capable of such a heinous crime, she'll hold out for a jury trial. I think she's just that stubborn and just that arrogant."

"I can see Leigh Ann taking the witness stand in her own defense. She's a good actress." I recalled all her *oohs* and *ahhs,* how she faked that line about how a French martini must be good simply because it's French. "Henri was a good actor, too. They were in collusion to project an image of a happily married couple. It was crucial so Henri could get his green card. It was also important for their business—interior design is an intimate endeavor. Customers want to buy more than furniture. They want to buy a lifestyle. They performed beautifully. No one knew the truth. It might work for her on the stand."

"Do you think you should have been able to figure out that it was all one big lie?" Wes asked.

"No. If people are talented and committed prevaricators, there's nothing someone else can do to avoid being taken in. It's why con men succeed."

"Do you believe that?" he asked.

"I don't know," I said. "I've gone back over every clue I missed. When you trust someone, you skip over anomalies, you know? You want the reality you hope for to be true."

"You got snookered again, Josie."

"Don't be crude, Wes. I didn't get snookered. I trusted people."

"You bought into an illusion."

Wes was right. I did—and that was something I planned to spend a fair amount of time thinking about.

Wes's prediction that Leigh Ann would insist on a jury trial was wrong. I was turning off the interstate en route to work when the local radio station broke into its regular programming to announce that Leigh Ann Dubois had just agreed to plead guilty to second-degree murder in return for a reduced sentence. Instead of facing life without parole, she'd be up for parole in fifty years.

THIRTY-FOUR

I LOOKED AT my handiwork, a two-foot-tall pink heart to which I'd glued a doily border and type I'd printed in a girly font. The front read:

I Love You

I opened the handmade card, my arms stretched wide.

With All My Heart

I nodded, pleased. It was simple and clear and exactly what I wanted to express to Ty this Valentine's Day. I signed it and slid it behind the sofa, out of sight.

I looked around the room. The candles were lit. The champagne was chilled. The steaks were marinating. I was wearing a new red dress and my mother's ruby studs. I was ready for Valentine's Day.

"I feel pretty silly," Ty said, stepping into the living room, "wearing a red sweater just because it's Valentine's Day."

"You take my breath away," I said. "Red sweater and all."

"So do you. You're so gorgeous, Josie."

He hugged me, then looked deep into my eyes and kissed me, a soul kiss, leaving me all fluttery inside.

"I love kissing you," I said.

He popped the champagne cork and said, "I love kissing you, too."

I gave him my card.

"I love it," he said, kissing me again, a longer one this time. "Here's yours."

The outside was decorated in red flocked velvet and read, *Feel beautiful. Feel treasured.* I opened it up. *Because that's what you are and always will be to me.*

"Wow," I said.

"I mean every word of it," he said, and as he leaned in for another kiss, I knew this would be a moment I'd remember forever.

* * * * *

ACKNOWLEDGMENTS

SPECIAL THANKS GO to Adèle Bové, an associate at Verdura, who provided invaluable details about Fulco di Verdura and his remarkable jewelry. Thanks also to Verdura's Patricia Kayne. Ongoing thanks to Leslie Hindman for her guidance about the antiques appraisal process. Any errors are mine alone.

Special thanks also go to Gail Nardin of LIM College for her ongoing support and to Katie Longhurst for her meticulous reading of the manuscript. Thanks also to LIM College's Claudine Monique, who named this book's martini. For my pals in the Wolfe Pack and fans of Rex Stout's Nero Wolfe stories everywhere, I've added my usual allotment of Wolfean trivia to this book. Special thanks to my Wolfean partner in crime, Carol Novak.

Special thanks also go to Jo-Ann Maude, Liz Weiner, and Christine de los Reyes. Thanks to Al de los Reyes, Marci Gleason and James Nield, John and Mona Gleason, Linda and Ren Plastina, Rona and Ken Foster, Bob Farrar, Meredith Anthony and Larry Light, Dave and Cindy Scott, and Wendy Corsi Staub and Mark Staub.

Thanks also to Linda Landigran of *Alfred Hitchcock Mystery Magazine,* Barbara Floyd of *The Country Register,* and Wilda W. Williams of *Library Journal.* Special thanks also to Molly Weston and Jen Forbus.

Since this book is dedicated to librarians, I want to extend special thanks to my librarian friends David S. Ferriero, Doris Ann Norris, Mary Russell, Denise Van

Zanten, Mary Callahan Boone with whom I share a love of theater, Cynde Bloom Lahey, Cyndi Rademacher, Eleanor Ratterman, Jane Murphy, Eileen Sheridan, Jennifer Vido, Judith Abner, Karen Kiley, Lesa Holstine, Monique Flasch, Susie Schachte, Virginia Sanchez, Maxine Bleiweis, Cindy Clark, Linda Avellar, Heidi Fowler, Georgia Owens, Eva Perry, Mary J. Etter, Paul Schroeder, Tracy J. Wright, Kristi Calhoun Belesca, Paulette Sullivan, Frances Mendelsohn, Deborah Hirsch, Sharon Redfern, and Heather Caines.

Thank you to my literary agent emerita, Denise Marcil, and my fabulous literary agent, Cristina Concepcion of Don Congdon Associates, Inc. Special thanks go to Michael Congdon and Katie Kotchman as well.

My editor, Minotaur Books' executive editor Hope Dellon, offered invaluable insights about the manuscript. Special thanks also go to Silissa Kenney, assistant editor, for her shrewd perceptions and thoughtful feedback. I'm indebted to them, and to the entire Minotaur Books team. Thank you to those I work with most often, Andy Martin, Sarah Melnyk, and Talia Ross, as well as those behind the scenes, including my copy editor, India Cooper, and my cover designer, David Baldeosingh Rotstein.